I0818061

CHOOSING *the* HART

DANI RENÉ

Published by Dani René

Paperback ISBN 978-0-6398104-5-4

Cover Design by Raven Designs
Edited by Candice Royer
Proofread by Allyson, Main Manuscripts

The following story contains mature themes, strong language, and sexual situations. It is intended for adult readers.

This book is dedicated to all of you
that begged me to get it published.
Thank you for your support, encouragement, and love.

Prologue

Sitting back, I grabbed my glass of wine and took a long sip. The fire blazed in front of me, and as I watched the flames weave and crackle, I shut my eyes and basked in the warmth. He just messaged me to let me know he was on his way home. Memories flooded my mind as I watched the dancing red and yellow. The man was frustrating, a perfectionist, which drove me insane.

Since I graduated, I had my sights set on my marketing degree. It was the only thing I wanted to do with my life. The excitement of running an event and managing it from conception to completion became my passion. What worried me was actually landing a job after the fact. Once I had the piece of paper that told me I was qualified, I needed to find a company that would give me a chance.

The day I moved to New York was the day I started my life anew. The past was left behind, and I landed an interview not long after arriving. I had the experience, and I was versatile. That was why he hired me. It all happened so fast. When I walked into the office holding my portfolio and resume, I felt confident. I even had my reference letters all ready to wow him.

The owner of Je Te Veux Events was known to be strict and had specific criteria for his staff. Dressed in my black, knee-length skirt with jacket to match and a white blouse, I knew I would fit into any corporate environment. I wore my hair tied low on my neck, and although I wasn't a fan of makeup, I decided to add a light touch.

Yes, I walked into that meeting prepared, but I was completely unprepared for what met me on the other side. Stunned by the man who turned out to be nothing like I expected, young and handsome, piercing blue eyes that seemed to look straight into my soul, he unnerved me.

The interview was tough, to say the least. I was sure my frustration showed, because he picked and prodded at every part of my resume. I understood he wanted to be certain I was capable, and yes, I respected that, but this was a hands-on job, and my experience couldn't be seen on a piece of paper. I needed to show him first hand.

The perfectionist in him, and the pessimist in me, led me to believe I didn't get the job. I was ready to walk out with my head held high. By the end of the interview, I felt defeated. I waited for the "Don't call us, we'll call you", but he stunned me once more by asking me how soon I could start. Without thinking, I stuttered, "Immediately."

I started the following day. The love I had for the job allowed me to hit the ground running, and I didn't stop. I needed to prove myself. Landing the job nobody thought I could get, myself included.

Perhaps I should introduce myself. I'm Em, or Emily, but only my mother calls me that. Three weeks ago, I moved to New York to start anew. To leave behind a life that no longer served my purpose. My dreams led me here, to The Big Apple, to a city that never sleeps, and I needed to make it home.

I found an apartment as soon as I arrived.

The beautiful Manhattan, one-bedroom home had breathtaking views, and for the first time in my thirty-three years, I felt like I was living the life I wanted, watching my dream turn to reality.

I had the career, the apartment. The only thing missing was a prospect of love. Although, that was the last thing I wanted at the moment. My job came first.

Isn't that when love usually comes knocking? When you least expect it . . .

The darkness brings with it echoes of you,
I try to escape them,
but I realize I could never leave you,
Engraved on my skin, emblazoned on my heart,
You are forever part of me.

Chapter One

Glancing up from my computer, I could see him on a call. My desk was conveniently outside his office, and the large window is allowing me to see directly into it was distracting. He didn't look happy as he slammed his fist on the desk. Since I started working here, we'd been so busy I hadn't had a chance to talk to him properly. We had four events this week alone, and I was given the International Coffee Convention as my first major event.

Who knew they had conventions for the stuff? As much as I loved coffee, I didn't know much about it. As soon as I hit send on the email, his office door flew open, and my eyes locked on his. "Miss Reid, thank God you're still here. I need you. Get in here." He turned to stalk back into his office, leaving me staring after him.

I turned to Jessie, and she shrugged. She'd been his assistant for almost five years, and if she was confused, so was I. She mouthed "good luck" to me as I pushed up from my desk. Triston Hart was not known for his calm demeanor when something wasn't going to plan, and we both knew it.

Stepping into his office, I shut the door and looked at my boss. "Mr. Hart, has something happened?" He dragged his gaze up to mine, piercing blue sparkling in the ray of sunlight coming through the window, and it left me breathless.

"Ms. Reid, sit." His voice was hard, commanding even, and I found myself obeying easily. The plush raven-color chair opposite his desk was comfortable as I settled into it. His gaze raked over me, which had a knot tightening in my stomach. Butterflies freewheeled themselves deep in my core, and I found it hard to concentrate on anything but his intense stare.

"What can I help you with?" I fiddled with my pen, trying not to show any reaction to his intense gaze that only moments ago roamed every inch of me. This man had the power to unnerve me, to disarm me, and to make me feel something I'd long since forgotten how to feel. Dressed in a black suit tailored to his immaculate stature and a white button-up beneath, which had a few buttons undone because he'd taken his tie off, I caught a glimpse of a tattoo on smooth skin, teasing me from where I sat.

His strong chiseled jaw had a light dusting of stubble. And those eyes, my God, those eyes had the power to scorch with you just a mere glimpse. Shaking my head, I tried to stop the wayward thoughts. He was my boss. I needed to appear professional, even though my body was reacting in a very unprofessional manner at that moment.

"I've just got off with our client. The coffee convention set-up is starting tomorrow, and I need you there. I'm furious because I had lined up some new business meetings and would have preferred you in on them; however, it seems they'll have to be moved. I need you back here as soon as you're done with the set-up. Do you understand me?" His strained voice had a sexy rasp, and I found myself nodding. Something about this came across as strange. I'd been out of the office before. So, the tension was really uncalled for.

"Yes, I'll certainly head back as soon as I can. What time am I meant to be there tomorrow?"

He glanced at the page on his desk and mumbled, "You need to be there at six. They'll have the venue open and ready for the stalls to be erected. It's early. I'm sorry, but I'll have the car pick you up."

Shaking my head, I offered a smile. "No, thanks. I can sort myself out." Pushing off the chair, I rose and turned to leave when his voice stalled me.

"Ms. Reid, do you have plans tonight?" Startled by his question, I turned to regard him.

"No, I uh . . . I figured I'd have an early night since I've got to be up so early tomorrow." He nodded, shifted the pages on his desk, then looked back up at me.

"I'll take you for dinner tomorrow then. After work." I watched him pick up his phone and dial Jessie. "Make reservations for two at Candle 79 tomorrow at seven." He glanced at me with a nod, clearly dismissing me.

Still speechless, I opened the door and headed back to my desk. Sliding into my chair, I glanced at Jess, and mouthed, "What the fuck?" She put a finger to her lips to silence me.

"Later," she whispered.

Opening my calendar, I decided to concentrate

on work, but my mind kept drifting back to the man in the office across from me. I blocked out my calendar and opened my email.

The office door opened at five thirty, and I snapped my gaze to find beautiful pools of blue that reminded me of the ocean. "See you ladies tomorrow." His words directed at both of us, but his eyes were locked on me.

He strode past, and I couldn't help but take in the man. He was controlled and calm. So far, I'd gotten to know him through the other staff members, and what I'd heard was only good things. He was caring, no doubt about that. But I wondered why I warranted a dinner. Surely some flowers would have sufficed.

As soon as he was out of the office, I turned to Jessie. "Tell me!"

Her giggle was contagious because soon I was giggling too. "Okay, okay, I think he likes you. He's never taken any other girls to dinner before. And, he's never dated after what happened to his ex-fiancée." I stared at her open-mouthed, in shock.

"But he's . . . he's my boss?" The question was obvious to me, but not her.

She shrugged. "Hey, if he likes you, he's going

to get you. He can be . . . persistent."

Crossing my arms, I flitted my gaze between her and the door. "He doesn't know me well enough then. I don't just give in to anyone." I turned back to my desk and shut down my computer. Grabbing my bag, I turned to leave. "See you tomorrow? I'm out till late afternoon. I've blocked out my calendar."

She smiled and nodded. "Perfect. Good luck with setting up, and call me if you need anything." I nodded before making my way out of the office with my mind still running a million miles a minute.

As soon as I unlocked my apartment and stepped inside, I felt myself relax. Leaning against the door for a few minutes, I allowed my mind to play out the reasons for Triston wanting to take me to dinner. Tomorrow was going to be a long day, and I needed an early night, but my mind didn't wander far from those searing Arctic eyes. *Why would he want to take me to dinner?*

I was sure it was only a *welcome to the company* dinner. At least, that was what I kept telling myself. Although, wouldn't a standard welcome be flowers or a box of chocolates?

I opened the refrigerator. Leftovers would have to do as I was in no mood for cooking. I put the container in the microwave and walked over to my bag, pulling out my phone to check the social media notifications for the company. I needed to update the statuses and dates for the convention. As I unlocked my phone, I saw a text message from Triston.

Triston: See you tomorrow, I look forward to it.

Mr. Hart

I smiled. He was handsome and charming, but the more I thought about it, I didn't know if dating the boss was such a good idea. That's if what Jessie said was true. The microwave alerted me my leftover lasagna was ready. Grabbing a fork, I put my phone back in my purse before looping it through my arm and headed to the living room to sit down. I hated wearing heels. At least I could wear my flats the next day.

I opened my laptop and logged in. As I ate, I watched the notifications pop up on-screen. All the events were happening on the same dates, which meant we were busy. We had a few people taking shifts online. I grabbed my phone and hit reply to the message from Triston.

Em: So do I, Mr. Hart. Till tomorrow.

I put my phone down and carried on updating the statuses on our social media sites. As I scooped up the last of the lasagna, my phone beeped again. I picked it up and unlocked the screen.

Triston: Miss Reid, stop working and get some rest. I am online. Mr. Hart

I smiled at his message. He was so demanding yet sweet. I decided tomorrow would be a nice dinner, but I couldn't date my boss, and I would tell him tomorrow. I logged out of the work accounts and into my personal ones — nothing of interest. I hadn't heard from anyone back home since I left, and it had been almost three months. I hit reply on the text message.

Em: Thank you, Mr. Hart, have a good evening.

I giggled like a schoolgirl at the exchange between us. You would never believe he was forty-three years old. He acted like he was twenty-three. I put my phone on the sofa and got up. In the kitchen, I put the container in the sink and filled it with hot, soapy water. It would have to wait until morning.

I went back to the living room and shut down my laptop. Grabbing my phone off the sofa, I went to the bathroom to get ready for bed. My phone beeped again as I was crawling between the sheets. Another message. Did he ever sleep? He seemed to be awake till all hours of the night.

Triston: Not sure good is what my evening is. I am working. Sleep now.

How could I disagree with the boss man's orders? I made sure my alarm was on. Turning off my bedside lamp, I got under the covers. I lay on the bed, looking at the ceiling, my head spinning from this strange day.

I groaned at the sound of my alarm. Four thirty, and way too early for any sane person to be awake. I rolled out of bed and turned on the lamp. It felt like I had gotten no sleep at all. I needed two things, coffee and a shower, in that particular order. I stumbled to the kitchen and turned on the kettle. Making my way back to the bedroom, I picked up my phone. Opening my iMessage, I scrolled down to Jessie's number.

Em: What am I meant to wear to dinner?

I heard the kettle boil and walked back into the kitchen. I added the filter to the little AeroPress, scooped the coffee in and poured the water, filling it up. I loved the smell of the Colombian blend. It was rich, chocolatey, and strong, which was exactly what I needed. Walking into the bathroom, I turned on the light. Everything seemed too bright that morning. I set the mug of coffee on the counter and turned on the shower. I stripped down and stepped in. The hot spray hit me. It was relaxing and calming, but I couldn't enjoy it for too long. I needed to get to work. I couldn't believe I was awake before sunrise; it was a first.

I was ready by five thirty, I knew it would take me fifteen minutes to get to the venue in a cab, so I wasn't in a rush. I stepped out onto the landing and locked my apartment when my phone beeped.

Tristον: Miss Reid, the car is downstairs, I prefer if you let the driver take you to the venue. Mr. Hart

I walked down to the entrance foyer of my apartment block, opened the door, and looked out. The car was waiting for me. Charlie, our company driver, waved at me, and I smiled. I walked up to the car as he got out to open the door for me. "Charlie, you do not have to open the door for me!" I laughed, and he gave me a nod. "Mr. Hart instructed me to look after you, Miss Reid." I slid into the back seat of the Lexus SUV, and he closed the door. I guessed that Mr. Hart wanted me supervised. This was my first big event; I supposed he didn't trust me yet. I was going to have to prove to him that I was made for the job.

We pulled up to the venue at 5:50. I had ten minutes to spare. I hoped the coffee roasters were ready -- I needed another coffee. After I got out of the car before Charlie could get out to open the door for me, I waved goodbye to him and made my way to the entrance, where I saw Charlene.

"Miss Reid, good morning." Charlene smiled. We had met a few days prior in the introduction meeting.

"Hi, Charlene. Please call me Em." She shook my outstretched hand and smiled.

"Em, we need to get the guys inside up and ready by midday. They're going to bring in all the equipment. Also, the tables need setting up. I need you to supervise, or nothing will actually get done."

I nodded. "Coffee first?" She smiled, and we walked to the large cafeteria. The venue was large enough to hold five hundred people, and there would be at least fifty coffee companies exhibiting. There were already a few people milling around. I supposed they were some of the roasters that were joining the convention. We grabbed a couple of coffees when I heard a deep voice behind me. I turned to see where it was coming from, or who it was coming from.

I laid eyes on the source of my distraction. The man was talking to some friends and turned to catch my gaze. I looked into beautiful hazel eyes that had a naughty sparkle in them. A rugged, tanned god with dark hair, dressed in tight black jeans and a black T-shirt, which seemed to hug his muscled arms perfectly. He was handsome, not much taller than me, and I found myself blushing from his intense stare.

"Em, let me show you where the office is. You can set up if you need to work." Charlene startled me. I turned to face her and nodded. I hoped she didn't notice the flush on my cheeks. I tried keeping my eyes down, but I kept glancing at him from the corner of my eye. I followed her out of the cafeteria, but I felt the intense hazel-eyed gaze follow me.

The office was small, but there was enough space for both of us to get on with what we needed to. I set up my laptop, connected to the Wi-Fi network, and started downloading my emails. "What time do you reckon we will finish off here today?" I asked Charlene.

She looked up and shrugged. "About five, I think. It shouldn't be a late night. Why? Got a date or something?"

I smiled and looked at my laptop. "Or something . . ."

I handed my layout plans to the set-up crew coordinator and gave him the instructions. He was confident they would be done in two hours for set-up. That would take us to midday, which was perfect timing. Most of the companies that were participating had already arrived, the flooring for their particular stalls laid out. I walked around looking for those hazel eyes but couldn't find him. I wondered if he had already left. I supposed I could grab a cup of coffee from the cafeteria.

I walked around trying to decide on a coffee to get when I noticed they had set up some new blends. There were a few brews from local roasters featuring at the event. There was one I didn't recognize, Tribal Fuel, that sounded interesting. I poured some of the filter coffee they had set up, and the aroma hit me at once. It smelled amazing! I took a small sip and immediately got the mocha flavor. It was strong, yet the flavor of chocolate was gentle. This was definitely going to be my new favorite.

"I hope you like the coffee." A familiar deep voice startled me. I turned and was met with those intense hazel eyes. I nodded. "Yes, I think this just may be my new favorite coffee." A genuine smile creased the corner of his eyes and made him look younger than I thought he was.

"Well, that's good. I guess I did my job right. Sebastian, but you can call me Bash." He held out his hand. I shook it, and his big, strong hand engulfed mine.

"Nice to meet you, Bash. I am Emily. You can call me Em, though nobody uses my full name anymore. Your coffee is amazing; I haven't heard about it before. Is it new?" I stopped myself, realizing I was rambling. He let go of my hand, and I felt nervous. His gaze was intense; I felt myself flush. He nodded, his eyes never leaving mine. "Yes, our company opened a couple of months ago. So, I guess we're still new, but I have a lot of experience . . . with coffee. I hope I see more of you later; I have to finish setting up. Enjoy the coffee." He winked and turned to walk away. I watched his retreating form and found my appreciative gaze locked on his tight black jeans. He definitely filled them out perfectly.

I was running late. There were minor details I needed to finalize. I sat in Charlene's office, checking my emails when my phone beeped.

Triston: I trust your day has been productive Miss Reid? Your boss.

Em: It has been; I apologize for the delay in getting back. Your employee.

I hit send, and a smile crept up on my lips, "Boyfriend?" Charlene asked as she stared at me mischievously. I smiled. "No, it's, uh . . . It's just a friend." How was I meant to tell someone I was smiling like a teenager at a text from my boss? I opened my other messages. Jessie had replied that she had Charlie picking me up at five p.m., and there would be a dress in the car for me to wear. I sent a quick reply to thank her.

"I am about to go and check on the setup. Can I bring you anything?" I asked as I opened the office door.

"Yeah, sure, get me a coffee. Something strong. I'll be here a while." I nodded and walked out, closing the door behind me.

"Miss Reid, can we get your signature on these?" The contractor caught me as I made my way through the exhibition area. I signed the forms, giving them final clearance to finish the last structures. The venue looked amazing, and it smelled even better! I walked down to the cafeteria.

"Are you following me?" I turned to see the rugged Bash walking toward me. "I think you're the one following me, Bash." I laughed, he smiled, and his eyes twinkled. I couldn't help but stare at him. As I turned, he grabbed me, pulling me toward him. I had almost bumped into a contractor carrying a couple of long poles. "Shit! Thank you! I am not used to being awake as early as I was this morning." I looked up, and his face was so close to mine I forgot to breathe. His strong arms felt warm around me, and I felt myself relax into them.

"It's part of my job, you know, saving damsels in distress."

His face was a picture of amusement, and it made me giggle. "Oh, I am sure it's a job you quite enjoy." It was when he stood me up did I realize I was leaning into him.

"Thank you, again . . ." I stepped back. I turned to walk to the cafeteria with him following alongside. "Can I get you a coffee?" Bash asked, "There are some amazing blends here. How do you take it?" I smiled. He had gone from flirting to professional in a matter of seconds. "I love strong coffee, no milk, no sugar."

He nodded in agreement. "My kind of girl." Making his way over to the table with the Tribal Fuel coffee, he grabbed an unmarked bag and started grinding some beans.

"Is that your special stash?" I joked. He

finished up by setting the machine to boil and turned to me. "Absolutely! A special coffee for a special lady. That's my company motto. And it also might keep you from injuring yourself, since I won't be around once you go back to your fancy office." He winked and turned back to the coffee machine. I frowned at his strange remark. I wondered how he knew I worked in a fancy office.

He handed me a cup, and I inhaled the strong scent of rich chocolate and caramel. "This smells amazing." I looked up at him, and he looked pleased with himself, nodding and smiling at me. The warmth of the cup felt good, and I imagined that's how he would feel.

"Well, it tastes even better." I took a sip, and he was right; it was definitely mouth-watering.

"Do you try to impress all the girls with your coffee-making skills?" I narrowed my eyes at him.

He shook his head. "Only the pretty ones." He smirked at the incredulous look I gave him. "I better get back to work. See you around." And with that, he was gone.

Chapter Two

Since I didn't make it back to the office, Jessie told me to go straight home. I unlocked my apartment at five thirty, and I had some time to get ready. First, I needed a hot shower. I walked into the bedroom, unzipped the dress bag, and I pulled out the garment. It was beautiful. A simple, knee-length, black, off-the-shoulder dress, with a thin, silver belt around the waist had me in awe. It was stylish yet sexy. Jessie had amazing taste in clothes. I hung the dress on the door of my closet and pulled out my phone. I needed to call her and thank her. Unlocking the screen, I noticed I had a message from Triston.

Triston: I hope your day wasn't too tiring, Miss Reid. See you in a couple of hours. T

I didn't know what to think. He had my mind whirling with thoughts I shouldn't be having. Between him and Bash, I was sure going to have my hands full. Although, I had completely forgotten to get Bash's details. The only thing I knew about him was that he worked for a coffee company and a fantastic coffee company at that! I suppose I would see him over the next few days at the event.

Em: It was busy, as expected, I look forward to dinner. E

Shower time. I made my way to my modern bathroom. I loved the spa bath and large shower. Stripping down, turning on the shower, I waited for it to heat up and stepped into the hot, welcome spray. I closed my eyes and saw those beautiful hazel eyes. I thought about Bash. His rugged exterior, the flirtatious smile, and those naughty eyes that seemed to sparkle. He was absolutely handsome.

The hot water was calming, and I felt relaxed when I stepped out. Grabbing a towel, I dried off and wrapped myself in my bathrobe. Walking back to the kitchen, I turned on the kettle and walked back to the bedroom to find shoes to pair with my dress. I had about an hour left to get ready — plenty of time. My phone beeped from the bed. I picked it up and unlocked the screen.

Jessie: Have a good dinner. He was in an exceptionally good mood today… I wonder why ;)

Jessie did think Triston liked me; I wasn't sure. I still had reservations about dating the boss. It's not a professional thing to do. I made a cup of green tea and got ready.

I walked downstairs. Knowing Triston was in the car right outside the door made my heart race. I took a deep breath before opening it.

I had never seen him outside of office hours, and I genuinely wasn't sure what to expect. He always seemed calm and collected at work. I wondered if he was like that normally. Upon opening the entrance door to the street, my breath hitched. He was leaning against the passenger door, and he looked breathtaking. His shoulder length hair was shining. Dressed in black slacks and black leather, unzipped boots, a silver shirt with the first few buttons undone completed the look.

"Don't you scrub up beautifully, Miss Reid?" He smiled as he took in my appearance. He turned to open the door for me.

"Thank you, Mr. Hart. The dress is beautiful. Jessie's choice is perfect." I slid into the passenger seat.

"Actually, I chose it," he said and closed the door. My heart hammered against my rib cage. I couldn't believe he chose my dress! He slid into the driver's seat and looked over at me. I felt self-conscious under his gaze. "Well, you have good taste in women's clothing, Mr. Hart. As well as sizing," I stated, making a point of the fact that he had chosen a size that fitted me perfectly.

"It seems I do." His gaze traveled over my body appreciatively, and he smirked. His stare had my stomach doing flip flops, and my heart thudded so hard in my throat. He started the engine, pulling out into the street, and sped off.

He leaned forward to turn on the radio. I gazed down at his hands. They were so smooth with prominent veins pulsing just below the skin; I felt the need to touch them. The song started, and I recognized it from my running playlist. Pia Mia's song "Do It Again" was good. I loved her voice. As I listened to the lyrics, I blushed. I sat back as we made our way through the traffic. "So, what made you move to New York?" he asked over the music.

"I have always wanted to run off to the big city and make a name for myself. I finished university, and I suppose life got in the way of my dreams for a while." I trailed off, not wanting to share the painful details that brought me here.

"Life? Yeah, it has a funny way of fucking up your dreams. At least you're here now?" He reached over and touched my knee, feeling sparks surging through my body. He pulled his hand away quickly. "Sorry," he mumbled and put both hands on the wheel. He gripped it so tightly I could see his knuckles turn white and the veins pulse. "So, what happened to make you finally follow your dreams?" He glanced over at me. I shook my head in response. Everything seemed so fresh in my mind that I couldn't find the words to explain.

"Can we not talk about this now?" I looked into those steel-blue eyes, hoping he would let it go. He nodded and turned his eyes back to the road.

Triston pulled into a parking spot right outside the restaurant. It looked like a quiet little place, and I felt relieved. I was definitely not in the mood for a bustling restaurant to get to know him. Looking over at him, he seemed so casual yet sophisticated. He would fit in anywhere.

After getting out, he came around to the passenger side, opened my door, and held out his hand. I slipped mine in his and felt my skin tingle with an electric current surging through me. His hand was so smooth, soft and warm.

We walked alongside each other to the door. He stepped aside, allowing me to enter first. A perfect gentleman at all times. He walked up to the manager. "Mr. Hart. I have a reservation for two for seven p.m."

The manager smiled and nodded. "Please, this way sir . . ."

We followed the manager to a private table at the back of the restaurant. Triston pulled out my chair and grabbed my coat as I shrugged it off. His fingertips brushed my shoulders, and the hair on the nape of my neck stood on end. I felt goosebumps rise across my skin. He handed it to the manager who proceeded to place our menus and the wine list on the table. "Your waiter will be with you in a few moments." The manager smiled and walked off.

"Do you drink?" Triston's blue gaze was on me again, and my stomach fluttered. I nodded. "I do. I didn't think you did?" He always struck me as such a serious person, as I couldn't imagine him drinking at all.

"I do. Only on special occasions, though, like tonight. Would you like a glass of wine? Unless you're a beer girl?" He had a wicked smile that crinkled his nose, which made him look like a naughty little boy.

"Dry red wine, please." He nodded and looked at the wine list while I picked up the food menu. I glanced at his face over the top of my menu. He was definitely perfect.

A lanky, dark-haired waiter appeared at our table. "Good evening, I'm James. I will be your waiter this evening. If there is anything you need, please let me know."

Triston looked up and gave him a gracious smile. "James, please bring us a bottle of your Lenz Estate Merlot 2007 vintage. Give us some more time for the food order." James nodded with a small smile and retreated with the wine list.

Triston turned his gaze to me. I didn't look up from my menu, but I could feel his eyes as he observed me for a few moments before speaking. "Did you have a good day, Miss Reid?"

I looked up and smiled. "It was busy, but productive, Mr. Hart. Are we going to keep with the formalities tonight?" I asked him, curiosity getting the better of me.

His face changed to an amused smirk. "I didn't want to put pressure on you by assuming this was a date. I don't do dates, as I am sure Jessie would have mentioned when you two gossip."

My mouth fell open. "We do not gossip!" He laughed, a carefree look on his face. He seemed relaxed. I shook my head, my dark brown eyes meeting his steel-blue stare. I felt a flutter in my stomach, and my eyes fell to his clasped hands, which rested on the table. He looked so calm — nothing seemed to faze him. His emotions in check at all times. I wished I felt half as calm as he looked. "I didn't feel any pressure, Mr. Hart. I am a big girl. I can take care of myself, you know."

His eyes glinted with something. I couldn't tell what it was, but his smile deepened. "Oh, Miss Reid, I am well aware of that. Running away from home to a big city is proof of taking care of yourself." I felt a tug in my abdomen from the dark look in his eyes.

James returned with our wine and proceeded to open the bottle. "Shall I pour a taster, sir?" Triston nodded and watched the dark red wine flow into his glass. He picked it up and took a small sip. Mesmerized by his movements, slow, sensual, and sexy, my mind boggled at how a man could be so perfect. I was blatantly staring at him.

"Perfect, James. Please go ahead . . ." He motioned for James to fill my glass. The wine was the color of garnet, almost black in the dim light of the restaurant. Once James filled our glasses, he retreated once more. He mumbled he would be back shortly to take our order.

Triston picked up his glass. "I want to welcome you to the company, Miss Reid. I trust we will have a fulfilling . . . relationship." He stopped short, and I felt the tension thick in the air. It was consuming, just like he was. I picked up my glass and clinked his. Our eyes locked in a stand-off — I wasn't looking away, and neither was he. The air prickled with an underlying current.

"Thank you for hiring me, Mr. Hart. It's a

dream to work for an internationally recognized company like yours." He smiled, his eyes creasing. I stared at him. I knew I shouldn't, but I couldn't look away. There was something in his smile that drew me in. I felt consumed by his ethereal beauty. Lifting his glass, keeping eye contact with me, he took a sip of his wine. My eyes fell to his mouth. He pulled the glass away, and I watched the blood-red liquid stain his soft lips. I ached to kiss them in such a way it almost hurt, wanting to taste the wine there.

He licked his lips, and I watched his tongue move over each one. A fire furiously burned inside me. I ached to feel his tongue, and I squirmed in my seat. I could see his eyes flicker with the recognition of the effect he was having on me. He was aware of what he was doing and enjoying it.

"So," he broke the spell. My eyes fell to my glass. "Tell me about yourself. Your family, what do you enjoy doing besides running around after clients?" I looked into his eyes again. Did he want to talk about my family? After what he just did to me? How was I meant to concentrate?

I wondered if he could squirm, and I dared myself to find out. I wanted to play his game, to challenge him. Before I answered him, I took a sip of wine. Licking my lips, tasting the rich, fruity flavor. I noticed his gaze falling on my mouth. His eyes followed the movement of my tongue like a hunter watching his prey. We both knew the game being played. He seemed to enjoy making me squirm, but I knew I could give as good as he gave. Something in his eyes changed. I noticed the color deepening, the cerulean darkening to a midnight blue.

I smiled. "I grew up in a small town, nowhere near as exciting as New York. I'm an only child. What do I enjoy besides work? Well, uh . . . I guess I love being outdoors. Walking, hiking, anything that spikes the adrenalin. And you?" I grinned at his intrigued gaze.

"Mmm . . . I do know of a lot of activities that can spike the adrenalin." His smile was dark and devilish. I felt a flush on my cheeks. The apex between my thighs responded too, aching with need for this man.

"Oh, I'm sure you do, Mr. Hart." I tried to sound calm, but I think he could tell I was far from it. He was my boss for god's sake. What was wrong with me? What was wrong with him? I needed fresh air. The tension between us was too intense, almost magnetic.

"What about you?" I looked at him expectantly, changing the subject.

He shrugged. His long, slender fingers trailed the stalk of the glass. An image of his fingers trailing my arms caused a shiver to run down my spine. "Well, I quite enjoy the outdoors myself. So much fun can be had in nature." He looked up, and his eyes had filled with an invitation. I wanted to find out where to.

James chose that moment to interrupt us, and a thankful interruption it was. "What can I get you, folks, to eat?" Triston looked over at me.

"You trust me?" I nodded, and he proceeded to order the starters and mains. Once James had taken the order, he grabbed our menus and disappeared.

"You were saying?" I edged Triston on, hoping I could learn more about this mysterious man. I took another sip of wine. I watched his gaze flicker, and as I predicted, it fell on my mouth again. Licking my lips, his eyes blazed a dark, electric blue.

"Would you stop that?" he asked seriously, looking up, meeting my eyes.

I feigned an innocent look. "Stop what?" He

shook his head and smirked. The restaurant had a lively buzz now, and I felt more at ease with other people around.

"You are—" He stopped suddenly and picked up the bottle of wine, filling my glass and then his.

"I am?" I asked jokingly.

"You do realize I'm your boss?" His expression one of amusement, his eyes sparkled with mischief. "Did you forget that little nugget of information? While you sit there distracting me with your mouth, Miss Reid?"

I shrugged and watched his steel-blue eyes return to normal. "I do realize you're my boss, Mr. Hart. I do hope you realize I was merely drinking my wine. It's not my fault you were staring at my mouth when I did so." His gaze locked on mine, and we stared at each other. I felt the fire flare inside me. It was a feeling I hadn't felt in a long time, an ache I needed to extinguish because it was for my boss. I could see the amusement dance in his eyes, his lips curving into a mischievous smirk.

"Are you going to tell me about you? Or would you like me to beg?"

His smile grew, and I saw a naughty glint

in his eyes again. "Oh, Miss Reid. I would give anything to hear you beg." His voice was a deep, husky whisper. Molten lava trickled from my abdomen, collecting between my legs. I squirmed in my chair, squeezing my thighs together tightly, hoping to numb the ache.

I raised the glass to my lips. I licked the wine on the rim of the glass, my hands trembling, and I hope he didn't notice. I took a mouthful of wine and wet my bottom lip. His eyes flared with a need I myself felt at that moment. We were definitely playing the same game, and I loved it.

His gaze flitted away, and he looked around the restaurant. He took a deep breath. I could see him struggling with his emotions. I wondered what turmoil was raging inside his calm exterior.

James brought the starters. A platter of olives, hummus, flatbread, crumbed mushrooms, and some other dips. With a quick "Enjoy," he scuttled off.

The evening went by much the same, with a casual chat about work and clients. Between the mundane chatter, we still played our game. I was enjoying it. There was something about him that made me think he didn't like me challenging him, which made me want to do it so much more. I was stubborn like that! Tell me not to do something and trust I will do it as much as I could.

As we walked out to the car after dinner, I felt Triston's hand on my lower back guiding me in the direction of the car. His fingertips sent sparks through my body, and I shivered. The fire in my stomach flared at his touch. I was sure this was something I would not get rid of anytime soon. His touch was commanding yet gentle. He was used to being in control, and I wondered if he ever let someone else take the lead.

He opened the passenger door for me, and I slid into the soft leather seat of the black SUV. Triston got into the driver's seat and turned the engine on. "Did you enjoy dinner?" He turned to look at me.

"Yes, it was amazing. Who knew vegan food could be that good!" His laugh lit his face up in the most handsome way. I saw that boyish charm, and a wave of emotion washed over me. I realized I wanted him to kiss me. At that moment, I didn't care if he was my boss or not.

I wanted this man with a ferocity I hadn't ever felt.

He pulled out of the parking space and drove in the direction of my apartment. The night was over, and I felt sad. I wished we had more time. We hadn't spoken about his family, and I wanted to know more about him. I decided to take the plunge and ask him. "So, where are your family? All in New York?"

He shook his head. "No, my mom lives in LA. I don't think she will ever leave. And I have a brother. We, uh . . . We don't get along." I frowned. He had my attention now.

"You have a brother?" He nodded but didn't elaborate. His hesitancy made me decide to let it go. There was a story, but I didn't want to push it and upset him. We both reached forward at the same time to turn on the stereo. My hand brushed against his. Electricity sparked through my arm, and I pulled away. My skin on fire from his touch. "Sorry, I . . ." Why was I apologizing? I was tingling. He glanced at me and smiled.

"It's okay." He turned the radio on and sat back, speeding down the empty city streets.

He pulled up outside my apartment complex. Turning off the engine, he got out of the car. Making his way around to my side, he opened the door. Smiling at him as I got out of the car, he took my hand. I wasn't sure what to say or do. Generally, at the end of a date, there's a kiss. I didn't think that would happen with Triston. He closed and locked the car behind him. I walked a few steps ahead, but I could feel his presence at my back.

He caught up to me, and his hand once more found the spot on the small of my back. We walked up to the entrance of my apartment building. I stopped and turned to face him. "Mr. Hart, thank you for the evening. I enjoyed dinner." I took my keys out of my bag and looked up. He had stopped in front of me. He smiled. It was a genuine smile, and my heart raced. I wondered if he would kiss me. I wanted to tease him one last time and licked my lips. My teeth chew on my bottom lip, and I saw his gaze fall on my mouth, as it had so often over the evening.

"For god's sake Miss Reid, I told you not to do that!"

He grabbed my face between his soft, smooth hands, and I gasped at how warm they were — his face inches from mine. I inhaled his soft scent. It was hypnotizing as it consumed me completely. "You need *not* to do that, please?" The turmoil in his eyes was evident.

"Why?" I whispered, challenging him even in the state I was currently in, at his mercy.

"Close your eyes," he growled. I did as he said, my body trembling in anticipation. I felt his hot breath on my face and felt the warm, wet tip of his tongue on my lower lip, tasting me. I moaned involuntarily. The knot tightened in my belly.

As quickly as it happened, it stopped. He released my face and stepped back. "I apologize; I shouldn't have . . . I better go." He spun on his heel and ran back to the car. I stood in shock. I watched him get in the car and pull away.

Reeling from the feel of his tongue, the heat of his breath, and the intoxicating scent of him. The ache between my legs tugged, and I needed to find some release. What just happened?

I unlocked the door and stepped into the entrance of the apartment building. The door shut behind me as I made my way up the stairs.

My lip tingled. I licked it and tasted him on me, and the fire flared uncontrollably. I unlocked my apartment door frustrated. Turning on the light, I shut the door behind me with a loud bang. I leaned back against it, taking a deep breath. Closing my eyes and feeling his warm breath, I felt his tongue, and shivers ran through my body.

How was I meant to go to work tomorrow and act like that never happened?

Chapter Three

Grabbing at the loud, obtrusive sound next to me, I found my phone under a pillow and turned my alarm off. The thought of going into the office today was something I wasn't looking forward to. I wasn't sure how to handle seeing Triston. After last night, I didn't want to face him. I rolled over, looking up at the ceiling as the events of last night ran through my mind. I bit my lower lip, closing my eyes, feeling his tongue slowly, deliberately grazing my lip. I trembled at the memory.

I needed to get up. This was driving me insane. Rolling out of bed, I slipped on my dressing gown and went into the kitchen. I turned on the coffee machine and took the beans out of the refrigerator. My phone beeped in the bedroom. I set up the coffee to brew and walked back to retrieve my phone. Who could be messaging me this time of the morning?

Triston: Miss Reid, you're needed at the venue today. Charles will collect you at 7:30. I want you back in the office at midday. Understood?

Well, that answered my question. We were back to formalities. At least that gave me a few hours to ready myself to see him that afternoon. Hopefully, he would be at a meeting, and I wouldn't have to deal with him till the next day. I hit reply.

Em: Certainly, Mr. Hart.

I didn't see the need in mentioning last night if he didn't. The scent of coffee filled the kitchen. I grabbed my mug and filled it. Walking back into the bedroom, I grabbed a pair of jeans and a T-shirt from my closet and laid them on the bed. I wasn't dressing up if I was going to be working at the venue. It suddenly dawned on me that I might see Sebastian. I smiled at the thought of seeing those beautiful hazel eyes and that rugged exterior. My phone beeped again.

Em: Thank you for a lovely evening last night, Miss Reid. We should do it again soon.

I read the message twice. He was giving me

whiplash. Come here, let me tease you with my tongue! No, wait, let me run off into the night! Ugh, men!

I didn't want to reply to him right then. Let him suffer. I needed to get ready for work. In the bathroom, turning on the shower, I heard my phone beep again. I ignored it. I was sure it could wait until I was done. The hot water was relaxing. I closed my eyes, and the steel-blue gaze flashed through my mind, haunting me. I wanted to kiss him so much. I did want him, but he clearly didn't feel the same. So, I should just forget him and move on.

As soon as I stepped out of the shower, my doorbell buzzed. I wrapped the towel around myself and made my way to the door. The buzzing turned to loud knocking. Who the fuck was banging down my door this time of the morning? Not thinking, I flung the door open.

"*What?*" I gasped as I was met with the most intense blue gaze I had ever seen. His eyes traveled gradually from my face down my towel to my dripping wet legs. Apparently, I had picked the smallest fucking towel I owned this morning.

I shivered as the cold breeze blew through the

open door. "Triston, Mr. Hart, uhm . . . Hi, come in." I stepped back. My heart was hammering in my throat.

"Miss Reid, nice to" — he looked me up and down with a predatory grin — "see you again." He walked into my apartment, his eyes darting around the room, taking in his surroundings.

"Why are you here? I mean . . . What are you doing here?" I stumbled over my words.

He turned to face me, and I felt like the prey caught by the hunter. I wrapped the towel tighter, but it didn't budge. "I came to pick you up for work. If you'd answered your phone, you might have known that," he said matter-of-factly.

"I was . . . uhm . . . in the shower." I pointed to the door absentmindedly.

He nodded. "Yes. I can see that, Miss Reid. I sincerely hope you were planning on wearing more clothes than that to work? You never know what kind of vultures would swoop down and grab you." His eyes darkened. "Dressed in the smallest towel I have ever seen." His voice trailed off, and his eyes stopped on my wet legs. The towel was just covering the top half of my thighs, and I blushed.

"Yes . . . Yes, of course. I better go get ready.

Make yourself comfortable." I walked back to the bedroom and dresser to find underwear. My hands were trembling. I needed to get it together. *Shit!* I took a deep, steadying breath and got dressed.

Walking back into the living room ten minutes later, I found Triston sitting on my sofa typing on his phone. He looked up and smiled. "That's much better for work. I approve." He carried on typing. I ignored his comment and walked into the kitchen.

"Would you like a coffee?" I turned to look at him, and he nodded.

"Please."

I turned on the kettle. It would be easier than using the coffee machine since we were in a hurry. Preparing the two mugs on the counter, I took a calming breath. I knew I needed to eat breakfast, but I was too nervous to eat. I grabbed the bag of coffee and the scoop. I couldn't believe Triston was sitting in my apartment, on my sofa.

"Miss Reid." I jumped at his voice, dropping the bag of coffee in my hand. He swooped down and caught it before it hit the floor. His reflexes were perfect, as was everything about him.

"Mr. Hart, I didn't hear you." I took the bag from him, and my fingers brushed along his. The electric current I was getting so used to course through my body.

"You were miles away. Care to tell me where you went to?" He studied me. His piercing blue eyes amused at my discomfort.

"I was just thinking, about the event. I'm looking forward to trying more coffee. Are you joining me? I found an amazing new roaster who has a lovely blend. They're called Tribal Fuel." His eyes darkened, and annoyance crossed his face.

"No, I will be dropping you off and going to a meeting." He turned and walked back into the living room. Sitting down, picking up his phone from the table, he busied himself. He really was peculiar sometimes.

We sat quietly in the car as Triston made his way through traffic. I watched the people on the sidewalk hurrying to get to work. I thought about seeing Sebastian. I wanted to see those hazel eyes again. I licked my lips and realized I had forgotten my lip gloss on the kitchen counter. "Miss Reid, why do you persist on doing that?" His voice filled with irritation.

I turned to look at him. His profile was beautiful against the darkened window. "Doing what, Mr. Hart?" A smirk crossed his lips.

"Mmm . . . never mind. Leave it at that. Here we are. I wish you a good day. I'll see you back at the office at midday, no later. Charles will collect you." His eyes met mine.

"I am sure I can--"

He cut me off. "I said Charles would collect you. Have a good day, Miss Reid." I got out of the car.

"Thank you, Mr. Hart." I closed the door and walked toward the venue. I could feel his eyes on my back, but I didn't turn around. I heard the purr of the engine pull away.

I walked into the office and found Charlene at her desk. "Charlene, how are you?"

She looked up and smiled at me. "Great.

Things are going really well. Everyone is happy, so that makes me happy. I am so glad to see you. I need your help with some photos. Triston mentioned you are pretty good at that, so I figured you could take shots of the event?"

"Oh, Triston did? He never mentioned that he told you." She shrugged as she opened the cupboard door. "Well, you know how he can sometimes be." I nodded. Did I ever.

I walked up to the desk as she pulled out the camera. It was the brand-new Canon EOS 5D SR. One I had my eye on for ages, but it was way out of my price range. "Let me have a look. We would need specific settings for the indoor venue." Charlene handed me the camera and memory card, and I went through the various settings. "I'm going to grab a coffee first and then get to it if you don't mind? Triston wants me back at the office at midday."

"Yeah, sure. He can be such a slave driver honestly." She giggled. I could tell she had a crush on him, but I didn't say anything more. I smiled and made my way back down to the cafeteria.

I went straight to the Tribal Fuel section and grabbed a mug, "Wow, back so soon?" I spun around and saw Sebastian. Dressed in tight blue jeans and a black T-shirt with the company logo across the front, he looked hot, and I couldn't help but admire him.

"Well, you got me hooked to this amazing coffee. What can I say?" I smiled, and he laughed.

Giving me a cheeky wink, he said, "And here I thought it was my good looks and boyish charm that brought you back."

I blushed and took a sip of the coffee. "Sorry to disappoint you, Bash. I don't stalk just anyone, you know." His laugh was deep, and his eyes sparkled at the challenge. He stepped toward me, and my heart leaped into my throat. He reached behind me and grabbed a mug. I stepped aside. His spicy scent enveloped my senses, and I watched him pour his coffee. His hands big, strong, and rugged, utterly completely opposite to Triston. One thing I did notice they had in common were those beautiful pulsing veins.

"So, what brings you back today?" He turned to look at me and caught me looking at his hands.

"I, uh . . ." Holding up the camera, my voice had so obviously abandoned me. "Photos." I wanted the ground to open and swallow me as I sounded like a bumbling idiot. I was sure he would think I was crazy. Smiling, I hoped he didn't notice my fumble, but I knew he could see the blush that heated my face.

"Beautiful and talented. Is there anything you can't do?" He looked at me and smiled.

I thought about it for a second. "Well, I definitely can't ride a horse. Fell off once and never tried again."

He laughed, a deep sexy growl, and my heart raced. "Emily, can I ask you something?" I nodded, not sure of what was coming. "I want to take you out, to dinner, or something. Say yes?"

He looked so adorable.

"Mmm, do you normally pick up random girls at coffee conventions?" I asked and giggled at his pained expression. Watching him was like looking at a little boy begging for his favorite sweets. "Okay, okay. I will go to dinner with you as long as you supply me with coffee for the rest of my life?" His smile was contagious.

"Done deal! So that means you would trust me enough to give me your number?" he said excitedly.

I nodded. "I guess so since you will be picking me up. Ready?" He nodded and pulled out his phone. I watched him add the number to his contacts. He sent a text message, and my phone beeped.

"I had to make sure you weren't giving me a random number!" He winked, turned on his heel, and walked off. I stood there dumbfounded. Two dates in one week, that must be a record.

I pulled my phone out of my pocket and unlocked the screen, opening my messages.

Sebastian: Checking to see if you are real. Bash x

I smiled. I liked him. He was sweet and clearly interested. Unlike someone else who couldn't make up his mind what he wanted.

I spent the next two hours taking photos of the event. Every time I passed the Tribal Fuel stall, I felt Bash's gaze on me, watching me move through the crowds. Our eyes met a few times, and every time my heart raced.

I sat in the car as Charlie drove me back to the office, and the nerves had set in. I didn't know what to expect from Triston. I wondered why Triston insisted on calling him Charles. He was so sweet, and I think Charlie fitted him better. I took my phone out of my bag and saw a message from Triston.

Triston: Miss Reid, when you get in please meet me in my office.

I had felt guilty agreeing to a date with Bash, but Triston made it clear he wasn't interested. Since reading his message, I knew we were back to business. He obviously wanted a professional relationship which I could handle that. I just couldn't handle his tongue on my lips. A shiver ran down my spine at the memory. If he wanted to keep it professional, then we needed to stop the game that was so obvious between us.

"Here we are, Miss Reid. Have a lovely afternoon." Charlie pulled up outside the office. "Thank you, Charlie. Please call me Em?" He nodded, but I knew he wouldn't. I got out of the car and made my way to the elevator. I pressed the call button and waited.

When the elevator doors opened, I waited for it to empty before stepping inside. I pressed 20, and just before the doors closed, a briefcase wedged between them. As they slid open again, Triston stepped in, and my breath hitched. "Miss Reid, nice to see you clothed in more than a towel." His smirk was naughty, and I blushed bright red.

"Mr. Hart, nice to see you not banging down my door." He smirked, and the elevator lurched up. We stood in comfortable silence. My body reacting to the closeness of his body, my skin prickled with anticipation. I felt the heat radiating from him. Dressed in a black Armani suit and silver dress shirt with a black tie, he looked breathtaking. I felt the need to pull his tie toward me and kiss him. My mouth suddenly went dry. Without thinking, I licked my lips.

"For god's sake." Dropping his briefcase, he grabbed me by the shoulders. He pinned my back firmly against the wall, and his body pressed against mine. "You need. To stop. Doing. *That!*" His face was inches from mine. I felt his hot breath on my face. An ache tugged at my lower abdomen. The electricity between us was inescapable. We were clearly fighting something unavoidable.

I looked into his hot, blue gaze. "Doing what, Triston?" I breathed his name, deliberately licking my lower lip. His eyes darkened. "Fuck it!" he growled, and his mouth crashed onto mine, his lips devouring me hungrily. Our tongues tangled and danced. I sucked on his tongue, feeling him lick into my mouth. He growled, and I pressed my body against him. I needed him, aching to feel his touch.

The elevator came to a stop and dinged to alert us we had reached our destination. Triston stepped back and released his grip on my shoulders. Picking up his briefcase, he stepped out of the elevator as nothing had happened.

I followed him out of the elevator, still reeling from the kiss. He held the office door open for me, and I walked past him. Jessie turned and saw us walking in together. She raised her eyebrows, and I shrugged. He walked into his office. "Miss Reid, meeting, please. Bring your iPad."

I walked into his office. "Close the door, would you?" I turned to shut the door. Walking across the office toward his desk felt like walking the plank. His eyes were on me, and my knees still felt shaky from the elevator incident. Sinking into the black leather chair opposite his desk, I opened my Notes app and looked up at him. Lifting the lid of his laptop, he started typing.

Without looking at me, he explained, "We need to plan an important event. Working as a team, we will be in control of everything, from beginning to end. It's in two months. We have complete control over the look and feel, and I want it to be the talk of the city."

That sounded easy enough, and I nodded. "Okay, what is the event?" He motioned for me to come to his desk. "Come around here. Let me show you. The company that was handling it fucked it up last Year. I won the account, and now we have the chance to make megabucks, and it all goes to the charity of my choosing. We need this, Miss Reid, and you are the only one I trust to make it happen for me." I leaned over his shoulder, reading the information on the screen, trying my best to ignore his scent intoxicating all my senses. He turned to look at me, his face once again inches from mine. My gaze dropped to his soft lips that were on mine not that long ago. "Sure, I can . . ." I stood up quickly and smiled, walking around the desk and sitting in the chair again. I typed a few notes and hoped he couldn't see my hand shaking.

He stared at me for a while. Getting up, he walked around his desk, sitting on the edge, his hands gripping the dark wood. "Miss Reid, can I take you out this weekend?" I looked up and stared at him. His face filled with an unreadable expression. He sounded as indecisive as I felt at his question. I was going to need a neck brace with his back and forth. I remembered I had a date tonight with Sebastian. I couldn't date two men; this was going to get ridiculous. I decided to get to the bottom of it.

"Is this a date? Or will it be a professional meeting?" I cocked my head to the side, curious to hear his answer.

He looked thoughtful while he stared at me and smiled. His eyes were beautiful, sparkling blue pools. "A bit of both, Miss Reid. I hope that suits you?"

I nodded. "Fine, a professional date. Do you take all your new staff on professional dates?" I enquired. Acting braver than I felt. His eyes narrowed and darkened at my challenge as my heart raced. I shouldn't have pushed him. Finally, he smirked. It was dark and dangerous. "Do you like to challenge me, Miss Reid?"

I shrugged innocently, praying he couldn't see my heart hammering in my chest. "I was just wondering. No need to answer me if you don't want to," I answered cheekily. He gave a slight nod, acknowledging my statement.

"Stand up." I obeyed his instruction, expecting him to dismiss me. My breath caught in my throat as he straightened and took a step toward me. My pulse quickened with the sexual tension radiating from him. He leaned down, and I could see the beautiful, hypnotic cerulean irises gazing at me. He brought his fingertips to my jawline, slowly tracing the line from my ear to my chin. His eyes followed the path of his fingers.

Lifting my head, making sure our eyes met. His gaze flickered, and he dropped his hand. My mouth went dry again. I licked my lips, and his eyes darkened. He leaned down and licked my top lip, followed by my bottom. A moan escaped my mouth as I felt his tongue hot and wet on me. He flicked his tongue on the underside of my top lip, sending a sensation all the way down my body which ignited the heat between my legs.

He stepped back. "You may go now. Prepare a draft of the marketing plan for the event we spoke of. I want it emailed to me by five p.m. today." He looked at his wristwatch. "That gives you three hours. Plenty of time, don't you think?" His eyes met mine, challenging me to respond.

I nodded. "Definitely, Mr. Hart. You will have it by five p.m." I turned and walked to the door, opening it without another word. As I walked to my desk and glanced at Jessie, she mouthed "What the fuck" to me. I smiled and winked. As I sat at my desk, I gazed into his office window, which overlooked my desk.

He was on a call now. His eyes met mine, and we stared at each other for a few seconds before he broke eye contact and looked at his laptop. I put my earphones in and started up my iTunes. My messenger pinged, and I opened it.

JessieW: "You need to tell me what's happening?"

EmilyR: "We had dinner, nothing happened. He is not interested. It's just professional."

JessieW: "I don't believe that. I am sure something is going on, he is acting really strange."

EmilyR: "Believe it! It is just professional."

JessieW: "Weird… So, no kissing?"

I turned my head and looked at her with a

knowing glance. I felt my face heat up at her question. She laughed out loud.

JessieW: "I KNEW IT!!"

I giggled and closed my messenger; I needed to work. I opened up my Pages app and created a new document. I loved setting up marketing plans, and this was an amazing project. My messenger pinged again, and I opened it.

TristonH: "You do realize I can see you?"

I frowned. What was he talking about? I looked up and saw him looking directly at me.

EmilyR: "I do realize that. Why?"

TristonH: "Jessie and you giggling. I can only imagine what that was about…"

My face heated up again. Shit!

EmilyR: "An overactive imagination is not good for you, Mr. Hart. It might drive you insane."

I looked up and saw his devilish smirk at my response.

TristonH: "Mmmhmm, yes, that is indeed what you do to me, Miss Reid."

EmilyR: "I have work to do, Mr. Hart; my boss is expecting a marketing plan in a few hours."

TristonH: "He is? What a slave driver!"

EmilyR: "Yes he is… extremely demanding!"

TristonH: "You would do good to remember that, and remember that he ALWAYS gets what he wants."

My stomach flip-flopped at his words as I looked up at him through the window. His eyes met mine, giving me a brief nod. I smiled and looked back to my screen, trying to concentrate on my work.

I hit send on my email and turned to Jessie as she was packing up. "I'll see you tomorrow darling. Let's go for coffee after work?"

I nodded. "Yeah, sure, that sounds good!" The office suddenly felt abandoned. Triston and I were the only ones left. I shut down my laptop. Picking up my phone, I saw a message from Sebastian, sent thirty minutes before.

Sebastian: Dress casual, no fancy restaurants tonight, we're going to have some fun. Bash

I smiled. Sounded good. I was a tomboy at heart and was much more comfortable in jeans. I hit reply.

Em: Sounds like my kind of night, see you later

I locked the screen and got up. Grabbing my bag, I slid my laptop in and grabbed the charger. I had my back to Triston's office door as I didn't hear him approach me. "Date tonight?" I jumped at Triston's voice at my neck. I turned to look at him, his body inches from mine, and I could feel the heat radiating from him. I felt a familiar tug in my lower abdomen with him being so close to me.

"It's just a dinner, why?" He shook his head and stepped back. I felt myself release the breath I was holding. His soft, sweet cologne washed over me and had my senses in overdrive. It reminded me of a warm, fresh spring morning. One I wanted to be a part of so much, but he made it clear that wasn't what he wanted.

"Be careful. Let me know when you get home?" He didn't wait for an answer, but turned on his heel, walked back to his office, and closed the door.

I wore my blue Levis, black boots, and a blue tank top. I tied my shoulder-length hair in a low ponytail and kept my makeup natural, adding some lip gloss. I was ready when Bash buzzed the apartment. I walked downstairs and opened the entrance door. He looked so handsome I almost forgot to breathe. His short brown hair spiked and his hazel eyes sparkled. He was dressed in tight, ripped blue jeans, a black T-shirt with the company logo, and a leather jacket. He had black biker boots on, and I noticed him holding a helmet.

"You look amazing! Ready, babe?" I felt a shiver race down my spine because of his voice which was deep and sexy. I nodded.

He handed me a white helmet as he grabbed his black one and put it on. I noticed an S on the side of his helmet, which resembled a lightning strike. He climbed on the black-and-red Ducati 550 and held out his hand to me. I climbed on and instinctively put my arms around his toned torso. "Ready to ride?" He looked back toward me.

"Definitely!" I hadn't been on a motorcycle in years, but I remembered the feeling of the wind rushing past me. He started the engine and revved it a couple of times. I felt the vibration between my thighs, and the goosebumps rose on every inch of my skin.

When he pulled onto the sidewalk ten minutes later, we were outside a bar called Southpaw. I felt the adrenalin pumping through me from the ride. He helped me off the bike and kicked out the stand. Putting the keys in his pocket, he held out his hand to me, and I grabbed it. His fingers laced between mine, and we made our way into the diner. We were in Brooklyn, but that was as much as I knew. There was a queue to get into the bar. Bash walked up to the doorman, who greeted him and opened the barrier. He apparently came here often if the doorman knew him.

"Would you like a drink? We can order dinner as well." He pulled me against him and wrapped his arm around my neck. It felt so natural to be with him. He was so different from Triston.

"I don't mind; do you think we can get a table?" He smiled and nodded.

We walked up to the bar. "Hey dude, how are you doing? Table please?" The barman shook Bash's hand and motioned for us to follow him. We got a booth near the back of the large bar area. It was dimly lit with deep gold lighting, making the red furniture glow. "Beer?" Bash looked at me.

I nodded. "Yes, please."

He showed the barman two fingers and then he turned to me. "Well, here we are. I apologize, I'm not into fancy places I am sure you're used to. Those places I don't really step foot inside, unless my mother forces me to, and I never enjoy it anyway." I looked at his perfect smile as he laughed. There was a rugged handsomeness to him.

"Don't worry, neither do I! So where is your mom?" I giggled.

"She lives in LA. She hates New York, and she only visits a few times a year, when she comes to check up on me." His eyes filled with mischief.

The barman walked over carrying our beers. "Here you go, man. Let me know if you want food. The chef is finishing in an hour, so I need to get the food orders in."

Bash nodded. "Give us a couple of minutes.

I definitely want the burger and fries." The barman nodded and walked off to serve another couple who had just walked in.

"So darling, you ready to eat some junk food with me? They make the best burgers and fries here." His was face animated, the excitement evident in his smile.

I laughed at his enthusiasm. He reminded me of a child excited to open his Christmas presents. I remembered how different dinner with Triston had been, fancy vegan food and red wine. "Then naturally I better try it. You seem to have good taste in coffee, so you better impress me with your taste in food." I picked up my beer, taking a sip. It wasn't bad, I usually drank wine, but I wanted Bash to feel comfortable.

He sat back and stared at me. "Challenge accepted, darling . . . Just you wait and see." As he got up and walked to the bar, my eyes followed his retreating back. He did fill out a pair of jeans really well. My phone beeped. I pulled it out of my jeans and unlocked the screen. My heart started racing. How could a message from him do this to me?

Triston: Look after yourself please. I will pick you up for work tomorrow morning. Make sure you're

dressed this time. T

I stared at the screen, unsure what to say. How do I even reply to him? Bash slid into the booth. "Everything okay?" He gestured to my phone.

I looked up and locked the screen quickly. "Yes, just my boss."

He frowned. "Your boss always text you at night?" I shrugged. I didn't think about it, but I guess he was right. Although Bash didn't know I had gone to dinner with my boss.

"Yeah, um, it's just with all the events this week, we have been swamped." I smiled. "So, tell me about you?" I asked, hopeful to change the subject.

His face visibly calmed down. "What do you want to know?"

"Well, tell me about your love for coffee? How did you come to work for Tribal Fuel?"

He gave me a small smile. "Okay, well, I traveled a lot when I was younger. I, um . . . I had a lot of stupid interests, and when I pulled my life together, I found a love for coffee. The flavors, the aromas, it just intrigued me. I decided to see how it all started. I visited different farms, chatted to the roasters, and then I decided to open Tribal Fuel." His eyes met mine, waiting for my response to what he just told me.

"You OWN Tribal Fuel?" He nodded. "Wow, that's amazing! You said you had a lot of stupid interests? Do I want to know what they were?" He looked down at the table and shook his head. He was silent for a few minutes when we were interrupted by the waiter bringing our food. The burger was massive. I knew there was no way I would finish it, but it looked amazing.

"I hope you enjoy dinner. It's one of my favorites!" Bash grabbed the ketchup and drowned his fries in the red sauce. I giggled, remembering a family barbecue with my mom shouting at us for drowning our food in ketchup. "Did you want some fries with your ketchup?" I asked jokingly.

Bash laughed, his eyes creased at the sides, and I couldn't help but feel at ease with him. "Indeed, my mom always fights with us when we do this!"

I looked up. "Us?" His smile faded, and his eyes flickered with something I couldn't make out. He put the ketchup bottle in the holder, grabbing a couple of fries.

"Yeah, anyway, I hope you enjoy it!" He tucked into his burger, and I knew he was avoiding my question. I couldn't force him to tell me anything; we didn't know each other that well yet.

Bash pulled up to the sidewalk outside my apartment building. I was once again filled with adrenalin from the ride and feeling Bash's taut torso against me. He helped me off the bike and pulled off his helmet as he kicked out the bike stand. His hair stood in every direction, and I wanted to run my fingers through it. "Did you have a good time? Sorry, we have to cut the evening short, but I'm flying out to Brazil tomorrow to check out some coffee farms."

"That's okay. I have an early morning too, so I need to get some rest." I stood awkwardly in front of him, feeling like a teenager at the end of a date. He took a small step toward me, and the scent of his cologne washed over me. It was a mix of spice, coffee, and chocolate. It made me think of a cozy fire crackling on a cold winter night. His hand lifted my chin till my eyes met his. My heart raced in my chest, the knot in my stomach tightening in anticipation of feeling his lips on mine.

He gazed at me intently and leaned down. I felt his warm lips on mine, his tongue pushing between my lips. His kiss was soft, warm, and tender. There wasn't a sexual ache that tugged at me like Triston's kiss. There wasn't that ferocious hunger I felt when Triston's lips touched mine. Completely different in so many ways, even the feeling I had around each of them.

My lips felt cold when he stepped back. "I will see you in a couple of days when I'm back from Brazil. You busy on Saturday?"

I was about to say no when I remembered I was busy — with my boss. *Shit!* "Uhm, yeah, I have . . . work. How about Sunday?"

He smiled and nodded. "Perfect. Sunday it is."

He got back on the bike. Turning back to where I stood on the sidewalk, he tossed me the helmet. "Keep this for next time." I caught it. Thank god for netball at school.

"Is that a guarantee you'll see me again?" I asked. He nodded and winked.

"As a matter of fact, it is, darling." Pulling the helmet over his spikey hair, he turned on the engine, revved it a couple of times, and raced off into the night. I smiled, looking down at the helmet — a promise. One I wasn't sure how I could keep.

I walked up to the entrance and made my way upstairs. As I unlocked my apartment door, my phone beeped in my pocket. Pulling it out, I looked at the screen — a message from Triston. I walked into my apartment before unlocking the screen and opening the message.

Triston: Miss Reid, I trust you are home safely?

Was he keeping tabs on me now, seriously? He was so frustrating; I sighed as I hit reply.

Em: I am Mr. Hart. Thank you for your concern.

An immediate reply beeped.

Triston: I am indeed concerned about your well-being, Miss Reid. Sleep now.

For God's sake, he was so demanding. I was tired, but who was he to tell me to sleep? He was my boss, not my boyfriend, so he had no right to tell me to go to sleep. As frustrating as he was, a message from him sent the butterflies in my stomach into a fluttering frenzy.

Em: You are very demanding, Mr. Hart; I am not

tired

Triston: Early morning tomorrow. I need you 100%, please?

I smiled at the last message. He actually said please. Maybe he could stop being such a control freak and let me be myself like Bash. I felt so relaxed around him. They were both so different, yet they both were amazing in their own way. Triston made it clear he didn't want anything romantic between us. My phone started ringing, startling me out of my thoughts. "Hello?"

"Miss Reid, I didn't get a reply. I was hoping you were asleep." I walked into the bedroom. Sitting on my bed, I laid back, staring at my ceiling. "I was. You woke me up," I lied.

"I do not appreciate lies, Miss Reid. I can tell from the tone in your voice you were still very much awake. Now, would you please put my mind at ease and go to sleep?"

I stayed silent and thought about the deep, sexy voice on the other end of the line. "Well, I would go to sleep if you weren't on the phone with me." I knew he would have something to say to that, and I was right.

"Don't get cheeky with me, Miss Reid." His

warning sent shivers down my spine, and I wanted to challenge him. The familiar tug that Triston brought to my lower abdomen was there, strong as ever.

"Or what, Mr. Hart?" I replied, smiling.

"I will take you over my knee and show you just how respect is earned." I gasped at his threat but felt the heat in my core sending a delectable tingle straight to my panties. It felt deliciously wicked, just like Triston. I wanted this man. The ache inside was building, and I couldn't deny it anymore. I just wished he would stop being so frustrating and let me in.

"Why this sudden concern for me?"

"I don't have time for this. Go to sleep Emily. Goodnight." Closing off once again, I felt the frustration.

He hung up before I could reply. My stomach was doing flip-flops at the way he said my name. He was so direct with his deep, scratchy, sexy voice. He sounded so good at night. I dropped my phone on the bed and went to the bathroom. I needed to stop this effect he had on me. We could never work. He made that abundantly clear, but why did I still feel the need to challenge him. I knew I was in way over my head. He was my boss, but I wanted him.

I brushed my teeth and took off my makeup. Staring at myself in the mirror, the blush on my cheeks I knew was from my conversation with Triston.

Chapter Four

I decided on my black, knee-length skirt with my silver cashmere top for the meeting. My nerves took over. It was an important presentation, and Triston was counting on me to deliver. A prospective client worth millions! It was my time to show Triston I was made for the job. I wasn't sure what made me more nervous — being with him, or the presentation.

The apartment buzzer alerted me the car was here. Making my way down to the foyer, I took a deep breath before opening the door. The car was waiting, and Charlie was in the driver's seat. Triston was leaning against the door of the SUV in his black suit, wearing a black dress shirt and silver tie. His shoulder-length hair tied back in a bun, his steel-blue eyes sparkled. I decided being with Triston made me more nervous than the presentation. I walked up to him and smiled. "Mr. Hart."

"Miss Reid, you look . . ." His eyes roamed my body. His unfinished sentence hung in the air. I felt myself shiver. The fire ignited in my stomach, and I ached for him. He held out a hand to me. "Come on, beautiful, let's get this done." I took his hand, and he helped me into the car. I slid into the plush leather seat. "Hello, Charlie, how are you?"

He smiled back at me and gave a small nod. "Miss Reid."

Triston slid into the seat next to me. His leg brushed against mine, and I felt a surge of electricity. I wanted him. Right there in the back seat of the car, my whole body yearned for him. "Triston, I . . ." He looked at me, with his soft gaze.

"Emily, let's get through this meeting, and we can talk at lunch, okay?" I nodded. His hand found mine, and he squeezed it. I wasn't sure what to think anymore. I didn't know what to say to him. I liked Bash, but there was something about Triston that pulled me toward him. Something magnetic I could no longer ignore.

"Je Te Veux Events is the most prominent company in New York, with a reach worldwide. Our current event calendar and client lists are proof of that. Mr. Jacobson, we have the experience and the staff capable of handling international events such as yours. Mr. Hart prides himself in his hands-on approach with all the events we organize." My eyes met Triston's, and he smiled, winking at me. I felt a surge of confidence. "It will be in your best interest to entrust your worldwide events to us. Let me assure you Mr. Hart is demanding of his staff and runs a tight ship. We can do this." My eyes met Triston's again, and I saw them darken at my mention of him being demanding. I bit my lip to suppress the giggle threatening to escape. His eyes focused on my mouth with a devilish smirk curving his lips.

I stood at the front of the room, eight sets of eyes on me, but the most important were a bright steel-blue. I could see Mr. Jacobson debating what I had just told them. He was a short, stocky man with a kind face. He broke out into a broad grin, and I felt myself relax. "You're a little firecracker! I like you! Mr. Hart, congratulations, you have our account. I will have our lawyer draw up the contracts." He stood and shook Triston's hand. "As long as this beautiful young woman is handling my account." He smiled back at me, and I felt a blush cross my face.

Triston smiled. "Certainly, Mr. Jacobson. She is my best girl!" He looked over at me. He was beaming, and so was I. We did make an excellent team. "Well, you better hold on to her. Don't let her get away!" Mr. Jacobson walked across and shook my hand. He exited the conference room, leaving us to pack up. I shut down my laptop and slid it into the bag. Rolling up my charger cable, I turned as Triston grabbed me and swung me around. "Thank you!" His lips found mine, deep and hungry while his tongue was demanding entrance to my mouth. He licked into me, tasting me. I moaned, pushing my body against his rock-hard torso. He let me down but kept his arms wrapped tightly around me, pulling me into him. When he pulled away, he looked down guiltily. "Sorry. I, uh . . . let myself get carried away."

I reached up to touch his face. He grabbed my wrist and stepped back. "Don't! Let's get lunch." He turned and walked to his seat to collect his briefcase and laptop. Confused by his sudden change in emotions, I grabbed my bag and walked to the door. Why did he pull away like that? It just didn't make any sense! I was still reeling from the kiss when we stood side by side in the elevator. The current flowing between us was palpable; he needed to decide what he wanted.

"A bottle of champagne." Triston handed the menu to our waiter. He looked at me and smiled. "Thank you for today. You were amazing!" I blushed. I was excited that he saw my ability today.

"It's a pleasure. It was amazing doing the presentation. My dream come true. Thank you for giving it to me, Triston." The waiter brought our champagne, and Triston motioned for him to leave it. He picked up the bottle himself and untwisted the foil, popping the cork and pouring a glass for each of us.

"To us! We make an amazing team, Emily." We clinked glasses. His smile took my breath away.

My phone started ringing, and I looked

down. Sebastian's name flashed on my screen. I grabbed it as I set my glass down. "Just a sec." I got up, walking over to the bar area. "Hello?"

"Hey, darling, I just arrived in Brazil! It's beautiful and hot, and I wish you were here." Sebastian sounded excited. No unreleased tension filled me hearing him. He sounded like he was on holiday, and I smiled. "Well, I hope you have fun. I am having a . . ." I glanced back at Triston. He was busy on his phone. "Lunch meeting. I have to go. See you Sunday?"

"Sure. I just wanted to hear your voice. Chat soon, darling." The line went dead, and I took a deep breath. This was definitely not going to work. I walked back to the table and slid into the booth.

"Everything okay?" Triston inquired. I nodded and smiled, picking up my champagne and gulping it down. I didn't know what I was doing.

"Yes! A friend, just checking up to see how I'm doing." He frowned, nodding acceptance to my answer. He picked up his phone, scrolled down and held the phone to his ear. "Jessie, we will be out all day. Cancel my three o'clock. Miss Reid and I have somewhere to go." He hung up and looked at me. "You want to do something with me? To celebrate?" I wanted to spend every moment with him. How could he not see that?

I smiled. "Sure! What did you have in mind?"

"It's a surprise. We need to take you home, and you need to get changed." I looked into those beautiful eyes. He seemed truly happy.

I decided on my black denim shorts, a white tank top, and a pair of Converse. Triston said we would be walking, so I wanted to be comfortable. It was the end of May, and we were having amazing weather. I left my long brown hair loose down my back. When I made my way to the living room, Triston was sitting on my sofa working on his laptop. He looked up when I walked in and smiled. "You ready?"

"Yes! Are you going to tell me where we're going?" He shook his head. Walking back out to the car, his fingertips lightly brushed my lower back, sending a current through me. We slid into the back of the car, and Triston called out to Charlie, "To my apartment, Charles. I need to get out of this suit." His gaze fell on me at that moment, and I blushed furiously imagining him naked. The fire that seemed to be permanently burning inside me flared, and I squirmed as he drove me insane with wanton lust. I wanted to be with him, to get to know the person behind the mask that he held up. I wanted him to let me into that amazing mind, and maybe then into his heart.

We pulled up to Triston's apartment, and he told me to wait in the car. When I checked my phone, there was nothing from Bash; I guess he was busy.

Triston slid into the seat next to me ten minutes later dressed in a pair of gym shoes, a pair of tight black jeans, and a casual blue tee. His long hair hung loosely on his shoulders.

He told Charlie to drive us to the ferry. I wasn't sure where we were going, but I was excited. It had just hit midday, and we had the whole afternoon ahead of us.

We stepped onto the Staten Island Ferry fifteen minutes later. Triston still didn't tell me what we were going to do, but he did tell Charlie to take the afternoon off. "Are you ever going to tell me what we're doing?" I pleaded. I pouted and crossed my arms. "I will throw a tantrum; you do realize that?" I giggled, and he wrapped his arm around my waist, pulling me into him. Such a small gesture, but so perfect. It felt like we were a real couple.

"Soon!" he laughed. I rolled my eyes, and he leaned closer to me. He pulled me tighter against him, and his eyes seared into mine. I felt my body tingle. "You roll your eyes at me, Miss Reid, and I will take you across my knee right here on this ferry!" My body trembled at his threat. The thought of him taking such a dominant role over me had my heart racing. I looked into his eyes, challenging and teasing.

"Promise?" I cocked my head to the side and licked my lips. His eyes darkened, and I saw the desire dancing in them. He grabbed my wrist, pulling me to the back of the ferry. Since it was practically empty, no one ventured this far back. He pinned me against the wall and put a hand either side of my face. "Do you really want to challenge me, Miss Reid?" His voice laced with desire that tugged at my core.

I looked into his midnight blue gaze, and I

could tell things were running through his mind I ached to know. Naturally, in my stubbornness to obey, I nodded. "I do, Mr. Hart; I enjoy challenging you." He searched my eyes with a dark smirk on his face, his expression full of danger. I knew now he wanted me as much as I did him. He leaned closer, and I ached for him to kiss me, his warm mouth just inches from mine. My mouth felt dry, my heart racing at his closeness.

I licked my lips deliberately. His eyes flickered to my mouth, watching my tongue. I chewed on my lower lip, then released it with a coy smile. I couldn't believe his eyes could be any darker blue than they already were. He grabbed my bottom lip with his teeth and bit down gently. Currents shot down my spine, collecting between my legs, and I felt myself moisten at the pain. I moaned into his mouth. He softly sucked my lower lip into his warm mouth, and my knees trembled. Suddenly, he released me and stepped back. "Later."

We got off the ferry and hailed a cab to The

Conference House. This was where Triston wanted to hold the charity event. After the incident on the ferry, I kept the teasing at bay. I wasn't sure I could handle another one of his luscious assaults on my body.

We walked up to the beautiful historic house with lavish gardens. There was a forest in the distance, and a large gazebo, which could provide cover for a catering area. "This place is amazing!" He looked at me and smiled.

"Isn't it? I think it will be perfect for our fundraiser, and you, my dear, will be heading it all up. I wanted to bring you here to show you what you would be working with." He looked down at me and smiled. "Think you can handle it?" He winked, and I wasn't sure we were talking about the event anymore.

"Trust me, Mr. Hart, I can handle it!" I walked off in the direction of the gardens, and I heard his footsteps behind me.

"You're a stubborn girl, aren't you, Miss Reid?" I walked faster, my heart racing as he followed, his footfalls quickening to catch up to me. The gardens were vast with beautiful trees; it looked like a fairytale forest.

"I am, Mr. Hart. Think you can handle me?"

I teased him. Our good mood from winning the account was contagious. I felt carefree. I glanced back and saw him a few steps behind. I hadn't felt as excited and happy in such a long time. I felt like I couldn't stop smiling, mostly due to Triston. I ran into the forest area between the trees, the sun still high, and the shade felt good, cooling me down. I hid behind a large oak tree. "Miss Reid, I do like games. Very much so. But what do I get when I find you?"

"You will just have to find me and see for yourself, Mr. Hart!" I shouted as I darted behind another tree. I heard his deep laugh, and I listened to his footsteps on the grass. He was close. My heart hammered against my ribcage, and I giggled to myself. My phone beeped just then, and I knew he heard it, so I moved to another tree where I could see him from my hiding spot. I pulled out my phone.

Unlocking the screen, it was a picture from Bash. My smile faltered; he was on a coffee farm. I shook my head and shoved the phone back in my pocket. I could deal with it later. I turned to get a glimpse of Triston, but he had disappeared from my view. I frowned and turned the other way, crashing into something hard. I looked up into steel-blue eyes. "Boo!" He laughed and grabbed me around the waist. The closeness of his body had me trembling. He pinned me against the large tree trunk, my back flush against the tree. "Now, Miss Reid, what is it that I get?" He leaned in, and I felt his warm breath on my face. His intoxicating scent overwhelmed my senses, and I arched my body into him.

I smiled and looked into his beautiful sparkling eyes. My hand rested on his torso as I felt the hard ridges of his abdomen, and I felt the need to lick him, he felt so delectable. "What is it that you want, Mr. Hart?" I whispered.

His devilish smirk returned, and he leaned in closer. His mouth next to my ear, sending delicious tingles through me. "What I want might be something you can't handle, Miss Reid . . ."

His lips brushed my neck, and I moaned. Feeling every rock-hard inch of this handsome man pressing against me sent electricity flowing through me. The need I felt at that moment surpassed anything I had ever felt.

"Why don't you let me decide what I can or can't handle, Mr. Hart?" My voice was a hoarse whisper. His hands ran along my arms, causing me to shiver. He deliberately teased my lips with his tongue, the same way he did the first night outside my apartment.

His hands reached my hips, and he held me in a vice grip. Pulling me into him, his groin rigid against me, and I knew I was slick with desire. His mouth was warm; it covered mine, and he devoured me. Letting go of any inhibitions he may have had, he kissed me, and I let him. My hands tangling in his long silken hair. I felt his stubble on my chin. He growled into the kiss as he pulled me in tighter.

I plated the takeaway stir-fry on two plates and looked up. I smiled looking at Triston sitting on my sofa again. He was working as usual; I didn't think he ever stopped. We had just gotten back from Staten Island, and he wanted to buy dinner. I was too tired to go out, so we decided on takeaway. I enjoyed the afternoon with him. The kiss was incredible, but once we got on the ferry, it seemed like we were back to business. He didn't mention the kiss or anything else for that matter. "Triston, dinner is ready," I called to him, and he nodded. "Be right there."

We sat at the counter and ate in comfortable silence. I poured us each a glass of white wine. "Do we have any meetings tomorrow?" I inquired.

"No, but we need to work on the marketing plan. If we don't get it done, I think we may have to put in some hours tomorrow and Sunday." I looked up quickly. Sunday. "I, uh . . . have plans on Sunday."

He looked at me, clearly taken aback. "You do?" I nodded. "Right. We will have to finish everything tomorrow so you can go out on your date. Or whatever it is. We can work at my place. I have my office set up with two desks so that we won't get in each other's way."

I swallowed, watching his reaction. He seemed jealous. Trying to gauge his expression was difficult. He held a brilliant poker face. "Sure, sounds good." I licked the fork as the food was so good. I looked up, noticing that his eyes were dark and dangerous. "You are deeply distracting, you know that?"

I cocked my head to the side. "What do you mean?"

He looked down at his plate, smiled, and

finished the last of his dinner. I watched him, waiting for his response. He really did frustrate me, most times. Swallowing his food, he picked up his wine and took a sip. He caught my stare and smirked. "I meant exactly what I said. You're distracting."

"Distracting in what way, Triston?" I asked incredulously. He shook his head, got up, and took his plate to the sink. He started washing it. I smiled.

"Don't do that." He ignored me and proceeded to dry his plate. He opened the cupboards and found the one that held the crockery, placing his plate inside.

"Done!" He walked back to the counter and grabbed my empty plate. Following the same procedure, I watched him wash the plate, dry it, and pack it in the cupboard. He looked at his wristwatch. "I better go; it's late, and you need to sleep."

I stood, finishing the last of my wine. I leaned against the breakfast bar. "Do you like being so demanding?" I asked. His smirk answered my question. His gaze taking in every inch of my face, he finally settled on my eyes.

"I do. It's how I run a multi-million-dollar

empire, Miss Reid." He was frustrating me. He kissed me with such intent earlier that couldn't have been all business to him. I felt something more. "So this" — I gestured between us — "is just business?"

He folded his arms across his chest and looked at me. He leaned against the sink. We were at odds, standing opposite each other, neither one of us knowing what to say. He looked so sexy in his ripped blue jeans and too-tight tee. His muscles and veins were prominent and defined, and I ached to run my fingers along them. "You are my employee, Miss Reid." I felt physical pain in my chest as his words were cold. I couldn't let him see me cry, although I wanted to slap him.

"Well, Mr. Hart, I suggest you not kiss your employees in the future. It's not professional. And I suggest you leave now." My face hardened to him, and I could tell he was frustrated at my words. I felt the tears burning my eyes, but I refused to let them spill.

"Emily . . ." His voice was softer now, but I stopped him before he could say anything more.

"Good night, Mr. Hart. I will see you for work tomorrow." I walked over to the front door and held it open for him. He grabbed his laptop and phone from the living room.

His eyes betrayed him as he walked past me. I saw some emotion there, but he didn't let it show any further. He stood on the threshold and looked at me. "Emily . . ."

I shut the door in his face. Hearing his footsteps on the stairs, I slid down to the door as the tears flowed.

I arrived at Triston's penthouse apartment four hours earlier. It was perched high above Central Park, located at a sun-flooded corner of the tower. I noticed a wrap-around terrace with exquisite outdoor furniture. The open-plan living room and dining room were elegantly furnished. Modern furniture and masculine colors conveyed his style perfectly. Blacks, greys, and blues. A classic design with beautiful cityscape and Central Park views. The artwork hanging on the walls had beautiful accentuating colors. Reds, oranges, and purples. His office was old-worldly, furnished with two deep, mahogany desks, a wall filled with books, and a stunning Chesterfield sofa. He didn't make mention of the night before, and neither did I.

After making us both coffee and setting out croissants, we got to work. He was relaxed and professional with me. As much as it hurt, I knew I had asked for it. I just couldn't play his game anymore, not when my feelings were real, and his weren't. I knew I was falling for him, but he apparently didn't feel it. I couldn't do anything about it; I wanted this job. He viewed this as a business transaction, and I was not prepared to be one of his deals.

"Miss Reid, where are we with the layout plan?" he asked, pulling me from the painful thoughts in my mind. He looked up from his laptop, and when his eyes met mine, I felt a surge of love for a man who would never feel it for me. "I was about to email it to you, as well as the schedule for setup and breakdown."

He nodded and carried on typing. "Good." He didn't look up again, his voice clipped and serious. There was an icy tension in the room now, and it was distracting. My phone beeped. I picked it up and unlocked the screen. Bash.

Sebastian: Hey darling, hope you're not working too hard. Can't wait to see you tomorrow. Bash x

I smiled, feeling a blush heat my face, not caring if Triston noticed it. He shouldn't be bothered by me seeing anyone. We were professional after all, but deep down it tugged at my heart. As much as I wanted to ignore my feelings for Triston, I couldn't.

Em: Work is boring and busy. I can cook dinner tomorrow. x

His immediate reply beeped, and I felt Triston's gaze on me.

Sebastian: Sounds good. A girl that cooks, what a bonus… lol x

I smiled at his response and felt excited for tomorrow. I didn't feel the same magnetism I felt with Triston, but I liked Bash. He was sweet and relaxed, and he made me smile. I needed to give it a chance with Bash. I wondered what I should make. I knew he wasn't vegan, so that made it much easier. "Boyfriend?" Triston stared at me, his gaze demanding, but his voice was cool and calm. "Maybe. Who knows?" I answered nonchalantly. Something flickered in his gaze. Something dark.

"Mmm . . ." He looked back at his screen and

carried on working.

I closed my laptop and slid it into my bag. We had finished the whole marketing plan, and I was starting to see double from staring at the screen all day. I checked the time; it was six. I needed to get dinner. Take-out would be good. Triston came back into the office holding two glasses of chilled white wine, condensation clouding the glasses, and I felt the need to hold it against my face to cool me down. "Join me?" Handing me a glass, he turned and walked into the living room.

I followed him. "What's this for?" I held up the glass.

"A drink to thank you for today. Is that okay?" Nodding, I took a sip. The wine was crisp and refreshing after the long day.

"Sure. I will just have one, though. I haven't eaten." I sat on the sofa and watched him move to the docking station for the iPod. He scrolled through the albums and pressed play. "We can remedy that. I know a lovely little place—"

"No thank you," I cut him off. I recognized

the music filling the living room. The ethereal Icelandic band Sigur Rós. I had a couple of their albums. Hoping to change the subject, I gestured to the speakers. "I like them."

I took in his appearance as he stood at the stereo. Dressed in blue, ripped jeans that seemed to hug his hips and thighs, his white tee hung loosely on his upper body, making me wonder what was beneath. I couldn't help but notice how sexy he looked.

He nodded. "They're really good. I figured we could relax for a bit and talk." Making his way back toward me, he slid onto the sofa next to me. "Look, Em, I'm not used to being with anyone in any way other than business—"

I sat forward and looked at him. "Please, don't explain anything. It's okay. You are my boss. That's all. I understand." I stood up and put the glass on the table. I walked back into the office and grabbed my bag and coat. I didn't feel like doing this. I was already angry, and I didn't want to fight.

"Emily." He stood up and watched me walk past the sofa, but he didn't make a move to stop me. He had his chance, and he didn't take it.

"I better get going. See you Monday." I got

to the door and grabbed the handle. Turning around, I mistakenly looked back. There was a pleading in his eyes, and it tugged at my heart. All I wanted to do was run into his arms and never let go. I was so confused, what did he want? He made this choice when he said we were nothing more than boss and employee.

His smile had a certain sadness attached to it. "Goodnight, Emily." And there I had my answer.

Chapter Five

When I opened my eyes Sunday morning, I felt a dull ache in my chest from Triston's words the day before. What I needed was to forget about Triston and every romantic feeling I had for him. That was easier said than done, naturally. I turned on the coffee machine and opened the balcony doors, inhaling the fresh, early morning air. Closing my eyes, I willed myself to enjoy the day. I wasn't seeing Triston, and it was a small relief, although I would rather be near him. The beautiful blue eyes haunted my dreams in the night, always there, in the back of my mind.

My phone rang from the kitchen, pulling me out of my reverie. Picking it up, I saw Triston's name flashing on the screen. What did he want? Didn't he do enough damage last night? Swiping the screen, I answered the call. "Hello?"

"Miss Reid, I apologize for the interruption on a Sunday," his deeply formal voice greeted me. My heart tugged in pain. "I just got off the phone with Mr. Jacobson. He wants us to fly out to LA tomorrow. I want you packed and ready. I will pick you up at nine a.m." I stared at the wall, not sure what to say. Why would Triston take me to LA? "Uhm . . . LA? For how long?" I mumbled. Silence greeted me. Then I heard him typing. "He says three days. We need this, and you need to be there. He wanted you on his account."

I remembered at the presentation, Mr. Jacobson asked for me specifically. "Okay, sure, what about flights?"

"I have paid for them already. Think of it as a business vacation, Miss Reid. I will be at your door tomorrow morning. Please make sure you're dressed." He stayed silent for another few minutes. "Have a good day, Emily." His voice was soft, and there was a lingering sadness to the way he said my name. I felt tears burning my eyes and blinked them away.

I nodded. Realizing he couldn't see me, I mumbled, "Thank you. Same to you, Triston."

The doorbell buzzed at midday. I picked up the intercom. "Hello?" I heard the deep, sexy rumble of Sebastian.

"Hello, gorgeous!" Pressing the button to unlock the foyer door, I opened my apartment door and waited at the threshold. He came bounding up the stairs with a handful of beautiful white roses.

"Wow, Bash, they're gorgeous. You should go away more often," I teased him. He pulled me into a grip with his free arm and gave me a tight hug.

"Well, I might have to if all goes well with the suppliers I saw in Brazil! Also, my new investor is happy with the way things are going." His lips found mine, and I melted into his warm body. As soon as I started to relax in his embrace, blue eyes flashed through my mind. I pulled away, smiling, and let Bash in. He handed me the flowers and closed my apartment door. Taking the bouquet to the kitchen, I grabbed a vase and filled it with water. "Well, you might have to put up with not seeing me for a little while after today. I am flying to LA tomorrow." Arranging the roses in the glass vase, I turned and placed it on the counter.

Bash's eyes met mine. "Why?" He slid onto the barstool at the counter, watching me.

"I am flying to LA with my boss tomorrow. We have a new client to impress, and I was one of the prerequisites for us landing the account." He narrowed his eyes and nodded. He stood and walked around to me. Wrapping his arms around my waist, he pulled me against him. His body was solid. "A prerequisite. Wow, that's interesting. So, if I was a client, you could be my prerequisite?" he asked, winking and giving me his devilish smirk.

"Don't be cheeky!" I laughed, swatting his arm. "Let me cook now!" He released me with a quick kiss. I busied myself in the kitchen with the vegetables. Bash stood at the living room balcony. "You have an amazing view!"

"Yes, I love it. That was the main reason I wanted this apartment." I remembered viewing the apartment. I was excited for the open-plan living room-kitchen area as well as the amazing view. I put the deposit down immediately.

He nodded and walked into the kitchen. "So, my wench, what are you cooking for me?" he asked playfully as he wrapped his arms around my waist, his chin resting on my shoulder. My skin tingled from the feeling of his five o'clock shadow against my neck. It felt rough and sexy, like everything about him. "I'm making lasagna, my good sir. would that be to your satisfaction?" I replied, playing along. "And you can help yourself to a beer in the fridge."

He kissed my neck lightly and walked over to the refrigerator, oblivious to the effect his kiss had on me. "Wow, you bought beer just for me?" He pulled one out and shut the door.

"Yeah, I figured you didn't drink wine, so beer it is." He winked and pulled up a barstool at the breakfast bar, watching me prepare the vegetables. I turned to the stove and turned on the burner.

"So, tell me about the company you work for?" he asked. I heated the oil and added the vegetables. "I do marketing and event management for Je Te Veux Events—"

Bash spluttered and choked on his beer. I spun around. "Bash, you okay?" I grabbed some paper towels and handed it to him. I grabbed another sheet and wiped the counter. I stared at him in concern.

"Yeah, fine. I didn't realize you worked for Triston." My mouth fell open, and a cold chill filled my body as I felt goosebumps on my skin. I stared at him in shock. "You know Triston?"

Sebastian gave a quick laugh and shook his head. "You could say that, yeah." I waited for him to explain. When he didn't, I asked again.

"Bash? How do you know Triston?" He stared at me. I could see turmoil in his expression. I folded my arms across my chest to keep from shaking. What on earth? How would he even know who Triston was?

"He's my brother, Emily."

I stared at him, my mouth agape. A cold shiver rushed down my spine, and words failed me. What the fuck had I gotten myself into? I didn't think they looked anything alike. My memory played back, flashes of their smiles, the way their eyes creased when they laughed. It all started to meld together in one massive Hart collage. My brain hurt. I suddenly felt sick. What the fuck was I doing? I couldn't date Bash; this was a little too close to home.

"Em, you okay? You look like you've seen a ghost." Bash looked at me, concern written all over his handsome features. He reached out to me, and his touch felt like ice on my skin. Closing my mouth, I tried to find the words to answer him.

"Yes, I think I may have."

I turned back to the stove, adding the pasta to the pot that was now boiling. My hands were trembling; I had kissed both brothers. I didn't know, of course and I wouldn't have done it if I had known. I closed my eyes for a moment and saw Triston's handsome face. If he found out about this . . . I didn't want to think about it. I knew what he was like. I couldn't imagine what he would say. Or do, for that matter.

Bash's arms wrapped around me, and I jumped. "Are you sure you're okay?" He turned me around and lifted my chin. My eyes met his beautiful hazel ones. "What's wrong?" He searched my face for the answer. I felt numb. I was falling for Triston, and now I was standing in his brother's arms. "Nothing. I just didn't realize you were . . . He was . . ." I was at a loss for words.

He pulled me into him and hugged me. "Shhh, it's okay."

No, it wasn't, I wanted to shout, but I knew I couldn't. There was no way I could tell him what happened between Triston and me. Nothing was ever going to happen again anyway. Triston made that very clear. So why did it feel like I was cheating on them both?

We were sitting on the sofa after dinner watching the new Fast & Furious movie. Bash was loving the fast cars, and I was guessing the girls in bikinis too. His strong arm draped around my shoulders. He commented on Vin Diesel's car, "Now that is a beast!" I giggled at him, the tension from earlier gone. My landline rang. That was weird. I hadn't given anyone that number. I got up and grabbed the cordless phone from the wall charger. "Hello?" Bash was too engrossed in the movie to notice my face when I heard the voice on the other end of the line.

"Miss Reid, I need to talk with you. I am on my way to your place now." He sounded like he was walking or had been walking. He hung up before I could reply. *Shit!*

Sebastian looked at me. I looked up at him. "Gorgeous? You okay?" Concern etched in his voice. I shook my head and hung the phone back in the cradle.

"Your brother is on his way over. Now." His

face flickered, and I could see irritation etched on his rugged features.

"I better go." He got up and grabbed his jacket, walking into the kitchen. He leaned down and kissed my lips lightly. I didn't want him to go. I was finally at ease about this situation.

"No, don't go? Stay please?" I asked. Touching his arm, I felt the tension radiating from him. There was something between the brothers, something terrible, and the thought of them fighting pulled at me.

"It's not a good idea I see my brother."

What happened between them? It must have been something serious. "Okay, then wait in my room? He wouldn't stay long; I am sure its just to drop off more work."

He stared at me for a moment, considering my words. A knock at the door startled us both. "You don't have a choice now," I whispered. He finally nodded in resignation and went into the bedroom. My nerves were shot. I had one brother in my bedroom, and the other was at my door. I could do this; I just need to stay calm.

Taking a deep breath, I walked to the apartment door and pulled it open. My breath hitched, and I blushed. Triston was wearing a white tank top with a pair of gray track pants. He had his gym shoes on. The sweat glistened on his beautifully sculpted arms. It looked like he had been jogging. I took in his toned biceps. His forearms and hands were pulsing with thick veins that pulled at my core. His hair was tied back into a bun, and I could see his toned neck and shoulders.

I licked my lips. He was glistening, and I wanted to devour him right there. I felt heat surge through me, making its way down, collecting in a tight knot between my legs. "You going to just stand there staring at me, or invite me in?" he asked, amused at my blatant gaze drinking him in.

I nodded, gulping air into my lungs. "Yes, yes sure. Um . . . Come in?" I stepped aside. Aware of the fact that Bash was eavesdropping on everything being said. "What . . . I mean . . . Why are you here?" Triston's eyes fell on the roses. I saw his muscles tense, and his jaw clenched when he turned to me. He leaned against the kitchen counter, with his arms crossed over his chest. His stance only accentuated his muscles.

"I wanted to check on you. We leave tomorrow morning at nine a.m. Make sure you're ready.

Have you packed?"

I nodded. "Yes, I will be. My suitcase is out and ready to be packed. I'll do it later tonight, Triston."

He nodded. "Maybe bring along a swimsuit, you may want to go to the beach while we're there. We also will be having an exclusive dinner with Mr. Jacobson. I have bought you a dress for that. It will be delivered to the hotel in LA." His eyes glistened and roamed over me.

I nodded. "Okay. You could have told me that over the phone."

He smiled, nodded, and straightened up. "I know. I just wanted to see you. Goodnight, Miss Reid. Enjoy your date." He walked passed me, opened the apartment door, and left. I stood in shock. What just happened? My bedroom door opened slowly. I turned to Bash and shrugged. "He's gone." He smirked, walking toward me.

"Sounds like Mr. Ice Cold is crushing on you in a major way." He dropped his jacket on the back of the sofa. I could tell Bash was not happy about the situation.

"What? How do you know?" I shoved my hands in the pocket of my shorts and looked at him quizzically.

"I know my brother, Em. When he is that determined on someone or something, nothing stands in his way. I definitely don't want to be in the way." He lifted his hands in surrender.

"You're not in the way. We are just coworkers, boss, and employee. I am nothing more to him. He has made it clear." I knew my words let on that there was something more, but I couldn't change it now. Bash would have found out at some point anyway.

He looked at me. I could see the concern in his eyes. He was clearly worried about this. "Did you and my brother . . . ?" He didn't need to finish his sentence for me to know what he meant. "God no! We . . . We kissed." He closed his eyes like he was in pain, pinching the bridge of his nose. "Jesus, Em, he is going to fucking lose it. It is so obvious that he likes you. He doesn't just go around kissing girls!"

"I do not care what he wants. He made it painfully clear we have a working relationship, nothing more. Would you please stop worrying?" I walked up to him and wrapped my arms around his tight torso. My hands roamed his back and fell to his tight ass, and he was built just like his brother, from what I could feel.

His big hands grabbed my face, and he kissed me softly. Teasing my lips open with his tongue, I sucked his tongue into my mouth, and he groaned. His kiss became more urgent as his hands trailed down my arms to my hips. Lifting me by my ass, he made me wrap my legs around him while he growled, "I want you, Em." I heard the engines rumbling on the TV, but the movie was forgotten. He walked us over to the sofa and laid me down supporting his weight on his right arm, trailed my body with his left arm, causing me to shiver. His body on mine was warm, solid, and I felt his arousal poking into my hip.

He found the bottom of my tee and lifted it, pulling it up and over my head. I felt his big, rough fingers on my hot skin. I raised my body, and he unhooked my bra. Lifting it, he found my rock-hard nipples, twisting and tweaking them between his fingers. Electric currents shot through my body, all collecting in one heated spot between my legs.

I moaned against him, my hips lifting toward his. He moved away. With one hand, he pulled his tee over his head. His body was solid, his abs deliciously defined. He had a prominent V-shape that disappeared into his tight jeans. I sat up and unbuttoned his Levis. He smiled down at me. "You're so fucking beautiful. No wonder my brother wants you. But I get you first." He pulled my shorts off in one swift movement and smiled at my black panties.

He was standing in my living room wearing nothing other than his tight briefs now. I noticed they were about to explode from the large, rigid erection straining them. I sat up and reached out, pulling him toward me. I kissed either side of the V-line slowly and softly. His body shook. "Fucking hell, Em, you're going to kill me." I ignored him and slowly trailed my tongue down the ridges. Pulling his briefs down, I gasped at the size of him.

I looked up into his eyes. They were dark with wanton lust as I took him in my mouth. His head fell back, and he moaned my name. His left hand grabbing my hair, holding me in place, not moving, I sucked and licked him. "Stop, please, I want to be inside you." I laid back on the sofa. He picked up his jeans and pulled out a condom from the front pocket. Ripping the foil, he slid it over his rigid hardness. Supporting his weight over me on his right arm, his left hand found the moist entrance between my legs. He teased my slick entrance, sending shivers over my body while sliding two fingers into me easily, moving in and out steadily. "Mmm, nice and wet for me already. Good!"

I moaned out loud, my hips lifting into his hand. The friction was rubbing against my clit, and I climbed higher and higher. Suddenly, he pulled his fingers out and brought them to his mouth. His tongue was licking my arousal from his fingers. "So sweet, Emily." He smiled.

Without warning, he plunged into me, deep and hard in one stroke. "Bash!" I cried out. I had never felt so full before, completely and utterly his at that moment. He slid almost all the way out, teasing me and then plunging back in. I closed my eyes and saw steel-blue eyes staring back at me. I opened my eyes quickly. How could I be so stupid? I was in complete ecstasy with a hot man, but I was fantasizing about his brother. What was wrong with me? I grabbed Bash's face in my hands and kissed him. He slammed in and out of me, causing me to moan.

My body was trembling. I felt a fire inside my groin, and I knew I was close to the edge. "You feel so good around me, Emily. So fucking good." He slammed into me, harder and deeper, pinning me to the sofa. I dug my nails into his back as I felt my orgasm rise. "I want you to come for me, Emily. I need you to let go!" he growled, and I felt myself explode around him. His body went completely rigid, and I knew he had found his release.

As I came, the only person I saw in my mind's eye was Triston.

"Em, you awake, babe?" I opened my eyes to hazel ones staring down at me. I smiled, and the scent of freshly brewed coffee hit me. "Hello." His lips brushed against mine. "You need to get up and pack. My brother is going to be here in an hour, and I need to go."

I sat up looking at the time; it was seven forty-five. I had more than enough time. "I don't need that long to get ready." It doesn't take me hours to do my makeup. I laughed. Bash pulled the sheet down and placed a kiss between my breasts. I moaned as I felt my nipples harden. "But I do have to get up!" I giggled when he kissed my belly.

He stood up, and I rolled out of bed. Wrapping

my dressing gown around me, I walked over to Bash. My arms wrapped around him. "Mmm, you're so warm." He smiled and kissed my forehead.

"I need to jump in the shower, and then I need to go. My day is jam-packed with meetings." I handed him a towel and left him to it. He went into the *en suite,* and I heard the shower start. As I picked up my coffee, his phone beeped on the dresser. Curiosity got the better of me, and I looked at the screen. There was a preview of a message from "Shantay." I couldn't see the whole message, but what I could see made my blood run cold.

Shantay: Brazil was amazing, see you later…

I was sure there was an explanation for that; there had to be. I placed his phone back on the dresser and went into the kitchen for a refill of coffee. I decided to ask him about it when he got out of the shower because I needed to know what was going on. Walking into the bedroom, I pulled out my suitcase and started packing. I pulled out a few work outfits, and I found my black bikini. I was looking forward to going to LA. I was definitely going to the beach. Maybe

I could get Triston in the ocean. My thoughts always seemed to wander to him. He haunted my waking moments and my dreams.

"Babe?" I turned to face him. Bash was fully dressed, but his brown spikey hair was still wet. I watched him slide his phone into the pocket of his jeans, and I decided to test the water.

"What did you do in Brazil again?" I smiled, sipping my coffee. *Give me the right answer Bash; this is your chance,* I thought.

He frowned. "Work. I went to visit some coffee farms. Why?" There it was, no mention of anything other than work. I felt the distrust build in my heart, and I felt sick.

I smiled. "No reason." His lie was so obvious; it was written all over his face. Something was bugging me about the way his expression changed when I asked. I didn't like this feeling.

I walked with him to the door, and he kissed me again before he left, but it left me cold.

I had to finish packing and get ready. I grabbed some jeans and two tees. I didn't think I needed much else; it was only three days. My phone beeped from the bedside table. It was Triston.

Triston: On my way. See you soon, Miss Reid.

Chapter Six

Triston and I were seated in business class, waiting to take off. His mood was better than it had been the past few days. He turned to smile at me as the flight attendant went through the final checks. I was happy to have a window seat; at least it would distract me from Triston. The excitement of being away for a few days was tangible. Soon, Triston and I were giggling about shapes in the clouds. As relaxed as we both were, the sexual tension was still thick in the air between us. Having wanted to go to LA since I was a teenager, another one of my dreams was realized, thanks to Triston. The flight attendant brought us each a glass of champagne. I sipped mine slowly as I had skipped breakfast. I was too nervous at the thought of seeing Triston again. He made me feel like a teenager in love for the first time. The magnetic pull of his body next to mine was distracting. He was wearing a casual pair of black slacks and a silver-blue shirt. The first four buttons were undone, and I got a glimpse of his tattoo. I yearned to run my fingers over it. I was still so confused about Bash's lie about working while in Brazil. I gave him a chance to tell me something, and he didn't. I was angry. I knew I needed to concentrate on work these next few days. I wanted to show Triston we make a good team.

I took a gulp of champagne. The bubbles went straight to my head and made me feel dizzy. I needed to take it slow. Triston turned toward me. "A toast. To our first official business trip." He smiled sincerely, and I clinked his glass. Taking another sip, I was starting to feel the effects of the champagne. I needed something to eat.

As if reading my mind, Triston called the flight attendant over. "Can I get you anything, Mr. Hart?" She fluttered her eyelashes. Jealousy boiled inside me with such ferocity it shocked me. He smiled confidently. He knew the effect he had on women, and he enjoyed the control it gave him. "My girlfriend would like a sandwich, and one for myself, please? Vegetarian, vegan if you've got." Her face fell at the mention of the word girlfriend. She walked off with a sour look on her face.

"Girlfriend?" I stared at him in disbelief. He smiled and nodded.

"I needed to get her off my back. She was annoying me." He shrugged and carried on typing his email as if he had just said the most natural thing in the world. I stared at him for a few moments before starting with my interrogation. "Triston, you mentioned you had a brother?"

He stopped typing but didn't look at me. "Yes?" he said cautiously.

"Well, I was wondering—" I played with the stem of my glass. I didn't know what I wanted to ask or how even to question it.

He turned cutting me off. "Are you going to ask if I know you're fucking my brother?" My mouth fell open at his blatant honesty. I wasn't sure if I nodded in response, but he carried on.

"I do realize that, Miss Reid. I am not happy about it. You need to stay away from him."

I frowned at him. "What do you mean? Why?" He closed his eyes. Taking a deep breath, he looked at me directly, the blue of his eyes intense in the dim light of the plane. There was something he wasn't saying. It played across his handsome face. "If I show you something, I want you to take it and decide for yourself. I can't tell you to stay away from him. You are stubborn; that much is clear. So, I am giving you the proof you need to make up your own mind. I would never hurt you in any way if we were too . . . Anyway, if you want to be with him, I will wait until he fucks up, and then I will be here to put you back together."

I stared at him. How did he know Bash would hurt me? He couldn't know about the text message. They were brothers. Maybe Bash had done that before, and Triston knew. "What makes you think your brother would hurt me?"

He put his finger to his lips. "Miss Reid, keep your voice down." He gave me the softest and sweetest smile I had ever seen on his beautiful face. "This is what makes me think he will hurt you." He turned the laptop toward me. There was a photo of Bash in a Brazilian restaurant sitting next to a girl wearing next to nothing. I stared at the photo then looked at Triston. "How did you find this?" He closed his eyes. A serious expression burdened his beautiful features. "I looked into my brother because I knew you were dating him. I knew from the first night you went to the bar in Brooklyn. He's done this in the past, and I didn't want you to be another one of his fuck toys!" Anger flashed in his eyes, and I shivered. I had never seen him so angry.

"Triston . . . I am sure there is an explanation for this." I pointed at the screen, but even as the words left my mouth, I didn't believe them.

He turned to me. "Really? He is fucking around on the most beautiful woman to grace his presence. Now you're telling me there's an explanation. Excuse me." He got up and walked to the restrooms. I gasped at his words. He just called me beautiful. My heart raced, and I felt a blush on my cheeks. I pulled his laptop over to my tray and looked at the photo. The caption mentioned his name as well.

Sebastian Hart, owner of Tribal Fuel, on vacation with beautiful Shantay, model and actress.

It's her! He was all over her. There was no denying they were together. I couldn't stand to look at the photo for another minute. I minimized the browser window. There was a document open behind it. I knew I shouldn't snoop, but my curiosity got the better of me. What do they say? Curiosity killed the cat? Yup, that cat was me! The words I read brought tears to my eyes. My heart hammered in my chest. The pain in the poem was clear, the words tugged at my heart, and I wanted so much to hold Triston at that moment.

Not being allowed to touch you

is complete torture.

I would rather just kiss you than

to pretend I don't want you,

I have been fidgeting all day.

I can't stop tapping my fingers.

It feels like I want to scratch at my skin when

you're not around. I am coming down from a

high, that's exactly what it feels like.

You are a drug I have become addicted to and

it hurts that I can't be with you.

The only thing that satiates the craving is your

laugh, your smile, and your words.

It's so hard not to be with you.

It was so beautiful. I wonder who he was talking about? I looked up startled and saw his eyes blazing. "What are you doing?" He grabbed his laptop and closed it. I sat back, giving him a small shrug. Our eyes locked, and the electricity crackled between us. "Nothing. I just closed the photo and then, there it was . . ." I motioned to his laptop. I was completely lost for words as he slid back into his seat and put his hand on my knee, giving it a small squeeze. "Don't do that again, please? It is private." I saw the pain behind his pleading gaze. I wanted to hold him. I wanted to feel him against me and kiss him so much it hurt.

I looked into his intense stare. "Why? Who is it for?" I asked, his gaze burning into me. He shook his head just as the flight attendant arrived with our sandwiches. *Took her long enough,* I thought angrily. I grabbed my phone and saw a message from Bash.

Sebastian: Hey babe, just saying hi! B

I hit reply as I wasn't in the mood for his lies right now, I felt the anger flare in my stomach.

Em: Did you have fun with Shantay in Brazil?

My phone rang. Bash's name flashed on the screen, and I hit the cancel button. My phone rang again; I was simmering watching his name flash on my screen. "Answer it. I am intrigued to hear what he is going to say," Triston whispered in my ear. As angry as I was, his breath sent shivers through me. I looked at Triston in complete shock. He nodded.

"Hello?" Immediately I was sorry I even checked my phone. I wasn't in the mood for this.

"Babe, look. It's not what it looks like. We just posed for a photo." He pleaded like a guilty man. Why was it *'it's never what it looks like'*? It's captured on camera.

"That wasn't a posed shot, and she has your number too. Do not lie to me, Bash."

Triston looked at me then, shaking his head. He opened his laptop and messaged someone on his IM. A reply pinged, and he turned the screen toward me. There was another photo, not taken by the media. It was a PI photo. I read Triston's message to the unknown contact. "Show her the other pics."

Another pic came through. "Babe? You there?" Bash's voice was strained; he knew he was caught. The second photo was even more incriminating than the last. Shantay was sitting on Bash's lap, his hand between her upper thighs. "Bash, don't call me again." I hung up before he could say anything. Tears stung my eyes. Triston closed his laptop, lifted the armrest between our seats, pulling me to him. My phone started ringing again. Triston held out his hand. "Give it to me now!" he ordered, his voice in a low whisper. I passed it to him.

He answered the call. "What do you want? She told you not to call." I couldn't hear what Bash was saying, but it sounded like he was shouting. "Dear brother, if you come near her again, you will have me to answer to. Do you understand me." It wasn't a question, and he didn't wait for a reply. He powered off my phone.

He kissed my head softly. "It will be okay . . . You're with me." I wasn't sure what he meant, but I didn't care. I just enjoyed the closeness he offered.

"You definitely need to fix it!" Triston shouted at the receptionist. We were standing at the reception desk of the stunning Sofitel Hotel; Triston was not happy. Mr. Jacobson's assistant booked us into a suite instead of booking two separate rooms. Running his fingers through his hair, I could tell he was exasperated at the situation. I tugged on his arm, turning him to face me. "It's okay. It's only for a few days. Let's just take it." I was tired, and all I could think of was a hot shower.

When his eyes met mine, I could see he was tired as well. "Are you sure?" I nodded. He turned back to the trembling receptionist. "Check us in, and give me two key cards. I apologize for the scene." She nodded quickly and continued with the check-in process. Placing two key cards on the desk, she gave him a meek smile. Triston grabbed the key cards and nodded. "Thank you." Grabbing the handle of his suitcase, he turned to hand me one of the cards. I wasn't sure why he got two. It wasn't like I was going anywhere without him.

"My apologies for the confusion, Mr. Hart," she mumbled.

He looked at me with those steel-blue eyes. "Let's go, beautiful." My stomach fluttered at his words. Since the argument on the plane and Bash being a complete jerk, Triston was so attentive, more than he normally was. It was strange to see how quickly his moods changed. It was like flipping a coin. I wonder what went on in that beautiful mind? At the elevator, I pressed the call button and stood back. I blushed thinking about the last time I was in an elevator with him. When the car arrived, we stepped inside. "Floor?" I looked at him.

"We're on six," he replied, his voice soft and deep. We were sharing a room for three days. The thought made my heart race. My stomach fluttered at the thought of seeing Triston in nothing but his towel. I smiled and looked at the carpet in the elevator. "A penny for your thoughts?" His deep voice startled me out of my wayward thoughts.

I shook my head. "Just excited to be here." Biting my lip to keep from bursting into fits of giggles, I looked up at him. His eyes darkened, falling on my mouth.

"You need to stop doing that, Miss Reid." His control was seemingly faltering, his scratchy voice pulling at my core. I didn't even realize I was doing anything. I don't do it on purpose, but it made me smile that I had such an effect on him.

The elevator pinged, and the doors slid open. We stepped into the hallway and turned to our right. Walking passed a few doors on either side, we reached our room. Triston slid the key card in and opened the door, holding it open for me. The room was beautiful. With deep browns and blues, it felt relaxing, and I was looking forward to doing just that. There was beautiful dark wood furniture, which lent to the relaxing ambiance of the room, in a spacious living room area, with a sofa, table, and television cabinet. The separate bedroom was huge with an *en suite* bathroom, and a balcony that overlooked the ocean and the city below. I did notice there was one king-sized bed. My body trembled at the thought of sleeping next to Triston. With the deep-rooted tension between us, I could tell this was going to be interesting. Would he finally let me in? Was there a chance for us? My heart hoped for an opportunity.

"I will take the sofa; you have the bed. I am so sorry they fucked up the rooming arrangements."

I shrugged, putting on a calm exterior, hoping he would relax about it too. "No Triston, we're adults, and it's a huge bed."

He looked at me with those beautiful sparkling eyes and gave a brief nod. "We can talk about it later." His cool control back in full force.

An hour later, we were in a silver Mercedes SUV. Mr. Jacobson had his driver pick us up to escort us to the Jacobson mansion in Hollywood Hills. We pulled up to large, ornate, black gates that opened slowly, allowing access to the most beautiful sprawling estate I had ever seen. I gasped. Triston grabbed my hand and squeezed it. He leaned down and whispered, "Welcome to the other side, Miss Reid." I felt a shiver on my skin from his warm breath. My hand tingled at his touch, and I savored the feeling. I was conscious of the need I felt to have his warm, soft hands on me and how I ached to have them on me all the time.

I smiled at him. "Thank you, Triston. You have no idea how much this, and you, mean to me." The words tumbled out before I could catch them. My heart raced realizing what that must have sounded like. I scolded myself. Why on earth would I say something like that when he made it so clear there was nothing between us? I needed to keep my comments to myself.

"And you to me, Miss Reid." His eyes seared into mine. The heat in them was unbearable. Like when one stares at the sun, unable to look away. His words caught me off guard, my heart hammering in my ears, and I hoped he couldn't hear it too. He turned, opening the car door, and I realized we had stopped.

He came around to my side and opened my door. I slid out of the car, happy that Triston suggested we change before coming here. I was wearing one of the black, knee-length dresses I brought along, with black pumps. Triston looked terrific as usual in black slacks and a white dress shirt. He had a beautiful cerulean tie on, which accentuated his eyes.

He grabbed my hand and laced his fingers through mine. The gesture was sweet, and a sense of calm filled me. He exuded confidence, which melded into me, and all the tension between us disappeared. I loved this side of him; he was happy. There was something that seemed to make my heart smile. As we walked up to the large, dark wood doors, they opened, and Mr. Jacobson greeted us with open arms and a massive smile. "Ah, there are my two favorite people! Welcome! Please come in." He shook Triston's hand, and he hugged me and kissed my cheek. Triston pulled me alongside him, and I tingled from the feel of his body close to mine.

"Let's get some supper and talk business!"

We walked through the entrance foyer, which was the size of my apartment. The architecture took my breath away. Outside, the red face-brick, the interior was a mix of old-world charm and modern lines with dark wood mixed with glass. There were large, modern, paint-splattered artworks hanging on the walls and a large, sweeping staircase led to the second floor. Triston glanced at me and smiled as I walked through in awe of the home. His eyes creased at the corners, and that sweet crinkle in his nose made me smile.

Mr. Jacobson led us through a study and out onto a lush manicured garden. "So, tell me, is the hotel okay? I have only used them once before."

Before Triston could answer, I stepped in. "Yes! It's beautiful. The room is exquisite." Triston's gaze was one of amusement. He shook his head, squeezing my hand. I smiled, sticking out my tongue. His eyes burned into me again, and as they darkened, I knew there was something more between us.

We sat in the warm LA sunshine and had a light supper of tapas and a fantastic salmon salad. Mr. Jacobson toasted our business arrangement with a crisp white wine. We discussed the event and the requirements. We were going to have a busy day tomorrow, setting up the meeting plans. We needed to confirm all the scheduled dates with the venues. That was imperative to everything running smoothly. Since it was an international event, Triston and I would be getting in a lot of air miles.

After lunch, Mr. Jacobson escorted us back to the car. "Right, you two young'uns have yourselves a good evening. Tomorrow, we work!" We had the afternoon free, and I was excited to explore. I wondered what Triston wanted to do; maybe we should go to the beach? I thought of Triston in swim shorts, and I knew that would be a good idea.

"Did you have any ideas on what you wanted to do, Emily?"

I turned to look at Triston and giggled. "Have I been promoted from Miss Reid?" I asked him jokingly.

He smiled, leaning over, whispering in my ear, "You were promoted a long time ago, beautiful." I trembled. "Miss Reid I will keep for when you . . . frustrate me."

His hot breath on my ear sent delicious shivers over my skin. The fire he ignited in my stomach flared, and I squirmed in my seat. He traced the outline of my ear with his tongue, and I bit my lip to keep from moaning out loud.

"Jesus, Triston! The driver can see you!" I hissed at him, and he let out a carefree laugh.

"Oh, Miss Reid, you do make me laugh." He grabbed my knee, giving it a squeeze. Electricity zinged through me again. I shook my head and turned to look out my window, trying desperately to ignore the fact that his hand had my skin on fire.

The driver pulled into the drop-off area at the hotel ten minutes later. We made our way back to the room. I definitely needed to change — it was way too hot! "Did you want to go to the beach?" I asked Triston. I picked up my suitcase, too nervous to make eye contact.

"Yeah, that sounds good! You just want to see me without a shirt on," he growled. I giggled at his comment. It was like he could read my mind. Of course, I wanted to see him without a shirt on.

"Don't flatter yourself, Mr. Hart!" I retorted, picking up a cushion and throwing it at him. He caught it and winked at me. He was a lot more relaxed now, and I found the tension in my shoulders ease.

I unzipped my suitcase, rummaging through the clothes. I found my black bikini, black board shorts, and crocheted white top. "I am going to change." I closed my suitcase.

"You change here. I want to hop in the shower first." Triston walked passed me to the bathroom. He had black and silver swim shorts in his hand and nothing else. My mind wandered at the thought of seeing him in those. This was not going to help the sexual tension between us.

I waited until I heard the shower start. Stripping down, I changed into my bikini. It was a plain black halter top with a silver diamanté heart in the middle. The Capri bottoms were black with three straps over each hip holding together the front and back. There were diamanté on either side. I pulled my top and shorts on and decided to tie my hair up. I had my hair halfway into a ponytail when Triston walked out of the bathroom in nothing but his swim shorts. My breath left me, and I froze.

My eyes roamed the naked, taut torso of my boss. His arms and body were exquisitely cut. Striking, sexy veins ran from his forearms into his hands. His abs were rock hard and formed to complete perfection. There was a prominent sculpted V-shape pointing into his low-slung, black swim shorts. I drank him in, every exquisite inch of his perfect body. I wanted so much to run my hands and tongue over that torso. "Are you enjoying the view, Miss Reid?" he asked in absolute amusement. I averted my eyes. I felt the heat on my face, and I knew I was bright red.

"I . . . I . . . am . . ." His laugh was soft and friendly. I was at a loss for words. My whole body was on fire, yearning and aching to feel that rock-hard body against me. I spun around, facing the wall, trying to calm the knot in my stomach. I finished tying my hair and picked up my phone. I didn't turn it on. I just needed some distraction from looking at him.

"Is that stubborn mind of yours working overtime?" He was right behind me. I felt the heat radiating from his naked skin warming my back. I was trembling without him even touching me.

"No . . . no . . . certainly not!" My voice came out strangled. I cleared my throat and put my phone in the drawer. Triston laid his hands on my shoulders, and the searing heat that filled my abdomen was unbearable. The electricity that shot through me was intense, and I ached for more.

He turned me around to face him. His index finger trailing a feather-light line from the back of my ear along my jaw until his fingers rested on my chin, lifting it. My eyes met his intense gaze. "Will you have fun with me today? Forget Bash, forget work, and just have fun?" His caring nature was so beautiful as he pleaded with me, while I smiled.

I nodded. "Okay, Mr. Hart, I will do as you please." His eyes flared with darkness at my words. I was mesmerized at the midnight blue taking over his normally steel-blue eyes. I didn't dare look down. I knew if I saw his body again, I would probably drag him to the bed, and we wouldn't leave the room.

He kissed my forehead softly, which ignited little sparks on my skin, and I felt myself blush. "Okay, then it's settled! I do look forward to you pleasing me, Miss Reid." He turned around. I was stunned by his words. Watching the muscles in his back ripple as he moved, his broad shoulders flexed as he grabbed a T-shirt, pulling it over his head. I felt myself breathe again. "And leave that god damn phone right there," he ordered, the control returning to his voice. I smiled and shook my head.

The taxi dropped us off at Venice Beach. It was my first visit to the infamous beach, and it was everything that I thought it would be. It was a quiet afternoon. There were tourists snapping shots of their family with the beach in the background. The beachfront shops were selling some amazing trinkets and ice creams. We strolled around for a few minutes, stopping at a store to buy sunblock. It had a fantastic vibe, and I felt relaxed. "Triston!"

We both turned around to the sultry voice behind us. A beautiful, leggy, bleached blonde in a tiny bikini ran up to him. She threw her arms around him, and he gave her a reluctant hug, a bit of jealousy hit me hard. She was tanned and beautiful, and she must have been a model. "Jenna, how are you?" he asked in a guarded tone. I felt so short and frumpy compared to her.

She looked over at me with disdain. She flashed him her best smile and fluttered her fake eyelashes. "Good! I just landed the CK job! I am ecstatic. When are you going to do my shoots again! I miss you." She reached out and stroked his chest. I felt bile rise into my throat, and all I could do to keep from puking was to take a deep breath.

He grabbed her wrist, pulling it off his chest. Releasing it from his grip, he gave her a small smile. "I'm a busy man these days, Jen. This is my partner in crime, Emily." He gestured to me. I smiled and nodded, not wanting to talk to this woman who blatantly wanted Triston. She gave me a small smile and looked back at Triston.

Without a second thought, she carried on talking to him. "Will I see you while you're here?" He shook his head and grabbed my hand. He gave it a small squeeze. I wasn't sure if that was a sign of him reassuring me or to provide her with the idea we were together.

"Emily and I are here on vacation, planning a private event." His voice was clipped and serious. I glanced at him. What was he talking about? She frowned and leaned in closer to him.

"Don't tell me you got engaged!" She playfully slapped his arm. I could tell she was definitely not joking. She seemed shocked, and it made me smile.

"Not yet. I have to go, Jen. See you around." He gave a small nod and turned around.

He pulled me against him, and we walked off toward the beach. "Who on earth was that?" I asked him when we were out of earshot.

"Can we not talk about her, please?"

I stopped before we reached the end of the promenade. Triston halted mid-stride. "No, Triston, I'm asking you a question." His eyes glanced behind me, and he wrapped his arms around my waist. I reached up to push him away when he held on tighter.

"Just stand still, Miss Reid!" he ordered as I struggled in his embrace. "She is watching. Just smile and listen to me." I stopped and watched his eyes dart back and forth between me and the blonde who was clearly not taking the hint. "I slept with her on a shoot a few years ago. She was infatuated with me; the feeling isn't mutual. It was a long time ago, and she means nothing to me. It was a fling. She clearly thinks otherwise." As he told me, his eyes never left mine. The sincerity burned into me, and I felt at ease.

"So, you prefer blondes?" I questioned slyly. Seeing his eyes flicker with annoyance at my challenge, I giggled.

He leaned down, his tongue tracing the shell of my ear. I felt his hot breath on my neck, turning me on as my breathing faltered. "Miss Reid, if you continue to push me, there will be consequences!" he hissed, the words making the butterflies in my stomach do somersaults. His mouth found mine, and he kissed me deeply. The passion radiating from him made my body melt into his. His tongue caressed mine, and there was an urgency in his kiss. Pulling my body tighter against him, I felt his rigid arousal. The electric sparks that shot through my body were present as always.

When his lips left mine all I could do was stare at him. "Now do you think I prefer blondes?" he smirked and grabbed my hand. "Let's swim. I need to cool down." He adjusted himself, his erection straining the front of his shorts. We got close to the water when he pulled off his tee and dropped it next to his shoes. I took in the tanned, sculpted body walking into the water, and I ached to feel his wet skin against mine.

"You coming?" He ran into the water, and I watched the surf splash against him. I pulled my top off and slid my shorts down. Leaving my clothes in a heap with my flip-flops, I walked into the water. Grateful that it was warm, I stepped in farther, enjoying the waves against my hot skin.

Triston turned around. He was completely soaked, his shoulder-length, brown hair dripping down his back. As he stepped into the shallow of the surf, my eyes roamed his body, his sculpted abs dripping wet, his low-slung shorts heavy from the water, which seemed to pull them lower. The oblique muscles more prominent, I couldn't help but lick my lips. "Do you like staring at me, Miss Reid?" he asked with an amused expression. I nodded slowly. I couldn't hide it anymore — I wanted him, and he knew it.

"Mmm, we should do something about that. But first, I want to get you wet!" He grabbed me and lifted me against him. I squealed as he walked us into the water. I splashed water as I kicked back. His words and his body making the apex between my thighs moisten. I giggled as he spun me around in the warm, crashing waves. All the worries and concerns were melting away with his arms around me. We both laughed as he walked farther into the ocean. "Triston! Put me down!" I shouted. I held onto his strong shoulders, and I felt the muscles flex under my touch. He felt so good against me.

There had to be a chance for us. I did not imagine the feeling between us.

"I don't think that's an option, Miss Reid. I am not letting you go!" His words held more meaning than we both cared to admit. I held onto his neck and felt the warm water slowly soaking my hair. He reached up with one hand and pulled my hair tie off, freeing my long brown hair. I leaned back wrapping my legs around him, wetting my hair. It felt refreshing.

"You look better with it down anyway." He smiled as I pulled myself back up. Holding on to Triston's neck, his face inches from mine, his eyes a midnight blue. "You're beautiful," he growled in a deep scratchy voice that tugged at my core. I smiled and stared into his glistening eyes.

"You're handsome," I whispered back. He kissed me then, a deep soft kiss full of longing, with his tongue invading my mouth, stroking mine as they danced together. His lips felt like they were made to be on mine. He held me so close like I was part of him. My heart hammered in my chest, and my skin tingled at the current between us. I pulled away breathless. My lips felt cold at a distance between us.

"Then we make a good match. I just—" He looked away, pain so evident in his face.

"What, Triston? You need to be honest with me, please?" I begged. He nodded.

"Emily, I want you to know me. I want you to know everything. I'm just scared if you do, you're going to disappear. I'm not easy to be with, and I'm not used to opening myself up." His solemn expression made me sad. Something was hurting him, and deep down it pained me to see him like that.

I grabbed his face in my hands. "I am not going anywhere. Get used to it!"

He smiled. "You're a stubborn little one, aren't you?" I nodded.

Chapter Seven

"A bottle of your Hauté Cabrieré Merlot 2007." Triston handed the wine list to the waiter. He looked over at me and gave me a smile that made me melt. I spent the afternoon wrapped in his arms in the warm LA ocean. "Did you have a good day?" he asked seriously. I nodded and smiled. A blush warmed my cheeks as the memories of our day washed over me.

"How could I not enjoy myself? I spent the day in a beautiful city with you. I forgot all the things that bothered me, which was good." I blushed at my honesty.

He smiled. "Emily, I asked you to forget the world and be with me, and you did. Thank you. I keep pushing you away, but for some reason, I can't stay away from you. I don't know what it is, or what is between us, but I can't fucking think straight without you. It frustrates me because I feel" — he looked down — "out of control. You need to decide if it's me you want." His long slender fingers intertwined, I had never seen him nervous, but right now he was. "Before you do, though, there are things I need to tell you. If you choose me, I want you to know who I am. I need to be honest with you. Brutally honest." When he looked up at me again, his eyes held such sorrow I felt my own heartache.

"Triston, we all have demons in the closet. I have my fair share. Everyone has a past, but that's not where we live. And nobody is perfect." He nodded. The waiter brought our wine and opened it with a flourish, pouring a taste for Triston.

He sipped it leisurely. His eyes locked on mine. I watched him licking his lips — something that always stroked the fire inside me. He nodded at the waiter for our glasses to be filled, and Triston ordered dinner. He loved the control, and I let him have it.

The waiter disappeared, and we were left alone with our confessions. I wasn't near ready to share mine with Triston. It was something I needed to come to terms with. If I wanted a relationship with him, I had to be honest. I needed to tell him why I left home and why I could never go back. He picked up his wine glass, his mouth lingering on the crystal lip. I watched his tongue lick the drop of wine from the glass. The knot in my stomach tightened, and I wished his tongue was on me. He was deep in thought, and when his eyes met mine, a smile curved his soft lips. "So, I suppose I should start." I nodded. He was quiet for a minute as if collecting his thoughts.

"Triston—" I whispered. His soft gaze looked haunted.

"I am not the easiest person to be with as I don't do relationships. Since my ex-fiancée, I am somewhat . . ." He took another sip of wine just as my heart begins to race. He was engaged. I remember Jessie mentioned it. "I push people away, Emily. People who care are difficult for me to deal with. I'm not used to it. She didn't love me. I realized it when I walked in on her and my brother fucking." He was so blatant as I felt my heart constrict at this bit of information. "That is one reason why we don't speak anymore." He looked up again. His guard went up, and I could see pain evident in his handsome features. "I find being alone easier, less painful." I sat in shock. That's why the brothers were so hostile to each other. Something Bash said that night hit me like a rock.

"...no wonder my brother wants you, but I get you first."

He was staking a claim; I was even angrier now than I was before.

"I enjoy the control I have over my life and those around me. I guess that's what makes me a good businessman. It's the only way I know how to survive. I feel that if I don't control a situation or person, I can't trust it or them." His fingers twisted the stem of the wine glass. "I didn't have the easiest childhood. There are things I did, things which I am not proud of. When I was younger, I got mixed up with the wrong crowd. How cliché is that? I did and sold drugs, and I stole from people, even my own family. I was completely fucked up, Emily, in so many ways." His eyes burned into me, pleading.

I placed my hand in his when he reached out to me — feeling the familiar soft, warm skin, aching to hold him. I knew I had to let him get it all out before we could move forward. "I tried to kill myself, Emily." He averted his gaze, ashamed. My heart shattered into a million pieces. "I overdosed. I felt like I needed to stop doing what I was doing, and that was the only way." I wanted to tell him to stop. I could see this was hurting him, but he carried on. "I don't believe I'm capable of being loved or of loving anybody. I didn't believe it then, and I don't believe it now." His eyes met mine, challenging me.

"Nobody is brave enough to put up with my shit, Emily." His gaze on me was so intense my breath caught. "Except you."

I stared at him and nodded. I saw the pain disappear from his eyes. "Yes, I am brave, Mr. Hart, because I know what I want. I want you."

"Why?" His voice was a raspy whisper, his eyes darkening. He caught me completely off guard. Why would he ask me that? "I . . . I . . . don't know," I mumbled.

A look of frustration crossed his face. "Miss Reid, that is not an answer."

I looked into those beautiful, midnight blue eyes as they changed color in front of me. "What did you want me to say, Triston? Yes! Okay! I want you. Even in your most broken form, I want you! I want to pick up the pieces and put you back together!" My voice challenging him, his fist clenched, and I watched him take a deep breath. Frustration at me evident on his handsome face. I know he didn't want to hear me say that because he didn't believe he was worth it. I could see he was at war with himself, my words adding fuel to the fire. I didn't care. I wanted him to know I wasn't going to run away from him. What he had done was in the past, and I don't believe people should be judged.

"Are you sure about what you're saying?" His calm demeanor faltered, and he sounded almost hopeful. I nodded and smiled to lighten the mood. He smirked. Rolling my eyes at him, I giggled at how almost childlike he was sometimes.

His eyes darkened at my insolence. "I want to take you back to the hotel room right now and put you across my knee for such blatant disrespect!" His face took on a dark, dangerous look. I squirmed in my seat. Moist at his threat, my whole body was on fire. Squeezing my thighs together, I picked up my wine, sipping it. I looked up at him.

"Mr. Hart, I think you would enjoy that a little too much." I smiled sweetly at him. Taking another sip, teasing his gaze to my mouth. I licked my lips, paying extra attention to my bottom lip, chewing on it. His grip on my hand tightened. I smiled inwardly. I was enjoying the rush of making him feel so out of control. His eyes dark, almost black, and my body trembled at what lay before me and the choice I had just made. Triston called the waiter over. "Ask the chef to package the food. We need to leave urgently." The waiter nodded and ran off to the kitchen.

"What are you doing Triston?" I asked, completely shocked. Why would we leave we hadn't even had our starters?

He smirked at me. "We need to leave . . . Now!" Midnight blue eyes burned into me, and I squirmed again, my panties wet from the ache I felt for him.

"Triston, we haven't even had starters. And our wine—"

Cutting me off abruptly, his voice was a deep, low growl. "Fuck the starters! We are going back to the hotel for dessert."

We walked through reception at breakneck speed. Triston pressed the call button on the elevator. I was a jumble of nerves because I wasn't sure if he was angry or just plain frustrated with me. He didn't say a word all the way back to the hotel, and I didn't know what to say to him.

We stepped inside the elevator, and he pressed the button for our floor. I could feel the energy radiating off him. It was magnetic. I could feel the pull my body had toward him, and I couldn't deny it any longer, I wanted him, and I wanted him now. The elevator felt like it was moving at a snail's pace, and I urged it to hurry.

The elevator doors opened, and Triston grabbed my hand, pulling me behind him. I was still carrying our dinner in the take-out bag they gave us. As we made our way down the hall, I fell in step beside him. He released my hand and placed his fingertips on the small of my back. Electric currents zinged through me. My hand was shaking as I slid the key card into the door.

I walked into the room and placed the food on the cabinet. I stood at the desk sliding my shoes off when I felt Triston's body behind me, his hands on my shoulders. His warm breath on my neck, he whispered in my ear, "Now, Miss Reid, I am going to do things to you that will make you think twice about rechallenging me ."

His husky voice made me tremble. "I want

you to stay still; do not move. Do you understand me?" I nodded. As soon as he walked away, I felt cold. I heard him rustling around in the cupboard and then in his suitcase. I wondered what he was doing, but I didn't dare turn around. I was aching to feel his lips on mine again, but somehow, I knew he was going to take his time, teasing me.

It wasn't long before he was behind me again. "Close your eyes, Miss Reid." As soon as my eyes closed, I felt soft fabric covering my eyes. He tied it around my head. "Is that too tight?"

"No, Mr. Hart." I breathed, my whole body yearning for him.

He unzipped my dress. His fingers trailing down my spine, leaving goosebumps in their wake. He slides the straps over my shoulders, the fabric slipping down my body, and falling to the floor. He groaned. "I do love your taste in lingerie, Miss Reid." His tongue traced the shell of my ear, making me shiver. I felt self-conscious standing in my black lace bra and panties. He planted feather-light kisses from the back of my ear down my neck. When he reached my shoulder with his teeth, he gripped the bra strap and pulled it off. His hands, soft and warm, lingered on my arms.

He repeated the process on the other side, and I was entirely at his mercy now. I was aching, yearning and trembling for him. My body was on fire, and the heat between my thighs was unbearable. He unclasped my bra. "Take it off." I pulled the bra down my arms and dropped it on the floor next to me. The cold breeze made my bare nipples rock hard. With my sight taken away, all my other senses were heightened. I felt every nerve in my body respond to him. His fingertips trailed my arms again up to my shoulders. He unpinned my hair, and it fell down my back.

"Mmm, you are beautiful." His left hand slid over my shoulder, wrapping his fingers around my neck in a firm grasp. The act so dangerous, but so sexy. His right hand slid down to my breasts. His grip on my neck tightened, pulling me into his rock-hard body. I could feel he was as aroused as I was. He leaned in close to my ear, nipping it with his teeth. I was slick with desire, aching to feel him inside me. I arched my body and pushed my ass into his groin. His right hand pinched and pulled my nipple, sending shock waves flowing through me.

"Do you want me, Miss Reid?" His voice dripped with lust. His words were almost predatory, the darkness in them pulling at my core. I nodded. He tweaked my other nipple, sending another shock of electricity through me. "Triston!" I moaned out loud.

His tongue trailed a hot, wet path from the shell of my ear to my neck. "I want you to bend over. You will put your hands on the table, and you will not move. Do you understand me?"

"Yes," I whispered, my voice barely audible.

Triston placed a flat hand between my shoulders and eased me over the table. I was bent over at the waist, the top half of my body on the cold wood, my arms straight in front of me holding onto the edge of the table. I felt Triston's finger tracing a line down my spine, making me shiver. "You look fucking delectable." His voice was raspy and deep. "Now tell me, Miss Reid, do you still want me?" His hand moving over my ass, sensually. "Do you want the dark parts of me? You have to be completely honest. Understand?" His hand stopped on my lower back just above my ass.

"Yes, Triston." My voice was an unrecognizable hiss. He lifted his hand, and my skin felt cold where he had touched me. I heard the sound before I felt the sting. His hand came down hard, causing me to wince, alternating on each side, again and again. My legs were trembling. I was so turned on I was sure I would come undone as soon as he touched me. Thankfully, I was holding on to the table; as it was helping me steady myself. His foot pushed mine farther apart, and now I was completely spread in front of him.

He moved my soaked panties aside, and I felt his finger between my legs. He stroked my sex, teasing his thumb over the slick entrance. I whimpered. "Miss Reid, I do believe you were enjoying that." I heard him suck his thumb, moaning, "You are delicious!" The thought of him tasting me on his fingers had me so close to the edge. "Are you sure you want this, Miss Reid?"

"Please!" I begged.

I heard him pull off his belt, and I knew what he was going to do, shocked at how much I wanted it and how much I wanted him. The sting resonated over my skin. "Do you like challenging me, Miss Reid?" his voice low and scratchy. "Yes, Mr. Hart!" I couldn't contain myself. I needed it, submitting to him completely at that moment. The second sting made me whimper. He dropped the belt on the table next to me.

He placed feather-light kisses on my thighs. My knees were about to give way, and I gripped the table tighter. His soft, warm hands held on to my thighs. I felt his hot breath on the drenched opening of my body. "Triston . . ." I moaned.

I felt his tongue on me, and I came undone. My body shook with the most intense orgasm I ever felt. I squeezed my eyes closed so tightly I saw stars as my release washed over me. He didn't move, allowing me the pleasure of his skilled tongue on the most sensitive part of my body. He eased a finger inside me, and I felt the fire blazing through my body. "Triston!" I moaned his name louder.

"Miss Reid, I need you. I need to be inside you. Do you want me?"

"Yes, please. Please, Triston?" I begged shamelessly.

I heard him pull off his shirt, listened to the zipper of his slacks, and I knew he was almost naked, which coaxed the need in me. "Stand."

I stood up shakily, my legs like jelly. He untied the blindfold, and I blinked in the dim light of our room. "Hands behind you."

He proceeded in tying my hands behind my back. As he leaned into me, my palm was directly at his groin. I felt the rigid hardness that was about to be inside me. He was so big I didn't know how I would handle it. "Do you want that inside you?" he asked hoarsely as if reading my thoughts. I nodded.

Bending me over the table, he lifted the belt again, and I knew what was coming. The sting on my ass was harsh. It made me lift onto my toes, and the second one had the same effect. I felt his warm hand rubbing the ache, his touch soft, moving slowly over my ass.

His finger traced its way over my entrance, and I was dripping wet again. "Mmm, so hot and wet," I heard him drop his tight briefs. "Tomorrow, when you feel the ache between your legs, you will know you are mine."

He plunged into me, and I cried out at the invasion. "Yes, Triston!"

He filled me so deep it knocked the breath from me. He held on to my hands tied behind me as he plunged into me, easing out only to fill me again. He was right, I was his, and he possessed me completely.

He slapped my tingling ass again and again as he filled me. I could feel my orgasm building again as I am tightening around him. "Not yet," he warned me. I tried to concentrate on not coming, but he was feeding the fire inside me. I wasn't sure how much longer I could hold out.

He untied my hands and pulled me up by my shoulders. I was almost flush with his body, my hands holding me up. My back arched, and his hand gripped my neck. I felt his hot breath on my ear, and I was so close; he was hitting every nerve ending in my body. As he plunged into me one last time, he whispered in his deep, lust-filled voice, "Come for me! I want to possess you." I felt my body shake as a second, intense orgasm ripped through me. His hand tightened on my neck, and his teeth grazed my ear as he filled me with his release.

I opened my eyes and looked into Triston's sleeping face. He looked so peaceful and calm. His arm wrapped tightly around me, but as I tried to move, I felt the sting on my backside. Last night flashed through my mind, and I shivered. I reached up and touched Triston's face. His eyes opened, and he frowned. He looked so adorable. "Morning, handsome," I whispered, and he pulled me into him as he groaned sleepily. His leg intertwined with mine, and a smile spread across his face.

"Triston, we need to go to work!" I scolded him.

He rolled on top of me and rested his weight on his elbows. "Is that any way to say good morning to me, Miss Reid?" he laughed. He leaned down and kissed me, his tongue invading my mouth as he rolled his hips. He was rock hard, teasing me. I raised my hips toward him, and he growled into my mouth. I couldn't get enough of him. Even after last night, I was still aching to feel him inside me, his tongue licking into me, tasting me. His lips were soft and demanding, displaying the need in him.

Reaching between us, I gripped him in my fist. He groaned into the kiss as I stroked him. I positioned him at my soaking entrance. I was teasing the tip of him on my slick sex when he stopped the assault on my mouth. "You sure?" I nodded. He slowly pushed into me. I gripped the sheets as I opened to take him inside. My head fell back. He kissed my neck, and I moaned. "You feel so fucking good, Emily. Open for me. I want to be inside you all the fucking time," he groaned as he filled me. He rocked his hips back and forth, plunging into me, harder and harder. His hair fell across his face. I wrapped my arms around his neck, my nails digging into his back as I climbed higher. The coil tightened in my stomach, and I felt my release edging closer. I looked up into his lust-filled eyes, and I knew I was close to coming undone.

"I want you all the time, Triston. Every second of the day," I moaned, and I felt his body tense. He was close. I wrapped my legs around his waist and pulled him deeper into me. He pushed faster and harder, and I clenched around him. My orgasm ripped into me, and my body shook with the intensity.

"Fuck!" he groaned as he came inside me, my whole body spasming with him. Kissing me again, his lips moved over mine, down to my neck, and nibbling on my ear.

He rolled over next to me, and I felt empty as soon as he pulled out. We laid there for what felt like hours in each other's arms. I didn't want to move, but I knew we had to get to work.

"Triston?" I whispered, and his eyes opened.

"I'm awake angel; I just didn't want to get up." He smiled.

I leaned over him and checked the time on his phone. It was seven thirty. We had another two hours before the driver was picking us up. "Do you want breakfast?" I asked.

He nodded and pulled me closer. "Wasn't that what we just had?" he asked jokingly. His hips rolled into me again, and I giggled. He was insatiable.

"Not that breakfast. Mr. Hart, behave yourself!" I rolled out of bed and grabbed the bathrobe, tying it as I walked over to the phone. "What did you want?" I looked over at him, and my breath caught. His tousled brown hair framed his handsome face. The sheet just covered his hips. The beautifully tanned, sculpted body looked breathtaking on the white sheets. "You decide, angel. I'm happy with anything. Vegetarian is good if they don't have vegan." I nodded and called room service.

The silver SUV pulled up to Mr. Jacobson's

mansion at nine thirty on the dot. I wore a grey pencil skirt with a blue chiffon top, the color matching Triston's tie while he's dressed in a black suit with a grey dress shirt. We were greeted by a young man in his mid-twenties who introduced himself as Mr. Jacobson's assistant. He walked us through the lower section of the house to the study and opened the door to a large office. Mr. Jacobson was sitting behind his desk when we walked in, and his face lit up when he saw us. He got up and walked around his desk to greet us. "Hello, Mr. Hart, Miss Reid. I was just finishing up the contracts. You can have a read-through today, and we can make the amendments and finalize." He shook Triston's hand and gave me a peck on the cheek. Escorting us into the room, there was a large meeting table to the left of the office. "You can set up here, Miss Reid. You will need the cable as well." Handing me a power cable, I plugged in my laptop and powered it on. He pulled up a chair and gestured for us to sit. "Did you both have a good day yesterday?" I smiled and nodded.

"Yes, thank you. We ended up going for a dip in the ocean. It was lovely!" I blushed, remembering kissing Triston and feeling his strong arms around me. Memories of the night before, on the other hand, had my whole body on fire.

Mr. Jacobson got up and walked over to his desk. "That's great! Tonight, we party." I turned to Triston. He winked, causing a blush to heat my face. The magnetic pull of Triston's body next to mine was so strong as we sat next to each other. Mr. Jacobson brought over the paperwork, which Triston took and laid on the desk in front of him. I knew this was going to be a long day from the size of the contract. "Well, let's get to it. Miss Reid, you can start with the marketing plan. I have a copy draft here. We need the final dates and prep times. There will be set up and break down days, and we also need a final roll call on all the staff in attendance." I nodded and opened a new document. It was time to get started.

When lunchtime rolled around, I was starving. I stood up and stretched. We had been working nonstop for four-and-a-half hours. I had a forty-page document typed out with information about all twelve of the events. The staff brought our lunch into the office, and it smelled amazing. "I hope you don't mind eating in here. I figured it would be easier than shuffling outside." Our host smiled and moved the paperwork to his desk. The table was large enough to accommodate six people. Lunch looked like it was enough for six as well. I smiled at the spread in front of us. "Yes, it's perfect. Can you tell me where the restroom is?" I asked. Mr. Jacobson explained there were two on the lower floor, giving us directions to both. I walked to the office door with Triston close behind me. I turned to the left, and Triston followed, "Aren't you going to the restroom?" I asked, confused.

He winked and nodded. "Yeah. Yours sounds much more inviting!" I giggled at his naughty smirk and shook my head.

Opening the door to the immaculate bathroom, I stepped inside. Triston followed right behind me, shutting the door and locking it. He immediately pinned me against the wall, pressing his body into mine. Grabbing my wrists, he pinned my hands above my head with his right hand. His left hand lifted my skirt up to my thighs, his mouth on mine, devouring me. "Triston," I moaned into his kiss. He ignored my protest, although I didn't think it was much of a protest. His left hand stroked the crotch of my wet panties as my hips rocked with his movements. I was aching to feel his fingers, and my nipples strained against the soft lace of my bra. He growled wantonly, and I felt him harden on my thigh.

He pulled away suddenly. "Fuck!" His eyes were dark blue. He spun around and looked in the mirror, watching me recover from the kiss. "I needed to kiss you!" He turned to me again and smiled. Grabbing my hand, he placed it on his crotch, "This is what you do to me. The whole fucking meeting I was in agony!" he growled.

I smirked at him. "Good, now go! Before we get caught!"

His gaze fueled by desire. "That smart little mouth will be punished later!" He released my hand and stepped back, his hand on the doorknob.

"Promise?" I whispered. I knew it was a promise, and I looked forward to it.

He opened the bathroom door, and before stepping out, retorted, "You can count on it!" Triston closed the door behind him, leaving me breathless.

I closed my laptop at five p.m. The sun was still high, and I was famished again. We were escorted to the car by Mr. Jacobson's assistant. He mentioned the car would collect us in a couple of hours for the dinner we were meant to be attending this evening. It was our second night in LA, and I was enjoying it. I knew there was an exclusive event we were going to attend tomorrow, which was exciting. I was curious to know what the theme would be. "Thank you for your hard work today, Miss Reid," Triston said as we slid into the backseat of the SUV. His hand found mine, and he gave it a small squeeze.

I smiled. "It's been a pleasure, Mr. Hart." His smile melted my heart. I loved how his nose wrinkled and the edges of his eyes creased.

"Tonight is going to be interesting. I can't wait to see you in that dress." We were joining Mr. Jacobson and his wife for dinner at some fancy restaurant.

"I'm excited; I can't wait to see the dress myself!" I giggled.

He winked and leaned closer to me. "Angel, I'm looking forward to taking that dress off you!" My whole body responded to his words, and I squirmed in my seat. He was smirking, noting my unease.

"Don't push your luck, Mr. Hart. You do realize I'm your employee?" I challenged.

"Miss Reid, you are my employee. That means you need to obey my orders. Or there will be consequences." He bit my earlobe, and I felt the heat between my legs.

"Triston . . ." I moaned, biting my lip to keep from drawing attention from the driver. His soft hand fell on my thigh. He pushed my skirt slowly and meticulously up my legs. His expert fingers stroked my damp panties, yet I slapped his hand. "Stop it!" I hissed, and he laughed — a full, throaty laugh.

When we pulled up to the hotel, I opened my door and slid out. "Miss Reid, I would be happier if you waited for me to open your door." His tone was serious as he admonished me.

I smiled. "Sorry! I didn't realize it was a prerequisite that you open my door." He was so demanding sometimes it was driving me insane. I walked into the hotel, ignoring his protests. I walked past the elevators and opened the stairwell door. Slipping off my shoes, I fiercely started up the stairs. I heard him follow through the door.

"Em!" He ran up behind me. "Miss Reid!" I stopped dead at his tone and spun on my heel two steps above him. I looked down at his darkening blue eyes.

"What?" His eyes turned black at my raised voice.

"What is your problem?" I shouted at him, the echo resonating off the empty stairwell. I held onto the railing, waiting for him to respond. He stepped up to me, his body inches from mine, and I was too aware of him. He was distracting me from my anger. I took a step back, and he stepped forward until I backed against the wall. His hands on either side of my head, "Triston," I breathed, not sure what I wanted to say.

"You, Miss Reid, are going to be the death of me! I control so many things in my life, but you, you're the one thing I ache to control and possess. But you are always just outside my grasp. It makes me crazy!" His voice was louder than I expected. My heart tried hammering out of my chest. Pressing his body flush against me, I felt a hunger for this man, and I didn't know how to satiate it.

I looked up into those beautiful, dark blue eyes. "Triston, you do possess me!" I shouted. I didn't care if it angered him. "Don't you get that?" Stepping back, a look of shock crossed his face. I turned and walked up the stairs to the landing of our floor.

"Miss Reid, stop!" My hand was on the handle of the exit. I turned to him. He stared at me, oblivious to the effect he had on me. Those beautiful blue eyes held so much pain, but also so much love — a love he was so scared to give. I felt like shaking him and making him see how much I wanted him. How much I wanted to be his.

"I do?" His whisper, laced with insecurity. How on earth did a man filled with so much confidence still have insecurities? He reached the landing, standing in front of me. I nodded.

Releasing the doorknob, I grabbed his face in my hands. I held his gaze. "You do, Triston; you possess me in ways I never knew were possible." Grabbing my wrists, he walked me back against the wall, his mouth crashing onto mine. I arched my body into his, feeling his erection against my thigh. I ached to feel it inside me. Pinning my hands above my head with one hand, his other hand found my soaked panties. His growl emanated through his chest into the kiss. He stroked my panties, pushing the thin material aside, slipping two fingers inside me.

Pulling away from the kiss, he looked at me, his eyes filled with lust. "I love how wet you are for me, angel." Plunging his fingers into me, I bit my lip to keep from moaning out loud. I could hear people passing the door. My head fell back, and I savored the feeling of his fingers lifting me higher and higher. I heard his zipper, and when I looked down, he had freed his rock-hard erection.

"Triston—" I protested.

Placing a finger on my lips to hush me, he pulled his fingers out of me, licking them. His smirk was dark and devilish. "I need to be inside you, right now!"

He rammed inside me hard, leaving me breathless. His hands grabbed my ass, lifting me as I wrapped my legs around his waist. He slammed into me fast and deep. I needed this, and I needed him. To take me, possess me in only the way he could. I was so close I clenched around him, making him groan, "That's my angel. Come for me." His words were my undoing as my orgasm ripped through me. He pushed into me again, and I felt his body tense as he found his release.

He slowly let me down. My knees felt wobbly, and I wasn't sure I could make it to the room. "I guess we can get dinner now?" he asked, amused. After straightening up, we walked through the stairwell door toward our room. I giggled as we walked passed another couple who had just stepped out of the elevator. "Yes, let's go to dinner, Mr. Hart."

Chapter Eight

I dabbed lip gloss over my lips. I was in the dress Triston bought. It was long, black, flowing chiffon with the back open in the shape of a V. The straps flowed over my shoulders with a cowl neck, and there was a long slit from my left ankle ending mid-thigh. I slipped on my black diamanté sandals. I decided on my white gold and diamond earrings with a matching necklace. My hair was tied in a messy bun, and stray curls spilled down my neck, framed my face. The butterflies in my stomach are awake and now having a party. I took a deep, steadying breath. This was it. Triston and I were together, officially and I smiled at my reflection. Life felt perfect.

I walked into the living room. Triston looked up, and I twirled. "Do you approve, Mr. Hart?" I giggled hearing him growl. I faced him again as he stood. Music drifted from his laptop, and he grabbed me, spinning me around. I recognized

Ellie Goulding's voice. She sang the words I wanted to say to Triston. But it was too soon for me to say.

"I do have fantastic taste in clothes, don't I?" he asked in a low voice, pulling me out of my thoughts. I laughed at his question. He smiled appreciatively at me.

"Thank you, Triston. The dress is exquisite. I don't think I have ever worn anything as beautiful." Hooking his index finger under my chin, he lifted my face so our eyes locked.

"You are a vision tonight, and you should wear beautiful clothes all the time. I will make sure of that." I blushed and smiled at his promise. He pulled away and walked over to turn his laptop off. I took in his appearance properly for the first time tonight. Triston looked as if he had just stepped off a photo shoot for GQ magazine. He wore his pinstripe, black Armani suit with a silver dress shirt. The first four buttons of his shirt undone as he always did when he wasn't wearing a tie. His black, unzipped boots completed his look. It was elegant but rugged, and only Triston could have pulled it off. His shoulder-length hair hung loosely on his shoulders.

I was thankful I didn't need to take a purse along. He turned to me, his body close, and I felt his warm breath on my face. Leaning in, his lips on mine never failed to send sparks flying through me. When he pulled away, I felt a yearning for his body. Something else that didn't go away. "You ready to knock them dead, angel?" His eyes sparkled in the light of our room. He took my breath away with his exquisite beauty.

"I think I am."

We walked into the restaurant, and I'm blown away. The restaurant was luxurious. Coming from a small town, I had never been in a place like this before. Triston's fingers brushed against my lower back as he guided me through the tables. The heat from his touch sending shivers down my spine. I felt everyone turn to stare at us, and a blush heated my face. Walking next to him made me feel like a princess; he oozed confidence, which seemed to cover me. "Seems you're quite the head turner, Mr. Hart," I whispered to him.

"You're the one they're looking at, angel."

He leaned in close. "Even the women," he whispered in my ear. I smiled.

"Are you jealous, Mr. Hart?" I asked as we got closer to our table.

"Miss Reid, I can't be jealous. I'm the one who gets to see you naked," he rasped, sending a current through my body to my panties.

"Mr. Jacobson, Mrs. Jacobson." Triston straightened and greeted our hosts, kissing Mrs. Jacobson's hand, causing her to flush. No woman seemed immune to his charms. We sat down, and were immediately served with two large glasses of a crisp Chardonnay. Triston's right hand found a spot on my thigh, his thumb drawing circles on my skin. That was why he sat on my left. The slit fell open, and he had access to tease me all night.

The conversation flowed, and Triston impressed Mr. Jacobson with every answer. I was proud watching him. He was controlled and confident and oh so sexy. Mrs. Jacobson chatted to me as the men spoke business. She asked about my work and how long I had been employed at Triston's company. She caught us both off guard with her next comment.

"You two make a beautiful couple!"

Triston turned and gave her a dazzling smile. "Thank you, Mrs. Jacobson. She makes me look good." He winked and smiled at me. I felt my face flush bright red, and he squeezed my thigh, causing me to jump. He watched me, his hand never leaving my thigh. His teasing was relentless, and I figured I could play his game. I picked up my wine, taking a sip, wetting my lips. As always, his steel-blue gaze fell on my mouth. My tongue traced the line of my bottom lip, licking the moisture. His eyes glued to my mouth. He smirked, and his hand traveled higher up my thigh, and I almost moaned out loud. My eyes flickered to his. "Triston," I gasped.

He winked at me. Leaning in, he whispered in my ear, "Miss Reid, you do realize you're making me hard . . . in public!" He sat back, and I noticed his other hand adjusting the front of his pants under the table. I giggled. His gaze on me was intense, making me squirm.

I leaned toward him. My eyes darting to the couple at our table who were engrossed in a conversation about the wine. "I didn't realize that, Mr. Hart," I breathed in his ear. "I do apologize." My tongue teased the shell of his ear, and his grip tightened on my thigh. I sat back, pleased with myself. Nobody had noticed our little exchange, and I gave him a sweet smile. His eyes had turned a beautiful shade of midnight blue in the dim light of the restaurant. I knew I had won this round at least.

The rest of dinner was light in conversation as we finished a delectable cheesecake. I continued teasing Triston, licking the cream from my fork. His eyes were glued to my mouth almost throughout dessert. I felt powerful knowing I could affect him so much.

The band started soon after our Irish coffees arrived. "I am taking my girl for a dance! Excuse us!" Mr. Jacobson escorted his wife to the dance floor, leaving Triston and me alone. As soon as they were out of earshot, Triston turned to me. "Miss Reid, you do know you will be punished for your little display earlier?" His eyes flickered with lust, making me shiver. I didn't think I could wait until later. I was so turned on from our teasing I wanted him here and now.

"Mr. Hart, I count on it!" My eyes challenged him. His smirk was dangerous. I stood up, and my dress flowed around my legs. Looking down at him, I smiled. "You coming?" I took a step toward the dance floor and waited till I felt his body heat on my back.

"Angel, you bet I will be coming!" I gave a small laugh as he led me onto the dance floor.

The song changed, and I recognized Annie Lennox singing "I Put a Spell On You." It was appropriate, as he definitely put a spell on me. My arms wrapped around Triston's neck, and his warm, soft hands held on to my lower back. His body was inches from mine, and he was radiating his magnetic heat my. We swayed across the floor alongside other couples. It was everything I could hope for. I was with an amazing man, I had my dream job, and I felt happy — like I was in one piece again. "You do look delicious in that dress and those heels," he whispered. He spun me around, and we moved together effortlessly. It was like we were made to fit, made for each other.

"Thank you, Mr. Hart, I did think you preferred me better without the dress?" He smiled as he led me between the people. I didn't even notice them; all that mattered was him. There was nothing else or no one else I could ever want or need but Triston. His fingers traced feather-light lines up and down my spine. Goosebumps rose on my skin, and I trembled in his arms.

"I do, Miss Reid. I also like making my girl tremble." His voice was low and husky.

"Your girl?" I arched my eyebrow at him, and he smiled, pulling me tighter into him.

"Of course. Unless of course, you prefer someone else making you tremble?" He questioned, his eyes flickering with something. Insecurity? I realized he still didn't believe I wanted him and only him.

"I prefer you," I murmured, resting my head on his chest.

We sat side by side in the back of the car. Triston held tightly onto my hand. "Are you okay, Triston?" I looked over at him. H smiled and nodded. He seemed a million miles away, and I frowned.

"I was just thinking; I want to take you somewhere." His explanation didn't say much, but I left it. The driver pulled up to the hotel, and Triston got out. He walked around to my side and opened my door. I stepped out, placing my hand in his. "Thank you, Mr. Hart." He gave me a small smile. I wondered what had changed his mood so unexpectedly. He had something on his mind, and I could tell he wasn't ready to share it. We walked through reception and waited at the elevator. "You really took my breath away tonight, angel. Of course, you always do." He squeezed my hand. Stepping into the elevator, I pressed the sixth-floor button, and we ascended. I watched the lights change as we neared our floor. My heart was racing; I wanted to tell him how I felt. I wanted to say the words, but I knew he wasn't ready to hear them.

"Triston," I mumbled, and he turned to face me. "I . . ." My face flushed. "Thank you."

It was his turn to look confused, his frown creasing his handsome face. "Thank you for what, beautiful?" The elevator dinged to alert us we had arrived at our floor. We stepped out and walked along the hallway.

"Everything." I saw the confusion on his face, but I didn't think it was time to go into details. I couldn't explain what I meant, so I smiled and watched him slide the keycard into the door. Unlocking it, he stepped aside and let me enter first.

I walked into the bedroom and felt Triston follow close behind me. I faced the bed, slipping my shoes off. "Stop. Don't move." He pressed his body against me. I felt the heat radiating from him straight through me, his hot breath on my neck as he spoke, his voice low. "I don't know what you're doing to me, Miss Reid." His voice cracked with emotion. His fingers traced a line from the back of my ear down to my shoulder.

"Triston," I breathed his name.

"Shh, Angel, do not say a word." He slipped the dress off my shoulders, and the soft fabric slid down my body to the floor. "Tonight, I want to show you other pleasures I can bestow on that beautiful body of yours. Stand still, okay?" I nodded in agreement, my body already trembling in anticipation. It wasn't long before I felt the familiar fabric around my eyes. Butterflies fluttered in my stomach; I was nervous. I was acutely aware of him moving around the room, and I heard glasses clinking and then heard ice.

"You're going to lay down, angel, on your back." He helped me onto the bed, feeling the soft sheets. He had removed the covers. I laid back and felt the cold breeze from outside on my nipples, hardening them. He grabbed both my wrists, and it felt like the material of the blue scarf he was wearing wrapping around my wrists. He tied them to the headboard, which I remembered were wooden slats. He leaned over me on the bed, his tongue tracing a line from my ear down my neck, and I whimpered and moaned. I was naked except for my black lace panties. His tongue moved over my lips, and my mouth opened aching to be kissed. He sat back, and I shivered. "Mmm, my girl." His voice was raspy with desire. "Do I possess you as much as you do me?" His whispered question in the darkness surrounded me.

I nodded. "Yes, Triston."

He ran his fingers lightly from my neck down my chest, between my breasts, following a line down to my belly button. I squirmed under his feathery touch. His fingers were soft and warm, sending sweet sparks to every nerve-ending in my body. I felt alive and electric at his touch. The bed shifted, and I knew he had gotten off the bed. I heard the glass again and felt the mattress sink next to me. I could only guess he was kneeling beside me. A second later, he was leaning over me again. Straddling my hips, I could tell he had taken his pants off, but I felt the material of his tight briefs. His lips on mine caused my mouth to open to him. I tasted the wine from his lips as it slowly dripped into my waiting mouth. I moaned, swallowing the crisp, cold liquid.

I heard him take another mouthful of wine. I felt the cold liquid dripping down the line he traced from my breasts. Slow. Steady. All the way to my belly button. The cold caused goosebumps to rise on my skin, and my whole body tingled. "Mmm," he growled, and I felt his tongue dip into my navel.

"Ah, Triston!" My hips rose up to meet his teasing mouth. His teeth grazed my skin, and I felt the heat between my legs intensify. I knew it wouldn't be long till I came undone.

I felt him move again as he reached over me. Unexpectedly, I felt heat on my skin. I realized he was dripping hot wax following the path of the cold wine. "Oh god, Triston, please?" I moaned out loud.

The heat sent intense shivers over my body. I almost came undone when I felt the ice. He traced the line of the wax with melting ice until it reached my belly button. He started blowing back up my skin, his breath hot. I couldn't stand it anymore. The hot, the cold, it was driving me insane. "Triston, please!" I begged louder this time. I needed him so much as I was in complete exquisite agony. He moved over me, his fingers taking the cool wax off me.

"Miss Reid, you do recall the teasing you did at the dinner table?" His voice was so dark and dangerous. I knew he would get his revenge for that. And what a magnificent revenge it was. I nodded, not sure if he saw.

"Yes," I mumbled, giggling into the darkness. He grabbed my hips in one swift move, turning me over, spanking me hard. "Ouch!"

Another slap and I was about to come apart when I heard him growl, "Do you think it's funny, Miss Reid?" My body stretched as I kneeled in front of him. My hands are tugging on my restraints.

"No." My whisper was barely audible.

"No? No, who, Miss Reid?" He spanked me again, kneeling behind me. His lust-filled voice caused my whole body to react and tremble. I was dripping wet, and I needed him to take me. I needed him so much it hurt.

"No, Mr. Hart," I mumbled into the pillow.

I heard the sound of him pushing his briefs down. I anticipated his movements, but nothing could prepare me for him filling me, his hands in a vice-like grip on my hips. He plunged into me deep and hard. "Triston!" I screamed his name, so close to my release. He was unrelenting as he took me, fucking me hard.

His growl sounded animalistic, and it spurred me on. "You are so fucking tight. Feels so good around me." I was almost at the edge when he slowed. He wasn't allowing me my release. "Please, Triston?" He ignored me, continuing his exquisite torture inside me. I was close to delirium when his hand reached down, between my legs. His fingers circled my clit in slow, teasing touches, taking me back to the edge. I was almost there when he slammed into me once more. "Come, Emily. Give me your pleasure!" Biting onto the pillow, an intense orgasm ripped into me. I squeezed him inside me, tightening around him.

"Fuck!" His body tensed behind me, and he spasmed. I felt his hot release filling me.

I woke to the smell of pancakes. Opening my eyes, I rolled over to an empty bed. Triston was at the balcony door in his low-slung pajama bottoms, the muscles in his back looking tense.

"Good morning, Mr. Hart." I sat up. Covering myself with the sheet, I scooted up. When he turned to face me, I noticed he looked uneasy. "Are you okay?" I got out of bed wrapped in the sheet and walked over to him. I wrapped my arms around his waist and could feel the welcome heat of his skin.

"I should be asking you that." His voice was strained and clipped. Twisting in my arms to face me, he lifted my chin with his index finger. I look into those amazing steel-blue eyes and frowned. What did he mean? Why wouldn't I be okay? "Of course I am; why would you even ask?"

He released my chin and shrugged. "I don't know. I just . . ." As he pulled away from me, I knew something was wrong. Leaving me standing in the door of the patio, he walked back into the bedroom and stood at the cabinet with his back to me.

"What is wrong, Triston? Have I done something?" I frowned, watching him tense again. Something was seriously wrong. My heart was constricting in my chest. Had he changed his mind about us?

"It's nothing. We are going to be late for work

if you don't get dressed!" He turned to me and picked me up, spinning me around and kissing me deeply. His tongue stroked mine. I tangled my hands in his hair, and I heard the familiar growl in his chest. The concern in his eyes had disappeared, but I knew something was bothering him. I wanted to know what it was. He let me down and stepped back.

"Can I get you some coffee? They've just brought our breakfast." I nodded as he made his way back into the living room. I passed the cabinet and noticed my phone. I hadn't checked it since we arrived, but picking it up and pressing the power button, the screen lit up. I didn't remember turning it on. I was sure it was off for a few days. I unlocked the screen and saw my messages open. One from Bash sent that morning.

Sebastian: I am so sorry. Please don't let my brother steal you from me? I didn't mean to hurt you.

That was probably what was on Triston's mind. "I see you found it." I jumped at his voice behind me. Turning to face him, I saw the concern was back in his eyes.

"Triston, did you turn my phone on?"

He nodded, and I felt fear in my heart. Did he see the message and think we were over? That didn't make sense, though. "I shouldn't have looked. I am sorry. I got a message from him this morning, and I had a feeling he would have messaged you too." I was in shock. The man standing in front of me was so broken and insecure, yet he had no reason to be. I didn't have anything to hide from him. Why would he think I was angry about him looking at a message that I had no desire to answer? I had a feeling there was something else, though. There had to be.

"Is there something you're not telling me, Triston?"

He handed me the coffee and sat on the edge of the bed. "Remember when I told you I overdosed?" I nodded. "Well, it was my brother who found me." He was quiet for a few moments. I knew the confession was difficult for him. "When I woke up, let's just say I was less than grateful to him. I said some things to him, insulted him in a way I knew would hurt him. He never forgave me for it and yet I don't blame him. I don't forgive myself for saying what I did to him. We stopped speaking for years until my mother invited him to my engagement party. She thought it was time to mend fences."

"Okay, what did you say to him that was so bad?" I asked slowly. I held onto my cup, hoping it would stop my hands from shaking.

He looked up again. "I told him he was just like our father, and I guess he wanted to prove he was by cheating with my ex. Our father was a liar and a cheat. He also gamble and had addictions just like I did. He left my mother with nothing. He took all our savings and ran off with some girl he had found. Bash — when he was younger — was a bit of a gambler, and I feared he had turned into my father. He worked at a bar where he was stealing the tips to gamble. He is okay now, of course. I guess we're both broken kids." He didn't look at me. "I told him he was like our dad, and I knew it cut him deep. I said it on purpose. I wanted to hurt him. So, he hurt me. He took Krista from me."

As I stared at him, I saw a little boy aching for forgiveness from his brother, and my heart broke. I took a step toward him. "Don't. Emily . . ." His voice was commanding, and I stopped.

"Triston, everyone says things they don't mean in the heat of the moment. Yes, it might take years, but he will forgive you. And you will be able to forgive him some time. What did he say in the message he sent you?" I frowned. How could they hate each other this much? They were brothers. Everyone makes mistakes, but they overcome them. Don't they? He got up and grabbed his phone from the nightstand. "It's in the messages. I'm going to shower. Once you've read it, and you decide to stay, join me. If you decide not to be with me, I completely understand." His eyes never met mine as he walked past me into the bathroom.

Unlocking his phone, I smiled at the home screen photo. He had taken it the day we went to the beach; it was a photo of us smiling after we had our swim. I opened his messages and found the one from Bash.

Sebastian: Do you think she will want you after she knows the real you? The dark, demented person under those pretty blue eyes? Why do you think Krista chose me? I will get Emily too. Brother

I was shaking with anger, but also with confusion. I put the phone on the cabinet as thoughts whirled through my mind. What the fuck was Bash playing at? We spent one night together. Why did he think he had any say over me? I could make my own choices, and I wanted Triston. I dropped the sheet and walked into the bathroom. Sliding the shower door open, I stepped inside. Triston turned, his eyes betrayed him — he looked shocked that I was there with him. I realized he didn't expect me to be there.

"Em." I put my finger to his lips, my eyes never leaving his.

"I am here, Triston, with you. Now can we please get ready for work?" I smiled, trying to reassure him.

"Emily." He pulled me into his body, and I realized how much I ached for him. I wanted to fix him, to make him whole. I wanted to show him he was worthy of love. His past didn't matter anymore; I knew I couldn't be without him. "I'm not running away. Okay?" I whispered, leaning up to kiss him.

"You're my girl . . ." he said into the kiss, and I smiled. His hands cupped my ass, lifting me against him. I felt his arousal at my entrance, and I was ready for him to take me again. Under the hot spray, he pinned me against the wall, sliding into me slowly. It was so different from the night before. He was slow and gentle, sliding into me all the way, filling the ache inside my core. His mouth on my hard nipples sent waves of pleasure to my heated entrance. I tightened around him, and his growl vibrated off his chest. His teeth bit lightly on the hard bud, and I cried out.

He was lifting me higher, fixing me the same way I fixed him. The only way we knew how was by having him inside me. He moved faster and deeper as I dug my nails into his shoulder. His eyes burned into me. Without breaking eye contact, he whispered, "Come for me, angel." His words sent me over the edge as I tightened around him, his release filling me.

The day was long and busy. We had finished the complete marketing plan and revised the contracts. When five o'clock rolled around, I was ready for bed, but Triston and I had to go to a masked ball. This time, I was entirely out of my depth. I had never been to a special dance of any kind. Triston called Jessie earlier with instructions to order my dress and his suit, as well as masks, which would be delivered to the hotel for our arrival back after our day at the office. Mr. Jacobson threw a lot of parties, and this was the most opulent of them all. As a tomboy, I wasn't used to wearing dresses every day. I was much more comfortable in sweats and a pair of gym shoes.

We also still had to talk about Triston and Bash's past. I knew he wasn't looking forward to it. I was sure I was about to learn the darker side of the man I was falling in love with as I looked over at him in the seat next to me. Feeling my eyes on him, he turned. "You okay, angel?" His hand found mine, and he laced our fingers. I nodded and smiled.

I couldn't shake the feeling that something was going to happen. Something bad. I hated that feeling. I remembered it so well from my own past. That dread that fills your stomach, waiting for the blow to knock you down. I just hoped that when my past comes knocking, Triston would be able to handle it. The driver pulled up to the hotel, and we made our way to the room.

I stood at the dresser in the bedroom and stared at myself in the mirror. I had just finished my hair and makeup, "Triston, I feel out of my depth. Tonight is a lot to take in." I watched his reflection in the mirror as he turned to look at me.

"Angel, you are perfect. It doesn't matter what you're doing or wearing." He stood behind me, and I looked at our reflections. We looked good together, like we fit. His warm hands held my shoulders, and his lips kissed my neck. I melted into his body and electricity surged through me. I needed him and only him. His eyes lifted as he lightly bit on the sensitive spot on my neck. I moaned loudly. We needed to stop, or we wouldn't leave the room. "Come on, we need to leave soon." He read my mind as he always did.

Fastening his tie, he winked at me, and I flushed. He was in black and white, his hair tied back in a bun, and he looked like a young James Bond. I stepped into my dress, sliding it up my body. It was a long, black, silk halter neck with diamond studs in the center from my breasts down to my belly button. I was wearing my small diamond earrings and the diamond necklace to match. "I got you something, angel." I turned to face Triston, and he smiled. It was warm and engaging, and I knew I wanted to see that smile forever. The thought took me by surprise. I really was in love with him.

I shook my head. "A gift? Why?" I asked, puzzled.

"Because, Miss Reid, you are special, and I want to spoil you." I flushed at his compliment. He handed me a long, thin, black velvet box. Flipping it open, I saw the most beautiful bracelet. It was white gold with princess and rose-cut diamonds. I couldn't even imagine what it cost, and I didn't really want to know. I took it out of the box. "Let me help you." I watched his long slender fingers clasp the hook around my wrist. It was sparkling under the light of the bedroom. "Perfect!" He pulled me into him and gave me a lingering kiss.

"But, Triston, I mean . . ." He put his finger to my lips, copying my earlier action in the shower.

"Let's go, Miss Reid." I grabbed my purse, and we made our way down to the waiting car.

Chapter Nine

We walked into the opulent ballroom, and it was absolutely breathtaking. I started doubting that I belonged there. Triston's hand fell on my lower back, and his confidence poured into me, like a waterfall rushing into a silent river. He pulled me into his world as if I was always meant to be there. As an elegant, sophisticated woman, when deep down I felt like a girl out of my depth. My eyes darted around, taking in everything. I was having an out of body experience; I was sitting on my sofa in my sweats, watching Cinderella at the ball with Prince Charming. The only part that worried me was, what happened at the stroke of midnight? We stopped at the entrance to have our photo taken with our masks on, as per the rules, they are kept on all night.

A waiter offered us glasses of champagne with floating strawberries. Triston took one for himself and handed me a glass. "I want to toast to us, Miss Reid." His steel-blue eyes were striking in the black domino covering half his handsome face.

"To us, Mr. Hart." I clinked my glass to his. Those blue eyes burned into mine, and I felt myself flush. His stare was intense. I wondered if he would ever stop having that effect on me. We made our way through the crowd, his hand never leaving me. Typically, being in a room full of strangers would weigh on me, but next to him, I felt at ease. Triston took my hand and laced his fingers through mine. We walked over to the chart with seating arrangements and found our names. We would be seated with Mr. Jacobson and his wife and a few other people we hadn't met before.

We took our seats and saw Mr. Jacobson walking up to the stage. "Good evening, fine people! Please take your seats. If you're not sure of the seating arrangement, we have ushers to assist." Everyone made their way to different tables, and a hush fell over the large room. Once everyone was seated, Mr. Jacobson started his speech. Triston took my hand as we listened. I sipped my champagne and felt happiness bubbling inside. Maybe it was just the champagne, but I smiled to myself. My mind had been working overtime with thoughts of what was going to happen when we went back home. I looked at Triston's beautiful, steel-blue gaze, and his smile was genuine, easing my worries for the time being.

Music started after an enjoyable dinner, and people were dancing, laughing, and drinking. It was beautiful seeing the black and white dresses and suits flowing across the dance floor. "Miss Reid, would you care to dance with me?" Triston turned to me, holding out his hand. I slipped mine in his, and we walked to the dance floor.

He pulled me into him. The song changed, and a slow melody began. David Gray's voice filled the large ballroom, and my heart raced. The song always brought me to tears. The lyrics were haunting, tugging at my heart as I swayed with Triston. Something in his eyes changed as he looked at me. I couldn't quite pinpoint what it was. The lyrics of "This Year's Love" echoed from the speakers and I looked into his eyes knowing I was in love, but was he?

Feeling his rigid body against mine, I ached for him again. He radiated his magnetic heat. His hand on my back, tracing a line up and down my spine as we spun around. "You look breathtaking tonight, Miss Reid," he whispered in my ear. His lips brushed my neck, and I shivered. He pulled away, and his eyes met mine, his stare searing through me as it so often did.

"And you look magnificent as always, Mr. Hart." I smiled up at him. Following Triston's lead, we danced across the floor. As the song ended, we made our way to Mr. Jacobson to thank him for the evening. "Triston, I'm going to the restroom. Meet you back here?" He smiled and nodded, kissing me on the cheek.

"Yes, angel. I'll wait here so you can find me again." He winked, and I giggled. How could I not find him? He was the only person here with those striking steel-blue eyes!

I walked out of the ballroom and into the hallway and followed the signs to the restroom. People were milling around, and I saw a few women walking in the direction I was headed. A sudden voice ripped into me and made me want to retch. "There she is!" I spun around at the familiar gruff voice. My heart plummeted, and the bile rose into my throat. I was met with the familiar, startling green eyes. My past hit me all at once, and sudden breathlessness knocked me hard. "Did you think you could run off with your blue-eyed millionaire and I wouldn't find you?" he sneered at me, and I knew I needed to get away. Anger flashed in his eyes, and I realized he was out for revenge. I took a deep breath. I needed to try and calm him down somehow. Thoughts whirled through my mind. I wasn't sure how I was going to do this. Even though I was so used to his temper, I still found myself defenseless.

"Blake, I . . . What are you doing here?" I asked softly.

He gave a deep, gravelly laugh. "I wanted to come to LA to see prospective clients. When I saw your name on the guest list, I thought you would welcome me with open arms. Didn't you miss me?" He walked toward me, and my heart started racing. I couldn't run -- he would catch me. I didn't want to cause a scene. I knew if I didn't get back to Triston, he would come looking for me, but I didn't want him to see Blake. I couldn't let him see my past so soon.

"Oh, well I better get back." I turned to go back inside the ballroom when Blake grabbed my arm. "Blake, please let me go? I need to get back," I whispered, hoping not to anger him.

"Not even a hug for your husband?" He pulled me into him.

"Ex-husband, Blake." I could smell the whiskey on his breath. He pulled me into him, giving me a tight hug. When he released me, I saw the evil glinting in his eyes.

"That's a technicality. I'm sure you missed me." He stepped back. "I'll see you soon, missy. Don't forget that!" He turned and stalked off down the hallway. I stood shocked, unsure what to do. I knew I needed to speak to Triston about him, but how on earth did I even begin? I walked back into the ballroom and found Triston in the same spot I had left him.

He turned to look at me; his eyes flickered with concern. "What's wrong, angel?" He took my hand, his eyes searching mine for an answer.

I shook my head slowly. "I'm not feeling too good. I think it's a migraine." I gave a small smile, hoping he would decide to leave immediately. I couldn't risk having him bump into Blake because I was not giving up my future for my past.

"We are leaving; I don't want you at a loud party if you're not feeling well." Triston held my hand, and we walked through the crowds to find Mr. Jacobson. I felt terrible for lying to Triston, but I didn't know how else to stop him from running into Blake. I didn't want him finding out about my past in public. He was going to blow a gasket.

We sat quietly in the car on the way back to the hotel. I needed to talk to him; I just didn't know how to bring it up. He lifted my hand to his lips and kissed my knuckles. "I'm going to make you some tea, and you need to rest. Tomorrow is our last day here, and I want to take you somewhere special. Since we aren't working, I want you to have a relaxing day." I smiled and nodded, resting my head on his shoulder. His energy radiated through me, and I felt calmer.

The driver pulled up outside the hotel. Triston got out and came around to open my door. Holding my hand as I stepped out, he laced his fingers through mine, and we walked through the reception area. The elevator ride was excruciating. My mind whirling with thoughts on how I could even begin telling Triston about Blake.

On our floor, Triston unlocked the room door, and I went straight to the bedroom. I slipped off my shoes, and I felt him behind me. "Let me help you, angel." He slid my dress over my shoulders, and I shivered at his warm touch.

"Thank you," I mumbled. I left Triston in the bedroom as I walked into the bathroom to get ready for bed. When I came back out, Triston had found some painkillers and a bottle of Evian. "Drink those and get into bed." It was a direct order, but his voice was soft and loving. I smiled. The way he cared for me made my heart fill with love.

I slid into bed. "Sit with me?" I pleaded with him, not wanting to be alone after seeing Blake again.

"Of course, I will. Let me brush my teeth, and then we can get some rest." A few minutes later, he slid into bed next to me wearing only his tight briefs. He slid his strong arm over me while his rhythmic heartbeat lulled me into a calm I needed. I took a deep, steadying breath. This was it. The moment I may lose the man I love.

"Triston?" My voice was low. My heart was racing. Fear tugged at me. I felt like I was about to puke. Closing my eyes, I saw that vile green gaze. The menacing look on Blake's face chilled me to the bone. I couldn't let him come near Triston. I needed to save Triston from the man who almost killed me.

"Mmm, what's up angel?" His voice was soft in my ear.

I leaned up on my elbow. "I . . . um . . . Can we talk?" His frown was adorable. I watched his brow crease, and I knew it was now or never. I needed to tell him. This was the defining moment. I didn't want to lose him, but after I told him about Blake, he might never want to look at me again, and I wouldn't blame him.

"Of course. You can tell me anything. You know that." I smiled, nodding slowly.

"Earlier, at the ball, when I went to the restroom." My gaze fell to the sheet, twisting it around my fingers. I felt my heart hammering its way out of my chest.

"Emily, you're scaring me, what's wrong? What happened?" There was concern in his voice, and I could see it etched on his handsome features. He was so beautiful sometimes it hurt to look at him. He sat up now, trying to look into my eyes.

I took a deep steadying breath. "I saw my ex-husband." The words fell out of my mouth, and I couldn't look up. I didn't want to see his expression. I heard his sharp intake of breath. I closed my eyes waiting for the worst.

"Ex-husband? Okay, so?" I looked up at him, his eyes searching my face. Here goes nothing.

"He is the reason I ran away from home, Triston. He . . ." I couldn't get the words out. My throat tightened, and I was sure I was going to pass out. Tears burned my eyes, and I tried blinking them away. Instead, they slowly rolled down my cheeks. He sat up straighter. Knowing something was amiss, he pulled me into him. "I'm here, angel, please tell me? I'm not leaving you, no matter what you tell me."

"I was with him for five years, married for two. He was . . . um, possessive. He . . ." I hadn't spoken to anyone about this. Now I wasn't sure telling my boyfriend was the best idea. I didn't even know what Triston was to me besides my boss. His arm tightened around me, with my head against his chest. I closed my eyes, and the words came out easier. "He was abusive for most of our relationship. Triston, I left because he put me in the hospital. I had been knocked unconscious. I had a few broken ribs, a broken arm, and a few cuts and bruises. They said I was in a coma for two weeks." I felt his body go rigid beneath me. He was so tense, but his arm never let me go. The temperature in the room dropped, and I felt ice cold.

"What?" His voice hissed through his teeth. I was trembling now. Clearly, he was angry, and understandably so. The tears flowed down my cheeks, and I knew Triston could feel them on his chest. My body shook with emotion as my sobs came faster. I didn't want to lose Triston; I couldn't survive that.

"I'm sorry, Triston," I mumbled. He pulled me up and turned me to face him, grabbing my face in his hands. His eyes blazed with fierce emotion. I could see the anger but also something else. Something I couldn't read through my tears.

"Sorry? You're sorry? For what, angel? This fucking dick better not come near you, or I will see to it he never walks again!" I shivered at his venomous words, but my heart stopped racing. His anger wasn't directed at me. I relaxed, taking a deep breath. He wasn't leaving me?

"I just thought . . ." I trailed off. I wasn't sure what I thought. Well, that's not true. I thought he would walk out the door and leave me and my baggage.

"How can I ever be angry with you? How could someone call himself a man doing that to someone he loves?" Triston's body was radiating and trembling with intense anger. It scared me to the core. "Oh my god!" He released my face and pinched the bridge of his nose. It looked like he was now directing the anger at himself. I was confused. "What, Triston?" A frown creasing my forehead. He lifted his eyes, looking directly at me.

"We . . . You let me . . ." He wiped my tears with his thumbs. I still didn't know what he was talking about. "You let me do those things to you! Oh god, Emily, I am so sorry!"

I smiled at him, hoping to calm him down. He was angry at himself for what we had done.

I ran my fingers over his chest. "Triston, I wanted that. I wanted you! That stuff we did, I wanted that." A deep growl resonated in his chest when my fingers reached his abs. I ran my finger over the lines of his beautiful torso.

"Emily, be careful," he said, motioning to my hand. His warning was husky, dripping with anger and lust. It was a heady combination, making the fire within me flare with intensity. I wanted him now. I wanted him to take me and fix me. I wanted him to put every shattered piece of me back together, and I knew only he could do it.

"Oh, Mr. Hart, I am very careful," I whispered, leaning down and kissing the soft, smooth skin of his torso. I felt his hand grip my hair, pulling back slightly so I could face him. "I want you, Triston. Let me?" I begged him. Did he not see how much I wanted him?

"Miss Reid, you are completely distracting. I am coming to terms with everything, and now I can't think about anything else. Now all I want is to be inside you." He released his hold on me, and I smiled at him. His eyes took on that darkness I had become so familiar with.

I laid soft kisses on his chest, moving my way down his beautiful body. I looked up and saw his eyes close, and his head leans back on the pillow. I kneeled next to him, licking the sculpted lines of his torso. Finding the beautiful V-lines pointing somewhere below the sheet, then tracing both lines with my tongue, from his taut hips down to the sheet.

A low moan escaped his lips, and I saw his hands grip the sheet as I pulled down the one covering him to find he was hard as steel. I moved down the bed as my tongue licked the length of his erection. Taking him in my mouth, I slowly sucked him deeper till I felt him at the entrance to my throat. "Fuck." His growl was deep and scratchy. I continued my assault on him, sucking and licking every inch of erection. His knuckles were white as his grip on the sheet tightened, the veins pulsing in his hands. Every part of him was perfect. He tasted like honey and strawberries.

I watched his face, the expression of pure ecstasy and lust evident on his handsome features. Suddenly, his eyes opened. "Miss Reid, stop! I need to be inside you!" Pulling my mouth off him, I gave a final flick of my tongue. The salty sweetness of him in my mouth, I slowly licked my lips as he watched me, a devilish smirk etched on his face.

"Come here." He pulled me astride him. I could feel him at the entrance to my body, his hardness pressed against my panties. He teased them aside, and the tip slid over my slick entrance. "Mmm, Miss Reid, you are delectable. So ready and so wet for me." He gripped my hips and pulled me onto him. I cried out at the fullness of him. He hit my sweet spot, and my body shuddered. He plunged into me, deep. I rolled my hips back and forth, building a steady rhythm. His hands traveled up my body and tweaked my nipples, sending waves of pleasure to my core. "Open your eyes; look at me," he rasped.

Our eyes locked, making the moment so much more intense than ever before. "Don't you ever not tell me something!" His voice was so husky. He spoke as I moved on him. "I need you to be honest, Emily. That's the only way this will work. Okay?" I nodded. His soft hands moved up my back, pulling me closer to him. His lips on mine, I felt his tongue push its way into my mouth, sucking on it, teasing him. He moaned into the kiss, and I smiled. The power I had over him . . . Making him want me was a heady feeling. He gripped my hips again. I moved faster, feeling my release building inside me, taking me higher and higher. I felt him spasm, and I knew he was close as well. He tugged off my tee, and his mouth devoured my rock-hard nipples. Alternating between them, biting and licking, flicking his tongue over them, making me tremble.

I tangled my fingers in his soft, long hair. The feel of our bodies moving together, the way we fit together was perfect. "Emily," he moaned. I sat back, feeling him hit new depths inside me. His dark blue eyes stared into my dark brown ones. It was almost as if I could see his broken soul inside, and I wanted to pick up every piece and put it back together.

"Triston!" Grabbing me, pulling me to him, his lips crashed into mine. I could feel his chest against mine as he rocked his hips, plunging into me, faster and faster. I was on the precipice, about to fall.

"Angel, I'm going to fill you. Come for me. Do it!" His words are pushing me over the edge. I clenched around him, feeling him tense and fill me. "Jesus, Emily!" His words got lost in my neck as I bit his shoulder to keep from screaming out loud. My body shook as he tightened his hold on me. Biting on my neck in return as we ascended together.

Standing in the hallway, my heart thudded in my chest. He was angry again, the bottle of Jack Daniels shattered on the floor. There was glass everywhere. "Come here, you fucking bitch!" Tears flowed down my cheeks. I needed to get out of here, but he had the keys. He rounded the corner and stalked toward me. "Please, don't do this? I am so sorry!" His laugh was maniacal. I shivered; it was so cold, freezing. My ripped tank top hung from my body.

"You fucking do this. You make me angry! It's all your fault!" he accused. When he reached me, his body pressed me against the wall. His big hand on my throat was lifting me against the plaster. My breaths stopped slowly as he squeezed. "You are going to fucking pay for throwing my whiskey in the sink!" Spittle flew from his mouth as he spoke, and I could smell the stale beer stench from his mouth. I wanted to throw up. I couldn't get enough air. "Please, stop,"

my voice wheezed. If he could just let go. Stars floated across my vision. I knew I was about to pass out. "Fucking bitch!" Dropping his hand, I fell to my knees. "Get up!" I stood slowly. As I straightened the punch winded me. I gulped in air, his laugh echoing in my ears. "No! Please! Stop!" Another punch landed on my cheek.

"Emily! Wake up! Emily!" I sat up with a start. I turned to face Triston in the dark. He sat up next to me, wrapping his arm around my shoulders. "Are you okay, angel?" I nodded slowly, trying to shake off the nightmare. Triston got out of bed.

"Where are you going?" I looked at him, alarmed.

"Getting you some water, angel." He went into the living room, and I heard the bar fridge open and close. He walked back into the bedroom. I couldn't help but stare at his naked body. It distracted me from the horror of my nightmares. Illuminated by the moonlight shining through the windows, he looked like a statue, a perfect sculpture. He slid onto the bed next to me. Opening the bottle, he handed it to me. "What were you dreaming? You scared the shit out of me." His soft hand landed on my back. I felt calmer now, knowing he was here next to me. I wasn't sure I could tell him what it was about; it was still so fresh in my mind. I sipped the water slowly. My throat felt dry, and it hurt as the cold liquid went down.

"What's the time?" I looked at him, and he reached over and grabbed his phone from the bedside table. He pressed the home screen as I peeked over. It was four a.m. I wasn't going to get to back to sleep at that point. "Angel, do you want to lay down again?"

I shook my head "No, I can't." The room was hot. Too hot. I put the water down and got out of bed. Slipping on the tee we discarded earlier, I walked to our balcony door and opened it. The fresh air hit me, and it felt good. I stepped out onto the balcony and looked out at the sparkling lights of the city. It was beautiful. I was so broken; why would Triston want me?

I felt Triston behind me, radiating heat onto my back. He wrapped his arms around me and held me tight. I had never felt safer than when he was holding me. He leaned his chin on my shoulder. "I am here whenever you want to talk, okay?" I nodded as tears welled up in my eyes. He was so sweet, and still, I didn't deserve him. How could such a perfect man want me? The thoughts tumbled in my mind, and I couldn't shake the feeling. He kissed my neck, causing me to tremble against him. His hands slid over my breasts, tweaking my nipples, and they hardened in his expert fingers. "Triston!" I scolded.

"I'm sure I can make you feel better if you let me?" And this was why I needed him. He fixed me; he made things better. My ugly nightmares pushed to the back of my mind as I felt Triston grow hard behind me. Pushing my ass back onto him, the ache I had for him burned my core. I wanted him now. I wanted him to take me, to possess me.

"I'm sure you can, Mr. Hart, but you need to get some rest, don't you?" I smiled, feeling his teeth grazing my neck. His tongue is slowly licking its way up to my ear. I moaned as his hands traveled along my body, grabbing my bare ass under the tee as I pushed back into his hands. "Does my girl want to play on the balcony?" he whispered in my ear, sending shivers down my spine.

"Maybe," I breathed.

I felt his erection pushing between my legs. I pushed back onto him. "Triston, make me yours," I pleaded with him, aching for him to make me forget. His soft, warm hands glided up and down my body. His left hand slipped between my thighs.

"My girl. Only mine. Do you understand?" I nodded. "So wet, just for me." His deep voice was husky in my ear as he slid two fingers into me, in and out, causing a moan to escape from my lips. My head fell back onto his shoulder. Pulling his fingers from me, I watched him lick my arousal from them. "I want to fuck you now, Emily." His eyes filled with desire, tugging at my core. I nodded. He slid his hard cock into me. I held onto the balcony, steadying myself as he plunged into me.

"Triston, yes, please, harder," I moaned, louder this time. I was so lost in the feeling of him sliding inside me, with a view of LA stretched out in front of us. His hands gripped my hips, pulling me back onto him.

"Emily, you are mine! I love how you fit around me. So tight and wet, just for my cock." His words were pushing me closer to the edge. I was close. I needed the release only he could give me. His hand slid down between my legs. His expert fingers are touching the sensitive spot between my thighs, eliciting a moan.

"Shh," he leaned in and whispered in my ear. I was so lost in the sensations flaring through my body that I didn't care who heard us. I felt the familiar fire intensifying in my stomach. I pushed back onto him. Matching his rhythm, aching for the beautiful release his body gave me every time he was inside me. The release that broke me into a million little pieces then pulled me back together. "Triston." My ragged whisper edged him on as he slammed into me. His fingers never left the wetness between my thighs.

He slammed into me again and again, deeper and harder. "Come for me, Emily. Give me your pleasure!" His words were my undoing. My body shook, and I felt his release as I came undone around him. He pulled me back toward him, his mouth on my neck. "You are truly fucking amazing, Emily Reid."

We stood watching the sunrise on the horizon as we came down from the high of our release, his arms around me, and the nightmare wholly forgotten. He scooped me up and walked back into the bedroom, laying me down on the bed. I felt tired, and sleep took hold of me.

I opened my eyes to sunlight streaming through the window. "Good morning, sleepy head." Triston walked into the bedroom with a breakfast tray. "I was about to wake you up. I want to take you out today. It's our last day in LA." I scooted up, resting my back against the pillows. He placed the tray on my lap. There were two cups of coffee, two glasses of orange juice, toast, and a few spreads. I grabbed a piece of toast and spread some hummus on it, savoring the taste. I realized I was starving. *Might be all the exercise lately,* and I giggled at the thought.

Triston smiled. "I love hearing you giggle." I drank the orange juice as he watched me.

"Thank you, Mr. Hart. I love seeing you smile." I finished the toast and picked up my coffee. Taking a sip, I watched his steel-blue eyes burn into me. I couldn't believe that such a handsome man could be so broken. "What are we doing today?" I smiled, holding onto the warm cup.

"I want to take you somewhere special. I

have rented a car for the day." He stood up and walked over to the window. "Looks like we're in for a hot day as well, which is perfect for what I have in mind. Come on, get your sexy ass out of bed!" I giggled. Finishing my coffee, I placed the cup on the tray and grabbed my phone. Turning it on, I saw five missed calls, all from an unknown number, and one message from Jessie.

Jessie: I do hope you and the boss man are having fun! Didn't I tell you?! xo

Smiling at the screen, I felt myself flush. She was right. How I didn't notice it before was beyond me. I hit reply.

Em: You were right, well done. We are having an amazing time! Thanks for the dress by the way!! xo

"Are you two going to giggle about me all day?" Triston's amused gaze made me laugh. How on earth he knew what we were saying I would never know.

"Don't flatter yourself, Mr. Hart!" I retorted. I stuck my tongue out at him, and his eyes narrowed. Putting my phone on the bedside cabinet, I walked over to him. Leaning on my toes I gave his cheek a quick kiss. "I'm going to get ready!" I announced and walked into the bathroom. I wondered what we were doing?

Stepping out of the shower twenty minutes later, I wrapped the towel around me, staring at myself in the misty mirror. I looked happy. Smiling, I walked into the bedroom to find Triston sitting on the bed in grey cargo pants and a black tank top. His muscles look exquisite against the black material. His tattoo peeked out like it was begging to be licked. My tongue darted out, imagining what I would like to do to him. Triston's eyes flickered toward me, taking in my appearance. "I do love when you pick those small towels. They definitely suit you." He winked cheekily. I poked my tongue out at him as he passed me to get to the bathroom. I felt a slap on my ass.

"Hey!" I spun on my heel. His laugh was infectious.

"You weren't complaining the other night!" Pulling me into him, his lips crashed onto mine. His tongue in my mouth made me moan as he devoured me. Reluctantly pulling away, his voice was low and raspy. "Get dressed, or we may never leave this bedroom, Miss Reid." Opening the closet doors, I pulled out my blue denim shorts and white tank top. It had the script "Los Angeles" on the front. I dressed while Triston finished up in the bathroom. When he joined me in the bedroom again, I turn to face him.

"This suitable to wear on this surprise trip, Mr. Hart?" I spun around, giving him a three-hundred-sixty-degree view.

"Yes. Perfect as always. Wear comfortable shoes. We're going walking." He walked into the living room, and I grabbed my sneakers. I decided to wear my bikini, just in case we ended up at the beach. I would love to see him dripping wet again.

I tied the laces of my black and white Converse sneakers. Grabbing my phone and sliding it into the back pocket of my shorts, I walked into the living room. "Ready!" I announced, and his eyes lit up.

"Finally! Let's go, angel!" Triston laced his fingers in mine, and we headed out on our adventure.

Sliding into the passenger seat of the black

little Mercedes SLK, I took in the beauty of the car. Excitement for the day ahead caused my stomach to flip-flop. "You have amazing taste in cars, Mr. Hart," I commented, turning to him. He started the engine and pulled out of the hotel garage.

"I have amazing taste in a variety of things, Miss Reid, including my newest addition, woman." He turned and gave me that sexy devilish smirk, causing electricity to course through my body.

"Oh really? Well, that's interesting, Mr. Hart, because just recently I found out what good taste I have in men. This is such a coincidence; don't you think?" I giggled at the expression on his face. He nodded earnestly.

"Miss Reid, aren't you lucky to have landed yourself such an amazing man? And he's wealthy too." His eyes met mine for a split second. I knew he was joking around, but I needed him to realize I wasn't with him for his money.

"That's not why I'm interested in him. I hope he knows that." I answered him seriously. He certainly didn't know I had money of my own, even though I refused to use it. But I didn't want to think about that right now.

"Miss Reid, he knows that, trust me! He can see what a beautiful, honest, and trustworthy woman he has on his arm. He isn't about to let her get away either." He put his foot on the gas as we drove up into the Hollywood Hills. As we passed the beautiful mansions and estates, I gasped. I couldn't believe some people could afford these amazing homes. I had never given it much thought, but I could buy one of these. The money that was paid out to me from Blake's family could probably buy a lot more than that.

He pulled up into a parking spot at the bottom of the main hill. He got out and came around to open my door. Triston had his Aviators on, hiding his beautiful blue eyes. The view was already breathtaking. You could see most of the city below. As we got higher, the view opened before us. "I wanted to bring you here a couple of days ago. I thought you might appreciate the view." It was a clear morning, and the sky was ice-blue without a cloud in sight.

"This is really amazing, Triston, thank you!" We finally got up the hill, and I saw why he wanted to bring me here. We were at the back of the Hollywood sign. I had dreamed of standing in this exact spot so many times when

I was younger. It was one of those teenage dreams you're never sure you would get to experience. "This . . ." Words failed me. I was so overwhelmed that tears were threatening to spill. I pushed my sunglasses up to take in the view without restriction. Triston turned toward me. "Oh no, I didn't mean to make you cry!" His arms wrapped around me tightly, and I smiled.

"It's tears of joy, Triston, really. I am just overwhelmed. I promise." He leaned down and kissed me. When he pulled away, he stared at me.

"I never want to hurt you." His voice was sincere. "Emily, you know what type of man I am. You know I'm into things that aren't exactly '*vanilla*.' If ever we're doing anything you're not comfortable with, tell me okay? Promise me you will!"

My heart leaped into my throat, and I nodded. "I promise." I knew he meant when his darker side came out.

His phone started ringing then, interrupting the moment. "Shit!" Pulling his phone out of his pocket, he answered the call in a gruff voice. "Jessie?" He listened for a few moments. His eyes met mine, and he nodded. "Yes, get him in the office. I'm back tomorrow, and I'll brief him. I need this done ASAP." He listened to her reply. Turning away from me, I heard him whisper, "He comes near her or my company, there will be hell to pay!"

I watched him hang up, and he slid his phone into the pocket of his pants. "Triston? What's wrong?" My hand on his arm, I could feel the tension radiating through him.

His eyes met mine, and he gave me a small smile. "Nothing. Let's take in the view. We still have somewhere to go." Lacing his fingers in mine, he pulled me toward the large white letters. The view was spectacular, exactly what I had always thought it would be. I couldn't believe I was standing up here. Finally, and with the most amazing man I could ever ask for.

As we made our way back down the hill to the car, something was bothering Triston. I could see it, but he didn't want to tell me what. I pulled out my phone and unlocked it. Opening the messages, I hit reply to Jessie.

Em: Okay, you need to tell me what's going on.

Why is T so angry?

I didn't need to wait long for a reply.

Jessie: It's better that he tells you. Just enjoy your last day there and deal with it when you're back. Please?

This was so frustrating. Why wouldn't anyone tell me what was going on?

"She won't tell you Em. I asked her not to. I want you to enjoy your day. So, would you please respect my wishes and stop asking?" He glanced over at me, and I nodded quickly. There was nothing I could do. I knew when Triston set his mind to something, nothing could change it. When we got into the car, I noticed the time was only ten thirty. It was already so hot that I wouldn't mind a dip in the ocean. Triston pulled onto the I-10 toward Santa Monica moments later. "I am sorry, Triston. You just look worried. I don't like that look on you. I'm concerned." I felt the need to say something. The tension was not helping me enjoy my day.

"I know, angel. I'll be fine. Just let it go, okay? Trust me?" He put his hand on my thigh and the electric current that his touch always brought shot through me.

"I do trust you. I just don't want you upset." I looked at him and saw his smile creasing the edges of his eyes.

"Okay, I'll smile more. Does that help?" He flashed me a beautiful, flawless smile, and I giggled. He stuck out his tongue, and I immediately wanted to kiss him. "Don't stick out your tongue, Mr. Hart; it's rude!" I admonished him.

He laughed out loud. "You weren't complaining this morning when it was tracing lines down your neck." His words trailed off as we neared the Santa Monica Pier. The memory was fresh in my mind. The feel of his tongue made me tingle, licking the softest and most sensitive spot behind my ear. "Well, Mr. Hart, if you're going to stick your tongue out, at least put it to good use!" I teased him, running my hand up his thigh, and I felt him tense.

"Miss Reid, I'm driving! Please refrain from distracting me." I giggled at him.

"But, Mr. Hart, I do love keeping you distracted." I held onto his toned thigh as he pulled into the parking lot and turned off the engine.

He turned to look at me and smiled. "Now, Miss Reid, did you like distracting me?"

I smiled, winking at him. I turned to open my door. "Miss Reid, stop." His demand was low, deep and sexy. My stomach flip-flopped as I turned to face him. He grabbed my face in his hands and kissed me, hard. His tongue pushed into my mouth, eliciting a moan from me. Pulling away slowly, I noticed his eyes had tiny flecks of dark blue. It was almost as if there were two of him hidden in that amazing body. "Let's go, angel or I might just fuck you right here in the car." He got out, ran around the hood, and opened my door.

We joined the crowds walking along the pier. Triston grabbed my hand as we stopped at the end of the boardwalk. "Emily, I wanted to speak to you about something." His tone was suddenly so serious, and it felt like something terrible was coming. My heart constricted, and my breath stopped. I knew we were headed back to work tomorrow, and maybe this whirlwind romance was coming to an end. Of course, it was, who was I kidding? He was my boss after all. I suppose he didn't want to be dating his staff. I steeled myself for the blow. This was going to crush me. I knew I was falling for him or had already fallen for him.

I closed my eyes and took a deep breath. "Yeah sure, what's up?" I tried to sound calm, but a storm brewed inside me.

"We go back to New York tomorrow, and I have made some decisions." His voice trailed off, and he looked out at the waves crashing below us. I didn't want to hear this. I couldn't hear that he was leaving me. I felt a physical pain in my chest, and I needed to get away.

"Triston, stop! Please? Don't." I pulled my hand out of his and ran up the boardwalk. My legs felt like lead, but I forced myself forward.

"Emily!" I heard him shout after me, but I didn't stop. I ran as fast as I could.

I passed a few small stores and ran into a small alleyway. I needed to catch my breath. Silence surrounded me, and I didn't hear him anymore. Maybe he had given up. I leaned against the wall. Wiping my face with my hand, I noticed it was wet. I was crying. I must look like a mess. I rested my head against the wall, and as I closed my eyes, I saw Triston's face. His somber expression and those incredible blue eyes. I knew he was breaking up with me, and I ran. How was I going to face him after this? I couldn't do this; I would need to find another job.

I startled when my phone started ringing

in my pocket. I forgot I had it. Pulling it out, I saw Triston's name flashing across the screen. My hands were shaking. I unlocked the screen. "Hello?" My voice was a hoarse whisper. My throat burned, and so did my eyes. Tears spilled over my cheeks.

"Miss Reid, where the fuck are you?" His voice was harsh and bit into me. "Where the hell did you run to? Tell me where you are now!" Flinching, I could hear the noise around him. He must be about two blocks away. "Emily! So help me . . . !"

"I am here . . ." I stepped out of the alleyway. As I looked up into his cobalt eyes, I could tell he was angry, rightfully so. He stared at me for a while before grabbing me and pulling me into him. "Jesus, Emily, don't you ever do that to me again!" His words muffled as he kissed the top of my head. I felt my breath leave my body as he squeezed me.

"Triston . . . can't . . . breathe . . ." He released his grip and held my face in his hands.

"Do. Not. Ever. Run. Again." He enunciated each word with his gaze locked on mine. I nodded slowly. His look was fierce like he was about to kill someone he was so angry.

"I just . . . I didn't . . . I know what you want to say." I looked down, not wanting to meet his gaze. I toyed with my phone in my hands to keep myself distracted. The tears burned my eyes, and I needed to get away from him. His hands felt hot on my face.

"No, you don't, Emily. You have no idea what I was about to say. You jumped to conclusions, and I can only imagine what it was." He leaned down. "Look at me." Lifting my head, he kissed me softly. He dropped his hands and laced his fingers through mine. He pulled me along the boardwalk. "Come on, we're going to talk without you running away this time." We walked in silence down to the beach. There was no one along this stretch. When we got far enough from the crowds, he stopped and turned to me. "Look, Emily, we are going back, but I don't want you to feel awkward with me being your boss. So, we have made a shuffle within the department."

"What do you mean? What shuffle?" Confusion was evident on my face. I frowned, waiting for an explanation.

"Uhm . . . Well, I promoted Jessie. She will be heading up the Sales and Accounts department.

This is something she has been working toward, and I think the time has come." That sounded great, but why was he so nervous? The thought hit me all at once. He was firing me! Of course!

"Emily? Are you listening?" I shook my head, as I was so lost in my thoughts I didn't hear him. "I said you're going to be head of the Marketing and Events department and my personal assistant."

It took a while to sink in. "Wait, *what?*" A promotion? Me? *Shit!* That was amazing! I jumped up, wrapping my arms around his neck. "Oh my god, Triston! Thank you!" His hands on my ass held me up as I wrapped my legs around his waist. My face was in his shoulder as he spun me around. I started giggling, and his laugh vibrated through his chest.

"It's only my pleasure, angel. You are amazing, and I want you with me at all times!"

The plane had just taken off, and while climbing to cruising altitude, my mind was reeling at how much work I needed to do. The prospect of my promotion has me excited. Once the seatbelt lights were turned off, I took my laptop out. Triston was sleeping next to me. We were up most of the night talking, deciding on how to best introduce "us" to the staff. Since we were going to be traveling together so much, I was setting up our itinerary. We had a busy few months ahead of us. "You working?" he mumbled beside me. I turned to see his sleepy expression. It was adorable, and my heart filled with emotion.

"Yes. You do realize my boss is a demanding slave-driver, don't you?" A devilish smirk spread across his handsome features.

"Yes, he is, but that's not all you can do to keep him satisfied, you know?" He stroked my thigh, and I knew what he was thinking. My body responded, but I needed to work. He was going to distract me the whole time, and I couldn't even hide in my office. "I am working, Mr. Hart!"

"I have something more important for you to work on. Two minutes. I will wait for you." He got up and walked toward the restrooms. Business class was empty this time of the morning. I looked around, and the few people who were there were asleep. I closed my laptop and slid out of my seat, following the path Triston had just taken.

I tapped on the door, hoping it was him on the other side. I heard the lock click, and the door opened. He pulled me inside. Locking it behind me, he pinned me to the door. His kiss was forceful, his tongue dancing with mine. He tasted of green tea and peaches.

His right hand slid into the front of my shorts, and I moaned. "Shh . . .," he hushed me. He stroked my thin panties. "You're so fucking wet for me, I love it," he hissed. He unzipped my shorts and pulled them down along with my panties. Standing back up, he unzipped his jeans. I looked down as he freed himself, hard and pulsing. I ached for him to fill me. He lifted me onto the small counter. "Hold on," he breathed. Opening my legs, his eyes darkened. He slid into me, and I gripped the edge of the counter. Leaning back against the mirror I felt him hit my sweet spot, sending shivers over my body.

He pounded me, rough, hard, and fast. "I love fucking you, angel." His voice dripped with pure lust. I was about to come undone at the danger of it all. We could get caught! He slammed into me, and I felt myself clench. My body started shaking, and my pulse quickened. I leaned forward, grabbing him. He lifted me and pinned me against the wall. I watched his ass flex in the mirror as he slammed into me. "Come for me, angel." His words sent me into delirium. To keep from screaming out, I bit into his shoulder hard, and I felt his release fill me. "Fuck," he groaned, his curse muffled by my hair.

As we relaxed, he let me down and helped me slide my shorts back on. We made our way back to our seats separately. I slipped back into mine and opened my laptop as the flight attendant came around. "Are you okay, miss? Would you like some water? You look a bit flushed." She smiled sweetly.

I nodded. "Yes, I'm okay. Thank you. Water would be great. I think it's just a little too warm here." Triston was walking back and heard our exchange. Coughing at my comment, he tried to hide his amusement. She smiled and handed me the bottled water. I couldn't believe I had just joined the mile-high club with my boss. Triston slid into his seat, and I giggled. I knew I was blushing furiously. He leaned over and whispered, "Now, that is how you enjoy a flight."

Chapter Ten

I unlocked my apartment door, stepping inside. Triston carried my suitcase in as I closed the door behind him. "Let's make some tea. Can you please put the kettle on?" I asked him as I walked to my bedroom.

"Sure, angel." He nodded. Leaving my luggage in the living room, he walked over to the kitchen, and I heard him fill the kettle, turning it on. It was strange hearing him do such normal, domestic things. He always looked so far removed from it.

Carrying the mail that was left at the door, I scanned the envelopes. Most were bills, apart from one that was a plain white envelope with no return address, with my name scrawled on the front. I didn't recognize the handwriting. Ripping it open, I found a photo from my wedding. My blood ran cold. There was a thick, black X drawn over my face with a marker. I froze. Who the hell would do this? "Angel, I—" Triston walked up behind me, grabbing the photo out of my hand. "What the fuck is this?" His voice seethed anger.

"I . . . I don't know. It came in the mail." Triston was visibly shaking. He walked back into the living room, grabbing his phone. I followed him, watching him in silence. He found the contact and dialed. Turning to look at me, he gave me a reassuring smile.

"James," he spoke into the phone. "I need your help with something urgent." He listened for a few seconds before replying, "Yes, it's a matter I know only you can handle for me. My girlfriend" — his eyes met mine as he said it, and my heart skipped a few beats — "has received a threat, and I need you to sort it out." He turned away and walked out onto the balcony. I went into the kitchen and waited, but I could still hear him. "The fucker needs to be taught a lesson, and I want it to hurt! Okay, call me when you're free tonight."

He walked back into the apartment. "Angel, I want you to pack a bag." I spun to look at him. I knew it wasn't a request but an order.

"What? Why?" I frowned at him.

"You're staying with me until James can sort this out. I don't want you here alone. That is not a request. You're not safe here alone." I folded my arms across my chest, staring at his steel blue eyes. "And if I want to stay? I have security." Closing his eyes, I knew he was about to lose it.

"You are not staying here alone. I will put you over my shoulder if I have to." I smiled and walked toward him. I wanted to distract him. It was mainly to get my mind off what happened, but, of course, I did enjoy our little game as well. "Miss Reid, you do know what happens when you defy me." His smirk was devilish.

I nodded and smiled, licking my lips slowly. His eyes darkened, and I turned, walking into the kitchen. "But I do enjoy the consequences so much." I filled teacups with boiling water. A growl emanated from his chest, and I knew I had gotten to him. I picked up the tea and handed him a cup. I sat at the breakfast bar watching him. "I will pack after tea, and we can go to your place." I took a deep breath to steady my nerves. I was scared, but I had faith that Triston wouldn't let anything happen to me.

"Good. Then I'm going to show you a few consequences I have in mind." My body trembled in anticipation of what he was planning. I couldn't wait. He winked and walked back out onto the balcony. I could see this had shaken him. I wasn't sure why Blake was doing this, but I knew he wouldn't stop until he ruined my life.

Triston pulled into the garage of his apartment complex and parked the car. He turned to look at me. "I'm glad you're here. I want you safe. I will find him, and he will regret coming into my life, I promise you that." His eyes blazed with anger, and I shivered. "I know, Triston. Thank you, for . . ." I didn't know what to thank him for. A job, keeping me safe, making me feel like love is possible?

"Don't, not here." He got out of the car and walked around to open my door. He pulled my bag and his suitcase from the trunk, grabbing both bags in one hand. He laced his fingers through mine with his free hand as we made our way up to the penthouse apartment.

He unlocked the large steel grey door. "Welcome home." He ushered me inside.

I stepped into the apartment I walked out of

last week. I didn't think I would ever be back after that night, but so much had changed. Triston and I were together, officially, and it felt good. "Make yourself at home. I'm going to put the suitcases in the bedroom."

I walked to the large patio doors. The whole wall was made of glass, as the city was sprawled out in front of me. I smiled, remembering the last time I stood looking out over a city with Triston behind me. My body tingled at the memory. "We can play on the balcony later if you want?" His voice low and lust-filled, it was as if he was reading my mind. I giggled.

"Mr. Hart, what would your neighbors think?" I turned to face him.

His eyes darkened. "I don't have neighbors. My apartment doesn't have any prying eyes. We can make as much noise as we want." He winked with a devilish smirk, and my body responded in the only way Triston could make me feel.

He leaned down, and as his lips touched mine, his phone rang, interrupting us. "Fuck it!" he cursed loudly. I giggled at his frustration. He pulled his phone out of his pocket. "I have to take this. Get some wine in the refrigerator and decide what you want for dinner." He walked toward the office. "James, thank you for calling me back." The rest of his sentence disappeared with him as he closed the office door.

I walked into the modern stainless steel and granite kitchen. Opening the refrigerator, I was shocked at the number of ready-made meals in Tupperware. He must have had a personal chef. I noticed there was a small compartment of white wine, and I decided on a crisp Chenin Blanc. Closing the door, I rummaged through drawers, looking for a bottle opener. Everything was packed perfectly in neat compartments. I finally found it in the third drawer and started opening the bottle. I heard Triston opening a door. He padded into the kitchen, and my breath caught. He had changed, wearing only his ripped blue jeans. I couldn't help but stare at his perfectly toned body. My hand slipped, and I felt the sting of the cut from the corkscrew. "Angel!" He ran to my side, grabbing the kitchen towel and wrapping my hand in it.

"It's okay. I'm okay, just—"

"We need to rinse it. Come here." He pulled me toward the sink and opened the tap. As the blood washed down the drain, I noticed the cut was tiny. It always seemed the smallest cuts were the bloodiest. "It's okay, Triston. I am okay. I am just clumsy." I blushed, remembering it was my own fault. I was too busy staring at Triston to notice the corkscrew wasn't secured in the cork. He kissed my hand, the skin between the index finger and the thumb sensitive to his attention. I melted into him. My body constantly wanted him, needed him. How was that even possible? I wanted to know about his phone call, though.

"What did James say?" My eyes locked on his face.

"Nothing you need to worry yourself with. He knows what he's doing. It will sort out soon enough." His voice was serious, and I knew not to push him. "Did you decide what you wanted for dinner?" I shook my head, indicating the bottle on the counter. "I was still trying to open the wine, when—" I cut myself off and giggled.

"I can't leave you alone for a second!" He smiled. I watched his eyes crease with amusement. I loved the crinkle in his nose when he smiled.

"I'm so glad I amuse you so much, Mr. Hart, but I could have died, you know!" I teased and stuck my tongue out at him.

"Miss Reid, do you know that sticking your

tongue out is rude? Someone once told me that." His eyes darkened, and I knew we may not make it to dinner if I kept this up.

"It is? Well, what are you going to do about it?" I challenged him, my eyes unblinking, watching a look cross his face. He grabbed my hips, pulling me into him.

"Do you really want to do this now? In the kitchen?" I nodded. His face was so close to mine I forgot to breathe. Opening my mouth slowly, I leaned closer to his ear and brushed my lips over the soft skin.

"I do, Mr. Hart. More than you know," I breathed.

His grip tightened on my hips. "Good, because I am going to take you now!" He hissed in my ear, biting my earlobe. I moaned loudly at his words. "But first." He took a step back and walked to the breakfast bar, opening the bottle of wine. Grabbing two glasses, he poured the clear liquid in each. He handed me mine and took a sip of his. "Now, Miss Reid, I think it's time I showed you why it's rude to stick out your tongue. Sit!" He pulled out a barstool and pointed at it. I sat down, watching him. He circled it without restriction.

His eyes were dark blue, like the midnight sky, twinkling like there were stars in them. He pulled my top over my head and unclasped my bra, tossing them both on the floor as his mouth devoured me. He teased my hardened nipples, then he grabbed my wrists and held them behind my back. My body trembled as he kissed his way down to my bellybutton. "Stand up!" I obeyed. He unbuttoned my shorts and pulled them down with my panties. My body shivered at being naked in front of him. "Sit back and hold onto the counter behind you." I sat and leaned back against the edge of the cold marble. Triston kneeled in front of me, opening my legs wide. I watched his mouth slowly tease its way down my stomach. Flicking his tongue on my bellybutton, it took all my strength not to grab him.

His stubble on my inner thighs made me moan even louder. He kissed every inch of my skin, slowly licking and nibbling down to my ankles. I knew I was dripping wet for him; I needed him. "I can smell you, Miss Reid. You smell good enough to eat," he growled, pulling my barstool so I was leaning back even more. He took his wine glass and poured some between my breasts. Goosebumps rose on my skin at the cold liquid as it dripped down my stomach and between my legs. His tongue slowly licked its way from my breasts down to my belly button. He followed the trail of wine but stopped at my slick entrance. I wanted his tongue on me, but he was teasing me; I knew he was. My whole body was on fire. "Triston," I moaned.

He repeated the action again. The third time, his tongue licked at my pussy. "Triston, please?" I begged him as I needed him inside me. "Do you know why it's rude to stick your tongue out Miss Reid?" he asked in a scratchy voice. He put the wine glass on the floor as he kneeled between my thighs. His thumbs stroked me while his tongue slid into me. My breathing quickened, and my pulse was erratic. The rough feel of his stubble on my inner thighs caused my body to ignite from every nerve ending. My hips bucked against his mouth. His tongue plunged inside me. "Jesus, Triston, please, I need you!" I cried out as I came undone on his tongue. I was still shaking when he slid two fingers inside me, hooking my sweet spot, sending another orgasm ripping through me. I gripped onto the counter like my life depended on it.

Triston stood up, licking his lips. It was the most erotic thing I had ever seen. "You taste like honey, Miss Reid." He leaned down to kiss me, and I tasted myself on his lips. I was so turned on I was sure I would explode again. He stepped back. "Stand and face the counter." I obeyed him. Standing up, my legs wobbled, and I leaned onto the counter. I felt his hands move over my back. He pushed my feet apart with his. I heard his zipper, and anticipation shot through my body. He slid into me, slow and steady — the exquisite torture was sending my body into a spiral — inch by inch until he was buried to the hilt inside me. He pulled out again, and I felt empty.

"Triston, please. I need you," I begged him. He plunged into me suddenly, causing me to scream out as he filled me. He pulled me back onto him as I gripped the counter. He reached forward and gripped my neck, pulling me up till my back was against his rock-hard chest. "I love being inside you, Miss Reid," he hissed in my ear. His hand tightened on my neck as he rammed into me. His other hand traveled down my stomach then down between my thighs, teasing my clit. His five o'clock shadow rough on my cheek. The intensity of him electrified my nerves. I was teetering on edge with my pussy clenched around him. "That's my girl. Come for me." His words pushed me over the edge, and I came hard. "My turn. I am going to come inside you!" His voice cracked as he came undone and filled me with his own release.

Rolling over in soft white sheets, I looked up at Triston's sleeping face. He looked ethereal sleeping next to me. I could get used to this, waking up next to him every morning. I was jumping ahead of myself. I was only here so that nothing happened to me. I knew Triston cared for me, but deep down, I wasn't sure if he felt what I wanted him to. Could he ever love me?

"Good morning, beautiful." His voice pulled me out of my dark thoughts.

I smiled up at him. "Good morning, handsome." He rolled over and wrapped his arm around me.

"You do realize that waking up next to you is the best thing that's ever happened to me?" His words made my heart race.

"Nope, I really don't think so. You have a

multitude of amazing things in your life. Like your company, apartment, your cars."

Triston lifted himself against the pillows, sitting up, pulling me up against his chest. "Em, look at me." His voice was soft. I turned and faced him, my arm around his waist. "Yes, I have what everyone thinks is a perfect life, but" — he took a deep breath — "I have never really been with anyone. I . . ." He closed his eyes. He seemed to be struggling with what he wanted to say. I was so eager to know, but I didn't want to force him to say anything he wasn't ready to say.

"Triston, it's okay. You don't have to—"

"No, Emily, listen to me? I have never been with anyone I have cared this much about. The thought of someone hurting you." He closed his eyes again, and I felt the anger radiating through him. "For the first time, I feel really happy. Just don't run again, please?"

I nodded, understanding. I wished I could tell him how I felt, but it was way too soon. We had known each other for three months. Dating, if you could call it that, for a just over a week. "I won't run, Triston, I promise." I looked into his eyes. I wanted to keep my promise to him. I just hoped nothing would make me break it.

His phone rang right at that moment. "What the fuck is wrong with this phone?" He reached over and picked it up. I saw James's name flashing on the screen. He answered immediately. "James?" He got out of bed, and I wrapped the sheet around me. I watched his body tense. "*What?* I want everything in that room! Do you understand me? Thanks!" He hung up and turned to face me. I looked at him expectantly. Shaking his head, I knew he wasn't going to tell me. "It's going to be okay. I just need to relax. Let's shower?" Not waiting for me, he walked into the bathroom. The lousy mood evaporated as quickly as it started. I got up and followed him into the *en suite*.

I stepped into the shower and wrapped my arms around him, placing kisses on his back. He turned in my arms and I kissed his chest. Then moved down his body till I reached his hardening cock. It was beautiful to look at, and I wanted to please him the way he pleased me last night. "Emily." Ignoring him, I licked the tip of his arousal, loving the taste of him. Taking him into my mouth, I swirled my tongue over him. The velvety feel of his erection caused an intense shiver to wash over me. His eyes blazed with desire as he watched me. I felt him at the back of my throat. I sucked hard. "Jesus, Emily, you need to stop. You're going to make me come." His fingers gripped my wet hair, and I pulled my mouth off him. Licking him from base to tip, I tasted his saltiness on my tongue. Taking him in my mouth again, I stroked his length, sucking the head of his erection. I wanted to make him lose control. It turned me on watching his face as he climbed higher.

Taking him all the way to my throat, I sucked harder, my head bobbing back and forth. A growl vibrated through his chest. It was one of the sexiest and most erotic sounds I'd ever heard. Moving faster on him now, I felt him tense. "Emily, I am going to come in your mouth." His warning spurred me on, and I sucked him harder and deeper. My throat tightened around the tip, and I heard him growl as his release shook through him. I tasted the warm salty-sweetness of his release, swallowing every drop. I pulled my mouth off him slow and steadily, flicking my tongue over the tip as he softened in my hand. I stood up and smiled at him. "You are a fucking goddess!"

It felt exciting walking into the office next to Triston. We turned heads. Everyone stopped what they were doing as we walked in like we were this invincible duo. We were both dressed in black and white, and I had my red Chanel bag Triston had given me that morning. It was a gift he bought when he had decided on giving me a promotion. He was wearing a black Calvin Klein suit, white dress shirt, and red silk tie. His hair was loose on his shoulders, and he looked breathtaking. I was nervous, and at the same time, it felt like I was on cloud nine. There was a lot of work that needed to be done, but I was definitely up for the challenge. We stopped at my desk. Triston leaned in and gave me a chaste kiss. "Later, angel." He walked into his office. I watched him for a few seconds, in awe of the man that was mine. I slid into my chair and powered on my MacBook. Jessie appeared from around the corner. "Oh my god, I missed you!" she shouted, and I knew Triston would have heard that. I giggled and stood up.

Hugging her, I smiled. I didn't have a friend in New York and having someone to talk to would definitely be fun. "I missed you too! It's been an insane few days."

She looked at me and winked. "Oh, I am sure it has. Spill!" I laughed as I glanced in Triston's direction. He was on a call, so I had a few minutes. "Well, I have a promotion. I have a boyfriend, and I am so happy! Maybe we should talk some more at lunch?" I asked, looking at Triston's office again. He had left his door open, and I noticed he had finished his call. She nodded.

"Jessie! Emily! Get in here!" We looked at each other, and she shrugged. I grabbed my iPad, figuring I would have to take notes. We both walked into the office, and I closed the office door. Before I had a chance to sit down, Triston started. "Jessie, what the fuck is this?" He handed her a folder. I looked at him, and I knew something was wrong. I took a seat next to her, watching his reaction. It must be huge; he seemed really angry.

"Triston. Mr. Hart, I mean. It's a new client. I thought you would be happy we landed these events?" She looked up unsure. He got up and walked around to the front of his desk. He sat on the edge, holding onto the dark wood. I noticed his grip tightening on the side in frustration as his veins bulged. I knew he was not happy at all.

"Do you realize that Emily will be doing these events? Do you know who owns that company?" He gestured to the folder. I was so confused. Why would a new client be such a bad thing, and why would me handling those events cause such a problem? Jessie looked down. "Yes, the owner is . . ." She rummaged through the file and looked up, meeting Triston's intense gaze. "Oh!" I saw her flush a bright shade of red.

"Okay, guys, what is going on?" I couldn't take the suspense anymore; I needed to know. I reached over and grabbed the folder from Jessie. Opening it, I chewed my bottom lip. Now I knew why Triston was so unhappy.

"Triston, I can handle this. Come on, it's a client. A working relationship." The gaze that fell on me knocked me breathless. The steel-blue was shimmering in the ray of sunlight on his face. He was exquisite. I shrugged, hoping he would calm down.

"I would rather you not have *any* relationship with my brother! Since you feel okay with it, then we can run their events. I do not want you alone with him. Is that understood?" That was not a question, but I nodded. I closed the folder.

Getting up, I placed it on Triston's desk.

"Great, because we have a meeting with him in thirty minutes," Jessie said as she looked at me. I smiled, but my stomach flip-flopped. I hadn't seen Bash since he left my apartment, and I wasn't sure what to expect.

"Okay, can I go and get ready for my meeting?" I looked at Triston. His expression was calmer now, but I could tell he was still seething. Jessie got up and walked to the door.

"See you in there, Em." I waited for Jessie to leave. When she closed the door, I turned to face Triston. "Triston, please relax? It's only a meeting. It's work; nothing more." I walked around to him still perched on the front of his desk. Leaning over, I kissed him on the cheek. He pulled me into a tight embrace and held me. His breathing was slow, and I felt his pulse return to normal. "You are mine; I just want you safe." His words sent a feeling of calm over me. He was claiming me, and it made my pulse quicken. His voice was low and husky. I nodded, and I locked my gaze on his.

"I know." Kissing his soft, warm lips again, I left him in his office.

Twenty minutes later, I grabbed my laptop and looked up at Triston. He was on a call. He gave me a small smile and nodded. It was time for my meeting. Walking toward the conference room, I felt nervous again. I opened the door and noticed Jessie wasn't there yet, but Bash was. He stood up as I entered. "Emily, I—"

"Mr. Hart, how are you today? Welcome to Je Te Veux Events." I set my laptop down and smiled at him. He looked good, handsome, dressed in a charcoal suit and black dress shirt. He sat back down and nodded. "We can wait for Jessie unless you want to start. I have all the documents here." I indicated the file on the table.

"You're in charge, Emily. I don't mind." His hazel eyes burned into me, and I felt self-conscious. His smile was distracting, and I needed to get this over with. I could be professional; I needed to be. I couldn't let Triston or Jessie down.

"Right. Okay, I noticed you have five events over the next eight months. What we can do is set up a theme to run through all. Alternatively, we can have event-specific themes. The first thing I noticed is that you mentioned different locations for these. You would need an onsite team to assist with all setup and break down." I looked up. "What do you think, Mr. Hart?"

"I do need a team, and I want you on that team. You are my prerequisite." He remembered the conversation we had in my kitchen. My pulse quickened. I smiled. "I requested you handle all events, and I want you on location. And I prefer Bash. My brother is Mr. Hart. I would also prefer it if you heard me out?" His voice was deep and his gaze molten lava, which causes me to shiver.

"Fine. Bash, what is it that you want to say?" I stared into those hazel eyes, challenging him.

"The photo you saw; it was a promo shot. I wasn't with her for any reason you were thinking. I like you, Emily. My brother does this all the time. Everything I ever wanted he has taken away from me. Just give us a chance?" His voice was so low it was almost a whisper. I shook my head slowly; it didn't matter what he said.

"Bash, I am with Triston. You do realize that, don't you?"

He nodded slowly. "I see."

The door flew open, and Jessie bundled in with her laptop, "Sorry I'm late. I got caught in another meeting. Mr. Hart, I hope you are well?" She set her laptop down and shook Bash's hand.

"Please, call me Bash." He held on to her hand for a moment longer than he should have. I knew what he was doing — making a play at Jessie, trying to make me jealous. "Miss de Ware, so nice to see you again." He flashed her his sexiest smile, and I noticed Jessie blush.

She was falling for his charm. "And you too, Bash. I hope we can please you with our ideas for the events." Jessie sat down next to me, and I took my cue to continue. I gave him the rundown of the rest of our plans, explaining the marketing and sales. As I spoke, I felt his intense gaze watching my every move. He did affect me, there was no doubt about that. I needed to get this wrapped up as soon as possible.

An hour later, I stood up. Just then, the door opened, and Triston walked in. The brothers' eyes met, and there was an undeniable chill in the air. He turned and looked at me. "I need you."

I smiled. "We were just finishing up here anyway. Jessie will show you out, Mr. Hart. Have a good afternoon." Bash stood up. Walking over to me, he grabbed my hand and shook it. "Thank you, Miss Reid. You were enthralling as always." His voice was low on the last two words, but I knew Triston heard him. I nodded. He let go of my hand, and I turned and walked out.

"What the fuck was that?" Triston was fuming as we walked down the hallway.

"Nothing! He was trying to annoy you, and it clearly worked!" I stared at Triston, his expression was deadly. He stalked down the hallway with me. "Triston!" I pulled his arm, turning him to look at me. We stopped, and when his eyes fell on mine, they softened. "Please? Just accept that I am working with him? I told him we are together, so he knows. He won't do anything to jeopardize our contract. His company needs us."

He nodded, grabbing my face in his hands and kissing me lightly. "Ahem . . ." We pulled away to be met with the hazel gaze that seemed to be haunting me now. "Mr. Hart." I nodded and walked away in the direction of my desk, leaving the brothers alone together. I wasn't going to be a referee.

As I walked up to my desk, I took a deep

breath. That was one of the most intense presentations I ever had to give. Those two were going to be a handful to work with, especially now that we were handling Bash's events. I plugged in my MacBook and opened my email. I was sure I had hundreds to catch up on. Triston walked back in. He had taken his tie and jacket off; his shirt buttons were halfway undone. "Miss Reid, my office, please?" He disappeared through his door, and I followed, closing it behind me. I turned around, and Triston grabbed me, pinning me against the closed door. "You drive me insane!" His mouth crashed into mine, pressing his solid body flush against mine, our tongues fighting for dominance. He tasted like strawberries, sweet. He pulled away moments later leaving us both breathless and panting. "Triston, what the hell was that for?"

"You, working with my brother. I don't like it." He walked back to his desk, and I noticed his hand on the front of his trousers. He rearranged himself, and it made me giggle. "It's not funny, Emily." He turned his steely gaze on me.

"I know, I know. I wasn't laughing at . . . I was laughing at your . . . Uhm . . . predicament?" I gestured toward the rigid erection in the front of his trousers. He gave me a devilish smirk.

"Oh, that . . . predicament, as you put it, is all on you, Miss Reid." He crooked his finger, calling me to him. I walked over to his desk. His bulge was so straining in his pants. I was aching to feel him inside me. He pulled me closer, grabbing my hand and placing it on his rock-hard bulge. I gasped at the feel of him. "This is what you do to me. Even when I am angry, all I can think of is you. Laying you across my desk and—"

There was a knock at the door, interrupting the moment. He released my hand and winked, sitting behind his desk. "Come in!" I stifled the giggle that was threatening to escape. "Mr. Hart, my apology for the interruption, but it's urgent. I have James here for you. He says you called him." It was Amelia, one of the receptionists.

Triston nodded. "Send him through." He turned to me. "Angel, I want to handle this alone. I will call you when I'm done." Leaning down, I gave him a soft, lingering kiss.

As I was leaving the office, I saw James. He was a tall, bulky man. He looked like a bodyguard, dressed in a black suit and white shirt with an emerald green tie. Maybe he was ex-military. He certainly had the gait. I sat down at my desk and tried to concentrate on work.

I looked through Triston's office window. It already seemed heated, and James had just arrived. I wondered what's happened and if he had found Blake. I opened my mail and noticed I had an email from Bash.

From: Sebastian Hart

To: Emily Reid

Date: June 15 - 2:05

Subject: Pre-Event Meeting Dinner

Dear Miss Reid,

To thank you for the successful business meeting today, I would like to invite you and Miss De Ware to dinner to celebrate our new client relationship. I have made reservations at The House on East 17th tomorrow at 7 p.m. I do hope you can make it.

Let me know if you would like me to have a car pick you up.

Sebastian Hart

CEO - Tribal Fuel

I stared at the screen, speechless. Triston was going to flip out over this. I knew there was no way he would let me go. Although, I wouldn't be alone. Jessie would be there. Of course, I had to go. It was a client inviting me to dinner.

From: Emily Reid

To: Sebastian Hart

Date: June 15 - 14:30

Subject: Re: Pre-Event Meeting Dinner

Dear Mr. Hart,

I can join you tomorrow. Thank you for the invite. The car would be appreciated.

Emily Reid

PA to CEO Triston Hart - Je Te Veux Events

Chapter Eleven

"No fucking way! There is no way I am going to let you go to that restaurant and have dinner with my brother! Do you understand me? I do not care if he has invited Jessie as well!"

I stared at him pacing. I expected this exact reaction. I couldn't refuse the invite; I didn't tell him I had already accepted. It was a brand-new client, one of Jessie's first as the Sales and Accounts Manager. It would not look good on the company. Of course, Triston knew this. "Look, Triston, I know you're angry. I know you don't trust him, but you have to trust me. You do trust me, don't you?" I pleaded with him to see sense.

He stopped. He looked at me intently with concern. I didn't just see anger in his eyes, but I saw fear as well. He was scared his brother would try and talk me into giving him a second chance, and he wouldn't be there to stop it. He needed to trust me. He couldn't keep me away from every male client we had.

"Angel, I trust you. It's my brother I don't trust. I just—"

"So then, relax. You can have some time on your own to relax, read a book . . ." I trailed off at his amused expression.

"Do you really think I'm going to be relaxed? Knowing you're sitting at a romantic restaurant with my brother?" He leaned down and kissed me.

I pulled away. "And Jessie!" He ignored my protest and kissed me again. I wrapped my arms around his neck, feeling his beautiful body against mine. It had been a long day, and being at home with Triston was perfect.

The doorbell interrupted the kiss. "Must be dinner. I'll get it." Triston walked to the front door. I decided to get the plates ready and open the bottle of Merlot on the counter, pouring two glasses. He stepped back in, but by the look on Triston's face, it was definitely not the take-out we had ordered.

He put the box on the counter. "It's got a card, for you." He stood back, waiting for my reaction. "If this is from my brother!" Frowning, I slid off the bow and untied the card while pulling out the small note from the envelope. My heart raced reading the words scribed on the inside.

****You will regret running from me. I will make sure of it****

"It's not Bash." I looked at Triston. I didn't know what to say. Grabbing the card, he read it.

"*What the fuck?*" He looked back at me. "This is the end. I am going to fucking kill him!!" He stalked to the living room and grabbed his phone from the sofa. I knew who he was calling.

"James, I need you at my apartment. Now! It's urgent." I watched Triston as I pulled the lid from the box. I gasped. There were a dozen dead red roses tied with a black ribbon. The room spun around me, and I felt faint. Triston hung up and rushed to me, grabbing me around the waist. "Triston, this is . . ." I didn't know what to say. It felt like I had been punched, winded, completely and utterly destroyed.

He held me in his strong arms. Kissing the top of my head, he mumbled into my hair, "I will never let anything happen to you, do you understand me?" I tried to nod, to acknowledge him, but he was holding me too tight. I didn't complain. I felt safe in his arms.

I sat in on the briefing that Triston gave James. I listened as the two men spoke, but I didn't provide any input. Everything seemed far away. James was going to trace the flowers back to the florist and find out where Blake was. He obviously had a plan in mind, and I knew he was resourceful. My mind was working overtime. I was right about my earlier assumption; James was ex-military. I lifted my feet onto the sofa and wrapped my arms around my legs.

When James left, Triston refilled our wine and opened the balcony doors. "Angel?" I looked up and rose from the sofa. Stepping onto the balcony, the fresh air enveloped me. The view from the penthouse was spectacular. He handed me my glass of wine. "I wanted to tell you that you have nothing to worry about. We will find him, and I will personally put a stop to him." Triston's eyes held the promise, and I knew he would keep it. He looked out over the city, and I could tell his mind was busy. He never stopped thinking. I wondered if he ever felt exhausted from constantly thinking.

"I know, Triston, I know. I trust you." I sipped my wine. "Do you ever just stop?" I asked, giving him a small smile. "Look at me." He turned at my request, and those steel-blue eyes burned a hole inside me. Straight to my heart, reaching into my soul, making me whole again — that's what he always did. "Remember what you said to me in your office earlier? What I do to you?" He nodded, a frown on his face. "Well, you do the same to me. Except, I keep waiting for you to disappear. I mean . . ." My words trailed off. I wasn't sure how to say what I wanted to say without saying too much. My heart was racing. "I just, you know . . ."

He turned, his body flush with mine. "No, I don't know. Why would you think I would disappear?"

I took a gulp of wine, hoping for some liquid courage. I felt his eyes on me, and I knew I needed to say something. "Everything I have ever had in my life that's made me happy. Everything I ever cared about has disappeared. So, naturally . . ."

"Emily, I am not leaving you." He put his glass down, and his hand lifted my chin. My eyes met his. "You need to understand that I haven't felt like this about somebody in a very long time. When I care about someone, they are everything to me! Okay?" I nodded, and suddenly his lips were on mine. I didn't have time to reply. I felt the electric spark that was so evident between us as it shot through my body, making me moan into his mouth. His lips curved into a smile, and I knew it was one of his sexy devilish grins.

He pulled away, his eyes dark with desire, igniting the fire inside me. "Now, can I take you to bed and fuck you into next week?" I couldn't find the words to answer him. All I could do was nod. He scooped me up and carried me into his exquisite bedroom.

"Angel?" I opened my eyes. Triston was standing next to the bed in his briefs with a mug of coffee. A girl could get used to that view every morning. I smiled up at him.

"Can I request this treatment every morning?"

"Of course you can, but I don't come cheap, you know!" He set my coffee down as he leaned over me, his lips brushing mine. Teasing, leaving me wanting more, as he did every time.

"I'm sure I can afford it." I winked. Taking a sip of coffee, I notice his gaze is on my mouth. Grabbing the waistband of his briefs, I pulled him toward me. "Does the coffee delivery come with breakfast, Mr. Hart?" I asked, giving him my most innocent face. Placing the mug on the nightstand, I kneeled on the bed in front of him, and his smile appeared.

"Miss Reid, I can definitely give you breakfast." I licked my lips as I slowly slid his tight briefs over the growing bulge. I leaned forward, taking him in my mouth. I loved the taste of him. "Oh god, Emily." His head fell back, and he moaned. He grabbed my hair, holding me in place as I sucked him into my mouth. He hardened as I flicked my tongue over him. "Emily!" His body was rigid. I took him as deep as I could, feeling his length at the back of my throat.

"Fuck." His voice was so deep and scratchy. I enjoyed the power I had over him, moving my mouth up and down his hard length, tasting every inch of him. His abs and hips flexed as I watched him tremble. My hands held onto his hips, feeling him tense under my fingertips. "Jesus, Emily, I am . . ." I sucked harder, taking him even deeper in my throat. I knew he was close. I felt the spasm of his release filling my mouth as his groan vibrated through his chest. "Shit!"

His moan was husky as he filled my mouth. I moved off him slowly. Licking my way to the tip, flicking my tongue, causing a shiver over his body. I sat back, completely satisfied that I had just made him feel the way he usually did me.

He opened his eyes. "Emily, I . . ." Shaking his head, he gave me a warm smile. "You are something else, Miss Reid." He grabbed my face in his hands, kissing me. He stood up again, pulling his briefs back up.

"I do enjoy breakfast at this establishment. Very satisfying," I said, giggling at his expression. I laid back and watched amusement dance across his face.

"Emily, I have never had a better breakfast in my life!" he said seriously.

I slipped on my knee-length black dress since I was going to dinner after work, and I figured something more professional would be best. "You look too sexy; you can't wear that to dinner." Triston walked back into the bedroom.

I turned and looked at him incredulously. "Seriously? I am dressed like a nun!" I turned around and looked at my reflection. Yes, I was dressed like a nun. "Help me with my zipper?" I asked, my back toward him.

"A sexy nun!" he said, standing behind me, pulling the zipper up my back. I started giggling at him. His face was that of a petulant little boy.

"Babe, you need to relax. You're the only one who finds nuns sexy." I looked at him, trying to stifle the laugh threatening to escape.

"Miss Reid, must I remind you that I can bend you over right now and spank you for your rudeness?" Giving him a quick kiss, I tried to hide the tremble that shook my body at his threat. I grabbed my phone and bag. "Later, sexy, let's get to work. Just because you're the boss doesn't mean you can be late." I walked out of the bedroom before he could change his mind and we ended up spending the day in bed. As much I would enjoy that, there was a lot of work to get through.

The elevator descended to the garage, and the doors slid open. Triston walked toward the black SUV and unlocked it. "I need to take the SUV today, angel." We had taken the silver V8 Vantage the day before, one of my favorite cars. I slid into the passenger seat of the large black BMW. Triston closed the door and made his way to the driver side.

The engine purred to life, and we headed into rush hour traffic. "So why do you need the SUV today?" I asked as I turned the music on. Scrolling through the playlists, I found one I liked and settled back in the seat. I loved watching him drive. The way he commanded the steering wheel, the way his hand flexed on the gear stick.

"I am meeting James today, and we need the space."

"Do I want to ask why?" He shook his head and turned to me, winking.

"You don't need to know anything about it." I nodded. I didn't want to know what they were up to.

I spent the morning setting up meetings with various clients, venues, and suppliers. At midday, my phone rang. I looked up, but Triston was busy on a call. I wondered who it could be.

"Good afternoon, Je Te Veux Events. Emily Reid speaking, how may I help you?" I toyed with the pen in my mouth.

"Emily, hello. It's Bash. I'm so happy you're coming this evening. I wanted to find out if you would like the car to pick you up from the office or your apartment?" I didn't want to mention that I was staying with his brother. He sounded different. I wasn't sure what it was. Maybe he was looking forward to dinner.

"Sebastian, the office would be great, thank you. My boyfriend is in meetings, so he will have the car." My use of the word boyfriend would show him that I was serious about my relationship with Triston. Or so I hoped.

"Perfect. I look forward to seeing you again," he answered without hesitation. I suppose he was expecting it.

He hung up before I could reply. "Emily!" Triston called from his office.

I got up, grabbing a notepad and pen. Walking up to his office, I stopped at the door. "Please close the door?" I stepped inside, turned, and shut the door. "I do like the use of the word boyfriend." He looked at me amused.

"You were listening?" I gasped at him. "You are seriously driving me insane! Do you have to spy on everything I do? And I can handle your brother." He shook his head slowly.

"I wasn't spying. I heard you from here. My office door was open, Emily. I also hope that you will not be handling my brother in any way." He gave me a serious look. "I need you to set up our flight schedule for next month. We have a couple of weeks, but I would like everything confirmed as soon as possible."

I nodded. "Sure. We will be flying to Europe first, and we'll then come back for the last few events." He nodded and made a few notes. I slid into my usual seat opposite his desk. "Bash wants me here for his first event." I trailed off when Triston's head shot up at the mention of his brother's name. "Look, I'm running the event. I need to be there; I don't have a choice, Triston."

He put the silver Parker pen down and stared at me. "Fine. Then I will be there too." I knew that was not up for discussion. I could only imagine how that was going to go down. Triston and Bash in the same room for more than five minutes; we may need a referee because I was not going to be one.

"Okay, but you need to let me do my job when you're there. No hovering!" I smiled, sitting back in the chair. He picked up his pen and made a few more notes before he got up and walked around his desk, handing the page to me. I saw he had written down the dates we were flying and the times he preferred.

"Those I want to be booked this afternoon before you go off gallivanting with my brother." He narrowed his eyes watching me, and I smiled.

"Yes, Mr. Hart. Anything to please you." I stood, and he smirked.

"Oh really? I want you to keep that in mind for when you get home after dinner. I have a way you can please me."

I walked to the door. Opening it, I turned around and looked into those beautiful steel-blue eyes and smiled. "Mr. Hart, you are such a tease. I was just thinking about this morning's breakfast." I licked my lips. "It was delectable." I winked and walked out of his office, closing the door. I left him to simmer in the heat of our exchange.

Amelia at reception called at six p.m. to tell me Bash's driver was waiting, so I packed up and grabbed my bag. I walked into Triston's office. "Bye, babe. I'm off. I'll be home about nine." He smiled and nodded, then stood up to kiss me. "I'm meeting James now. I'll pick you up from the restaurant. Don't leave without me." His eyes filled with concern. I knew he was still worried about Blake trying to hurt me.

"I won't, I promise." He didn't have to worry; I would be in a crowded place. At least I knew I would be safe with Bash.

I met the driver at reception. He walked me down to the car. It seemed both brothers had terrific taste in vehicles. A charcoal Mercedes SUV with blacked out windows was parked outside the offices. Traffic had died down slightly as we made our way to the restaurant. My phone beeped with a text from Triston.

Triston: I do hope you enjoy dinner, missing you already. T xo

I smiled and hit reply.

Em: Thank you, handsome, I will see you soon. Miss you too xo

The driver pulled up outside the restaurant. He got out and came around to open my door. "Thank you." I smiled, and he nodded. I walked into the restaurant, and it was beautiful inside — an intimate, low-key venue with amazing art on the walls. "I'm meeting Sebastian Hart," I stated, grinning at the young man who was welcoming guests.

He smiled and nodded. "Follow me."

The table was in a private area at the back of the restaurant, with soft lighting making everything feel almost ethereal. Bash was dressed in black slacks and a white shirt. His spikey hair was pointing in all directions, a just-got-out-of-bed look, which suited him. "Emily!" He stood when he saw me. Leaning down, he gave me a peck on the cheek. I felt goosebumps rise on my skin. I didn't like that he still affected me.

"Sebastian, how are you?" I smiled, sitting opposite him at the booth in the plush chair. "It's beautiful in here. I didn't realize how big it is. Looks a lot smaller from outside." I suddenly felt nervous. I wondered where Jessie was. Maybe she was running late.

"I love it here. It's my favorite restaurant. Would you like a glass of wine?" He smiled, holding up the bottle of white wine.

"Yes please, that would be lovely."

Our waiter appeared. "Good evening, folks. I'll be your waiter this evening. My name is Duncan." He smiled at Bash and me.

"Thanks, Duncan, we need a few more minutes. You can bring the starter I arranged in the meantime." Duncan nodded and disappeared into the throng of people who were arriving. "I wonder where Jessie is?" I said softly as I felt his eyes on me.

"Oh, you didn't know? She couldn't make it this evening. I thought she would have told you." Bash smiled, filling my glass. My heart raced at the thought of being here alone with him all night. Triston was going to freak out. At least we were in a busy restaurant.

"No, she didn't mention it. I actually haven't seen her today, It's been busy," I said, taking a sip of wine. His eyes never left me, and I felt myself flush. I knew this was going to be a long dinner. Duncan returned with our appetizer, an amazing seafood platter with various dips, olives, and French bread. "Wow, Bash, this looks amazing!"

He smiled. "I had to thank you somehow

for taking on my events. I did invite Jessie; she couldn't make it. I hope you believe me?"

"Yes, of course, I believe you. Why wouldn't I?" I stared at him. His face changed between anxiousness to happiness.

"I just figured you and Triston would think I was trying to come between you. My brother and I don't have the easiest relationship. I'm not sure if he told you?" I nodded. "Well, since we're here alone, I would like to tell you my side of the story. Then you can decide for yourself." He looked at me expectantly.

"Okay, Bash, what's your side of the story?" I sat back and picked up my wine. He looked determined. I knew he wasn't here to make a play for me. He was here to try to win me back, no matter what. I took a large gulp of wine, hoping to steady my nerves.

"When we were growing up, my brother was always the outgoing one. When he wanted something, he would go for it. He ended up with the wrong crowd in college. He didn't want to listen to our advice. I was dating a girl not long after Triston moved out. We were together for about six months when Triston came back, asking for a place to stay. He was in a bad way, and I said okay." He took a sip of his beer, fidgeting with the glass as he set it down again.

"I tried helping him until the day I came back from a job interview and found him fucking her, my girlfriend." His eyes met mine, and I could see the pain that was so evident. This all sounded like what he did to Triston, so that was an act of revenge. "I loved her, Emily. I was going to propose to her that night, but Triston and I had a fight, an ugly one, and I walked out."

He took a deep breath and sat back. Why didn't Triston tell me? Why did he hide this bit of the story? I always knew there was more, but this is a lot more. "I came back the next day to find Triston on the floor. He had overdosed, and I tried saving him. I took him to the hospital. That didn't go down very well . . ."

I nodded. "He told me the part about your dad." Bash nodded, taking a swig of beer. He called the waiter over. "Please bring me a Glenfiddich twelve year old, neat." Duncan nodded and skittered off.

"I did get something from my father. My gambling problem. I did do things I'm not proud of . . ." He trailed off, his voice barely audible. "I miss my brother, Emily." When his eyes met mine, I knew he was serious. "But he is determined not to have me in his life, and that's okay. I just want you to be happy."

"What about Krista? What happened to her?" I saw the recognition on his face. "And why would you say that you got me first, Bash? Do you remember the words you used that night we fucked?" I used the word crudely. I felt angry suddenly beneath the calm exterior, and he could see it. "Did Triston walking in on you and Krista make you feel better? Was that the revenge you needed?" I finished the wine in my glass, hoping it would calm me down.

"Emily, I—" He shook his head.

"Don't Bash, just leave it. Let me call Triston, and he can pick me up." I pulled my phone out of my bag.

"No, wait! I will tell you about Krista. I'll tell you anything you want to know. Just don't leave?"

I sat staring at Triston's number for a moment. I needed to hear this, whatever it was. Locking my phone, I looked at Bash. "Fine. Tell me. Then I need to leave. I want all the sordid details about you and your revenge on Triston, and I want it now."

He nodded. "Okay." He picked up the bread on the platter and broke a piece. Dipping it in one of the bowls, he held it up. "Try this first?" I looked at him skeptically. "Trust me, please?" I leaned forward and took a bite.

"What the fuck is this?" I choked on the bread in my mouth as I looked up into cold blue eyes. "Emily, we're leaving! NOW!" Triston's arctic gaze fell on his brother, and I shivered.

I grabbed my phone and bag, looking over at Bash. "I have to go." Triston grabbed my arm, and half pulled me out of the restaurant.

"Triston, what the hell was that?" I slid into the back seat of the SUV. Triston was radiating anger. He closed his eyes as if concentrating on the words that were about to come out of his mouth. "Emily . . ."

I turned to him, needing to calm him down. "Babe, please, it was just dinner. Nothing happened. We didn't even have dinner." I reached out to him, and I felt his hand shaking. "Triston, you need to calm down," I spoke softly, hoping he would realize that I was okay, and I was with him.

He turned to me suddenly. "I'm not angry you were eating with him. I just found out why

Blake is here!" He spat the name out like it left a sour taste in his mouth.

"Why? What happened?"

He pulled me closer, holding me in his arms. "Emily, my brother and Blake are partners in his company. Blake bought forty-five percent shares in Tribal Fuel."

I sat up, opening my mouth to say something, and closing it again. I was speechless.

"He contacted Blake about two weeks ago. They met last week when we were in LA. Blake found out you were with me and flew out as well. James found an apartment where Blake has been staying. It's not pretty." He pulled me into him and held me for the rest of the way home.

Our driver pulled into the garage of Soho Grand. Charlie got out and came around to open my door. I stepped out, and Triston held onto me like I was a piece of China. "I can stand, Triston." But as soon as he let me go, I felt wobbly. My knees gave way, and he scooped me up. "Charles, can you call James and finalize details for tomorrow?" I saw Charlie nod, and Triston turned to make his way into the building.

When we got to the elevator, Triston set me down. His arm wrapped around my waist, holding me against him. "He didn't even say anything!" I finally found my voice. "I mean, he must know who Blake is?" I turned to Triston; his face was hard with emotion.

"Emily, let's just get into the apartment, please?" The doors opened, and we stepped out into the hallway. Triston unlocked the door and scooped me up, carrying me into the apartment. "I'm putting you in bed." He walked straight to the bedroom and set me on the bed. "Did you want a glass of wine?" He looked at me, giving me a small smile. I nodded and laid back on the pillows.

I was so confused. Why would Bash do this? It didn't make sense. Surely he knew that Blake was my ex? Unless Blake wasn't completely honest with him. I got up and grabbed my phone from my bag. Unlocking the screen, I had a message from Bash.

Sebastian: Not sure what happened, I hope you're okay. Please give me a chance to finish my story? B

I hit reply.

Em: I am okay. I have questions for you, and I want complete honesty! Talk tomorrow.

Locking my phone, I set it next to me. I needed to see Bash and get the story from him. I hoped he would be honest with me. Triston walked back into the bedroom holding two wine glasses. "Angel, I don't want you near my brother. I don't know what he's up to."

"Look, Triston, I want to talk to Bash. I need to hear it from him. I know you don't approve, but this involves me." I looked at him, and I could tell he was not happy about it.

"No, Emily, let James and I sort this out. I don't want you near him, and that's final!" Triston was angry again, but I needed to hear it for myself. I decided to talk to him about what Bash had said earlier. "Bash told me about the time you lived with him. He told me about his girlfriend that you slept with." He nodded slowly, and his eyes met mine.

"Emily, I made mistakes. I told you this." I nodded. I knew he did, and I wasn't judging him; I just wanted to understand.

"He misses you, Triston. He told me that himself, and I know he wasn't lying." I reached out and held onto his hand. Triston closed his eyes. I knew he was fighting with a lot of emotion right now, and my heart ached to make it all okay.

"No, Emily, he is playing on your emotions for him, and I can see he got to you. If he missed me so much, then he would talk to me." His voice filled with emotion, and I knew he missed his brother. Why were they both so stubborn? They both frustrated me so much.

"Why don't you take the first step?" I asked softly.

"Did he put you up to this?" He stood up and walked over to the window. "Emily, if you want him in your life, then you don't get me. I'm sorry, but I can't do this again." I stared at him in shock. Was he giving me an ultimatum? He knew I would choose him any day. Why would he even say that? Unless he thought I would cheat on him.

"Do what, Triston? Do you think I am your ex? You think I am going to go and fuck your brother?" My anger was at boiling point. I stood up and stared at his back.

He spun around, his eyes on fire. "I didn't say that, Emily!" His hands clenched with anger.

"Then what, Triston? I can't talk to other males because you said so? Get over yourself!" I made my way to the bedroom door when Triston grabbed my shoulders, spinning me around to face him. “Let me go, Triston!” I warned in a low voice.

“No! I don’t want you leaving. It’s not safe! Stay here!”

I shrugged out of his grasp. “Just let me go! You clearly don’t trust me, and I can’t be with someone who doesn’t trust me!” I took a step back, staring at him, willing him to stop me. He dropped his hands at his sides. “I figured. I have to go!” I spun around and walked out of the bedroom. Grabbing my jacket, I shrugged it on.

“Emily.” Triston followed me to the living room. He looked so sad, but I couldn’t be with someone who couldn’t believe me. I turned and slipped on my ballet flats. “Emily, look at me, for god’s sake!” I spun on my heel. I was so angry I felt tears spilling from my eyes.

“What, Triston? You have made it very clear where we stand! I’ll go to my apartment; you can have your fucking space!” I walked toward him now, my anger giving me the confidence to be honest with him. “I never wanted anyone but you since that first day in my interview. Every fucking moment of being near you is like nothing I ever felt before! You fix me. You make me feel whole. You make me feel loved! But that's not what you do, is it? *No!* It's not! Do you even know what that feels like? To fucking let someone in?" I realized I was screaming at him. My face was wet, and he looked blurry through the tears. He grabbed my shoulders and shook me as he screamed in response to me.

"Yes, I fucking do! Because I am falling in love with you!" His voice boomed through the expanse of the open-plan living room and kitchen, his whole body shaking. I stopped. My mouth agape. *What?* My heart thudded through my ribcage. He loved me?

Chapter Twelve

Triston sat on the sofa, his head in his hands. I was speechless. I stood in front of him, unsure how to react. I wanted to tell him I loved him, but he seemed so angry when he said it.

"I'm sorry, Emily; I didn't want to say it like that." He looked up, staring at me with those intense, blue eyes. He loved me. He was falling in love with me. It crashed over me like a wave. I flopped onto the sofa next to him.

"Triston . . ." Reaching out, I put my hand on his shoulder. It was tense. "Please look at me?" When he turned his head, the emotion was evident in his eyes. He was serious about this.

"I . . ." I looked at the vulnerability of this amazing man who had swept me off my feet. "I love you too," I whispered. "Well, I mean . . . You know . . ." I trailed off again. What was I even doing? How could I be mumbling when this is what I wanted to tell him days ago.

"You are adorable when you're speechless, but you don't have to say it back." He smiled.

"No, Triston, I'm not just saying it. I mean it. I do love you. I mean, I'm falling for you too," I rambled on, noticing the amusement in his eyes. "What?"

"You've just made me the happiest man alive, do you know that?" He pulled me into his arms. His kiss was soft and slow. His lips moved across my neck, sending a shiver over my body. "I want you, outside." He stood up, pulling me to my feet. "Take off your shoes." He gestured at my flats, and I kicked them off immediately. I shivered from the cold, hard tiles below my feet. He grabbed my hand and pulled me to the balcony. "Hold on to the railing!" His voice was deeper now, and I knew he was turned on.

"Triston—"

"Miss Reid, I need you to be quiet. Unless you ask me to stop, I do not want to hear another word. Do you understand me?" I nodded. He had me at his mercy. I wanted him so much. I smiled as I watched the city lights twinkle below us. Slowly he unzipped my dress; It was agonizing. As he pushed the sleeves over my shoulders, his lips brushed my skin in feather-light kisses. Goosebumps rose on my body, and I trembled. "You, Miss Reid, are amazingly beautiful. I love you."

He whispered in my ear, and I felt his teeth on my earlobe, eliciting a moan from my lips. "Did I not say you should be quiet?" I nodded. "And how, pray tell, do you think I am going to punish you now?" His voice was laced with desire, his hand flat on my back, pushing me down. Bent over at the waist, the twinkling lights of New York were in front of me. Triston spread my legs wider just as the sting came suddenly. His hand swatted my ass hard, twice. I bit my lip to keep from moaning out loud. "Miss Reid, do you like me doing that to you?" His voice deep, husky, and so sexy. I was so turned on my panties were soaked. The knot in my stomach had tightened, and I was ready to feel him fill me.

Triston gripped my hair, pulling my head back. "I asked you a question, Miss Reid?" I nodded. I felt his other hand slowly trace a line from my neck in a slow, sensual movement down my spine. "I think I'm going to find my sweet girl is soaking wet already." His words were taking me higher. I could come just by what he was saying to me. His fingers found the heat between my legs, moving my panties to the side and plunging into me. "Triston!" I cried out; my body shook. I was seeking the release only he could give me, aching for it.

"Miss Reid, you're always so fucking wet. So hot and sweet, ready for me." He pulled his fingers out, turning my head to watch him as he slid them into his mouth. My knees shook as I gripped the railing tighter.

Our eyes locked. "Now, Miss Reid, I am going to fill you. I am going to" — he leaned in closer, his hot breath on my ear — "fuck you!" I was hovering over the edge. He was behind me in an instant. Hearing the zipper of his slacks, I shivered in anticipation. Suddenly and quickly, he filled me. "Triston!" I cried out, not caring anymore. I watched the city below us as the man I loved took me and pushed me over the edge. He moved faster and faster. I couldn't hold on any longer, and I came undone over him. "That's my girl, the one I love." His words carried him over the top as he filled me.

Our bodies trembled as he pulled me up against him, brushing his lips over my shoulder. I looked at the lights below us. "I love you Triston." My words were barely audible, but I knew he heard me.

How am I back here? Where's Triston? I ran into the room to find Blake and Triston. I saw a gun shimmer in the light. "What the fuck are you doing here, Emily? You're my wife!" Blake sneered. "You're coming with me!" My eyes darted between the two men. I couldn't go with Blake. I loved Triston. I needed Triston.

"No, Blake, I am not your wife. I'm with Triston. Please just let me go!" I begged, pleaded. His eyes were dangerous, and I knew he wouldn't think twice to use that gun. I took a step forward, and Blake grabbed Triston, an arm around his neck.

"Em, go to the living room. Now," Triston choked out. I shook my head; I wasn't leaving him here. I couldn't.

"Get your stuff. We're going, Emily! Or I kill your blue-eyed boy!"

"Blake, please? Don't do this." Lifting the gun to Triston's head, his finger squeezed the trigger. I shut my eyes and screamed.

"No! NO!!!! DON'T!!!!"

My body was shaking. *"No!"* I sat up with a start, my face moist with sweat. I looked into beautiful blue eyes. "Triston! Oh my god, you're okay!" I wrapped my arm around him. His pulse was racing.

"What are you having nightmares about?" His voice filled with concern. "Please, angel, talk to me?" I leaned back against the headboard, closing my eyes and taking a deep breath.

"Triston, I just . . . Can we not?" I turned to face him in the dim light of the sunrise creeping in through the blinds. "I just can't talk about it right now."

"Angel, you're going to have to tell me sometime. I can't be in the dark about this. You have told me about your ex, and I know it's about him. You can tell me anything." He opened his arms, and I slid into the warmth of his bare chest.

"I know, Triston, but I just need to breathe. This has shaken me." His soft hand on my shoulder slowly trailed lines up and down my arm.

"When you are ready angel." I looked up, and even in the dim light, I could see his eyes were filled with love. I closed my eyes and savored the feel of him. "You're taking the day off tomorrow, and I don't want any arguing about it. Now let's try and get some more sleep." I laid my head on his chest. Closing my eyes, I let sleep claim me once more.

"Right, sleepy head, you need to get up . . ."

I opened my eyes, noticing the sunlight streaming through the window. I scooted up, sitting with my back against the headboard. "What time is it?" My head felt heavy like I had a hangover. Triston handed me a steaming mug of coffee. "It's not late. Just after 9. I wanted to let you sleep for a bit." I nodded, holding the mug, inhaling the amazing smell.

"I have work to do today, Triston." I knew he didn't want me to work, but there was so much to do. I couldn't just take the day off. I pushed the covers down and got up and walked to the window. It looked like it was going to be a beautiful day.

"You're not going into the office. You can stay here and work in the study. I have a meeting with James, and I would rather know you're here, safe. Then I don't have to worry about you being unprotected." I nodded, knowing I wouldn't win this fight, and I felt too tired to try anyway. So much happened the night before. I was exhausted.

"So, I can work wearing this?" I gestured to my tank and panties. A smirk crossed Triston's handsome face as he crossed the room toward me. "Miss Reid, I would rather have you wearing nothing." He leaned down to kiss me, his lips crashing into mine. Grabbing my ass, he lifted me in his strong arms. I held onto his shoulders as he walked me back to bed. Landing on the soft sheets, his body hovered over me. "Now, where is that breakfast you promised me?" His voice is filled with amusement and lust.

"You're supposed to come and get it, Mr. Hart," I teased, shifting higher on the bed out of his grasp. I rolled over to the other side and got up. We stood on either side of the bed now, staring at each other. The dark lust flickered across his face; he loved playing these games.

"I will get it, Miss Reid; you can count on that. Then we will both come." His words ignited the fire inside me instantly.

I ran toward the living room giggling. Triston caught me at the doorjamb, holding my back flush against his half-naked body. I could feel his pajama pants straining in the front. "Miss Reid, you do realize I was never going to let you get away?" he hissed in my ear, causing the heat between my legs to worsen. I turned my head, kissing him. He held my neck with one hand, his tongue invading my mouth. His other hand found the apex between my thighs, causing me to moan into the kiss. My body was his, completely. I was trembling as his fingers moved deftly inside the front of my panties, his mouth on mine. He pulled away slightly, his eyes burning into me. "So wet, so perfect. I love it." His words added fuel to my fire as I let him stroke me. His fingers are circling my clit, teasing my entrance, plunging into me. I was slick, and his fingers moved easily inside me. I was so close. "Come for me, angel." His whispered order sending me soaring.

My body trembled in his strong arms as he held onto me. He removed his fingers from my panties and spun me around. Lifting me up, he walked us to the living room wall and pinned me against it. "I need you, Emily. I need to feel your hot tight pussy around me." Pushing his pants down, his erection sprang free. He moved my panties to the side and rammed into me hard. My head fell back as I felt every hard, exquisite inch of him inside me.

He slammed into me, harder and deeper. "Emily, look at me." I lifted my head. As our eyes met, I felt the electric current shooting through my body. We were made to fit together. I watched his shoulders flex as he held me against the wall, his veins pulsing. His smirk was sexy and dark, and I knew I was about to come undone for the second time that morning.

"Yes, Emily, come for me. Give me your pleasure!" His voice was a hoarse whisper, and I felt myself spasm. "Triston!" My body shook violently, and he held me tight. His lips were on my neck, moving up to my ear. "You. Are. Mine." With the last word from his mouth, I felt his release inside me. We stayed in each other's arms until we had come down from the high. Triston looked into my eyes and smiled. "You are amazing, do you know that?" I flushed at his words.

"Nope, I'm just a girl." He let me down slowly. I still felt wobbly but completely satisfied.

"An amazing, beautiful girl, who drives me crazy." Triston stepped back. "Now I need to get to my meeting, and you need not to distract me."

I smiled up at him. "I did no such thing, Mr. Hart. You started it."

Triston left for his meeting with James, so I decided to start working on the schedule for our trip. I sat in Triston's office with a mug of coffee and hit play on the playlist I had just created. I had a smile that wouldn't go away. I still couldn't get over the fact that Triston loved me. I shook my head. I needed to concentrate on work.

I hit send on the booking email to our travel agent when my phone rang. Bash's name flashed on my screen. I took a deep breath and answered. "Hello?"

"Emily, are you okay?" I could hear the worry in his tone.

"Yes, why?" I frowned. Why would he think I wasn't okay?

"I was just in the office. Jessie said you weren't in today, and I—"

"You what, Bash? You were worried?" My voice was incredulous. Anger seethed through me. I wanted to believe he didn't know who Blake was, but I couldn't be sure until we had figured all this out.

"Yes, I'm worried. My brother storms into the restaurant last night, dragging you with him, and you're not in work the next day. What must I think?" His voice was low and angry. Then I realize he thought that Triston hurt me. My body radiated with anger. I closed my eyes, trying to calm myself. I didn't want to fight with him, but he needed to step back from whatever he thought of his brother.

"Bash, your brother would never hurt me! How dare you even think that! Why don't you ask your fucking business partner about hurting me? Unless you already know!" Not waiting for a reply, I hung up. I couldn't believe Bash had the audacity even to ask me that. Why on earth would he think Triston would hurt me? It didn't make sense. My phone started ringing again, but I hit ignore and carried on working.

At midday, I had finished most of the work

I had set out to do, and I needed lunch. My phone beeped with a message from Triston. He was going to the office to meet with a client and would be home at three. The apartment was so quiet without Triston, but I needed to get my mind off Bash and his accusations. I turned the kettle on and opened the fridge. There were a few ready-made meals which I could heat up. I decided on the veggie lasagna and put it in the microwave when the doorbell buzzed. I wondered who it could be.

"Hart residence."

"Emily, it's me. Open up, please?" My heart raced. What the hell was Bash doing here? Triston would freak out if he knew his brother was at the door.

"What do you want, Bash?" I folded my arms across my chest and realized I wasn't dressed for visitors.

"Just open. We need to talk."

I pressed the buzzer to open the entrance door. I looked at my appearance. Shorts and a tank top shouldn't be too bad. I hoped. Bash appeared at the door. He was dressed in a white tank top, which showed off the tattoo on his upper arm. The black slacks he wore hung low on his taut hips, and I remembered his sculpted V-line. He looked like he had just walked out of the gym, glistening with sweat as I took in his muscles.

"What are you doing here, Bash?" I turned and walked into the apartment as he closed the door. "You do realize your brother will totally flip if he walked in and you are here?" His eyes roamed the apartment, and I knew he had never seen the inside of his brother's place before.

"I needed to see if you were okay! And I needed to find out what you were talking about earlier, about my partner?" He looked genuinely confused.

"You don't know who Blake really is, do you?" He shook his head slowly, walking over to me. I turned to face him with my arms crossed over my chest. His eyes flickered down to my braless chest, and I felt my face heat. He looked up again, locking his gaze on mine.

"He is part of the team who helped me get out of the red last year. He arrived about two weeks ago, and he has been roaming around the company. We are not friends. My financial backer hired him. So I have no idea what you're talking about, Emily." He stepped toward me, and his warm scent enveloped me.

"Bash . . ." I stared at him, and I saw the honesty in his eyes. That same honesty that he showed me last night. "Blake is . . ." I wasn't sure if I should tell him.

"What, Emily? I need to know; this is my company we're talking about." He was standing too close to me now. I turned to face the window. I couldn't look into those hazel-brown eyes. "He is my ex-husband. I left him because he almost killed me." I closed my eyes, waiting for the onslaught of questions.

"*What?*" Bash spun me around. His eyes were filled with concern, and I felt the tears fall down my face. "Emily, I am so sorry. I had no idea. I swear to you!" He pulled me into a tight embrace. I believed him, but I knew he had to leave. I didn't want Triston to come home and lose it. I pulled away and giving him a pleading look.

"Triston can't find you here, Bash. Please, can you leave? I'm sorry to do this, but after the threats, I don't want to upset him." I stepped back and gripped the countertop. I breathed in his scent again, allowing it to calm me.

He narrowed his eyes. "Threats? What threats?"

I finally locked eyes with him again, his hazel brown with tiny flecks of green. I stared at him for a few moments, watching the range of emotions wash over his handsome features. I had to tell him. "Blake has been threatening to hurt me. That's why Triston told me to stay home today." He nodded as if understanding his brother's decision. I walked him to the door and unlocked it. "Thank you for coming over, Bash. I appreciate it."

"You call me if you need anything, you hear me?" His tone was serious, yet demanding, reminding me of Triston, and I smiled. "Thank you, Bash. I mean it."

He smiled and leaned forward, his lips brushing over my cheek. "Any time, princess." He turned, and I closed the door behind him.

I heard the door open and close. "Angel?"

"I'm in the study!" I heard his footsteps on the tiles. As I turned, I saw his beautiful face. He had taken his tie off, and his hair was loose. He looked so handsome. "How was your day?" I smiled as he leaned down to give me a kiss.

"Busy, I had so much to do. I met with Mr. Jacobson. He is looking forward to the trip next week. He wants to meet with us on Friday, so you will have to come with me to the office. Did you enjoy working at home?" He sat down next to me, watching me finish up an email.

"Yes, it was good. It's so quiet without you here." I closed the laptop and looked at him. "Did you see James?" I wanted to tell him about what Bash had said, but I didn't think it would be a good idea. That would mean I would have to tell him that Bash was in the apartment.

He nodded. "He has found Blake's employment details. Apparently, he works for a financial backer that my brother used. He has contacted him, and they have also found the florist. Blake is clever, but he will get caught." His fingertips stroked my arm leaving goosebumps in their wake.

"Can we go out, like for a walk or something?" I stood up and stretched. "I'm feeling lethargic from being cooped up all day." My tank top rode up, and Triston kissed my stomach. His scruffy chin tickled me, and I giggled.

Triston smiled. "Sure, let me get changed, and we can go to the park." Putting his briefcase down, he walked into the bedroom. His phone beeped from the desk. Picking it up, I looked at the screen. It was James. "Babe!" I ran into the room as Triston pulled his tee over his head. "Babe, it's James."

He grabbed the phone and answered. I pulled on my hoodie and sneakers, watching Triston as he walked into the living room. "What have you got for me?" He was quiet for a little while before I heard a glass smashing. I ran into the living room and saw Triston staring out the window. "Triston? Are you okay?" I walked over to him. He spun around, his eyes dark. "When were you going to tell me my brother was here?" My heart leaped into my throat, and it felt hard to swallow. My face heated. James must have seen Bash arriving or leaving. That's what the call was about.

"I wasn't, because of this." I gestured toward him and the broken glass on the floor.

"Jesus, Emily, I'm trying to keep you safe, and you open the door to—"

"To what, Triston? To your brother? He came to see if I was okay! He didn't hurt me! He explained about Blake. He didn't know who Blake was! You can't keep me locked in a cage forever, Triston!" I felt the tears rolling down my face for the second time that day. Walking into the kitchen, I grabbed the dustpan and brush. I kneeled down, sweeping up the mess at Triston's feet. "Are you happy now? Is this what you wanted?" I looked up at him through my tears. His gaze softened.

"Stand up, Emily." He pulled me up, wrapping his arms around me. I could feel his heart racing. "I don't want this; I'm so sorry. I never want to make you cry. I just want you safe."

Pulling away, I stared at him. "Then why are you so angry? Your brother won't hurt me." My voice is softer now. I knew he was trying to protect me.

"No, he won't." He stepped back and walked to the balcony.

"Then what, Triston? This doesn't make any sense. Why are you so angry? Because of the past? Isn't it time you got over it and spoke to him?" I stared at his back. I could see how tense he was, but I wanted to know. He needed to be honest with me, and he needed to do it now. "Triston? Talk to me!" I wanted to reach out to him, but I knew it wouldn't change anything.

"He will make you fall in love with him!" He

spun around and watched my reaction. I wasn't sure what he wanted me to say.

Wait! *What?* "Well, that's too fucking bad, because I am in love with you!" I stormed into the bedroom. I couldn't be near him right then. Triston followed me into the bedroom. "Emily, I know you love me. I'm an idiot, okay?" He turned me to face him, and I nodded in agreement. The amusement was evident on his face.

"I know you are. Can you hold me now?" I mumbled. He pulled me into a warm embrace and chuckled.

His lips were on my neck. I felt his tongue on the sensitive spot behind my ear. "Do we get to have makeup sex now?" he whispered, and I giggled at him. The fight was forgotten, and I was in his arms, where I wanted to be.

"What about our walk in the park? I need to get some exercise." I looked up at him.

"Trust me, I can give you some exercise! Go and put your bikini on. We're going for a swim."

I was confused now. A swim? I saw the excitement sparkle in his eyes. "Go!" he shouted, slapping my ass hard.

"Ouch! Okay, okay! Keep your pants on!" I was excited to be doing something fun with him as the past few days had seemed so dire.

He followed me into the walk-in closet, laughing. "I thought you liked me without my pants on, Miss Reid!"

"Mr. Hart, I love you without your pants on!" I laughed and started changing.

Moments later, he covered my eyes and led me into a private elevator and out onto a landing. I could smell fresh air, and I knew we were outside. "Triston, I seriously need to see!" I giggled as I cautiously stepped ahead of him. He led me to a step, and we stopped.

"You will soon. Stay here."

I heard something sliding, maybe it was a door, then his hands were on me, again guiding me forward. "Okay, stand here." I heard him moving around, and I heard a lock clicking into place. I felt his body against mine, his heat radiating over me. I leaned back into his sculpted chest, his hands resting on my shoulders. "You are mine. Every." His lips brushed over my left shoulder. "Single." Then the right. "Inch." And slowly up my neck. His fingers were stroking my bare arms, and I felt my nipples harden. His hands brushed light circles around the hard buds. My mouth opened, and a soft moan escaped into the darkness.

My body is trembling in anticipation. "Triston," I whispered, feeling his warm breath. Electric currents shot through me. He slowly untied the blindfold, and I blinked in the dim light of the vacant room we were standing in, a large swimming pool lit up in front of us by blue underwater lights. The roof looked like it had stars twinkling above us. The room was magical. The walls around the pool were all made of glass, and I could see most of New York sparkling below us. "Triston, this is beautiful. Where are we?" I turned to look at him, the shadows on his face danced across the sharp contours of his nose and jaw. He was breathtakingly beautiful. "We are on the rooftop pool. Come." He held out his hand, and I grabbed it. We walked along the side of the pool to the large glass wall. He slid one panel open, and we stepped out onto the concrete roof. We had an almost three-hundred-sixty-degree view of the city. "Oh my god, this is amazing!"

"Emily." He turned me around, taking both my hands in his. "I am sorry about earlier and about everything. I know you trust my brother. I have a hard time accepting that because I'm scared you're going to fall in love with him." The broken man inside surfaced, and I ached to hold him, to make him see how much he meant to me.

"I think you need to start trusting me. I love you, Triston. I'm not running off with your brother. Now, can we swim?" I smiled, hoping he would relax and enjoy our time together. I understood where his worry came from since it's happened before. His ex-fiancée slept with Bash, but I loved Triston. He smiled and nodded.

We went back inside, and Triston released my hand, jumping into the pool. I was definitely not jumping in. He was almost childlike sometimes, playful and carefree. This was the side that made me fall in love with him. Not to mention the dark, lust-filled side too. I stepped into the water, surprised it wasn't cold. He stood in the center of the pool and held out his arms as I waded into the water. Wrapping my arms around his neck, I kissed him. His hands lifted me up, and I took the cue to wrap my legs around him. "This is so beautiful," I breathed. He spun us around in the water and walked over to the deep end, the water coming up to our necks.

"You are beautiful, Emily." His lips met mine. Jolts of lightning shot through me. His shoulder-length hair was dripping wet on his shoulders, his body slick against mine. He untied my bikini top and left it on the side of the pool. "I think you are way overdressed, Miss Reid." He whispered in my ear, giving me feather light kisses down my neck to my shoulder. I giggled at his naughty side was clearly taking over.

"Well, you better do something about that Mr. Hart," I whispered, my voice filled with desire for the man I loved. He untied each side of my bikini bottoms, and they joined my top in a wet puddle on the tiles.

"That's much better." His voice was dark and dangerous. Kissing every inch of my neck, he moved around in the water, making his way back to the steps. He sat down with me astride his lap, and I felt his arousal between us. After pushing his swim trunks down, I reached down, grabbing it and fisting my hand around him. A growl vibrated in his chest, and I smiled. I stroked him in slow sensual movements, causing him to moan. "I do like making you moan like that, Mr. Hart." I giggled.

"Do you now?" Amusement was evident on his face. I continued stroking him and felt his hips buck in response to my hand. "Miss Reid,

I suggest you stop now," he insisted, lifting me off him. "Stand on the last step; face me." I did as he asked and watched him move his lips over my body, alternating between soft kisses and lightly blowing on my wet skin, causing shivers to run over my body. His mouth moved over my stomach flicking his tongue over my belly button, making my legs tremble. He looked up at me. "I do like making you tremble, Miss Reid." He blew lightly on the heat between my thighs, causing me to moan loudly. "Triston . . ."

He grabbed my hips, spinning me around. "Bend over for me." That scratchy voice gave me shivers. Holding on to the side of the pool, I bent over in front of him. I was more turned on than ever before. He dripped water down my spine, making me shiver. I moaned again. "Shh . . .," he warned, and I knew I needed to be silent. I wasn't sure I could.

He dripped water from my neck down my spine again, and a soft moan escaped my lips. His hand landed on my wet skin and stung. I felt myself respond. I was teetering on the edge, and I was sure I was about to fall. He rubbed the area softly, and I pushed back onto his hand. "Mmm, my girl does love being bad, doesn't she?" I nodded. His fingers stroked the heat between my legs, causing another involuntary moan to escape my lips. The sting on the other side of my ass made my knees tremble with pleasure. His fingers were moving between my legs. "That makes you wet, doesn't it, Emily?"

I nodded again. He pushed two fingers inside me, and I felt the release wash over me. He grabbed my hip with his right hand, holding me against him as he plunged his fingers inside me. "You do love being a bad girl." His words are a hoarse whisper, and I whimpered. Another spank came down hard on my ass. He pulled his fingers from my sopping entrance. "I love the taste of you," he hissed in my ear as he licked his fingers, causing a wave of pleasure to shudder through my body. "Do you want to taste me, my love?" I nodded once more. I was at his mercy; he could do anything to me now, and I would oblige.

"Good." I turned around and dropped to my knees in front of him. Taking him into my mouth I heard his growl. I moved my mouth slowly up and down his hardness, tasting every inch of him. "Oh god Emily," his words only spurred me on, working my tongue over him. "Stop! I need to be inside you!"

I stood up, looking deep into his eyes, licking my lips. His eyes were black with lust, and I ached to feel him fill me. Grabbing my ass, he lifted me. Walking into the water, he pinned me against the wall, and I felt him slowly pushing into me, inch by exquisite inch. My head fell back, and his mouth devoured my neck, chest, and shoulders with soft kisses. His teeth grazed my nipples, and I felt myself teeter on the edge again.

He slammed into me, harder and harder. "Triston," I moaned, my eyes locked with his as he plunged into me.

"Come for me, Emily. I need you to give me everything!" His words pushed me over the edge as I came undone around him. "That's my girl. Come harder." His was unrelenting pinning my back against the edge of the pool. I cried out as another orgasm ripped through me. I bit onto his tense shoulder. My nails dug into his back, and I knew he was close. "My turn," he whispered into my ear, and I felt his teeth sink into my neck as his release filled me.

I took a sip of wine and watched Triston. He looked calm and relaxed as we sat on the balcony. After the swimming pool, we decided dinner was needed. The swimming pool was one of the most amazing experiences I ever had with someone. Intense, but so was everything Triston and I did. "Thank you for tonight. It was amazing," I said in a soft voice. His eyes lit up, and I could see the excited little boy beneath those pained blue eyes.

"I love every minute with you, angel. It's like I'm finally awake. Life means something more than it has in a long time." His hand squeezed mine, and I smiled. He was reading my mind again. Every time he said something, it was like he was inside me, listening to my thoughts.

"I know the feeling. It's the same for me. I can't explain it anymore." My ringtone blared into the silence. I saw Bash's name appear on the screen. What did he want? Why would he be calling now? He knew Triston was with me. My eyes flickered up to Triston, and I saw the recognition on his face. He knew who it was.

"I trust you." He nodded. Getting up, he turned and walked into the living room.

I hit the green button. "Hello, Bash." I sat back, waiting for his apology.

"Em, I'm sorry for calling so late. I know my brother is there, but I have some paperwork I need to show you. Can I come over?"

I looked into the living room at Triston, unsure what to say. He wasn't looking at me, but I knew he was anxious. "I don't know. Let me chat with Triston, and I can let you know?" I stood up and made my way inside.

"Okay, but Emily, This is about Blake. I found him." My blood ran cold; I didn't think Triston would mind Bash coming over with information like that.

"Come over."

I hung up, and Triston looked back at me. His face betrayed anger, but I needed Bash here. "Did you just invite my brother here?" I nodded. "Emily, I don't think—"

"He found Blake."

Chapter Thirteen

I sat on the sofa with my legs crossed, my laptop perched on my thighs as I typed out the marketing plan for Tribal Fuel. I glanced up, watching the brothers go through the paperwork Bash had brought. There was no mention of anything else between them, which was good. At least they were having a civil conversation. I observed their interaction; it looked so natural to see them together. Triston had called James, who was on his way over. They had a plan to go to the apartment and have Blake arrested. There was evidence in the documents Bash brought that could help our case. "I'm going with you, Triston." Bash was adamant he wanted to go, but Triston didn't want to hear about it.

"No, I want you here. Protect Emily. I want to be the one to knock this son of a bitch out!" I stared at Triston. He just asked Bash to stay with me. "If he knows we're onto him, he's going to try something," he continued. "Please brother?" He held out his hand. I held my breath. Was this the moment they finally made up? The seconds ticked by as I watched the exchange. Bash grabbed his brother's hand, and they shook on it.

Bash nodded. "I will stay with her." The buzzer went, and I knew James was here. I needed a drink. My nerves were shattered. I didn't want Triston anywhere near Blake, but I didn't want Bash near him either. Triston opened the apartment door, and it filled with testosterone. I walked into the kitchen; I couldn't sit anymore. I couldn't concentrate on anything.

Bash turned to me. "Em, I'm here, and I won't let anything happen to you." He took my hand, and I nodded and gave him a small smile.

Triston walked back into the kitchen. His eyes fell on my hand in Bash's, and I saw his eyes flicker with darkness. Pulling my hand away, I walked over to him. "Please be careful," I pleaded.

He wrapped his arms around me and mumbled into my hair, "Of course I will."

"Mr. Hart, we need to go." James's deep voice echoed in the open-plan area. He sounded serious, and I knew he was ready for a fight, although I hoped it didn't come to that.

"Sebastian, thank you for staying with her." Triston gave him a nod then looked down at me, giving me a soft kiss. "I have to go, angel; I'll be back soon." He turned and left with James. It hit me with sudden ferocity, and I felt faint. Bash's arms were around me in an instant. "Emily!" He scooped me up and carried me to the living room. Sitting me on the sofa, he walked into the kitchen. "Can I get you some water or tea?"

I shook my head. "Can you get us some wine? In the shelf over there?" I pointed to the wine rack and sat back. I turned on the iPod because I couldn't handle the quiet anymore. Insanely, I thought I should have gone with them, but I knew there would be no way in hell Triston would have allowed me to go.

Bash came back with two glasses of red. "Here you go." His smile was warm, his presence calming, and I relaxed a little. He sat next to me in comfortable silence, listening to the song. I guess he was waiting for me to say something. "Thank you for staying."

"Where else would I be?" His eyes locked on mine, and I saw it. I saw the look I didn't want to see on his face. I stood up, needing fresh air.

"Come with me." I walked toward the balcony doors and tried to slide them open with one hand, the other holding my wine. I felt Bash behind me. He reached out to help me, and his hand brushed mine. "Let me," he whispers in my ear, causing me to shiver at his proximity.

As soon as the door slid open far enough, I stepped out and away from him. "Bash, please don't?"

"I was helping you open the door." He frowned in confusion. He was completely unaware of himself, or he was just good at hiding it. I smiled and turned to face the city. We stood side by side, watching the last traces of sunlight on the horizon disappear. "It's beautiful up here." His voice sounded far away like he was deep in thought.

"Yeah, it is." The lights twinkled on as the sun finally set. "It was nice to see you and Triston talking this afternoon." I turned to him. "I mean, I was just happy you both didn't punch each other." I smiled at his amused expression.

"Well, he knows I could kick his ass. I'm sure he didn't want to have that happen in front of his girlfriend," he joked. His face betrays his emotions as he said the words. I knew he liked me; it was apparent, but I just wished it wasn't so difficult.

"Bash—" Before I could finish, we heard a loud crash in the bedroom.

"What the fuck?" Bash put his glass on the table and ran inside. I followed him in, Bash grabbing the large knife laying on the kitchen counter. He walked slowly toward the noise, and I followed close behind. My heart hammered in my chest, and I felt the prickle of fear over my skin.

Bash pushed the door open, and my breath caught when we came face to face with Blake. "Ah, there's my little wife. Got the other brother to protect you now? Drop the knife." He aimed the gun at Bash. The realization of the situation dawned on me, and I shook with fear. Bash dropped the knife. "What the hell do you want, man? Leave her alone!" Blake's eyes blazed with anger, his gaze flickering between the two of us. I silently prayed Triston and James would have forgotten something.

"Shut up! This has nothing to do with you! Come here, Emily." His sneer made my blood run cold. I knew I couldn't refuse him; he would hurt Bash. Walking toward him, I shivered. He grabbed my hand, pulling me next to him. I took a deep breath and my eyes locked on Bash's. "Now, you and I are going to take a little trip. If your boyfriend over here tries anything, I will show him who the boss is."

Blake's arm wrapped around my throat as he dragged me back toward the broken glass doors. "Emily!" Bash took two steps forward when Blake shot a warning into the ceiling. I screamed and shut my eyes, fear paralyzing me. "Go! There is a fire escape. You're going to climb down, and no fucking tricks!" I walked on shaky legs toward the stairs.

I was on the first step when I heard a shot. Spinning around, I noticed Blake had gone back inside. I heard a shout and something smashing. I ran back up and made my way into the bedroom. The two men were fighting, but I saw blood and fear grabbed my throat. Bash landed a cracking punch, and Blake flew into the glass door of the balcony, smashing it to pieces. My hands flew over my mouth. Blake's face was bleeding, and I blinked the tears away.

Turning around, I saw the gun lying on the floor and Bash's arm bleeding. I was in complete shock. “Call 911, Emily!” Bash shouted, and I snapped out of my shock. My whole body was shaking as adrenalin pumped through my veins. I grabbed the landline and dialed. “Yes, I have an emergency. There’s an intruder in my home, and someone has been shot. There’s blood. I don’t know. Yes,” I mechanically rambled answers to the lady on the line and gave her the address. When I hung up, I ran to Bash. I grabbed a scarf and tied it around his arm. The shot grazed him, but there was blood everywhere. My hands were red, and I started crying. Without thinking, I grabbed him in a tight hug. “Oh my God, I am so sorry!” His right arm embraced me, my tears soaking his T-shirt.

“Shh, babe, it’s okay.” I pulled away to see the blood on his face. I shook my head, he was hurt, and this was my fault. If he hadn’t stayed with me, he wouldn’t have been injured. My mind was moving at a million miles an hour.

“Let me clean this?” I mumbled. He nodded.

“Let me check on the douchebag outside.” He went to the balcony. I went into the bathroom and found the first aid kit. I went to the bed and sat down. Bash walked back in. “He’s out cold.” Sitting opposite me, he smiled. “Ouch!”

he winced. His lip was split. I pulled out a cotton swab and soaked it in antiseptic. I dabbed at his lip, cleaning his wounds, then dabbed at his eyebrow, and he winced again.

His eyes watched me intently as I worked. "You're so pretty." His voice was low, almost a whisper. My heart thudded. I knew I was blushing, and I shouldn't be.

"Bash—" He leaned in, and I felt his lips on mine. My eyes closed. It was a soft, chaste kiss, warming me after the cold I felt. His right hand stroked my cheek gently. He didn't do anything more. Just our lips touching was more than I could take right now. I opened my eyes in shock.

I stood up, shocked at my actions. "Bash, don't!" The buzzer went, saving me from something I shouldn't have been doing in the first place. I ran to open the door, and the world crashed down with the noise of medics and police.

The rest of the evening was a blur until Triston got home.

The silence was deafening. It was three a.m.,

and I hadn't slept. Every time I closed my eyes, I would see Blake, the gun, and Bash. The fear would envelop me, and then it was Triston with the gun shooting Bash. It played in my mind, over and over until I couldn't take it anymore. I got up and walked into the kitchen. I turned on the kettle, made a mug of coffee, and settled on the sofa. Unlocking my phone, I noticed a message from Bash.

Sebastian: I am sorry. I didn't mean to overstep, but I definitely don't regret it. B

It happened in the heat of the moment. It didn't mean anything. I kept repeating that in my head, hoping that would make it easier to forget. It happened, but it would never happen again. I couldn't do that to Triston. I couldn't do that to me. I didn't want to lose Triston over something stupid. Yes, Bash saved my life, and I would be eternally grateful. But he wasn't going to get me as a reward.

"A penny for your thoughts, Miss Reid?" I jumped at Triston's voice. "Shit, I'm sorry. I didn't mean to scare you." His expression was apologetic as he flopped onto the sofa next to me.

"It's okay, I was just a million miles away. I couldn't sleep." I explained why I was sitting on the sofa at three a.m. in the dark. Triston's hand stroked my leg slowly.

"I know." His voice was calm and relaxed. "I'm taking a few days off with you. We're leaving tomorrow; I have a plane on standby."

"What? Why?"

"You need to get over this, and frankly so do I. We need time off, Emily." He got up and walked into the kitchen. "I want you out of this apartment for a while. We can fly to Miami. Go shopping, swimming, whatever you want."

"Miami? We have so much work to do here, Triston," I protested, but I knew I would never win this one. He had made up his mind. He was right; I needed to get away.

"I know, but we can take two days. When we get back on Thursday evening, you'll feel a bit better, and Friday is our meeting with Mr. Jacobson." He made a strong case. I suppose it wouldn't hurt.

"If you're sure, okay." Triston smiled and nodded. It sounded like fun. Maybe it would be good to get away. Also, it would give me space from Bash before we started the events for Tribal

Fuel.

"I think it would be good."

"Good, now can we go to bed?" Triston scooped me up and carried me to the guest bedroom.

The car pulled up to a private airfield. Triston wasn't joking when he said he had a plane on standby. We hadn't pack anything. Apparently, it was a shopping spree vacation. I thought he just wanted to take my mind off everything that happened. He had James and his team fixing and securing the apartment. There was a new security system being installed as well.

I didn't reply to Bash's text, and I didn't plan on it until my phone rang before we took off. I knew it would be him. I hit the answer button.

"Hello, Bash." I stepped into the belly of the plane and slid into a seat.

"Emily, I just wanted to check in. You know, see how you're doing. I, um—"

"Bash, I am fine. And you?" I didn't want to prolong this conversation. I looked at Triston. He was watching me with a steely gaze.

"I am good; the pain is gone."

"Good. Listen, Bash, I can't talk right now. We're about to take off." Triston winked and got up to get us drinks from the bar.

"Why? Where are you going?"

"We're flying to Miami for a couple of days." I looked out the window. I needed this to end because I wasn't ready to talk to Bash.

"Oh. Please let me know when you're back?"

"Sure, I will."

I hung up before he could say anything else. "Everything okay?" Triston slid into the seat opposite me, placing a drink in front of me. I nodded. "Yeah, Bash was just checking in. You know." He gave a stiff nod and buckled himself in.

"You know, if Bash wasn't there last night, I—"

"Emily, you don't need to tell me about what would have happened if my brother wasn't there. I know. I trusted you last night, and I trust you now." He smiled. My heart sank at his words, and I suddenly felt sick. I wanted to tell him about the kiss, but after what he had just said I knew it would hurt him beyond words. It was at that moment I decided not to mention anything about the kiss. I grabbed the glass and downed the liquor in one gulp. I leaned back and closed my eyes, needing to get some sleep.

"Emily." Triston gently shook me awake. I opened my eyes and realized we had landed. "Wow, I slept right through that." I smiled up at Triston.

"Yes, but it's good. You got some rest." He grabbed my hand, and we made our way off the plane. It was a clear day, and I was excited to be spending time with Triston away from everything that happened over the last few weeks. It had been a crazy rollercoaster, and I wanted to get off. There was a car waiting to take us to our hotel. I watched the beautiful blue ocean speed past us as our driver made his way from the airport. "This is so beautiful, Triston, thank you," mentioning as I turned to him. He leaned down and kissed my cheek.

"Only for you, angel." His warm fingers traced circles on my thigh. I felt my body respond to him in the way it only knew how, the need for him almost crippling. I couldn't believe I would want someone as much as I wanted Triston. I leaned my head on his shoulder, inhaling his scent.

"You are amazing." I looked up at him, getting lost in his deep blue eyes.

"So are you. Don't you ever forget that, okay?" I nodded.

The driver pulled up to the beautiful Acqualina hotel. Located on Sunny Isles Beach, and I was sure Triston booked a sea-view room. The thought of the balcony facing the ocean made me smile. I couldn't wait to get our short holiday started. "Angel?" Triston was staring at me; I was lost in my thoughts. Grabbing his hand, we made our way to the reception desk.

I was right; our room had an ocean view. Furnished in light colors, the beautiful room gave a feel of being on an island. The pastel palette was calming, and I needed calm. I dropped onto the large king-sized bed, and the tension in my muscles eased. I looked up at the ceiling and took a deep breath. Sitting up, I caught Triston watching me with amusement on his face. I stood and walked over to the large glass doors. We had our own private terrace with a lovely two-seater bench, a small breakfast table, and two chairs. "This view is amazing!"

Triston pulled off his T-shirt and walked up behind me, the heat of his body radiating on my back. He leaned in and rested his chin on my shoulder. "It is. I have a few ideas of what we can do while looking at that amazing view," he teased. His tongue snaked its way behind my ear. I closed my eyes, savoring the sensation. His teeth began to bite my sensitive earlobe, and electric currents shot down my body, gathering at the furnace between my legs.

He pulled my tank up and over my head. Unclasping my bra, he dropped it on the floor, where it joined my top. Biting my shoulder and licking the tender skin, he moved his hands down my arms. I felt my nipples harden as his hands traveled back up my stomach and cupped my breasts. He tweaked and pulled at the hard buds, causing a small moan to escape my lips. I could feel his hardness pressing against my ass. I pushed back against his groin, and I heard the low growl escape his lips.

His caress moved back down my stomach and

found its way into the drawstring sweats I was wearing. His right hand slid into the waistband of my panties, and I felt his soft, warm fingers. "Triston," I moaned out loud. I placed my hands behind me, between us, and I stroked his erection through his jeans. His fingers played with my wet entrance, causing my body to ignite with wanton lust. He groaned as I stroked him. A smile curved my lips; I loved effecting him that way.

"Shh, angel . . . No noise." His voice was so deep and low. His teeth bit my neck, sucking the sensitive skin into his hot mouth. I was slowly losing control. Opening my eyes, I looked out at the ocean, watching the waves crash onto the shore as my lust burned. He plunged his fingers deeper inside me, hooking them as he massaged my sweet spot. His left hand tweaked my rock-hard nipples. Electricity shot through me; my nerves were tingling. I wasn't sure how much longer I could last. I moved my hands to the window, holding on as my knees started to buckle. "Give it to me!" He growled the order in my ear, deep and scratchy, causing my orgasm to rip through me with ferocity.

His assault was relentless as he continued to

plunge into my sopping entrance. I couldn't take another one. My knees felt weak, and I couldn't hold myself up. "I want every bit of your pleasure," he whispered. With his left hand, he pulled down my sweats and panties. They fell at my feet as he pulled away his right hand. "Turn around." I did as he said. My eyes locked on his midnight blue ones. He licked his index finger, then the middle. The sight caused me to shiver with lust. "I love the way you taste." His devilish smirk was haunting.

My eyes took in the bare chest of the man I loved, every inch of his perfectly sculpted body on show in front of me. He lifted me, carrying me to the bed. Laying me down, he unzipped his jeans. I laid back, watching him move over me. Kissing me hard, his tongue invaded my mouth, fighting for control, and I submitted to him. He ran his mouth over my neck, down to my stomach. He reached my thighs, kissing and blowing lightly on my skin. His beard felt scratchy against the sensitive skin of my inner thighs. Lifting my head, I watched his mouth on my entrance, his tongue flat against my hot, slick sex, lapping at me like I was his only nourishment. "Triston!" His teeth bit down on my clit, causing my hips to buck into his mouth.

"I said you need to be quiet!" he growled, continuing his assault on my pussy. I needed him, ached for him, and I wanted him to fill me right at that moment. As if reading my thoughts, he sat up, licking his lips slowly while watching me writhe on the bed. "On your knees! Now!" Obeying him, I got up and kneeled in front of him. Still shaky from my orgasm, I held onto the bed. "Do you need a spanking, dirty girl?" I nodded quickly.

A hard swat landed on my right ass cheek. I yelped, and I knew there would be more where that came from. The sound was loud in the silence of the bedroom except for my moans. Another slap, two, three, four, every part of me on fire. Suddenly, he slammed into me, causing me to scream out. I knew I was dripping wet by now. My mind completely lost. I couldn't think of anything else but the feel of him sliding in and out of me. Gripping my ponytail hard, he pulled me back against him as he filled me deeper than he ever had. "You're my bad girl, aren't you?"

"Yes" was all I could say.

"You like my hard cock inside you, angel?" His voice was dripping with desire.

"Yes," I breathed.

"You were made for me." He slammed into me over and over. I was teetering on the edge of a cliff, and Triston was going to push me over. "Come for me, hard!" His words were my undoing as I felt my release wash over me. My body shook with the pleasure only Triston could give me. He slammed into me again, grabbing my neck with his other hand holding me in place as he took me, making me his. His body went rigid and spasmed, and I felt him come undone inside me.

Chapter Fourteen

We laid on the bed until the sun was low on the horizon, the orange glow over the blue ocean. "Are you hungry, angel?" Triston lightly stroked my arm resting on his chest. I ran my fingers over the lines of his abdomen. The soft white sheet covered his hips.

"Yeah, I could eat." I giggled as I turned and met his amused expression.

"Good. Let's put some clothes on and get some dinner. We can go to Il Mulino; they have good wine." He got up, and I took in his beautifully naked body as he crossed the room to pick up his clothes. He pulled on his briefs and turned to look at me. "Enjoying the view?" he asked, amused.

I nodded. "Always." I got up and slipped on my underwear. "What am I meant to wear?"

"There should be a dress in the closet. I called Jessie to arrange to have some things delivered."

I walked over to the closet and opened the door. There were two hangers. One with a beautiful chiffon, halter-neck, red dress, and one with a pair of black slacks and shirt. There was also a pair of black heels for me. Jessie seriously was amazing.

I slipped the dress off the hanger. Stepping into it, I slid it up my body until the thin string was able to tie behind my neck. It fit perfectly, but I didn't doubt it would for a second. The shoes were a perfect fit and match for the dress. I left my hair loose down my back and tidied up my makeup while Triston got dressed.

Ten minutes later, we were walking down to the restaurant. The setting was perfect. "Wow, this place is amazing!" Our table was a booth on the patio of the restaurant, overlooking the beach. Triston slid in next to me as the waitress placed our menus and wine list on the table. I noticed her staring at Triston, as most women did when he was around. She gave him a bright smile. "Hi there, I'm Candice. I'll be your waitress tonight. What can I get you to drink?"

"We will have a bottle of your Merlot, the house blend, and a bottle of sparkling water. Glasses with ice and lemon. We need a few more minutes with the food order." She scurried off smiling, flushing from Triston smiling at her.

"Do you realize what you do to women?" I asked him seriously.

His frown answered my question. "What do you mean?" He picked up the menu.

"Just as I thought. Completely oblivious." I giggled. Leaning toward him, I whispered, "You drive every woman you meet crazy."

"Miss Reid, there is only one woman I want to drive crazy." His voice was low, and his hand slid up my thigh. I jumped at his brazen move, lucky for tablecloths. I slapped his hand and squeezed my thighs together around his hand. "You see, I know you're aching for me to touch you," he growled.

The waitress came back with our drinks; I was thankful for the distraction. "Would you like me to pour it for you, sir?" She gave Triston another megawatt smile.

"Sure, thank you. Can you please bring us the vegetarian platter for two?" She nodded, opening the bottle and pouring a small taster for Triston. Taking a sip of the wine, he nodded, and she proceeded to fill both glasses. Leaving the bottle on the table, she disappeared.

I picked up my wine, taking a sip. It was full-bodied and had an aftertaste of strawberries. I looked out at the ocean. The patio was lit up by the candles on the tables. Triston's hand rested on my thigh. I was aware that the dress I had on was short and the material was soft. His fingers played with the hem, and I knew what his intentions were. He was going to tease me into submission. "It's beautiful here." I tried changing the subject. Meeting Triston's gaze, he was staring at me. "What?" He gave me a boyish smile and shook his head, turning to look at the ocean.

"Nothing, I was just thinking."

"Oh, you were? What were you thinking about?"

He leaned toward me, his hot breath on my neck. "About how I would like to take you and bend you over the table. Then I would lift this tiny dress and fuck you." His voice was low and hoarse. Squeezing my thighs together, I squirmed in my seat. I felt the fire ignite low in my belly. "Then I want to make you come around me," he continued, and I felt the knot tighten in my stomach. "Until you feel me come inside you while I spank you hard . . ." His words trailed off, leaving me aching. The heat between my legs was unbearable. I squeezed my thighs tighter, hoping to sate the need inside me, knowing he could feel the effect he had on me. His eyes locked on mine, and I knew my pupils dilated with lust.

His smirk was devilish. The dark, bad boy beneath the cool exterior was teasing me, and he was enjoying every minute of me squirming in my seat. I took a large gulp of wine, knowing this was going to be a long dinner. I watched his hand play with the stem of the glass, his beautiful fingers tracing lines up and down the crystal. "Do you enjoy staring at me?" he asked with an amused expression.

"Yes, as a matter of fact, I do." I leaned toward him, wanting to rattle that calm exterior of his. As my teeth grazed his neck, I whispered, "I would love to feel those fingers of yours inside me. You do realize I am soaking wet right now?" My breath was warm on his bare neck, and I could see goosebumps rise on his skin. I sat back, pleased with the reaction from my words.

"Miss Reid, you are good. I give you that, but I can play this game much better than you." He turned to face me. His eyes creased as he gave me a naughty smile. I took that as a challenge, sliding my hand up his thigh, stopping just short of his crotch. I sipped my wine, his eyes darkening as he stared at me. His gaze flickered with that all-too-familiar lust as I licked the wine from my bottom lip. "We'll just have to see, won't we, Mr. Hart?"

Triston sat back. "I do love a challenge." He wrapped his arm around me, and we watched the waves on the shore. A few minutes later, our waitress returned with the platter. The food looked marvelous. It was then I realized how hungry I was. We hadn't eaten since leaving New York that morning. I grabbed one of the cheese breadsticks and dipped it in the hummus. As I brought it to my mouth, I felt Triston's gaze on me. I decided to tease him, licking the hummus off the tip and slowly biting into it.

He averted his gaze quickly. "Jesus, Emily!" he mumbled under his breath. I giggled, knowing I had affected him.

"What's wrong, Triston?" I asked him innocently.

"Nothing. I think I'm just hungry." He put a few starters on his plate. I dipped the bread in another salsa dip and copied my earlier actions.

Triston's eyes were glued to my mouth, and I felt my stomach flip-flop at the lust-filled expression on his face. He blinked, turning his head away, and proceeded to fill our glasses with water.

His hand went back to gripping my thigh, holding my leg in place, his fingertips caressing my skin causing goosebumps to rise all over my body. When I didn't stop him, he moved his hand higher up my thigh, trailing his feather-light touch on my hot skin. A soft moan escaped my mouth. "Need some ice, angel?" His voice was syrup sweet as he gave me a devilish smile. He made my body ignite. The game he enjoyed made me smile. He continued to surprise and excite me in so many ways.

"Yes, please." I scooped up a small block of ice from the glass. Holding it to my lips, I sucked on it, rubbing the ice over my top lip then my bottom. His eyes blazed again, watching the water drip slowly onto my cleavage. "Oops!" I wiped the water with my index finger, putting it in my mouth, sucking my finger with a smirk on my face. His eyes were mesmerized by my actions.

"Are we going to eat tonight? Or did you want me to take you into the restroom and fuck you?" He growled, and my body clenched in anticipation.

"Well, you did say you were better at this than I was. I was just trying to get ahead." I smiled, finishing the wine in my glass. Our waitress came back to take our food order. The temperature dropped, but I knew his mind was elsewhere as he ordered our dinner. When she left, I leaned my head on his shoulder. My teeth bit the smooth skin of his exposed neck. "I would rather have you for dinner, Mr. Hart . . ." My whisper trailed off, and I kissed his neck.

"Miss Reid, I'm going to be having you for dessert. Now behave, or there will be harsh consequences later."

I sat up straight, giggling at his expression. "Okay, Mr. Hart, I will try to behave." I gave him my most innocent smile. "I'm going to the restroom. Don't go anywhere!" I stood and walked to the back of the restaurant. My body was on fire, and my panties were soaked. I needed Triston more than I imagined possible. I walked down the hallway toward the restrooms. When I felt him behind me, I wasn't surprised. I knew he couldn't resist. He grabbed my waist and pulled me into the women's restroom, pulling me into a stall and locking the door behind us.

Pinning me against the wall, his mouth crashed into mine as his tongue licked into me. I arched my back, pushing myself into his firm body, feeling every rigid inch of him. His right hand held my wrists above my head. Pushing my legs apart with his knee, his left hand moved up my thigh, finding the heat between my legs.

A growl emitted from his chest as his fingers moved my panties to the side, finding me soaking wet. He pushed two fingers into me suddenly, causing my hips to move against him. I moaned into the kiss. We heard the door open and close, but his attention was relentless. He didn't stop for a second. I was about to come undone when suddenly he stopped. "Now, Miss Reid, we should go and have dinner," he whispered. He straightened his shirt and unlocked the stall. Making sure no one saw him, he dashed out of the restroom, leaving me panting and on edge.

When I walked back to the table, I gave him a small smile and noticed our dinner had arrived. I was so high-strung when I slid into the booth, and my arm brushed him, every nerve in my body was electrified. "You okay, angel? You look flushed." He gave me a naughty smile, and I stuck my tongue out at him. "Miss Reid, I will bite that tongue."

I picked up my cutlery. "Mr. Hart, what you did in there was so unfair. Not to worry, though. I will definitely get my revenge." I smiled and winked at him.

"I did nothing that you didn't want me to do." He put a forkful of salad in his mouth. I decided eating dinner would be best. I needed to distract myself from the feel of him pinning me against the wall and his fingers inside me. Picking up my glass, I took a large gulp of wine. "I want you to sit still and be very quiet, okay?" He turned toward me. Seeing my confused expression, he continued. "I want to try something."

He picked up an ice cube. "Carry on as normal. You don't want to attract attention to us, do you?" I shook my head, but my heart leaped into my throat.

"No, but you're scaring me." I giggled.

He took the ice cube with his right hand and circled it over my knee. He looked so calm, eating his salad while moving his hand higher on the inside of my thigh. I felt the ice melting from the heat of his hand, and it slowly dripped down my leg. "Triston!" I hissed at him. A naughty smile curved his lips. He moved his hand higher, the skirt of my dress pushed up by his hand as the ice reached the top of my inner thigh. "You really are my bad girl, Miss Reid." He cleared his throat, and I knew he was turned on as I was. The fact that we were in public made me tremble at the risk we were taking. Finally, I felt the last drops of water on my thighs as his hand came into full contact with the apex between my thighs.

A small moan escaped my lips. "Miss Reid, would you like some more wine?" he asked nonchalantly as his fingers stroked the moist material of my panties. I nodded, not trusting myself to speak. The waitress came back to our table. Triston's hand didn't move. I felt myself blush as she asked if everything was okay.

"Yes, thank you. Everything is amazing. Another bottle of wine, please?" Triston's voice was calm and relaxed, his fingers slowly stroking me. The knot in my stomach was so tightly wound. I squeezed my legs together, trapping his hand from moving. As she scurried off, Triston turned to me. "You're doing so well. You're close, aren't you?"

"Yes," I hissed, keeping my voice low.

He pulled his hand away quickly. "We can leave that for later." He slowly licked his fingers. "Goddamn, you taste like honey."

"Triston, please?" I begged him. I needed to find my release somehow. His eyes were locked on mine, and I silently pleaded with him. He stared at me, debating what to do.

Finally, he asked, "Can you be quiet?" I nodded. His hand snaked its way between my legs. Moving the tablecloth over my lap as his fingers pushed aside my panties. "Mmm, I love how wet you are," he whispered. He plunged two fingers inside me. I bit my lip to keep from crying out. "You need to be very quiet. Understand?" I nodded, picking up my wine and taking a small sip as he plunged into the soaking depths of my body. I watched as everyone in the restaurant went on with their business, completely oblivious.

Our waitress came back with the wine, which she opened and left on the table for us. "Thank you." Triston's voice was so calm. I was surprised at how he could be so relaxed. I felt a third finger filling me, and I felt myself teeter on the edge. I needed this so much. In the dim light of our table, I leaned my head on his shoulder. His fingers moved faster and faster. "Come for me, my naughty angel." His voice was hoarse and low — my release shuddering through me as I squeezed my thighs around his hand. I bit into his shoulder to keep from screaming as my body shook. He stopped moving his fingers and kissed my cheek. "You are so sexy, Miss Reid." Pulling his hand out from under the table, he licked his fingers clean as he stared at me.

Chapter Fifteen

We walked along the beach, Triston's hand in mine. "You surprise me every day, Miss Reid." Under the light of the full moon, his face looked angelic.

"I do? Why is that?" He stopped, turned, and faced me. Pulling me against his taut body, he wrapped his arms around me. "Because you're not afraid of me. You're always open to trying new things, and because I love you." He kissed me softly, teasing my lips apart with his tongue. I dropped my shoes, wrapped my arms around his neck, and tangled my fingers in his long hair. His scent was intoxicating, sweet and spicy all rolled into one. His fingers ran up and down my spine. He had a way of touching me so lightly my whole body shook in anticipation.

Triston pulled away. We were both breathless. "I love you too, Triston."

"Come on, I want to show you something."

Triston picked up my shoes, and we walked down the beach. It was a busy evening along the promenade. Bars and restaurants were teeming with people. "Where are we going?"

"To the park over there." He pointed next to the hotel. We walked in comfortable silence as I watched people passing by. Couples walking hand in hand, just like us. It was a strange feeling to be with someone after such a long time, to feel something this intense.

"Swing?" I asked Triston, pointing to the bench swing in the park we had just entered.

He smiled. "Sure." It looked over the ocean, and the lights from the hotels sparkled on the water.

"It's so beautiful out here. I wouldn't mind waking up to this view every day." I turned to Triston, my legs resting on his lap with his warm, soft hands feeling so good on my skin.

"It is. That's why I wanted to bring you out here. I wanted to talk to you about something." His face took on a serious expression. When his eyes met mine, they looked so solemn my heart raced. Why did he always look like he was about to break up with me? My mind started working overtime, and in those few minutes before he spoke, I held my breath. "Having you in my apartment this past week has been . . . Incredible. I was thinking about you going back to your apartment." He stopped and looked at me. "I don't want you to." His lips curved into a smile. "Will you move in with me, Emily?"

My whole body relaxed. I let out the breath I didn't know I was holding. "Jesus, don't ever do that to me again!" I slapped his arm. "Why did you look like you were about to say something bad?" I glared at him in frustration.

"I was testing you. I needed to see if you really wanted me!" An amused expression crossed his face, and I knew he was trying to frustrate me.

"Ugh, you are so frustrating! I'm going to the hotel." I got up and walked barefoot down to the sand. I heard Triston run up behind me. Grabbing me around the waist, he lifted me and spun me around. "Put me down!" I giggled. He slowly let me down and turned me around to face him. Grabbing my face in his hands, he lightly brushed his lips on mine.

"Let's go back to the room. We can sit on the balcony and have some wine." I nodded. I had a few other ideas of what we could do on the balcony.

Back in the room, I noticed the concierge service had turned down the bed and left mints on the pillows. I decided to change into my boy shorts and a tank top. When I came out of the bathroom, Triston was watching something on the television. He turned to me. "Did you want some wine now, angel?" I nodded, opened the small bar fridge, and found a bottle of Sauvignon Blanc. "Will this do, Mr. Hart?"

He squinted at the label as I held it up. I giggled at him trying to decipher the name on the label. "Yes, I think you have good taste, Miss Reid." He winked and got up, heading to the bathroom, leaving me to pour the wine. I picked up both glasses and opened the balcony doors. Stepping outside, the warm breeze enveloped me. I put the glasses on the table and looked at the full moon shining down onto the dark water. The color of the ocean reminded me of Triston's eyes when he let his darker side take over. My mind replayed the scene in the restaurant, and I shivered. "Is it cold?" His arms were around me, and I noticed he wasn't wearing a top, his hot smooth skin on my back.

"No, I was just thinking." I turned to face him. I knew I didn't answer him earlier. I looked into those startling blue eyes. "I was thinking about what you asked me down there." I motioned to the beach. "About moving in together." I kept my face as serious as I could.

A frown creased his brow. I could tell he was tense, waiting for my answer. "Yes, I remember. And what was the answer?"

"Well, I think it's . . ." His hands held my face, and his eyes locked on mine. "I think it's a brilliant idea!" I giggled as I saw the relief wash over him.

He picked me up and spun me around. "I knew you couldn't resist me any longer!" I giggled as he held me against his bare chest. I was fully aware of his toned body and the heat radiating from him.

"Like I resisted you in the restaurant earlier?" I winked.

"One of the top ten experiences of my life." He let me down slowly and picked up his wine. "To moving in together! This actually calls for champagne, but I guess the wine will have to do." We clinked glasses, and I took a sip. It cooled me down somewhat from the heat of the day, as well as Triston's distracting heat.

I turned to look at the ocean. "It reminds me of your eyes."

"What?" he questioned.

"The ocean, when you're . . . Uhm . . . you know?" I blushed, suddenly feeling shy in front of him. I wasn't sure why. After everything we've done together.

"When I am what?" He pulled me against him. My ass against his groin, feeling him grow hard against me.

"Come on, Triston, you know what I mean." I laughed. He leaned down and kissed my neck, his lips warm and wet. He left a trail of soft kisses up my neck. His teeth grazed my earlobe, biting gently, sending sparks through me. "Triston," I moaned loudly.

"You're the most amazing thing that's ever happened to me."

"And you to me, Triston. You should know that by now," I whispered, taking another sip of wine, my mind calming down from the stress of the past few days.

"I want to take you inside. I want to make love to you." He grabbed my hand and led me into the room. Triston hooked his fingers at the bottom of my tank and pulled it up over my head. He pulled down my shorts. I stood in front of him completely naked. His gaze traveled from my head, over my chest, down between my legs, and to my feet. "I want you so much, Emily. You have no idea what you do to me, every fucking day." His voice was low, but I could hear the lust dripping from it. There was something different about him tonight, and I was unsure what it was. "I want to try something, but I want you just to tell me if you want me to stop." I nodded. I trusted him with my life, and I knew he wouldn't do anything to hurt me. "Close your eyes." I did as he said, and I heard him move around the room. I felt the soft material cover my eyes and felt him tie a knot at the back of my head. He leaned in close and gave me a few soft kisses on my shoulder. I felt him move down, and I smiled in my darkness.

His lips were on my legs, soft, light, and warm, kissing his way up, and I felt his teeth graze the sensitive skin on my hips. I trembled at the attention his lips were giving me. His mouth traveled slowly up my body, over my hardening nipples, and to my neck. I felt his hot breath on my neck. "I love you," he whispered softly, and goosebumps rose on the back of my neck. I would never tire of hearing those words from him.

He took both my hands and led me to the bed. I laid back on the pillows, and he continued his slow torture of my skin. He moved between my legs, and his fingers stroked my entrance, my hips rising to his palm. His middle finger slid into me. He hooked it, and I shivered. He continued sliding his fingers into me, making me wetter than ever.

The heat was building inside me, and I was aching for him. He was taking his time, slower and softer than he usually was. The fact that I couldn't see what he was planning made me anxious. My other senses heightened to the point of ecstasy. I moaned his name.

He reached up and undid the blindfold. "I want you to see." His comment confused me, but not for long. He got off the bed and unbuttoned his jeans. I watched as they fell down his hips and noticed he was rock hard. "This is what you do to me every moment of every day." He crawled back over me, supporting his weight on his elbows. I felt him tease my entrance with his hardness, and my hips lifted to meet his. His smile was beautiful. "I want you too . . ." His words trailed off as he slid into me. It was slow, exquisite torture. He didn't enter me fully, sliding back out, leaving me panting and writhing beneath him. His hand gripped his erection and continued his teasing, rubbing up and down my slick entrance mercilessly. "Do you want me, Emily?" he whispered in my ear, his voice soft and calm.

I nodded. "Please. Triston, please?" I begged shamelessly.

He pushed into me again, kissing my neck. I wrapped my legs around his waist, wanting to pull him closer when he stopped. "Be patient, angel." I let my legs back down as he slid into me, filling me completely now. His hips thrust back and forth gently as it was delicious torture. He leaned back up. "I told you, I want to make love to you."

My body was on fire at his words. I watched his veins and muscles pulse as he continued his slow assault. He sat up, lifting my knees against his hips. My view improved as I watched his sculpted body move, pushing inside me. Every movement caused his abs to tense. I could have come undone just watching that. He started moving faster, and I lifted my hips to match his movements. Our eyes locked. His face was one of pure ecstasy. "You feel so fucking amazing around me. I love being inside you, angel." Our movements hastened as I felt my climax build. I watched Triston's body tense, and I knew he was close. He lowered himself over me again, and we moved together. I wrapped my legs around his waist, pulling him in deeper. Our lips were on fire as his tongue invaded my mouth. "Come for me, Emily. I need you to submit to me." At his order, my body exploded. He thrust into me again, and I felt his release fill me.

It was Thursday afternoon, and we were on the plane heading back home when I pulled out my laptop and powered it up. I had three emails which needed a reply. One was from Bash.

From: Sebastian Hart

To: Emily Reid

Date: July 24 - 16:00

Subject: Invitation - Sponsors Dinner

Emily,

I need your help. Because of everything that happened with Blake, I needed to source a new sponsor. They want me at their event tomorrow night, July 25, and, of course, I want you to be there. I'm not good with business and marketing, and that's what they want to talk about.

I will have the car pick you up, or I can. I don't mind. Please?

Bash xo

Sebastian Hart

CEO - Tribal Fuel

I looked up at Triston who was busy with his own emails. What was I meant to tell him? I took a deep breath. "Triston, I need to go to an event tomorrow night. With a client." I added that last part, so he didn't freak out too much.

He looked up and nodded. "Sure, which client?"

"Well, that's the thing. It's um . . ." I mumbled.

"Emily, spit it out," his voice a direct order.

"It's Tribal Fuel." I stared at him. His facial expression didn't falter. His eyes were like glass as he looked at me. He gave a small nod.

"Right, well you best please the client then." He looked back down and carried on typing. I wasn't sure what to do. I was expecting him to freak out, but this silence was disconcerting. What did he even mean? He sounded indifferent, which was so unlike him.

"Really?" My voice came out higher than expected, and I squeaked.

He sighed. "Emily, if he wants you to go to an event, I can't stop it. I am not happy about it, but it's work."

I hit reply and told Bash I would love to go, and I would prefer if he picked me up. I asked him what I should wear and hit send. I didn't have to wait long for a reply.

From: Sebastian Hart

To: Emily Reid

Date: July 24 - 16:15

Subject: Invitation - Dress

I will get you something to wear, to be delivered to Triston's apartment, I presume?

Sebastian Hart

CEO - Tribal Fuel

I replied yes and closed my laptop. Sitting back, I thought about going to the event with Bash. I remembered the kiss from that horrible night, and I felt nervous.

It was a long first day back at work, and Triston didn't mention that night's event, and neither did I. He had a meeting with James after lunch. After that, for the rest of the day, it seemed like his mind was elsewhere. Charlie drove Triston and me home. I needed to get ready for this evening. Bash said he would be picking me up at six p.m. I checked my phone. I had an hour to get ready. As we made our way to the elevators, I noticed a new car in the parking lot. "I wonder if they're our new neighbors?"

Triston grasped my hand. "I don't want you alone tonight at all! Okay?"

I frowned. Why was he so overprotective? Blake was in custody until the trial. "Yeah, sure, I'll be fine. Blake is behind bars," I reminded him, and he gave me a small nod.

"Emily, can you just obey me for once?" His voice was harsh as he unlocked the door. His eyes blazed with anger. I wasn't sure what was going on with him, and I wasn't in the mood for a fight. I didn't like the way he was talking to me right then. I thought he might be tired, but it seemed there was something more, something I couldn't quite put my finger on.

"Look, if you don't want me to go tonight, then tell me! Do not talk to me like a child!" I stormed into the bedroom and saw that Mrs. Morrison —Triston's housekeeper— put the dress bag on the bed. I unzipped it and pulled out the soft material. It was a beautiful black, strapless, satin dress. It would be too long for me; I would need to wear heels. I checked the time. I was running late.

Triston came up behind me. "I just want you safe." His voice had softened.

"I am not a child. Don't ever talk to me like one." I faced him, and I could see the hard line of his jaw. He was biting back something, which infuriated me more. "What?" He shook his head and left the room. I didn't have time, so I went into the bathroom to get ready.

Walking into the living room thirty minutes later, I heard the buzzer. Triston got up to open the door for Bash. He looked at me and smiled.

"You look beautiful, angel." I nodded. I was still fuming. Triston turned to open the door. Bash walked in, and my breath caught. I had never seen him in a suit. He was dressed in an immaculate, black suit with a crisp white dress shirt and a shimmering, silver-blue tie finished off his look. His hair was messy, spikey, and standing in every direction.

"Triston." They shook hands, and I could feel the tension between the brothers.

"Bash. Hey, is this okay?" I stepped forward and gestured to the dress. His eyes met mine, and I saw a mischievous glint in his eyes.

"Wow. Yeah, Emily. My assistant knows how to pick a dress!" He smiled. "We better get going. Traffic might be a nightmare." He stepped onto the landing. "See ya, Tris."

Triston turned to me as I walked toward the door. He leaned down and gave me a chaste kiss on the lips. I felt him radiating tension. "Be careful, please?" His voice was low, and I wasn't sure if he meant being with Bash or something else. I nodded.

"Okay, see you later." I turned and felt the tension following me as I stepped out of the apartment. Bash and I entered the elevator, and

I pressed the ground floor button. "Is something wrong?" he asked as soon as the doors closed.

"No, we just . . . see things differently." I gave him a small smile.

"You do look amazing, by the way. I mean, I didn't want to say anything in front of Tris, but man, he is lucky." His eyes roamed over me, and I shivered. The doors opened, and I saw a red convertible BMW parked in the visitor's bay of Triston's apartment.

"You're the one who chose the dress. Well, your assistant. It's beautiful. You know that. Thank you, Bash. You really didn't have to—"

"I did. It's my way of apologizing for taking advantage the other night. I didn't mean to." He unlocked the car and opened my door. I slid into the sleek black leather seat. The car smelled of Bash's spicy cologne and leather, a heady mix, and I felt calmer. My nerves had been on end after my argument with Triston.

Bash slid into the driver seat. "Look, Bash, it's okay. Don't apologize. I kissed you back, but we cannot tell Triston. Please?" He nodded as he started the engine and pulled out of the parking spot. "Noted. My brother won't find out."

Bash sped out of the garage and into the quiet

street behind the apartment block. "So, what is this event we're attending? I didn't think you did fancy." I turned to see him smile. Making his way to downtown Manhattan, I noticed there wasn't any traffic. We were headed toward the Upper Eastside, and I figured it was going to be one of those posh places.

"It's an investor interested in helping me out. I need the backing right now as we're taking off, and he is really into marketing and events, hence why you're here. I mean, why else would I ask you?" His eyes flickered to me, and I saw a naughty look on his face. His smirk was as devilish as his brother's, and I knew I needed to keep my head screwed on straight tonight.

"So, this is purely professional, right?" I stared at him.

"Of course, darling, why? Did you think I was trying to steal you from Tris?" His voice was soft and deep, almost a whisper. I shrugged. "Well, I wouldn't. I will not kiss you or touch you unless you ask me to, and when you do, I will make you forget everything. Even if just for a moment." His words sent an involuntary shiver down my body.

"Bash—"

"Okay, okay! I shouldn't have said it quite like that, but I'm not going to apologize. Emily, I think about that night we spent together every single day." Bash slowed down, pulling into the underground garage of a fancy-looking apartment building.

"If you keep on about that, I'm going to get a cab and leave." I looked at his rugged features. He was so different from his brother, but they had the same devilish appeal. He parked and turned off the engine.

"I apologize, darling. No more sexy talk, okay?" I giggled at his facial expression and nodded. He got out and came around to open my door. Slipping my hand into his waiting one, we made our way to the entrance.

"Mr. Hart, welcome." It was strange hearing someone say that and not refer to Triston. The usher escorted us to a large table when a tall, friendly man walked over to Bash.

"Hart! Welcome. I guess this is the lovely Miss Reid?" He held out a hand to me. I smiled and shook his hand. "I'm Mr. Richards. We're going to have a lot to talk about!" He laughed. "I'm going to welcome the other guests. Get yourselves something to drink." He left us and wandered over to more guests entering the venue.

"Come on, darling. Wine?" I nodded. Bash called the waiter over and ordered a glass of wine for me and a beer for himself. He turned to me. "Thank you for being here. It means a lot to me." His voice was serious and sincere.

"It's a pleasure. It is a work function, after all." His smile disappeared, and he nodded, pulling my chair out. I sat down, and he took his place next to me. Most of the evening was spent talking about work, marketing plans, and event schedules. Then our host got up and made a speech, announcing his investment into Tribal Fuel. He mentioned working alongside Je Te Veux Events for marketing and event purposes. When he left the stage, the music was turned up, and it seemed like the party was starting. There were only about fifty guests, but everyone was immaculately dressed and elegant.

"Do you want to dance?" Bash looked at me expectantly. I nodded, and he grabbed my hand, leading me onto the dance floor. The song changed, and I recognized the beginning piano of the Ellie Goulding song "I Know You Care."

The lyrics tugged at my heart, and I knew my feelings for Bash were still very much alive. My arms instinctively laced around his neck. I felt his left-hand slide down the side of my body, lightly resting on my hip. "Just let me know when you're ready to go. I don't want to keep you out too late. In case you get into trouble with Tris." We swayed to the song.

"Why would I get into trouble? He isn't my father, and I don't have a curfew." My voice came out harsher than I intended, and Bash gave me a strange look. I looked up into those warm, hazel eyes, and a smirk crossed his lips.

"Trouble in paradise?" he inquired softly as he led me across the dance floor. His grip tightened on my hip, and I felt my body respond.

"No, it's just . . . It's nothing. Can we not talk about it?" As the song ended, I dropped my hands from Bash's neck and stepped back, turning and walking back to our table. I felt his presence behind me, his fingers guiding me from the base of my spine. I took a deep breath, trying to calm my nerves. Why was he having such an effect on me? I sat down and took a gulp of wine and felt the liquid calming me.

"I'm sorry. I didn't mean to upset you." His voice trailed off, and I realized he must think I was angry at him for asking about Triston and me.

"You didn't. I just didn't want to discuss your brother with you. This is an event for you, so let's have fun." He smiled, and his face lit up. Those molten hazel eyes melted into me, and I turned away quickly. My phone rang in my bag. I pulled it out and answered the call. "Triston?"

"Are you okay? I haven't heard from you." His voice was low, and I could hear the anger radiating from it. "You should let me know when you're getting home." I felt my blood boil at him. We were at odds tonight, and I didn't know why.

"Later. Dinner just finished and I can't very well get up and walk out. I told you I might be late; I wish you would stop worrying!"

"Miss Reid, do not dare take that tone with me! Do you hear me? I will put you across my knee and spank your ass into submission!" His voice was dripping with anger and lust. I squirmed in my chair hearing his threat. I felt eyes on me, and I knew Bash was watching my reaction. I needed to end this call before I lost it.

"Triston, I will see you later, okay?" I pushed the red button, hanging up on him before he had a chance to say anything more. I knew I was in for a long night. Shouting at him was my first mistake. Hanging up on him was my second, but I couldn't have him embarrassing me in front of his brother.

"Everything ok? I can take you back if you need to go?" I shook my head. Picked up my glass of wine, I gulped it down. This time, I was the one radiating anger.

"Can we go somewhere? Just like, get out of here?" My eyes met Bash's, and he nodded, getting up and grabbing my hand.

"Sure. We can go to my place? Unless you wanted to go clubbing or something?"

I shook my head. "No clubbing. Your place sounds good."

We walked down to the car a few minutes later, and Bash opened the door for me. I slid into the car and pulled my phone out of my bag. No messages or calls from Triston. He was probably seething with anger, and frankly, I didn't care. He was infuriating, and I wanted to let him simmer. I would go home later. I didn't feel like walking into the apartment, feeling like a teenager getting ready to be grounded for going out.

"You sure about this?" Bash asked, and I knew it was completely opposite to what I should be doing. I smiled and nodded against my better judgment.

Chapter Sixteen

Bash unlocked the door to his Manhattan loft. I stepped inside and noticed it was the total opposite of his brother's modern penthouse. It felt warmer, with dark leather sofas and large, deep red rugs. There was a large fireplace in the open-plan kitchen-living room. The view was just as magnificent as Triston's.

He walked past me into the living room, and his scent hit me all at once. I was overwhelmed by it. "Can I get you a drink?" I nodded absent-mindedly. "I can have my driver take you home when you're ready," he added with a small smile.

"Sure. I am guessing you don't have wine?" I joked.

"I do, actually. It's a bottle I got as a gift a couple of weeks ago." He walked into the bar area as I explored. The art on the walls were painted with rich, dark colors that matched the furniture. Everything about him was warm and homey. I stared at one of the pieces hanging above the large, red brick fireplace. I got such a melancholy feeling as I stared at it. Although I felt a hint of sadness from it, I couldn't tear my eyes away. Whoever painted it must have been hurt and brokenhearted. The way the paint hit the canvas and the colors were vivid; the sadness reached out at you. "That's my favorite piece. I did it about three years ago."

I turned to face him. "You painted this?" He nodded and smiled. "Bash, this is amazing! You should sell your art!" He shrugged.

"I don't do it for money. I do it because I love painting." He put his glass down and turned on the sound system. The soft, rich voice of Lana del Rey filled the room. It was one of my favorite albums of hers, the new one called Honeymoon. "Stay here. I'll be right back." He disappeared down the hallway. I took the time to explore the rest of the apartment. I walked into the kitchen and noticed it was spotless. Of course, he wouldn't do much cooking since he seemed to work as much as Triston. I looked out at the city. Central Park was just below us as a dark, formidable shape.

Walking back into the living room, I noticed

a spiral staircase in the corner and wondered where it went. "Here you go. You need to change if you want to see up there." Bash walked back into the living room wearing only a pair of ripped blue jeans that hung low on his hips. My breathing halted, and I gasped. I drank in the sight of him.

I gulped down my wine and grabbed the tee and shorts he held out to me. "Thanks" was all I could muster. A devilish smirk appeared on his face, and his eyes twinkled in the dim light of the apartment.

"Emily, if you looked any harder you may turn me to stone," he joked and turned to pick up the beer he had left on the table.

I walked passed him and realized I had no idea where to go. "Where is your bathroom?"

He chuckled. "Down the hall, first door on the left."

I followed his directions and found a large bathroom with dark grey tiles across one wall of the two-person shower. In the other corner was a large spa bath. I stepped out of my heels and slipped the dress down, folding it. I pulled on the shorts and noticed they fit perfectly. They were like my black yoga shorts. Did he have a collection of women's clothes laying around? Did he expect me to come back to his place tonight? I pulled the tee over my head and noticed the pins in my hair slowly coming loose as curls escaped the knot.

Grabbing the dress and my shoes, I padded back to the living room. "Is this presentable? And do you normally keep women's clothes at your apartment?" I inquired, not sure why it bothered me so much.

He smiled and nodded. "It's extremely presentable. You look good in my top." I flushed at his compliment. "Yes, I have a collection of women's clothes. So that when I have random, beautiful women here I can have them change in my bathroom." He laughed at my facial expression as I stuck my tongue out at him. I set down my dress and shoes on the sofa. "The shorts are part of my merchandise. Come." He held out a hand and led me to the spiral staircase I saw earlier. "You first."

I was painfully aware of him behind me. "Are you enjoying the view?" I asked cheekily.

"Of course. Why else would I have you walk in front?" My body tingled at his words and my heart hammered against my ribcage.

I reached the landing and took in the scene before me. Paint everywhere. Three easels with large canvasses. "This is why you needed to change." Bash walked in front of me and smiled. "Welcome to my sanctuary. I have always had my art; it's been my go-to when things got . . ." His words trailed off, and he dropped his gaze. "Anyway . . ."

I walked toward the canvasses and noticed the largest one with blues and greens. It was so calming. There was a figure faded in the paint. A woman, abstract, but it was definitely there. I walked over to the sketch table. "This is . . ." I was at a loss for words as I moved the papers around, looking at the pencil sketches.

"Don't, not those." Bash walked up behind me, but before he could stop me, I found one. The one I guessed he was trying to hide. The likeness was unmistakable. I gasped, turning to face him, still holding the sketch. I opened my mouth to say something, but I couldn't find the words. I looked up into the molten hazel gaze, then back down to the sketch.

"You . . . I . . ." I muttered. Words really couldn't explain it. The sketch was beautifully raw and captured the moment so perfectly. I was breathless.

"I didn't want you to see that. Give it here, please?" He stepped forward and reached for the paper I held. I shook my head. My sudden awareness of his proximity to me was stifling. The fact that he was half naked wasn't lost to me either. I moved my arm behind my back, hiding the page from him. He leaned forward, and his arm wrapped around me. I felt his hot breath against my cheek. We were both frozen, his hand gripped my hand and the page, but he didn't move away. He leaned forward, and his lips brushed against my cheek so lightly I thought I might have imagined it. I stood frozen. I wanted him to kiss me. I wanted him to warm the chill I felt standing barefoot in his studio.

"Emily." His voice was a low whisper in my ear. "Give it to me, please?" I didn't budge. I couldn't move. I was scared of what was going to happen if I let go. My mind was lost to me at that moment. Maybe it was the wine, and perhaps it was the heat inside me. It was intensified to an unbearable sensation.

"No," I breathed against his cheek. My voice unrecognizable, and I ached deep inside. I saw the goosebumps rise on his tanned skin. The tattoo that covered the top half of his arm tensed, and I knew he was as affected as I was.

"Em." His voice a warning. "Tell me to stop?" I could hear the pleading in his voice. I shook my head slowly, unable to voice anything. "If you don't, you know what I will do?" It was a warning. He was giving me a choice. He took another step forward, and his body was flush against mine. I placed my right-hand flat against his rock-hard abs, his skin hot to the touch, and I felt him harden against my hip. My other hand was still engulfed by his, holding on to the sketch of me, naked laying on my sofa the night we made love.

"Bash," I whispered again, my lips on his shoulder. His skin was soft, smooth, and hot. He gripped my hip and pulled me into him. His mouth devoured me, moving over my neck. I bit into his shoulder as he licked the shell of my ear. Feeling his hot breath on me was enough to dampen my panties. I squirmed in his firm embrace. "Jesus, Emily, I need you so fucking bad right now." His hoarse whisper turned me on even more than I was before.

I closed my eyes, and deep in my mind, I saw those intense blue eyes, and it felt like I had been drenched with ice-cold water. "Stop!" Bash pulled away, his hardness evident in his tight jeans. "Bash, I'm sorry. I can't. I just . . ."

"I know. I know . . . You better go!" He spun on his heel and left me in the studio, breathless and entirely at his mercy.

I stepped out of the elevator into the foyer, then through the door. The lights in the living room were still on. I heard the faint sound of music, and I looked at the iPod, but it wasn't on. I frowned. That was so strange. I put my dress and shoes on the sofa and walked toward the bedroom. That's where the music was coming from. It sounded so sad. Triston wasn't in bed; the balcony door was open. I walked toward the door and stood captivated. Triston was sitting on a small stool with his guitar on his lap, strumming a melody by one of my favorite bands. I recognized the song immediately. It was my favorite acoustic songs they played called "Witness." The lyrics along with the melody always clenched at my heart. You could hear the pain so evident in the singer's voice. I stood mesmerized, watching him. He hummed along with the guitar, then sang the chorus softly into the dark night. His voice was amazing. I had goosebumps listening to him. Suddenly, he stopped and turned. "Emily?"

"Triston." I stepped out into the chilly night and stood next to him. He looked me up and down, and I shivered under his scrutiny.

"Why aren't you wearing your dress?" He stood up and laid the guitar on the table.

I took a deep breath. I needed to tell him. "I changed, earlier. I, um . . . Bash was showing me his studio and didn't want me to ruin my dress. So—"

"So he took it off for you?" Anger flared in Triston's eyes, and I wasn't sure telling him was the best idea.

"*No!* God, Triston, I took my dress off, in the bathroom, with the door closed!" My voice rose an octave, and I was glad we didn't have neighbors.

"And then? You fucked him?" His words were harsh and cut into me like a knife. I felt my heart constricting.

"No, Triston, I did not fuck him! I came home to fuck you! But I see you're clearly not in the mood, so I will go to bed!" I spun around. Before I could walk away, Triston grabbed my wrist, pulling me back toward him.

"Look into my eyes!" I obeyed his order and stared into those intense blue eyes. "Did you sleep with my brother tonight?"

"No."

"Good." He pulled me over to the table and gripped my neck, bending me over. "Hands flat on the table straight ahead of you." I did as he said. I felt the sting through the thin fabric of my shorts. Another slap, and another. "Count!" His voice was harsh, but it was laced with desire.

"One!" My voice came out louder than I thought. "Two, three, four!"

"Did you enjoy hanging up on me, Miss Reid?" His voice changed hearing the lust taking over. The heat between my legs intensified. I shook my head.

Slap! "Five!"

Slap! "Six!"

"Will you hang up on me again?" I shook my head. Triston gripped my neck, pulling me back up, his lips against my ear. I felt his erection straining against my ass, pressing into me painfully. I needed him. "I do not like being hung up on. Do you understand, Miss Reid?"

"Yes." My answer was soft and filled with my own desire. I felt the heat pool between my legs. I wanted him. I needed him. I was aching from the earlier confrontation with Bash and the spanking I had just received. I needed Triston to take me. *Hard!*

"Good!" His free hand groped my breast, tweaking my hardening nipple through the top, causing a whimper to escape. Copying his action on my other breast, another whimper escaped my lips. "Now, I am going to fuck you," he said hoarsely and bit my earlobe, and I nearly came undone. *"Hard!"*

My knees weakened, and I trembled at his words. He bent me over the table again and pulled my shorts and panties down. "Mmm, so wet, my dirty girl." I felt his tongue between my legs, and I couldn't hold out any longer. My orgasm shook through me, and I held onto the table to keep myself up. As soon as my orgasm subsided, I heard the zipper of his jeans. He slammed into me hard and deep, relentless with his assault.

He slid in and out, faster and faster. He gripped my hair and pulled my head back. His other hand gripped my hip as he slammed into me. I felt myself clench around him, tightening. I was once again on edge. "Emily!" His voice was so sexy, scratchy and hoarse. "You are so fucking sexy, bent over for me." He started with his dirty words, and I knew he was trying to push me over the edge. He didn't have to try very hard as I felt myself about to explode. "I love being inside you. You're so fucking tight, makes me want you all the time!"

I moaned loudly. He spurred me on. "Yes, angel, come for me. You are mine, all mine!" His words lay claim to me, nudging me, and I felt myself falling. My eyes rolled back, and my knees trembled. I gripped the edge of the table and clenched around him, wanting him to fill me. I didn't wait long.

I opened my eyes early Saturday morning. As I rolled over, I felt a familiar ache on my ass. Last night, Triston claiming me on the balcony, fresh in my mind. I scooted up and noticed the balcony door was open, and the sun was bright. It looked like a beautiful day. I knew autumn was on the way, and soon we would have the cold to deal with. "You're awake." Triston walked into the bedroom carrying a tray. "Come." He gestured toward the balcony. I swung my legs out of bed and realized I was still wearing Bash's T-shirt. I pulled it off and made my way to the walk-in closet. I pulled one of Triston's T-shirts from the drawer and slipped it on.

Out on the balcony, Triston had set up breakfast under the umbrella. The sun was hot, and it was only 9 a.m. "Are we working today? I know it's Saturday, but—" I asked. He shook his head.

"No, we are taking the day off. We need to sit and go through the arrangements for next week. We fly to London on Sunday next week, ready for Monday's set up, so we only have a week to prepare." I gasped. Of course, I had totally forgotten about it. I finished my bagel and looked up at Triston. He was watching me. "I want to apologize, about last night. I didn't think you had sex with him. I was just angry and jealous seeing you come home with different clothes. I jumped to conclusions."

"Triston, don't. You do not have to apologize to me. I shouldn't have gone to his apartment. I was angry with you, and I didn't want to come home." I picked up my mug and poured more coffee.

"I know. Look, there's something I need to tell you. Something I'm dealing with, and I don't want you to get angry." I looked up and saw his unease.

"Okay?" I answered cautiously.

"Promise?" I nodded. "I got a call from James, and, um . . ." He hesitated, and I felt my stomach drop. This must have something to do with Blake. The next words out of his mouth stumped me. "Krista is ill. I'm going later today to see her."

"What?" I met his gaze, and I could see the concern etched on his face. "You mean your ex-fiancée?" I was shocked. Why on earth would he visit an ex who cheated on him and left him for his brother? Something didn't make sense.

He nodded slowly. "She's in the hospital, and I want to go and see her, to know she's okay. Nothing more." He looked at me and gave a small smile.

"And what am I meant to do? Sit here and wait for you to finish seeing your ex? She left you, Triston!" I felt anger rising, and I felt sick.

"I want you to come with me." I could see the pleading in his eyes, but this was ridiculous. How could he show such concern for someone who did that to him?

"No fucking way!" I stood up and walked back inside. How could he even think I would want to go and see his ex? What was he thinking? He wasn't thinking! I went into the living room and grabbed my phone.

"Angel." Triston walked in after me. "Look, I'm sorry. You don't have to go. I just thought if you saw her and me together, you would know there isn't anything between us. I just wanted to make sure she was okay."

"Triston, let this go. I don't want to meet her, see her, or ever hear her name again. I need to go." I walked past him, back into the bedroom. Grabbing my sports bra and a pair of shorts, I walked into the bathroom to change.

"Where are you going?" He followed me into the bathroom. I stared at him, long and hard. My face must have shown my anger because he didn't come closer.

"I'm going for a run." He nodded and turned away, leaving me to simmer alone.

When I walked back into the bedroom, he

wasn't there. I pulled on a pair of socks and my gym shoes as I plugged in my earphones and found my running playlist. I walked into the living room and to the door. "Please be careful, angel?" Triston's voice was strained from the kitchen, I knew he was stressed, but at that moment, I didn't care. He could visit his ex, but I didn't want anything to do with it.

"Fine!" I slammed the apartment door and stepped into the waiting elevator. As the doors slid closed, I saw him open the apartment door and watch me leave.

Out on the street, I turned left and ran. My regular route around Central Park was quiet this morning. I decided on a second lap when instinctively I ran out the entrance on the opposite side. I found myself outside the familiar building without thinking about it. The doorman gave me a small smile and nodded. I greeted him and walked toward the elevators, pressing the call button. I didn't know what I was doing here, but I didn't want to go home.

I stepped into the elevator and realized I must be a sweaty mess, but I didn't care one bit. Pressing the sixth-floor button, I waited. As soon as the doors opened, I second guessed myself.

Did I really want to be here? Was this a good idea? I stepped into the hallway and made my way to apartment 6277. I knocked and waited anxiously.

When the door swung open, I was met by a surprised pair of hazel-brown eyes. "Emily!" He stepped aside, allowing me access. I pulled the earphones from my ears and pressed pause on my phone. My phone beeped a few times with messages and missed calls from Triston, which I ignored. I turned to look at Bash. His face filled with concern, but he didn't ask. "Sorry . . . I shouldn't—"

"It's okay. Come in. I was making coffee. Do you want some?" I nodded. We walked into the kitchen, and I slid onto one of the barstools at the counter. "Are you okay? What are you doing here? Not that I mind you being here, of course!" He smiled.

"I just needed some space. To think, you know?" He nodded and busied himself with the coffee machine. It looked like a fancy one as well. The smell of coffee soon filled the room, the aroma assaulting my senses. "Nice machine!"

"Yeah, it's new. I'm testing it out for the events we're setting up. I need to know how it handles everyday use so I can start selling them as well." He turned with a steaming mug of my favorite coffee.

"Thanks." I inhaled the aroma and felt a bit calmer. I opened my eyes, and his intense gaze was on me. "I'm really gross right now. I ran through the park." I smiled, exhaustion hit me after the drama last night and this morning.

"I wondered what the smell was!" He laughed as I stuck my tongue out at him again. He was too far to reach so that I couldn't swat him. "Joking, darling! You still look beautiful, even all sweaty." His appreciative gaze fell over my sports bra and stopped. I looked down and realized he was looking at the logo. It was similar to the symbol on his bike helmet, the lightning strike. I wondered what the connection was. "Nice brand."

"Yeah, I didn't realize they did bike accessories as well," I commented.

"They don't. It's a sticker. I was sponsored by them when I did a photography show in LA a few years back. They used the symbol as their logo for that range. It's actually my autograph." His face broke out into a large grin. "So, essentially, you're wearing me on your . . .

Uh . . ." he gestured toward my chest, and I felt myself flush.

"Nice coffee." I looked down at the mug, trying to keep from smiling, needing to change the subject.

"Yeah, it's good. Emily, I would love it if you would sit for me?"

"What? I am sitting." I frowned, and he laughed.

"I mean, I would love to paint you. If you don't mind?"

"It seems you have no trouble remembering what I look like." I gestured toward the studio, remembering the sketch of me. My body, naked on the paper, his pencil strokes capturing the intensity of the moment. He nodded and turned away, putting the mug in the sink. "It's okay, stupid idea. I just wanted to see you in blues and greens." I got up. Walking around the counter, I reached past him, placing my mug next to his. He didn't move. The proximity of our bodies heated my skin. My hand brushed against his as I pulled away, and he turned to face me — his body flush with mine. My breath hitched as his scent invaded my senses. His knuckles stroked my cheek. It was such a soft gesture that it caused a shiver to radiate through my body. He lifted my chin with his finger until our eyes locked.

"Emily, what are you doing here?" His question was heated, filled with need and desire, his face so close to mine I could see the tiny green specks in his beautiful hazel eyes.

"I don't know," I answered honestly. I really didn't know what I was doing there. I loved Triston. He was the one. Wasn't he? I pulled away and went to sit back down, the counter keeping us apart. It wasn't the only thing keeping us apart, and I knew he was thinking the same thing.

We stayed silent for a few moments. I wasn't sure what to say to him. "Maybe I should go." I stood up and looked at him expectantly. What did I want? Did I want him to stop me? Did I want him to tell me he wanted me? There was a lot I wasn't sure about right then.

"You seem to love doing that." He looked at me.

"Doing what?"

"Leaving." The air was thick, filled with anticipation. For what? I didn't know. If I weren't dating his brother, I would probably walk around the counter and—

Stopping myself midway through that thought, I smiled. "It's the easiest thing to do. I mean, I can't even be in the same room as you, Bash."

"You mean you can't be in the same room with me without letting me grab you, pin you against that wall, and devour you?" His voice laced with desire, and my own flowed through me. I willed it to stop, but it seemed to have a mind of its own. I didn't answer him, and he continued. "You mean that every time I touch you, your body responds to me? It aches to be taken. Your body wants me to fill you like I did that first night. To feel my lips on your hard nipples, teasing them, biting them? To kiss my way down that beautifully sweaty body and make you scream my name?" He gripped the sink, and I could see the strain in his hands. I was sure he would pull the sink apart with that vice grip he had on it. "Is that what you mean, Emily?"

I opened my mouth and closed it again. I certainly didn't trust myself answering him. He smiled, knowing he had me. I nodded in answer to his words. Of course, he knew he was right because he felt it too. We did have a connection. There was no denying it. I just wasn't going to hurt his brother. I needed to get out of his apartment. This was a mistake. "I think it is best that I go." Bash finally released the grip on the sink and walked toward me, nodding.

My mind disagreed with my decision, my body too. I took a deep breath and picked up my phone. We walked to the door, but as he reached past me to unlock it, I felt the heat of his arm near me. I turned to say goodbye, and suddenly I wasn't standing anymore. I was pinned against the door with Bash's hands holding me up. I wrapped my legs around his waist. "Emily, I am going to kiss you now, just one kiss. That will be it, and never again." I nodded. There was no way I was going to refuse him, not right now. His mouth crashed onto mine in a bruising kiss. His tongue teased my lips apart, and I gave him access. My fingers knotted in his spikey hair, tugging it. A growl vibrated in his chest against me, and my nipples hardened in the soft material. His erection pushed against my tight running shorts, rubbing against my entrance. When he finally pulled away, he let me down. We both stood breathless, his eyes like melted caramel, desire evident in them. "I need to go."

I walked around the park for an hour. Then ran another two circuits around the park. Nothing could douse the fire Bash had lit just two hours earlier. By the time I stood in the elevator taking me up to Triston's apartment, my legs felt like jelly. I looked at the time and realized I had been gone for almost four hours. Bash left me breathless, and I left him hard. Nothing more happened. I decided to bite the bullet. I was going to tell Triston what happened. If he broke up with me, it would be because of my own stupidity and my stupid reaction to his brother. I didn't deserve Triston or his love, so I was ready to come clean. I steeled myself as the elevator doors opened. I walked into the quiet apartment and made my way to the kitchen. Turning on the kettle, I noticed two mugs in the sink. I picked up the white one and saw the bright red lipstick stain. Strange since I didn't wear lipstick, and I definitely didn't have any on this morning when I had my coffee.

I walked into the bedroom and grabbed my

overnight bag. I didn't feel like staying here, and I didn't want to know whose lipstick was on that mug. I threw some clothes in the bag and a change of underwear. I walked into the bathroom to grab my toothbrush when I noticed a pink bikini laying on the floor inside the shower. I didn't own a pink bikini, and I felt nauseated. The room started spinning. Who was here? Did Triston bring someone back here? This didn't make any sense. Yes, we fought, but why bring someone here?

He knew I was coming home. Couldn't he tidy up after his fun? I felt the fury raging in my veins. I knew I fucked up, but at least I didn't throw it in his face! Grabbing my toiletries from the bathroom, I made my way into the office and grabbed my laptop. Putting my bags on the sofa, I went into the bedroom, grabbed Bash's T-shirt, and pulled it on over my sports bra. I walked back into the living room, grabbing my bags, just as my phone beeped — a message from Triston. I unlocked my screen and opened it.

Triston: Call me when you're on your way home.

T xo

I hit reply.

Em: No need. I found everything already. You should have cleaned up after yourself.

I walked out of the apartment and stepped into the elevator. My phone started ringing. "What Triston?"

"It's not what you think, Emily. Let me explain?"

"Don't bother. I hope she was worth it. Don't follow me!"

I hung up, something he hated, but I didn't care. My blood was boiling, and my body was shaking with anger. After all the shit we had been through, I guess it was too much for him. Of course, too good to be true.

I walked through the park for the hundredth time that day. When I got to the apartment building that I had left only a few hours earlier, the doorman smiled. I made my way to the elevators, wondering if this was a good idea. On the sixth floor, I knocked on the apartment door. When it swung open, I saw those molten hazel eyes, fell into his strong arms, and burst into tears. "Emily!" He pulled me inside the apartment and shut the door. "Come in, sit down." We walked into the living room and sat on the sofa. He held me as I cried, stroking my hair.

When my tears finally dried, I sat back. Bash's tear-stained T-shirt looked terrible, and I giggled. "You think it's funny?" He looked down and smiled. I nodded. "What happened, Emily?"

"I . . ." Shaking my head, I tried to get the image out of my mind. The thought of Triston with her was ripping into me. It felt like an open wound. "He . . . Uhm . . ." Bash's face was so concerned. "I got home . . ." Shutting my eyes, I hope the pain would stop. "There was a girl there.

"Well, not there, but, her . . . A bikini in the shower." I finally got the words out.

"What the fuck?" I looked up, and his eyes were filled with anger. "Are you sure he was . . . you know?" I shrugged. What else could it mean? Some woman was in the apartment; there was a bikini in the shower. "It doesn't make sense, darling. He wouldn't cheat on you." I knew Bash was trying to calm me down, but the little he could say now would make a difference.

I looked into his eyes. "Just hold me?" He nodded and pulled me into his embrace.

Chapter Seventeen

I rolled over and felt a soft cushion next to me. The smell of fresh sheets and Bash disoriented me for a moment. I opened my eyes and saw the blinds on the window, and the realization hit me. I was in Bash's bed! I pulled the covers up. I still had my clothes on. We didn't have sex. Of course not! My memory was slowly returning — I cried on his shoulder till about two a.m. We drank beer and listened to music. He played my favorite band, and he played "Witness". I cried some more, and he wiped away my tears.

Bash was a gentleman, allowing me his bed, and he took the sofa. "Good morning, sleepy." Bash walked in carrying a tray with coffee, fresh orange juice, and two painkillers. "Drink those. I made pancakes. We can eat in the kitchen." He sat down on the bed and watched me. I scooted up and grabbed the orange juice and painkillers.

"Thank you for everything. I'm not sure I

would be able to survive this alone." Washing down the painkillers with the orange juice, I grabbed the coffee, inhaling the amazing, rich aroma.

"Em, your phone has been going crazy. Don't you want to talk to him? Maybe give him a chance to explain whatever it is?" I shook my head. I was adamant not to talk to him; I couldn't. "Okay, well he called me this morning. He knows you're here," he said in a soft voice.

"What?"

"Don't worry. He won't come here. He just wanted to make sure you're safe." He smiled.

"I don't care what he wants! He's fucking some girl in the apartment he wanted me to move into, Bash!" I climbed out of bed, careful not to spill my coffee. I walked around toward the door. "I want pancakes." I stormed off into the kitchen. I heard him chuckle behind me, and it made me smile. The smell of fresh pancakes assaulted my senses as I walked into the kitchen.

I sat down on the stool at the counter as Bash followed me. "Right, little lady! Breakfast is served!" He put a large plate of chocolate chip pancakes on the counter with some whipped cream and chocolate sauce to go with it.

"This is definitely not going to help my diet!" I smiled up at him.

"You have a wounded heart. It needs something sweet." He refilled my coffee.

"I have something sweet." The words were out of my mouth before I thought about it. My gaze fell on him. "I mean, you know . . ." I mumbled and blushed.

"No, Em, I don't know. Why don't you . . . enlighten me?" I saw the naughty smirk cross his rugged features.

"Look, Bash, I don't know what's going on between us. I care about you, and the only reason I came here was that I didn't want to be alone. I just don't know anyone else in the city besides Triston and Jessie." I ate the piece of pancake on my fork. "Oh my god, this is amazing!" He laughed, staring at me for a few minutes, and his smile disappeared. He put on his serious expression, and my heart leaped into my throat.

"Look Em, I'm not going to lie. I'm glad you're here. And if all we can be is friends, I can handle that. Don't feel bad for needing someone to talk to. I will always be here for you, and if you don't want more than friendship, I'm not going to push." I nodded. We ate in comfortable silence until the phone rang. Bash walked over to the wall and grabbed it on the fourth ring.

"Hello?" He listened to whoever it was, and I had a feeling I knew. He turned to face me. "She's okay. I told you earlier." He listened again. "Hold on . . .

"He wants to talk to you." I thought about it for a moment. Getting up, I walked over, taking the phone from Bash.

"Triston?"

"Angel, please let me explain? Please come home?" I heard the plea in his voice.

"What happened? Why was there a bikini on the floor in the shower?" He hesitated, and I had my answer. "Seriously Triston?"

"Babe, she came on to me. She kissed me. I was angry with you. Can we please talk face to face?"

"No, I don't want to see your face right now! Why don't you ask her to move in with you?" I was radiating anger.

"Angel, I love you, only you!"

"I don't know if I love you right now!" There was silence on the other end of the line, and I thought he hung up when I heard him release a breath.

"You want to do this on the phone? Fine! It was a spur of the moment thing. I made a mistake. I was angry with you! After you left the apartment, I had you followed. I knew you were with my brother." He was quiet for a few seconds before continuing. "I saw Krista; she was being released from the hospital. I invited her back to *our* place thinking you would be back. When I saw you were not, I felt a rage I had never felt before. I thought you were at his place fucking him!"

"So you decided to get back at me? You decided to fuck her in *your* apartment?" I was screaming. I felt Bash's hand on my shoulder and his warmth calming me down. Tears streamed down my face, and I felt my heart tighten in my chest.

"Our apartment!" he retorted. "You were with my brother, Emily!"

"I didn't fuck him, for god's sake!" I slammed the phone against the wall. Bash pulled me into his arms, holding me against his chest.

"Em, I'm sorry," he whispered. I knew he was unsure what to do. Turning me around, he wiped the tears from my face. My eyes burned, and I blinked hard. I grabbed his face and pulled him to me, kissing him hard. His tongue invaded my mouth, and I welcomed it. I wanted to dull the pain my heart was feeling. Bash pulled away slowly. "Let's not do this, Em. Not like this."

"I want to, please? Just make the pain go away?" I pleaded with him. My eyes were melting into those beautiful hazel ones as he lifted me in his strong arms and carried me to his bedroom. Laying me down, he leaned over me, his weight resting on his elbows. "Emily, I don't want to do this because you're angry with my brother. I want to do this because we are together." He leaned down and kissed my cheek. Pulling himself back up, he stood and watched me.

"Bash," I whispered. Sitting up, I pulled the T-shirt over my head. I laid back down wearing only a pair of running shorts. His eyes blazed. "God, Emily, you are a fucking temptress!" I scooted up in the bed and watched him pull his T-shirt off. He was wearing his ripped painter jeans. He slowly undid the button, and they dropped to his feet. He was wearing tight black, CK briefs. He reminded me of an underwear model, toned, tanned, and filling out the briefs with a large package. I giggled at the thought in my head. Drinking in the sight of that V-line pointing into the black briefs, my mind wasn't my own anymore.

"You know, when I'm standing in front of a girl in my underwear and she giggles, I feel very self-conscious," he said faking the hurt on his face.

"Shh. You know that's not why I was giggling!"

He leaned down, hovering over me again. "You're so beautiful." I raised my hips, rubbing myself against his growing hardness.

"And you're . . . handsome!" He leaned down and kissed me again, this time they were soft and tender. My tears began to flow again, but as I closed my eyes, I saw an icy-blue stare. My heart hurt so much it felt like I couldn't breathe. Just as his lips found my neck, there was a knock at the door.

"Fuck it!" He stood up pulling on his jeans and a T-shirt. I grabbed my T-shirt and pulled it over my head. He waited till I was decent then turned to the door. I knew who it was, and when I heard his voice, my body went cold. I wiped the tears from my face and listened.

"Where is she, brother?"

"In my bed." Bash's voice was cold, harsh, and then I heard something crash. *Shit!* I ran into the living room and saw Triston had punched Bash. "Jesus, Triston! What the fuck is wrong with you?" I ran to Bash. His nose was pouring blood down his T-shirt.

"It's okay, Em." Bash stared at his brother. Ignoring Triston, I walked into the kitchen and grabbed an ice pack from the freezer. Bash smiled and sat down, holding the ice pack to his nose.

"We're going! Now!" Triston looked at me, his gaze sending a shiver down my spine. He was infuriated, but I didn't care. He chose this, not me.

"No! I told you to leave me alone!" My voice was raised. How dare he come here and punch Bash for looking after me.

"And I told you, we are going! Nobody walks away from me. So get your stuff, and let's go!" Bash stood up, his hand on my back. "Why don't you talk here? I will go to the other room." His eyes met mine, and I nodded slowly. He winked and left Triston and me in the living room.

"Triston, look, I really can't do this." I looked at him, and the anger in him seemed to evaporate. He was so calm it was almost unnerving.

"Emily, I love you, do you understand that? I love you!" His eyes were filled with love. I saw it there every time he looked at me. I decided to come clean. I needed him to realize what I had done.

"I kissed him, Triston. I kissed Bash. A few times. Before you knocked on that door, I was ready to sleep with him. Is that what you want to hear?" I watched the look on his face, waiting for the anger to kick in, but it didn't. He just stood there quietly. He was deflated, and I knew he was as hurt as I was.

"If that's what you want, then I can't stop you from living your life. I want you to understand something. Krista and I was a mistake. As soon as it was done, I regretted it. I don't even know why I did it! Well, I do. I did it because I was angry with you. You never slept with him while we were together, did you?"

I shook my head, and he looked at me, his eyes locked with mine. "I regret doing it, but it's done. I can't undo it. If I could, I would." He grabbed my face and kissed each cheek. "I never want to make you cry again. I love you, only you, forever. Do you understand me?"

I nodded. There were things I wish I could

undo as well. "We need time, Triston. I need time. Can you give that to me?"

He nodded solemnly. I could tell he was wholly resigned to me walking away. I didn't want to lose him; I just needed time to think. "Sure, if that's what you need. We can take a few days, completely separate. Four days of single life doing what you need to. Be with him, spend time with him if you think it will help. You decide who you want, and if it's me, I will never, ever hurt you like this again. I swear on my life. When you are ready, you know where to find me." His body was visibly shaking, and I knew the pain that racked through me did the same to him. He kissed my forehead and left. I stood staring at the door for a while. I needed to go back to my apartment later. I needed time to think.

When Bash walked back into the living room, I turned to face him. "Is it safe to come out?" I nodded, giving him a small smile. He walked through with the melted ice pack. The bleeding had stopped, but his T-shirt was ruined.

"He gave me four days, Bash."

"What do you mean?" Bash sat down, watching me closely. I wasn't sure if he was scared I was about to fall apart or if I was about to smash everything within sight.

"He gave me four days. I need to decide who I want. You or him." I looked over at him, and I saw his smile.

"Well, that's easy!"

"Bash—" I admonished him.

"I know. I know . . . I didn't mean it like that. I just wanted to make you smile." I did.

"I can't believe he punched you!" I looked at his face, and he shrugged.

"I did deserve it. I told him you were in my bed. I would have punched him if it was the other way around."

"So, I guess I'm kind of single right now. Weird feeling. What do I do now?" I sat down next to him on the sofa. He put his hand on my knee circling his fingers slowly. "I have a few suggestions." He winked. I rolled my eyes and stared at him. "Emily, you do realize rolling your eyes is rude?" I nodded. "Do you know what happens to rude girls?" I smirked and nodded again. He pulled me to my feet.

"Wait!" I stopped halfway to the bedroom. "I know what we can do!" He frowned. "I can sit for you!" He gave me a megawatt smile.

"Yes! Do you want to stay the night? We can get take-out and just relax with a large canvas and some oils." He looked so excited, but I wanted to go home tonight. I needed time on my own. Time to think things through, and I couldn't do that with Bash.

"I wanted to go home, spend some time on my own. I need to think this through, Bash. I don't want to hurt you and give you hope of something, and then leave. You know?"

He pulled me into him, his body flushed with mine, and I felt his response so clear between us. "I told you earlier, Em, I understand. Even if I were given twenty-four hours with you, I would be happy. Now, can you stop being so sad and smile? We don't have to spend the night together. I will take you home and pick you up tomorrow. I know this isn't an easy decision, so take your time." I looked into his warm gaze and smiled. "That's the smile I want! Now, are you going to finish your pancakes?"

I smiled and nodded.

"Bash! Can we take a break? It hurts!" I whined for the third time. He stood up and looked over at me, shaking his head incredulously, making me giggle. It was late Sunday afternoon, and I was starving.

"Okay, let's get lunch?" He walked over to me and handed me a robe. I was sitting in the same position for three hours, and I felt stiff. I needed to stretch and get some fresh air. The smell of turpentine was making me feel woozy. I tied the robe around me and smiled. "Can I see what it looks like?" He shook his head, spinning me around, pointing me in the direction of the spiral staircase.

"So unfair!" I complained, and he chuckled. "What are we doing for lunch?" I slid onto the stool, which seemed to become my second home. Picking up my phone, I unlocked it — a message from Triston.

Triston: I hope you have an amazing few days. I respect your decision, whatever it may be, as long as you are happy. Talk soon angel. T xo

My chest tightened, and I closed my eyes,

remembering our trip in LA. We were set to fly to London next week on Sunday. I had a week and I needed to decide before then. I needed to choose between two amazing men. My heart was torn. It felt like I was being ripped in two. How did I fall in love with two brothers?

"Emily!" Bash pulled me out of my reverie.

"Sorry, shit . . . I was miles away. What did you say?"

Narrowing his eyes at me, he asked, "Was that him?" I nodded. "You love him, Emily. I can see it. You two need to work it out." His words felt like swords slicing into me. I closed my eyes and took a deep breath.

"I am in love with him, yes, but . . ." I stopped. I knew as soon as I said it I could never unsay it. I couldn't hide it anymore though. It was so obvious.

"But what, Em?" He turned to face me now, and I knew I had to give him an answer. I needed to at least be honest with him. He had always given me that.

"I am in love with you too." My voice was barely audible or recognizable. I felt nausea kick in, and I didn't know what to do. I needed time away from them both.

"Emily." He came around to me and pulled me into his arms. "I love you, darling. I do, but I don't want you to have to choose like this. I want you so much, you have no idea, but you need to think this through on your own. I am going to take you home. Go and get dressed."

I sat on my sofa for the first time in weeks. It was only five p.m. Bash said he would pick me up at seven for dinner. He was truly amazing. My mobile started ringing, it was Jessie.

"Hey, Jess!"

"Emily! What the actual fudge is going on? The man is on the warpath. I have so much work to get through this coming week!" I closed my eyes. This was my fault. No! It was his fault too!

"He slept with Krista. I kissed Bash. A couple times. So, Triston and I are on a break for a few days." Everything sounded so foreign when I said it out loud. How had it come to this? How was I sitting on my sofa alone when I had two incredible men vying for my attention?

"What?" she screamed into the phone. Then lowering her voice, she said, "Shit, now he's

looking at me. I guess he knows I'm on the phone with you. Wait, you kissed the hot brother? Spill the deets. Was it good?"

"Jessie! Well, yeah, it was!" I giggled for the first time in days. "He's amazing, Jess. He hasn't taken advantage of the fact that I am in turmoil. He even brought me home to think things through."

"Wow! Gentleman! So, what are you going to do?"

"Honestly? I have no idea! Bash is taking me out tonight for dinner."

"Okay, think about it this way. Close your eyes and remember the time with both of them. Who makes you happy? Like, I mean, truly happy? Also, think about if you saw either one of them with another girl, dating, kissing, whatever. How would it feel? Which one can you not see with someone else? And lastly, if either of them went down on one knee today. Which would you say yes to? Enjoy the dinner tonight. See how you feel, and if you're going to bang him . . . I want the details! Tomorrow is Monday. We will go out for cocktails, and you can tell me all! I know it's a weekday, but after work tomorrow, I may need those cocktails to survive!" She giggled, and I shook my head. She seriously had a way with words.

"Wow, Jess, you should become a counselor or something." We both laughed at the thought. I decided that going out with her would give me some more time away from Bash and Triston. Just what I needed. "Yes, cocktails sound perfect!"

"No way, chick, I can't handle all that drama. I will pick you up at your place, say six? Also, if you choose our boss man, let me make the bro feel better. I have some amazing medicinal skills."

"Ugh, Jess, TMI. Seriously! See you tomorrow! And Jess?"

"Yeah?"

"Thanks! I don't have friends here, but you've been amazing!"

"Anytime, sweets. Anytime. Tomorrow we drink!" Her voice reached new highs, and I giggled. We hung up, and I sat back on my sofa. I had a lot to think about.

I spent the last couple of hours on the sofa, flicking through bad movies on cable, eating ice cream, and drank green tea. My eyes felt like they had gone back to normal. After all the crying, it looked like I had been punched. I opened my messages and hit reply. I was ready to message him.

Em: Thank you for your message earlier. I spent the day at my place, thinking. Talk soon

Bash was going to be at my place in about fifteen minutes. I decided to wear a pair of skinny black jeans and a black halter neck. The weather was terrific, and I wanted to enjoy the last few days of summer. My phone beeped.

Triston: I am glad you're thinking. I have been doing the same. SO much I want to tell you. I hope we do talk soon. T xo

I smiled. Hitting reply, I decided this would be my last message tonight.

Em: Maybe we can meet on Friday night? I will work from home this week. Email me if needed.

The buzzer went, and I took one last look in the mirror. I was as ready as I would ever be. I opened the door and saw Bash with shopping bags. "What is all this?"

"Dinner, babe. I decided I'm cooking dinner for you." I laughed as he entered my apartment and made his way to the kitchen. He started unpacking the groceries, and I saw he had bought a bottle of my favorite champagne as well. I closed the door, and the buzzer went again. "Do you have more coming?" I asked. Bash shook his head and shrugged.

I opened the door and saw a dozen red roses. Triston really didn't play fair. "Delivery for a Miss Reid?" The poor delivery guy was hidden behind the bouquet. I said that was me and signed the tablet he held out to me. "Thank you!" I grabbed the flowers from him and closed the apartment door.

"Wow! He's going all out, isn't he?" Bash said when he saw the flowers. Placing them on the kitchen table, I grabbed the vase from the living room table.

"It seems that way." I filled the container with water. Grabbing the scissors from the kitchen drawer, I went to the table. Cutting the ribbon, I arranged the roses in the glass vase and placed it back on the table. "They're beautiful, Em."

"Yeah, they are." I pulled the card out of the tiny envelope.

I know I was an ass. A stupid ass. Forgive me?

Remember, sometimes you end up stronger at the broken places.

I don't want to be at my broken place anymore.

I want you.

T xo

I stared at the card, my fingers shaking. "Em, you okay, darling?" I looked up and realized there were tears in my eyes. I am broken and completely shattered. Bash walked up to me then and held me as I cried. Big, nasty tears flowed from my eyes, and I felt myself break. I loved Triston, so much. I needed to find it in my heart and mind to forgive him. I pulled away and noticed Bash's T-shirt was soaked. I giggled and looked up at him. "Are you okay?" I nodded. I needed that. I needed him to hold me, to hold all my broken pieces together just for a moment.

"I want to finish the painting, Bash." I looked up at him through my eyelashes.

"Em, we don't—"

"I want to. I need this. I need you, even if it's just for this short time." He nodded. He understood exactly what I was saying without saying the actual words.

Bash carried on cooking, and I picked up my phone. I hit reply on Triston's message.

Em: Friday. The Penthouse. 10 AM*

Turning my phone off, I headed back to the kitchen.

"Emily, turn your head more to the left. Yes, that's it, now don't move!"

I had to suppress a giggle. I didn't know how models did this. I couldn't sit still for five minutes, never mind the hours needed for one of those portraits you see in museums.

"Okay, we can take a break. I reckon another two days before it's perfect." I inwardly groaned.

"This better be good, Mr. Hart!" My heart ached when the words left my mouth. "Bash, I mean . . ." He smiled.

"It's okay, Em. Coffee?" I smiled and nodded as I tied the silk belt of the robe around me. I was so glad Bash could do this painting with me in a bikini. I don't think we would have gotten through it if I was naked.

I walked into the living room as Bash busied

himself in the kitchen. "I'm just going to the bathroom!" I called to him. I walked down the hallway, passing his bedroom. I noticed the door opposite the bathroom yesterday. I wondered what was in here. I grabbed the handle and opened the door. It was a study. I could see a large dark wood desk and his computer. I walked in and found one of the walls filled with books. I scanned them slowly. There were some amazing titles, classics that I loved. "This isn't the bathroom." His voice was soft and amused.

"Really? I didn't notice!" I rolled my eyes.

"Emily . . ." His voice was a warning. I felt the heat travel over my body.

"Yes, Bash?" I walked up to him till my body was flush with his. I closed my eyes and inhaled the spicy, warm scent of him. It assaulted my senses, and every nerve in my body was on high alert. I felt my nipples harden against my bikini top.

"Ask me to stop . . ." His voice was a low growl. My eyes locked on his, and I shook my head. He grabbed me roughly, and his mouth crashed onto mine. I reached up and tangled my fingers in his short, spikey hair, pulling him closer to me, deepening the kiss. His tongue danced with mine, and I felt the heat pool in my stomach, my bikini bottoms wet with need. "We don't—" he spoke into the kiss. I pulled away slowly. His eyes searched mine for an answer, and I smiled.

His gaze seared into me. "Finish this." My voice was ragged with lust. He gripped my ass and lifted me up, carrying me toward the bookshelf, pinning me against it.

"Hold on to the shelves." His mouth was on my neck, kissing me, licking his way behind my ear. I wrapped my legs around his waist, pulling him tighter against me. I could feel the button of his jeans rubbing me. I was so high I felt like I was flying. I leaned my head back and closed my eyes. This is what I asked him for. I wanted this. I needed to get my fill of him, get him out of my system, and I didn't know any other way to do it.

I heard his zipper, and I knew I had only a few seconds to stop this. I pictured Triston fucking Krista in the shower, and I made my choice. I felt him inside me instantly, and I bit down on his shoulder hard as my body shook with release.

He slid into me, filling me, stretching me. I moaned onto his hot, tanned skin, watching his muscles flex as he held me up. "Bash," I moaned as he started moving faster, deeper, filling me. "Emily, you are so beautiful." His voice strangled as he held onto his sanity. I gripped his tense shoulders, my nails digging into him. I felt myself close to another earth-shattering orgasm as he plunged into me. My body clenched around him, and I felt my release take over.

"Emily." His voice was a deep growl as he filled me.

Chapter Eighteen

The day had felt torturous, and I hadn't been able to concentrate on anything. I worked from home, and I didn't need to talk to Triston for anything today, which was good. I had enough time to dwell on the last few days. Tomorrow, I was spending the night with Bash. We needed to finish the painting. I couldn't wait to see the final product. Slipping on my T-shirt and sweats, I walked into the kitchen and got the blender out. Jessie and I decided on homemade cocktails. They were usually more lethal. I was looking forward to having a night with her. I thought about what happened this afternoon with Bash, and I shivered. Him, pinning me against the bookshelf, filling me. I shook my head; I needed to stop thinking about it. We still had to finish the painting.

There was a buzz on the intercom, and I pressed the button to open it, unlocking the door as Jessie reached the top of the staircase. "Oh my god, I missed you!" Her voice echoed in the empty foyer. We hugged, and I smiled. She was so amazing; I was glad to have someone to call a friend that didn't have the last name Hart. "Come in. Did you bring the whole liquor store?" I giggled at the number of bottles in her shopping bag.

"Well, you did say you wanted to get drunk!" She set the bag on the counter and unpacked. I noticed vodka and white wine with cranberry, strawberry, and orange juices. There was also a bottle of some sort of sours; it looked like the peach flavor.

"Uh, well, wine and vodka? And shots?" I picked up a bottle and unscrewed the cap. Giving it a sniff, I coughed. "What the hell, Jess?" I giggled at the look on her face. She really was adamant on getting drunk. "How was work?" I looked at her, and she knew I was asking how Triston was.

"He's . . . I don't know, darling; he's really broken up about this. I can tell." She looked at me seriously, and my heart ached. I wish it weren't like this, but we both made stupid mistakes. We needed time apart.

"I know. So am I. He just . . . It's just so fucking complicated, Jess." I gave her a small smile. "I mean, Bash is . . ." I didn't even know how to describe him. He was perfect in his rugged way, and I didn't know how I was going to say goodbye to him.

Then, on the other hand, I wasn't sure how I would say goodbye to Triston.

"Darling, I know it's difficult, but like I said. Drinks!" She started opening drawers. Grabbing the corkscrew, she started opening the wine. "Glasses?" I nodded, getting two wine glasses out of the cabinet. I placed them on the counter and watched the light-yellow liquid fill the glasses. "Now! A toast. To men!" She giggled, and her good mood made me feel better. This liquid was good. We drank to men and giggled.

We sat down after making the first round of cocktails. We raided my liquor cabinet and found some other mixers. I turned on the sound system. "I still can't believe everything that's going on. I mean, it just feels surreal, you know?"

"I know, babe. I am so sorry you're going through this. To be honest, I can't believe the boss man did that!"

"Well, I mean, I slept with Bash." I looked at

her.

"Yes, you did, but only *after* he went and banged his ex!" We drank to that. "Okay, so let's do this!" Jessie got up, grabbing a notepad and a pen from her bag. I noticed our company logo on the notebook and chuckled.

"You stole stationery from the office?"

"It's not stealing. It's borrowing! I doubt Mr. Grumpy Pants is going to notice since his girlfriend is gone! Ugh! Shit, sorry babe! You know my head and my mouth don't work well together!" I shook my head. It was true. I was gone, out shagging his brother.

"It's okay. I am gone. It's just weird thinking about it." I knew I had to decide, but in my state of mind, I wasn't deciding on anything except what I wanted to drink next. I got up and went into the kitchen, grabbing the jug of cocktail Jessie mixed, filling my glass.

"Oh my god. Okay, come on, we have to make a list of pros and cons!"

I woke up early Tuesday morning with a massive hangover. My head was pounding, and

I didn't think I deserved to live. I wasn't sure how Jessie was feeling being in the office, but I was definitely not feeling good. I rolled over and hugged the pillow. I closed my eyes trying to ease the pain.

BANG-BANG-BANG!

Who the hell was at my door?

I rolled over and pulled on a T-shirt. Padding to my apartment door, I pulled it open and gazed into the intense steel-blue eyes I missed so much. My heart lurched, and I felt sick. Leaving Triston standing at my door, I ran to the bathroom and proceeded to puke my insides out. I felt like death. Hugging the porcelain god, I wiped my mouth and dropped the tissues in the bowl then stood on shaky legs. Flushing the toilet, I grabbed the mouthwash. Looking at my appearance, I was far from the beautiful girl Triston was in love with.

Making my way back into the living room, I found Triston on my sofa. "There she is!" I looked at him with a pained expression. "Jessie looks as bad as you do. I brought you breakfast. If you promise not to puke on me." He chuckled, and my body ached to be held. I wanted his arms around me.

"What are you doing here?" I grabbed the painkillers he left for me and downed them with water. Orange juice and I were never going to be friends again.

"I came to see you at your worst. You know they say, if you love someone at their worst, you can love them at their best." His voice was low, sending delicious shivers down my spine.

"Triston—"

"I just wanted to make sure you're okay. I still love you, by the way." He sat forward, dropping the magazine on the table.

"I'm fine. I'm a big girl. We're supposed to be apart." My voice came out harsher than I expected, and I winced. "I mean, you shouldn't be here."

He nodded. "I know. I'm leaving now." He stood and walked to the door. "Soon, angel." Opening the door, he left.

"Bash, I cannot do this!" I giggled, hearing him groan. He had me twisted, and I had been sitting for at least two hours.

"Okay, darling, you can move. I think I only

need another day. I swear!" He held his hands up in resignation at my expression. "How about I take you out to thank you?"

"Thank me? For what?"

"For . . . being here." His voice gave away more than it should, and I smiled. It was Tuesday, and we were running out of time. My heart hurt. I wanted more time with Bash, but I knew it could never be more.

"Okay! Let me get changed." I grabbed my clothes.

"Emily." I turned and looked at his beautiful eyes. "I'm not stupid. I know you're going back to him. I just want the time I can get."

I nodded. My heart hurt for him and me. I loved him more than he knew, but I could never tell him. It was a secret I would have to carry to my grave.

"Bash—"

"Go and change, woman! I need to take you out!" His smile was handsome, but it didn't reach his eyes. I turned and walked into the bathroom. Locking the door behind me, I slid down, and the tears flowed. I couldn't do this anymore. I was hurting them both when it was the last thing I ever wanted to do.

"Emily!" I started at the sound of Bash's voice.

"Yes?" I stood up and realized I was still in the bathroom. What the hell?

"Are you okay? Open the door!"

I unlocked the door and pulled it open. "I . . . I don't know what happened."

He grabbed me and pulled me into his embrace. Bash's arms felt warm and safe. "I want you, Emily. I want to be inside you." His words stoked the fire inside me, and I knew I wasn't going to say no. He grabbed my hand and pulled me into the bedroom. He turned to me and held my face in his hands. Leaning down, he planted feather-light kisses on my lips. My mouth opened to him, allowing his tongue entry, and licking me in a movement that was slow and sensual. His hands came down to my neck and slowly slid the robe down over my shoulders. His hands were hot to the touch. He undid the string of my bikini top and dropped it next to me.

His lips were on my neck, shoulder, sending shivers over me. He sat on the edge of the bed pulling me forward, and I stood between his thighs. His lips on my hard nipples elicited a moan from me. His five o'clock shadow on my soft skin tingled. He undid the belt of the robe, and it fell, pooling at my feet. He kissed his way down my belly slowly. I ran my hands through his soft hair when I felt his mouth on the apex between my thighs. "Bash . . ."

His fingers hooked in the waistband of my bikini bottoms and tugged them down gently. This was so different from yesterday in the office. I stood naked in front of him, and he growled in appreciation. "You're perfect darling. So fucking perfect." His mouth was on my wet entrance, licking slowly, and I almost came undone. He stood up, his eyes locked on mine. "Lay down." I obeyed, not saying a word. I climbed onto the bed, lying back, watching him. His smile was devilish, he kneeled between my thighs, and my back arched. He stroked my slick folds and lapped at my wetness. He plunged two fingers inside me, and I came undone. He stood up and unbuttoned his jeans, letting them fall to the floor. His rock-hard erection stood proudly, and I wanted him. He climbed between my thighs and grabbed his hardness, stroking my now soaked sex. It was slow and deliberate, taking me higher. I lifted my hips, and a smile curved his lips. "Is someone in need of me?" I nodded shyly, a blush heating my cheeks. Supporting his weight on his left arm, he positioned himself at my entrance. As he slid into me, I moaned. He was taking his time, teasing himself inside me, inch by inch. "Slowly babe." His mouth was at my ear, sending torturing shivers over my body. Once he had bottomed out, buried to the hilt inside me, his hips rolled, hitting my sweet spot. I grabbed his neck, pulling his mouth to mine. His kiss was heated, and I could taste my arousal on his lips. Our tongues danced in unison, and I felt the knot in my stomach tightening.

"You feel so good, Emily," Bash growled in my ear. His thrusts hastened, and I knew he was close. I wrapped my legs around his waist, pulling him in deeper. I closed my eyes, and Triston's face stared back at me. And as I came undone, his face was the only thing I saw.

"Bash, this is beautiful!" We were standing at the top of the Chrysler Building. "But isn't this closed off to the public?" I turned to see a sparkle in his eyes.

"It is, but we're not public. My new investor,

Mr. Richards, has offices up here, so I have access." He wrapped his arm around me and held me close. His intoxicating scent washed over me and sent my senses into overdrive. The view was magnificent. "I have an idea." He walked over to the computer in the conference room we were standing in and started typing. The speakers around the room came to life, and I recognized the song. It made me smile, but deep down, it tugged at my heart. The song was called "One Last Night" by Vaults. "Dance with me?"

I slipped my hand in his as he pulled me close, with his one hand on my lower back. I closed my eyes and rested my head on his chest, taking him in.

"Bash." I looked up as the song came to an end. His caramel eyes burned into me. "Thank you, for giving me this."

"It's not me giving it to you, Emily. This is all you. You know how I feel about you, but I know you love him. I just wish we had met first."

I stepped away and closed my eyes. The tears that threatened to spill burned. "Maybe." He turned me around, and my eyes locked with his. "I love you, Bash, I do. So much. I just . . ." My voice trailed off, and I didn't know how to say it.

"Just?" His gaze was inquisitive.

"I just love him more." He nodded. It was evident how I felt about both brothers. I would never love anyone the way I loved Triston. It was an all-consuming love. The thought of never seeing him again pulled at my heart, and it winded me.

"Tomorrow we finish the painting." His voice laced with sadness.

"Well, we have till Thursday. So, I mean . . ." I found myself not wanting to let this end. I didn't want to lose him. He would still be a client, but that wasn't the same thing. "Unless you want to finish tomorrow?" Why did I feel like a love-sick teenager? Maybe because I was acting like one.

"No, I want as much time with you as possible. Will you stay over tomorrow night?" I nodded. He pulled me into his warm embrace as we swayed in the silence of the room.

Groaning at my phone alarm, I picked it up and shut it off. Bash had dropped me off at home just after midnight. Unlocking my phone, I found a message from Triston.

Triston: Friday, 10 am at the penthouse. I can't wait to see your beautiful face. T xo

I hit reply, staring at the blinking cursor, toying with my words.

Em: Are you flirting with me, Mr. Hart?

I got out of bed and padded to the kitchen. Coffee was needed. I had some work to finish, and then I had to get ready for my last day with Bash. The kettle boiled, and I took it through to my office just as my phone beeped.

Triston: Miss Reid, if flirting will get me your forgiveness then yes, I am*

He was distracting me now. I was going to forgive him, but I wanted to tell him face to face. We had the most amazing chemistry. He made me feel whole, like I was the only thing in his life that kept him going. I hit reply.

Em: Well, I suggest you should continue the flirting, Mr. Hart. Now I have work to do. My demanding boss is such a slave driver.

I giggled. I knew he would have something smart to say about that. A knot of anticipation tightened in my belly as I watched my phone.

Triston: It will continue until you're screaming my name... Oh wait, that's not flirting, is it? ;) This boss of yours sounds terrible.

I giggle at his reply. The butterflies were going wild in my stomach.

Em: No, Mr. Hart, that is most definitely not flirting. You better think about this carefully.

I opened my laptop and logged into the email system — only six new e-mails. Nothing I couldn't handle and have finished by midday. I was excited to see the painting as Bash was so talented I was sure it would be amazing.

My buzzer startled me from my book at midday. "Hello?"

"It's me." Bash's deep voice came through the intercom. I buzzed him up. Opening the door, I waited for him to reach the landing when my heart stopped. Dressed in his ripped painter jeans and a black tank top, I took in his appearance and flushed. "You look a little flushed gorgeous."

"I was just, um . . ." I stepped back and let him in. I couldn't tell him he had me blushing.

"I'm sure you were." He winked and flopped down on the sofa. "Are you ready to get dirty?" His smirk was devilish, and I could tell he was in a good mood.

"What?"

He chuckled at my shocked expression. "Painting, darling. Were you thinking about naughty things again?"

"No!" I giggled. His expression was disbelieving. He leaned back, crossing his hands behind his head and his tank rode up. His toned abs peeked out the top of his jeans, and I licked my lips.

"Would you like to join me?" I walked toward the sofa and straddled him, his strong thighs below me. "I like this position. We need to try this later." Grabbing my ass, he pulled me to him. His kiss was warm, his tongue licking my lips. I could feel his arousal between us. Rocking my hips, I rubbed against his jeans, causing a deep growl in his chest. "Or right now!" He tugged at the tank top I was wearing and pulled it up over my head. "Oh god, Emily." His voice was laced with desire when he saw I wasn't wearing a bra.

His mouth assaulted my hardened nipples.

I moved my hips back and forth over him. He was rock hard, the front of his jeans straining against the zipper. "Bash . . ." I moaned when his fingers found my heated sex. He pushed two fingers inside me. I rocked back and forth on his fingers.

"Come for me, gorgeous. Give me your pleasure this last time." His words brought tears to my eyes. I moved faster as his fingers brought me to the edge.

"Bash!" I cried out as he stroked my sweet spot, pushing me over. My orgasm ripping through me.

"That's it." Pulling his fingers from my sweatpants, he gripped my hips, holding me to him. His mouth crashed on mine as he devoured me. My heart felt physical pain as I kissed him.

"Don't cry, Emily. It's okay." I shook my head because I didn't trust my voice. How had I fucked this up so much? "It is. Don't be sad. Let's go paint!" I looked down at his erection still very much at attention, and I giggled. He looked at where my gaze had landed and smiled. "That you can take care of later." It felt like I was riding on an emotional rollercoaster, and I wanted to get off now.

"Let's go." I got up and grabbed my phone and keys. "I don't need anything, do I?" He shook his head as we went downstairs.

Chapter Nineteen

Bash unlocked his apartment, and I stepped inside. "Did you want a drink, darling?" I nodded. Walking to the kitchen, I slid onto the stool.

"Can I have a beer?" Bash turned. The look of amusement on his face made me giggle.

"Yes, sure." He walked to the refrigerator. "So, you ready for the last session?" I nodded. I wasn't ready. Far from it. Bash handed me the beer, and I drank it down. I want to find some dull for the ache.

"Can you put some music on?"

"Sure, darling. Are you going to get changed?" I nodded, downing the rest of my beer. I went into the bedroom, and I found the robe on his bed and smiled. This was it. I pulled off my tank top and tugged my sweats down. Pulling on the robe, I tied the belt around my waist and went back into the living room. Bash had taken his tank off and already had paint splattered on his chest. "Ready? I was getting another drink."

"Yup, I am ready; I will have another drink, please. Meet you up there." I took the spiral staircase slowly and dropped the robe on the table. Sitting on the stool, I got into position and waited. When I heard Bash's footsteps on the metal steps, my heart raced.

"Emily! My god!" His eyes roamed my naked body, and they burned with a fire I came to know so well.

"I thought you should finish it properly." I smiled, feeling a blush on my cheeks.

"Wow, darling. You didn't have to do this, you know?" I nodded. He handed me the beer, and I took a swig. Liquid courage, as they say.

"Can I see it when you're done?" His eyes met mine as he picked up the paintbrush. Mixing the green and blue, he smiled.

"You can."

"That's it!" Bash announced. My heart was racing. Grabbing the robe, I wrapped it around me and tied the belt. Walking around the canvas,

I gasped. It was one of the most amazing works of art I had ever seen. It was an abstract version of me, and it was beautifully romantic. The colors were vibrant and calming if that even made sense. The passion in the way the colors blended, the serenity of the strokes. Everything about it was magnificent. Tears threatened to spill. I had never seen anything more beautiful made for me, or about me.

"Bash . . ." My voice was a ragged whisper. My throat tightened from the emotion I felt. He really loved me. I could feel it scream at me through the canvas.

"You don't like it, do you?" He sounded tense.

"It's perfect!" I turned to face him. He was only an inch away from me. I looked up into his hazel eyes. "I love it like I love you." The words were hushed, but the emotion I felt saying it was raw.

"I love you too, my sweet girl." Grabbing the belt of the robe, he pulled me toward him. I wrapped my arms around his sweaty, paint-splattered torso and held on tight. The song that floated through the speakers felt like it was meant for us. The lyrics holding us in a moment that felt so perfect and imperfect all at once.

Bash and I stood swaying slowly till the song ended and the next one started. His hands felt warm on my back, slow strokes down my spine. I looked up at him, and his mouth crashed onto mine. Lifting my hands, I tangled them in his spikey hair, pulling him into me, taking him one last time. His tongue tangled with mine in an erotic dance. Untying the sash of the robe, his hands slid beneath, cupping my breasts in his strong hands. My nipples hardened to his touch. I arched my body into him, wanting to feel every part of him against me. My mind repeated my goodbye. He spun us around, pushing the papers onto the floor, lifting me onto the drawing table. Dropping the robe from my shoulders, he stepped back, taking me in again, almost as if he was committing my appearance to memory.

"This I want to savor." He kissed his way down my body with slow and sensual licks, nibbles, and his fingers followed the trail. My skin on fire. When he got to my slick sex, his tongue snaked its way inside me. I moaned, leaning back, closing my eyes. My heart was calm, and at that moment, as I came undone on his tongue, I knew what this was. It was the end.

He stood up, unbuttoning his jeans. My eyes

locked on his as he slowly entered me. The finality gripped me, and I knew I would be okay. I was going to be with Triston. As much as I loved Bash, I did love Triston more.

I watched the screen silently as the movie didn't make sense anymore. The painting was finished. Bash had dropped me at home about an hour ago. Tomorrow was Friday, the day I would tell Triston the truth, and if he still wanted me, then we would be together. I wrapped myself in a blanket on my sofa. Bash wanted to stay, but I couldn't let him. We said our goodbyes. Tears ran down my face. I knew I had fucked up, but it still hurt. More so than I wanted to admit to him or to Triston.

A knock on the door startled me. I wasn't in the mood for company. Who was at my door so late anyway? I got up and padded to the door. I knew I looked like a zombie, but I didn't care. I wiped my face with my blanket and turned the door handle. I looked up into ice-blue eyes.

"I couldn't wait till tomorrow." He took in my appearance, and I saw the concern etched on his face. "Shit! Angel, what happened to you?" I shook my head and turned, walking back to the sofa. Triston closed the door, dropped the bag he was carrying and joined me. "Emily?"

"I slept with him, Triston. We fucked. I wanted to. I let him." The words spilled out of my mouth. I didn't care anymore. I knew Triston would leave. It was only a matter of time. I didn't deserve him or Bash. The tears I held at bay every time I saw Triston spilled now. My vision blurred. I just sat there looking at him. I had nothing else to give him.

He flopped onto the sofa next to me and pulled me into him holding me tight against his chest. "Triston, I'm sorry." I cried. My heart broke into tiny pieces. Everything felt out of control. I couldn't breathe. It felt like someone had punched me, winded me.

"Emily." He pulled me up and grabbed my face in his hands. "Look at me!" I opened my eyes. His face was filled with every emotion I could think of. Anger, love, rage, lust, desire, and need. "I want you! I don't care what you did. I told you to do it. I told you we were apart!" His voice broke through the pain I was feeling and melded into me. This is what Triston was for me.

He was my healing ointment, and he made me better, healing me from the inside out.

"But—"

"Would you fucking obey me for once?" He didn't shout out of anger. His eyes were filled with desire. This was pure, unadulterated lust.

"Yes, sir." The words I uttered affected him, and suddenly I found myself on his lap, straddling him.

"Finally." He grabbed my tank top and ripped it open. Yes, ripped, shredded. I gasped. He had never done that before. He groped me lustfully, his mouth assaulted my hardening buds, and I moaned. My body yearned for the pleasure from the pain Triston was so good at giving. His teeth grazed my nipples, causing me to whimper. My fingers tangled in his long hair.

He looked up and smirked. "I need to punish my naughty girl for leaving me, don't I?" His voice dripped with lust and desire. I nodded quickly.

"Get up." His voice was urgent, and I could see his arousal evident in his tight jeans. He pulled me into the bedroom. He tugged my sweatpants down, leaving me in my thin black panties. "Lay down and close your eyes." I climbed onto the bed and laid back, my eyes closed. "Don't move."

I heard a bag rustling in the living room, and I remembered he had one when he arrived. The bed dipped, and I knew he was back. "Lift your head." I did, and I felt soft leather covering my eyes. He moved again and grabbed my wrists, tying them together above my head. "Emily, do you trust me?" I nodded. "Good. I will never hurt you, okay?"

I nodded again. I heard him undress — the zipper of his jeans and the sound of them dropping to the floor. I felt his hot breath on my skin, and I jumped. "Are you nervous?"

"Yes," I whispered.

"Do you love me?" I nodded. Suddenly, I felt the soft sting of leather. "I asked you a question?"

"Yes, Mr. Hart."

"Good. Tell me, Emily, were you going to leave me tomorrow?" I shook my head. The sting was harder this time, and I felt myself tingle. The heat between my legs intensified.

"No, Mr. Hart."

He grabbed my legs and turned me over onto my stomach. I felt the leather tips on my skin, teasing, torturing. Once, twice, and by the third time, I was moaning loudly. "Do you like that, Emily?"

"Yes, Mr. Hart." My voice was soft, waiting for the next one.

Third, fourth, fifth, sixth . . . My skin was on fire, and my sex was slick with desire for him. He dropped the flogger and tugged my panties, ripping them into pieces. I felt his fingers at my entrance, and my hips rose up to his hand. He leaned next to me and whispered, "I'm going to show you why you should never leave me again!" He hissed into my ear, sending delicious shivers over my electrified skin. Every nerve in my body was awakened by the man I loved.

He gripped my hips, lifting me onto my knees. He slammed into me hard. I was breathless for a second. I gripped the rope, feeling the knot in my stomach tighten. His vice-like grip on my hips felt like heaven. His soft, smooth fingers stroked my back, and I felt myself drip with desire. "You're going to give me all of you, from this moment. Do you hear me?" I nodded.

SLAP!

"Yes, Mr. Hart," I whimpered.

"I give you all of me, do you hear me, Emily?" I nodded.

SLAP!

"Yessss, Mr. Hart," I choked out in a daze. I was aching to come.

"Now give it to me! Come for me!"

SLAP!

I clenched around him, feeling my release shoot through me just as my body shuddered. I felt his release claim me, and I was his. He was mine.

"Would you hurry?" I shouted through the window at him.

"We need coffee; I'm not getting on that plane with you about to pass out on me!" Triston ran into the coffee shop, and I watched him. He looked so good in jeans, especially from behind. We had spent most of the weekend in bed, and I giggled at the thought. I flushed, remembering what we did. It was late Sunday evening, and we were on our way to the airport. I made the right choice; I kept telling myself that. I knew it was true. As much as I still loved Bash, I loved Triston more.

Triston slid back into the car, setting both

coffees in the cup holders. Putting the car into drive, he pulled out into traffic. I checked the time. We had about an hour to get to the airport. I leaned back, closing my eyes. I didn't get much sleep this weekend and was looking forward to sleeping on the plane.

"Drink your coffee!" His voice interrupting my snooze.

"Okay! Keep your freaking pants on!" I grabbed the takeaway cup and lifted the lid. It was too hot; he knew I hated drinking coffee too hot. I blew into the liquid. My mind was elsewhere since Bash texted me that morning wishing me a safe flight. I didn't reply, and I didn't tell Triston. I just wanted to move on, and I hoped Bash realized that.

"That's not what you said these past few days." Triston's hand rested on my knee, his soft hands that I craved all over my body. "Are you okay, angel?"

"Yeah, just tired." I leaned back and took a sip of the cooling coffee.

"You can sleep on the flight; we have no stop-overs. It's about ten hours, and then we'll be in London." I nodded. "You seem distracted. Are you sure this is what you want?" His question caught me off guard.

"What do you mean?"

"Us. Me?" He was so unsure of himself.

"Of course I want you! Why would you say that?" I turned to look at him. His ice-blue eyes burned into me. I knew he could tell I was feeling sad, but he didn't know the real reason.

"I just want you to be happy, and I hope I can do that." He gave me a small smile.

"Triston, we have had this conversation. I love you! I want you! You make me happy. Don't you know this already? I was torn for a while, but I am yours. Only yours. You make me who I am. You heal me. You make me feel like I'm worth the love you give me." I held his warm hand. It was so soft, smooth to the touch. Like the rest of his beautiful body. He smiled and drove on, turning on the iPod. I watched the city pass by as we made our way to the airport.

"Okay." I giggled. After my outburst, all he could say is okay.

He pulled into the JFK parking lot and found a space close to the departures entrance. "Triston?"

"Yes, angel?" He cut the engine and turned to me.

"What do you want?" I knew he wanted me, but somewhere deep down the whole debacle with Krista, it still scared me.

"There are four things I want." He was so serious; I didn't like that face.

I frowned. "And what would they be?"

He stared at me, his eyes searching mine. A smirk formed on his lips. "To love you." He kissed my cheek. "Touch you." Slowly, he rubbed my thigh with his warm hand. "Taste you." He licked the shell of my ear, sending shivers down my spine. Then he whispered, "And be inside you."

I squirmed in my seat. Squeezing my thighs together, my panties were suddenly moist. "Jesus, Triston, we're getting on a plane in a few minutes. I can't walk through security all wet and horny!" I admonished him, and he laughed. His smile wrinkled his nose. I loved seeing that smile. It gave him the innocence and the naughtiness I knew he was capable of.

I turned and got out of the car. I needed fresh air! "Come on then. Do you want to fly across the world with me or not?" I leaned down looking at Triston.

"Let's do this, little lady!" He got out and

opened the trunk, pulling our suitcases out.

"Can I get you anything?" The flight attendant smiled down at me. I knew I needed to have something, but I didn't feel hungry.

I smiled. "A sandwich would be great, and, um . . ."

"She will have a salad. I will have the same, and can we have two orange juices, please?" Triston slid back into his seat as the flight attendant walked off to get our dinner.

"Okay then! Someone's feeling bossy!" I stuck my tongue out at him.

He leaned toward me, and I felt his tongue trace the sensitive spot behind my ear. "I'm always bossy, angel, you know that." I shivered. Nodding, I closed my eyes, taking in the sensation of his hot breath.

"Triston," I moaned. He sat back with a satisfied smirk on his face. "Ugh, you are so frustrating!" I slapped his arm, and he chuckled at me.

"And you're so sexy. And you do know what planes do to me?"

I shrugged innocently. He leaned in closer and whispered, "They make me want to fuck you really fast and really hard." I whimpered, covering my mouth with my hand, hoping nobody heard me, my eyes as wide as dinner plates.

"Triston!" I hissed at him as he gave me a cheeky wink and sat back in his seat. The flight attendant brought our salads and disappeared down the aisle. This was going to be a long journey.

"Wake up, angel." My eyes fluttered open. I turned to see Triston's hot gaze.

"What's wrong? Have we landed?" He shook his head. I sat up and looked around. The cabin was dark. I looked out the window and saw we were still in the air. "Triston, what's wrong?" I whispered.

"I love you." He leaned in and kissed my neck softly, teasing his way down my shoulder. "I need you." His teeth grazed my ear. "I want you." His teeth bit down harder, and I felt the heat between my legs.

"Triston!" I was squirming in my seat, hoping everyone was asleep. I knew he wasn't going to stop there. His hand stroked my thigh in slow, deliberate movements moving higher between my legs. I squeezed my thighs together. "Angel, open your legs," he hissed in my ear and instinctively my legs released his hand. When his fingers reached the apex between my thighs, my hips rocked against his fingers. "That's my girl." He stroked my entrance, and I bit my lip to keep from moaning out loud. Thank god for the blankets that covered us. He continued his slow torture, stroking and pressing against me; a fire ignited inside me. I needed him now.

I opened my eyes and looked into his midnight blue stare. "Triston, please?" I pleaded shamelessly. He shook his head, and I knew this was going to be him enjoying the teasing. I needed to figure out a way to get revenge.

"Not yet, angel. Just breathe and enjoy it." His fingers continued to tease me. Shifting my panties to the side, his fingers slid into my wetness. My head fell back, and I bit my lip to keep from moaning out loud. I needed to feel some release. I leaned over and rested my head on his shoulder, inhaling his intoxicating scent. I was about to come when he stopped. I opened my eyes and stared at him, frustrated beyond belief. He gave me a naughty smile and winked. "Five minutes. Follow me." He moved the blanket off his lap and walked to the restrooms.

My body was electric, and I needed the release only he could give me. I couldn't wait a minute longer. I got up from my seat, my legs like jelly, and made my way to the restrooms. I knocked softly when he opened the door. Pulling me inside, he quickly locked it behind us. "I do love fucking you on a plane," he hissed. Tugging my skirt down, pushing me up against the counter. He spread my legs with his knee. Pushing his thigh against my heat. I held on to his neck, feeling the pressure of his muscled thigh taking me higher and higher. I tangled my fingers in his soft, shoulder-length hair.

Stopping again as I reached the precipice, I pouted at him. "Don't pout!" His voice was urgent and dripping with desire. His hand slid into the front of my panties and stroked my sex. "So wet. So fucking wet!" His smile was dark and devilish. Pulling his hand from my panties, he placed his two fingers in his mouth, slowly licking them. His eyes blazed with a darkness that made me want him even more. "You want to come?" he whispered. I nodded. "Do you deserve to come?" I nodded again, not trusting my voice.

His hand dipped into my panties again. His middle finger sliding into me easily. His thumb rubbed my sensitive clit, causing the ache inside me to ignite. "Ready, dirty girl?" I nodded wildly. I needed it so badly. "Good, because you're going to come." His fingers assaulted me deliciously. I dug my nails into his back, and my mouth bit onto his shoulder hard to keep from screaming. "Do it!" My body convulsed around his fingers. He held onto me until I stopped shaking, his strong arms around me, keeping me from falling. My legs were shaky, and my pulse raced. As I came down from my high, I looked into the steel-blue gaze that I loved.

"God, you are beautiful, angel." He kissed me softly as he removed his hand from between my legs. I watched him lick his fingers clean with a smile on his face. "You owe me." He winked and left me completely satiated.

Our hotel, The Arch in the center of London, was gorgeous. We had The Abbey suite, and when I saw the bedroom, I wondered if Triston had specially requested it. The large four poster bed had my mind whirling as to all the things he could do to me while tied down, and I smiled. "A penny for your dirty thoughts?" Triston wrapped his arms around me, and I giggled.

"How do you know they were dirty thoughts?"

"Well, you were looking at the bed and smirking, so I figured they must be." He kissed my cheek.

It was almost dinner time, and I was starving. "Can we get room service? I'm exhausted."

He nodded and walked into the bathroom. "Sure. Order whatever you like."

I grabbed the menu and dialed nine from the telephone on the desk. I ordered dinner and a bottle of champagne, also asking them to send some strawberries and chocolate sauce. I had an idea in mind, which was going to be delicious. I thought of Triston's beautifully sculpted abs. I was going to get him back tonight. I couldn't wait.

"Did you order?" He walked into the living area wearing a pair of low-slung black shorts and nothing else. All I could do was stare at the handsome man in front of me. "Miss Reid, if you are going to persist on staring at me, we will never get any work done!" He smiled walking to the desk to grab his laptop.

"It's not my fault you're half naked!" I decided two could play that game. I went into the bedroom and changed into my black lace panties and matching corset. I grabbed his blue shirt and wore it over my underwear. Leaving the first three buttons undone so he could just get a glimpse of the lace. I knew Triston hadn't seen them yet. I thought of his expression when he took the shirt off later. It would be priceless.

I walked back into the living room a few minutes later to find our room service had arrived. It smelled amazing. "Champagne, angel? Are we celebrating?"

I nodded. "Yes, I think we need to." Triston turned, and I watched his gaze roam over my body, the steel-blue igniting in front of me, and I smiled. I grabbed my laptop while he opened the champagne.

"Nice shirt," he commented as he took a seat opposite me.

"Thank you. It's my boss's shirt. I think he loves seeing it on me."

His smile was filled with desire and amusement, "I think he likes seeing it off you even more." He placed the glass of champagne next to me.

"He'd better behave because I am working." I leaned forward, giving him a glimpse of black lace. An audible groan escaped his lips. "Are you okay, Mr. Hart?" I asked innocently. Picking up my glass, I took a small sip. It was delectable, dry and ice cold.

"I'm just fine, Miss Reid," he growled. I gave him a sweet smile.

We sipped the champagne, watching each other above the lip of the crystal glasses. The shirt had ridden up my thighs, and I saw Triston's gaze fall to my legs. I felt the heat of his gaze travel from my bare feet up to the hem of the shirt, which was just covering my panties. I turned and started typing my email reply to Jessie about the flight and her date with Bash. It seemed he had moved on, I was glad. I could still feel Triston's eyes on me. I ignored him and carried on typing, slowly licking my lips, knowing full well it would incite desire in him. I loved playing his game. I chewed on my lip while I typed my email, thoughts of the hot chocolate sauce invading my mind.

"Are you hungry?" His voice was low but controlled, as he always was.

"I could eat," I replied not looking up. Picking up my champagne, I took another sip. The bubbles traveled through my body, causing me to shiver. I hit send and looked up at Triston. "Are you hungry?" I twisted in my seat, giving him a quick flash of the lacy panties beneath his blue shirt. His eyes darkened, and I felt the knot in my stomach tighten. I stood up and walked to the trolley of food.

I removed the covers from the dinner plates. Triston's body pressed hard against me, his arms on either side of me, trapping me against the food trolley. "Do you like torturing me, Miss Reid?" His voice is dangerous, and I tremble. I feel his arousal pressing into my ass, and I smiled. He couldn't see my face, but he knew that I was having fun.

"I was merely offering you dinner, Mr. Hart. Whatever are you talking about?" I smirked, looking at the delicious food that had been delivered.

"There is something I'm hungry for, and it's not on those plates." His words ignited my desire. I took a deep, cleansing breath and calmed myself.

"I suggest you have some dinner first, Mr. Hart." I turned and handed him his plate. I had ordered vegetarian wraps with salad, but I left the strawberries and chocolate sauce covered.

"What's in there?" He gestured to the other plate.

"Nothing. Eat your dinner!" He narrowed his eyes at me but turned and sat down at his computer. We had so much work to get through, but all I wanted to do was drag him into the bedroom and devour him.

I looked up from my screen to see Triston watching me. "Mr. Hart? Can I help you?" We had been working through dinner. I had finally finished all the correspondence for the next few days.

"Miss Reid, you can definitely help me." He got up and walked over to the trolley. "Do you think I don't know what's under here?" He smiled.

"It's a surprise for later. Do not touch!"

"Fine. Can I rip that shirt off you now?" He walked up to me, pulling me to my feet. He leaned down and kissed me hungrily, wrapping his arms around me, the soft, smooth skin of his bare chest against me. His hands grabbed my ass, pulling me against him. I felt my nipples harden as his tongue invaded my mouth. His shoulder-length hair was loose, providing a curtain around us. I ran my nails down his back, eliciting a growl from his chest.

He stepped back, grabbed the shirt, and ripped it open, the buttons popping in every direction. "Jesus, Emily!" His eyes were on fire as he took in my appearance — a tight black lace corset with panties to match.

"Yes, Mr. Hart?" I spun around. When I met his gaze again, it was as dark as the midnight sky. My body was yearning for him to take me.

"My god, you drive me crazy!" His smile was infectious, and I giggled. I walked over to the trolley, grabbing the warm chocolate sauce and strawberries. "Are we going to get dirty and sticky?" He gestured to the sauce.

"Oh, yes we are, Mr. Hart. Sit." I ordered, and he promptly flopped onto the sofa. I put the strawberries next to us. Straddling him, I grabbed his face kissing him softly, lightly. I dipped my finger in the chocolate sauce and rubbed it over his lips. I licked his bottom lip in slow, teasing licks. Another deep growl escaped his lips. "No touching!" I ordered, and he nodded with a smile on his face.

I took the small spoon and scooped some sauce, drizzling it over his chest. I followed the sticky trail with my tongue, lightly biting his nipples. "Fuck," he cursed in a low voice. His hands twitched at his sides, gripping the sofa. I watched his veins pulse as I undid the button of his shorts and slowly pulled them down. Kneeling before him, I looked up into those beautiful, sparkling eyes and gave him a wicked grin. I reached up and dipped a strawberry in the chocolate, holding it to his mouth, watching him sink his teeth in.

The heat pooled between my thighs. I brought the half-bitten strawberry to my mouth, sucking it, keeping eye contact with him. "Another one, Mr. Hart?" He nodded. I grabbed another strawberry and did the same, feeding it to him, watching him bite into it. I grabbed a spoonful of chocolate sauce and drizzled it over his rock-hard abs, licking and biting him, moving my way down to my prize. I could feel his arousal in his briefs, and I smiled.

"Emily," he grunted as I dipped my tongue into the left side of his sculpted V-line, licking down to the waistband of his briefs, moving my mouth to the other side, copying my actions. His head fell back on the sofa. His hands moved to grab me, and I looked up at him. "No touching, Mr. Hart!" His hands dropped back to his sides, gripping the material of the sofa.

"Emily." It was a warning. Ignoring him, I tugged on his briefs, pulling them down. I looked up, and he was concrete. I licked my lips. I drizzled the chocolate over his hardness.

Moving my mouth over him, I flattened my tongue, licking him from root to tip, taking him in my mouth and sucking his rigid erection. Flicking my tongue around him, another growl escaped his lips. He reached out and grabbed my hair. I stopped and pulled my mouth off him. "I said no touching." He dropped his hands back to the sofa.

"You are going to get fucked, Miss Reid! I am going to make you scream my name!" His words made me shiver. I felt the moisture in my panties. Taking him back in my mouth, I tasted the drizzled chocolate and him. The mix was intense, and I wasn't sure I could hold off anymore. I needed him. Taking him deeper and deeper, I licked every bit of chocolate off him, sucking him into my mouth. I watched his eyes roll back as he growled. "Fuck this!" He looked down and grabbed my hands. "Get up!" I stood up, and he spun me around to face the table, bending me next to his computer. He slapped my ass hard, twice. "Do you want to tease me?" I nodded as I pushed myself against him, moaning loudly. I was aching for him.

Pulling my panties to the side, he slid into me in one swift motion. He grabbed the string of my corset, pulling me back as he slammed into me hard. "You are a very"— he enunciated the words as he slammed into me harder and faster — "bad girl!" His other hand gripped my neck, pulling me up against him. My back arched, feeling his body heat as he filled me. His lips were at my ear, and his soft hand around my neck. Pounding into me, he uttered each word carefully. Hissing in my ear, his hot breath turned me into hot liquid. "I . . ." *Slam*. "Fucking . . ." *Slam*. "Love . . ." *Slam*. "You!"

Bringing his other hand down between my

legs, his fingers expertly teased me. His fingers knew my body so well. "Come, Emily, come on me!" My body started shaking as he bit into my neck, sucking on the sensitive skin. He slowed as I shook in his arms. "Now I can fill you!" He slammed into me one more time, filling me with his hot sticky release.

Chapter Twenty

I woke up to Triston and coffee on Tuesday morning. I could definitely get used to this. Every single day. "Good morning, gorgeous."

"Hey, handsome." Smiling up at him, I grabbed the coffee.

"Listen. James called. The trial is coming up next week on Monday. So, you need to be prepared for what may come." I feared this day for so long. Blake was going to trial. I knew he would get a few years, if that. I didn't think I could ever be ready to face him. "Angel?" Triston pulled me from my dark thoughts. "We can get him put away for a long time, angel. Please don't worry about it." I nodded, giving him a small smile. I didn't want to talk about Blake. I just wanted to be here with Triston. I would think about it when we got back.

"So, work today! I can't believe we're setting up already." He nodded.

"Come on, I think we need a shower." Giving me a naughty wink, he got up and walked into the *en suite*. Now that sounded like my kind of morning. I got up and followed him into the bathroom.

We ran up the steps to The Roof Garden, a lovely conference venue about two minutes away from Kensington Palace. I had always loved London, the rich history and beautiful buildings. Triston gave our details to the manager and was led into the venue. We found Mr. Jacobson delegating to the support staff.

Not long after our arrival, the madness started. Setting up was always a nightmare. Nobody knew where anything went. I spent most of the day on the phone or shouting at contractors. When lunchtime rolled around, Triston found me outside on the steps, standing in the sun. "Angel." Grabbing me, his lips crushed mine. He pulled away, giving me a beautiful smile.

"How is it going in there?"

"It's okay. Busy. We should be ready for tomorrow's opening. Are you hungry?" He nodded, and we walked down the road to a small Starbucks. Triston went in to order our lunch and coffees, and I grabbed a table outside. My phone rang, and I noticed it was Jessie. She was up early.

"Jess?"

"Just wanted to let you know, I'm on my way home. You were right. The brother is amazing!" I laughed out loud.

"I am glad you had . . . Uhm . . . fun?" I heard her giggle and I felt a weight lifted off my shoulders He was okay. That was all that mattered. Triston came out with our lunch. "I will talk to you soon. Take care!" I hung up.

"Who was that?"

"Jess. She's just checking in." I smiled, opening the sandwich wrapper.

"It's a bit early for her? Or late?" He was curious, and I knew he was going to find out sooner or later.

"She spent the night with Bash. They went on a date." He looked up at me in shock. "What?" I asked quietly.

"He certainly moved on quickly." He looked back down, opening his own sandwich. His words cut me with such ferocity I was breathless.

"Thanks, Triston!" My voice sounded harsh. For some reason, his indifference hurt me. I felt the tears threatening to spill, but I blinked them back.

"Emily." A warning, "I didn't mean it like that. Just relax." I couldn't look at him. I picked up my sandwich and coffee and left him at the table. "Emily!" I ignored his call and carried on walking into the park. I found a quiet spot under a tree and sat down. I closed my eyes. It shouldn't have affected me like that, but it did. I wish Triston would realize or think about things before he said them. I opened my sandwich and took a small bite. He came running up to me. "Angel, I seriously didn't mean to hurt you."

"Well, you did. I know it's weird, but I just . . ." I took a swig of coffee, not wanting to finish the sentence. I savored the strong flavor.

"I am sorry!" I stared into his ice-blue eyes and stuck my tongue out at him. "You are infuriating woman!" He grabbed me, pulling me into him. "Look at me!" Our eyes locked, and I saw the love shining in his. "I love you so damn much, you know that?"

"Nope, I didn't know. I was under the impression you're only with me for the sex."

He started tickling me, and my shirt rode up, exposing my belly, his soft fingers tickling the sensitive skin. My body reacted to him, and I knew I would soon be aching to feel him fill me.

"Well, that is a bonus!" His teeth nipped at my belly.

"Triston, stop! It's indecent exposure!" He laughed out loud, pulling the hem of my top down, covering me. "Thank you!" I sat up, leaning into his strong arms. "Do we have to go back to work?" I pouted, wishing we could spend the day lazing on the grass.

"You do realize you just asked your boss that?" he said in a mock-serious tone. I giggled.

"It's okay. He will forgive me if I get him some chocolate sauce." His eyes darkened at the mention of the night with room service. I loved making him lose control.

"Don't start that right now! I don't want to walk into the office with a hard-on!" Pulling me up, we stood under the tree. His lips were soft as he leaned down to give me a lingering kiss.

The hotel restaurant was quiet; I guessed

because it was Tuesday evening. The day went well. We had everything set up for the conference. We had another three days in London for work and decided to stay until Saturday as well. I wanted to do something touristy. Triston agreed to fly back to New York on Sunday morning and got Jessie to change our flights.

"Can I please get a bottle of sparkling water, and you can bring us the starters?" The waiter disappeared to get our order. "You look exhausted, angel. Early night for us. No funny business!"

I laughed. "Funny business? Really?" He nodded. "Fine, you can sleep on the sofa, and I will have that amazing king-sized bed!"

"You wish! I'm never leaving you alone in bed, ever! I'm never leaving you, at all. Ever. I can't. Last week was the worst days of my life. I . . ." His expression tugged at my heart. "I fucked up, Emily. I swear to you; I will never do anything to hurt you again." His eyes met mine, and I saw love, sincerity, and resolve. "I never want you anywhere but by my side. Do you understand me?" I nodded. "I will never walk away from you again."

"I hope not." We sat quietly staring at each

other. There was something he wasn't saying; I could see it in his eyes. The waiter returned with our water and announced the appetizers were on their way. Triston nodded. Filling our glasses with water, he picked his up and took a large gulp. He was nervous. Why would he be nervous? "Did you want wine, angel? I didn't think, sorry. I want wine. Maybe a whiskey?" I watched him ramble on. It was strange to see him in such a state. Almost like he feared something. He called the waiter over and ordered a bottle of red wine.

"Are you okay, Triston? You seem on edge." He smiled and shook his head. "You sure?"

"I'm fine. Of course. Why wouldn't I be?" I shrugged. The waiter returned with our starters and a bottle of Merlot. Filling our glasses, he left the wine on the table.

"Let me know when I can bring the main course." He smiled and turned, leaving us in uncomfortable silence.

"Mr. Hart, you're being strange tonight. Is it something I said?"

"No, Miss Reid." He took my hand, his eyes locked on mine, and my heart started racing. "I need to tell you something. Or ask you, actually."

I nodded my head, not sure I wanted to hear this. What on earth could be so bad? "What is it, Triston? I love you. You know that, right?"

He smiled. "I know, angel. I want you to think about it. Don't say anything until you're sure, okay?" His expression was dead serious, and I wasn't sure I could handle it. I remembered the last time he did this. He asked me to move in. Of course, after everything that had happened, I wasn't sure that was still on the table. Maybe he was going to reiterate that. I was definitely going to say yes. Why on earth would he look so sad?

"Triston, you're scaring me. What's wrong?"

"I do want you to move in with me, but, I don't want to be in the penthouse after everything that's happened. I have bought us a house." The news sank in. I opened my mouth then closed it. I didn't know what to say. A house.

"What about the penthouse?" He shrugged.

"I don't really need it. The only thing I need in my life is you. So, when you're ready, the house will be too." I smiled. The adorable look on his face made my heart fill with more love than I ever knew possible.

"Well, I suppose since you went through all the trouble . . . I mean, maybe I should move in with you." I giggled at his expression.

"You will be the death of me, woman!" A smile spread across his face, crinkling his nose and creasing the edges of his steel-blue eyes.

We walked along the river, the lights of the London Eye reflecting on the water. It was magical. My heart was filled with love for the man next to me. He turned, and we stopped at the edge of the bridge, watching the party boats float past. "Emily." He turned to me and smiled. "Since you're going to be moving in with me, there's something you should know." This again? Couldn't he just come right out and say something without giving me heart failure? He took my left hand in his and kissed my knuckles, sending sweet shivers down my spine. Pulling out a small velvet pouch from his pocket, he dropped to one knee. "Emily Reid, I love you. I never want to spend a moment without you by my side. You have shown me what real love is. After everything that's happened between us, my heart, mind, body, and soul are yours. I give you all of me. Will you be mine forever?" He opened the pouch and pulled out a shiny, white gold, princess-cut diamond ring, and held it up to me.

My breathing hitched, and my heart leaped into my throat, hammering in my ears. Did I hear him right? I stood in shock and awe of the man kneeling by my feet.

"Triston . . ." My voice was ragged with emotion. "Of course! Yes! Oh my god, a million times, yes!" He stood and picked me up, spinning me around. I didn't notice the crowd that had formed behind us until they cheered. He let me down and slid the ring onto my finger. I looked up at him.

"I love you so much. Even time away from you, I was never really away. My heart, mind, body, and soul are yours, Triston Hart. I can't believe you did that to me!" He looked down at me, amused by my reaction.

"Well, how did you want me to do it?"

"Exactly like that!" We stopped at the bottom of the London Eye. I looked out over the water; I still couldn't believe it.

"See, it's only because I know how your mind works. And I knew you would say yes if I asked you in public!" Triston laughed.

"Gee, thanks! So, you kind of forced me to agree to be Mrs. Hart?" I looked down at the princess-cut diamond on my left hand and smiled.

"I had to. I wasn't taking the chance of losing you again!" He pulled me against him, and he kissed me. We walked farther along the river and up onto the bridge, watching the water below us. " Do you want to go back to the hotel soon?"

"We can, but I want to do something first." His voice in my ear was raspy, and I had a feeling this was going to be risky. "Stand facing the water and don't make a sound." Pressing his body against mine, I felt his arousal.

"Triston . . ."

"Shh, angel." His left hand moved down my stomach, tracing slow circles over my bellybutton and slipping into the front of my skirt. His fingers deftly stroked the crotch of my panties. "So wet for me," he hissed in my ear, stroking and teasing me, taking me higher and higher. "Open your eyes. Watch the water and feel my fingers." Moving my panties to the side, he stroked my sex in slow, deliberate movements. I bit my lips to keep from moaning out loud. I was so glad it was quiet on the bridge. "You feel this?" Suddenly, his finger slid into me, and my knees buckled. Triston held me up, and I felt the smile on his lips against my cheek. I nodded. "And this?" He slid another finger inside me. His expert touch sent my body and mind spiraling out of control. "Now, you're going to give me your pleasure. Understand?" I nodded again. "Come for me, angel." His order was laced with desire. Plunging into me again, I felt my release take over, and I came undone on his fingers. He slowly pulled his hand out from the front of my skirt.

"Now, I want to take you back to the hotel and celebrate." He spun me around and kissed me hungrily. Pressing his body into me, I felt his erection digging into my stomach. He pulled away breathless and smiled.

"Oh really? Why can't we celebrate right here?" I giggled at the look on his face.

"Well, Miss Reid, if my future wife wants to do it out in public, I am not going to deny her the pleasure." Big Ben chimed at the stroke of midnight as Triston pushed his body against mine. He whispered in my ear, "You make me so hard, angel," then placed feather-light kisses on my neck. The feel of his stubble against my sensitive skin made me shiver. "I need to feel you," he moaned, nibbling on my neck. I was squirming by then; he knew the effect he had on me. I felt the smile on his lips.

"Triston!" I moaned, hoping he would stop. It was quiet, but people were still walking by, and I felt myself blush.

"I thought you wanted me now, babe?" He laughed and stepped back, leaving me panting. "Let's get a cab. I can't wait." Triston hailed a cab, and as we slid in next to each other, he pulled me next to him.

We got back to the hotel and made our way to the room at lightning speed. Triston opened the door and pulled me inside. "Now, Miss Reid. I want to take my future wife to bed and explore her body. But first, I think we need to get you out of these clothes!" He pulled at my top. "Lift your arms!" I did as he said as he slid it off, dropping it on the floor. Unclasping my bra, he dropped it in a trail as we walked to the bedroom. He unbuttoned his shirt and pulled it off. I couldn't get enough of his body. I ran my fingers over his taut torso, savoring the feel of his sculpted abs. He pulled his hair out of the bun, and it fell to his shoulders. He looked rough and sexy; I was already aching for him.

We stood at the foot of the bed. Triston shed his jeans and briefs. Sitting on the edge of the bed, he pulled me onto him. I straddled his hips and felt his fingers pull my panties to the side. I was already moist, and I felt his arousal at my entrance. He slid into me in slow sensual strokes. I moaned as I held onto his neck and moved back and forth. "Triston!"

He gave a primal growl as he grabbed my hips slammed himself into me.

"My fiancée. So fucking sexy." His lips found my nipples. Sucking them one by one into his hot mouth, I felt his teeth graze the hardening buds. Moving my hips faster, I was on the brink of coming undone. The heat was making my whole body tremble and tingle. "Come for me babe, hard!" His words sent me to my release, and I exploded on him. He was still rock-hard, holding me as I descended. "I'm not done yet." He set me on my feet and walked over to his closet. Grabbing his scarf, I watched him walk over to me, his body exquisite in the dim light of the bedroom. Bending me over the end of the bed, he tied my wrists to the post. "Now, my angel, you can't move." His voice laced with lust.

I felt him slowly slip my panties down as I was dripping wet. Triston gave me feather-light kisses on my calves. The back of my knees was so sensitive. I almost lost control when he kissed them. Grabbing my legs, he spread them wider. "You're such a naughty girl, aren't you, Emily?" I nodded, realizing he couldn't see me when his hand came down hard on my ass.

"Yes, Mr. Hart!" I cried out. I heard him moan, his fingers traveling up the backs of my thighs, and I wanted to melt. His fingers found my heat and stroked me slowly. I was about to lose control again as he pushed two long fingers inside me. His tongue lapped at my sex, pushing me to the edge. "Mmm, my beautiful girl." He kept up his slow torture on my body. My legs were trembling, and I was not sure I could stand for much longer. I gripped the post I was tied to and held on as Triston brought me to an earth-shattering orgasm with his expert fingers. "That's it, babe. Come for me!" My body started shaking uncontrollably, and I was absolutely soaked.

He reached over and untied my hands from the post. "Stand up." I obeyed him, feeling his body against me. He reached in front and between my legs. He whispered in my ear, "This is mine, forever." I nodded. I was still coming down from my high when he started stroking me again, taking me higher than I had ever been. I was delirious with lust, aching for him to fill me. "I love how you react to me. Trembling. Shaking. I love how you come on my fingers." His voice was a low hiss, dripping with desire. His words made me tremble.

"Triston . . ." I wasn't sure I could take another one. He wrapped his arms around me and pushed into me from behind, stroking himself in and out of me slowly. The torture was exquisite. His movements were teasing, taking me right to the precipice and stopping, over and over again. Pulling out, leaving me whimpering, I felt his smile on my cheek.

"You are all mine." His words washed over me. I was his. "I love you, angel." His voice was scratchy as he impaled me from behind, fast and deep. "I'm going to fill you. Do you hear me, angel?" I nodded. "You make me so fucking hard

I want to bury myself inside you all the time!"

He started plunging into me faster and harder. I knew he was close, and my release rose with him, both our senses heightened by the intimacy of the situation. I clenched him inside me. "I love you, Triston!" I cried out as my orgasm sent me spiraling. He slammed deep into me. I felt his orgasm rip through his body as he spasmed inside me. Gripping my neck, he held me close against his chest. We both found our release with each other.

Connected. Forever.

I missed him. I needed him.

I love him.

My Ace of Harts

About the Author

Dani is a *USA Today* Bestselling Author of seductive and deviant romance.

Her books range from the dark to emotional, but every hero is alpha, and each heroine is strong-willed, bringing the men down to their knees. She now lives in the UK, after moving from Cape Town, exploring cemeteries and old buildings while plotting her next book.

When she's not writing, she can be found binge-watching the latest TV series, or working on graphic design. She has a healthy addiction to reading, tattoos, coffee, and ice cream.

www.danirene.com
info@danirene.com

Find Dani Online

Do you follow me?

If not, head over to any of the below links,

I love to hear from my readers!

Amazon

BookBub

Facebook

Facebook Group

Goodreads

Twitter

Pinterest

Instagram

Website & Store

Newsletter

Spotify

Other Books by Dani

For a full list of Dani René's incredible titles visit her website www.danirene.com or find her on all major retailers.

www.ingramcontent.com/pod-product-compliance
Lightning Source LLC
Chambersburg PA
CBHW030333310726
48979CB00001B/3

* 9 7 8 1 8 3 8 1 7 9 4 6 5 *